A HEIST

ON THE ICE

A KENNEDY REEVES

MYSTERY

MJ MAC

Paperback Edition 2023

ISBN: 979-8-9870479-4-1

eBook Edition 2023

ISBN: 979-8-9870479-5-8

To Dan, for believing.

Sunny Dayz Cruise Line

THE MALINA

ITINERARY

DAY 1: DEPART SEATTLE, WASHINGTON, USA

DAY 2: AT SEA

DAY 3: JUNEAU, ALASKA, USA

DAY 4: KETCHIKAN, ALASKA, USA

DAY 5: AT SEA

DAY 6: VANCOUVER, BRITISH COLUMBIA, CANADA

Kennedy Reeves, cruise director for the *Helio*, was standing in the empty lobby, having bid goodbye to the last of the passengers. The ship had just completed a trip to Mexico, and the staff and crew were looking forward to a well-deserved day of rest before their next cruise when they would return to shepherding passengers to Nassau, Grand Turk, the Dominican Republic, and then back to reality in Port Canaveral. Their most recent journey had been a rollout for the new partnership between the Classic Style Network and the Sunny Dayz Cruise Line, and although there had been some dramatic moments, overall, the cruise had been successful.

Kennedy looked over her never-ending to-do list. Besides the staff meeting with Alfred in an hour, everything else could wait until later. She wanted to find Mila, her best friend, to see if they were still having dinner in Port Canaveral that evening. She took the steps to deck six and walked into Oaza. Before she could get past the retail area, Anna Marie, the spa's receptionist, called out that Mila was on the pier accepting a delivery.

"The passengers wiped us out of products again," Anna Marie grinned. She picked up a few bottles from the box on the floor and placed them on the shelf before her. She eyed the row critically and straightened the bottles so they stood like toy soldiers. "People just want to take home a piece of the spa, even if it's nothing more than a candle or an eye mask."

Kennedy looked around at the bare shelves. "Not a bad

problem to have. Will you be able to get off the ship? We don't have any passengers until tomorrow afternoon."

Anna Marie's eyes lit up, and she nodded. "As soon as the boss lady comes back. A bunch of us are going out for margaritas and karaoke, and the more margaritas we drink, the better we sound."

"Then I'll go find her on the pier and tell her to hurry up. Where will you songbirds be? I might stop by. You know I'm always looking for new talent for the shows," she grinned, and Anna Marie gave her the location as she pulled out more bottles to put on the shelf.

Kennedy left the spa, skipped down the main staircase, and walked quickly through the lobby. She stepped outside and stood on the gangway. The busy pier reminded her of an ant hill as workers and forklifts hurried from the dock to the ship delivering the food, liquor, and other items needed for the next cruise.

Standing in the middle of the organized chaos was Ali Asad, the ship's storeroom manager. He was wearing his typical scowl, and Kennedy watched as he hurriedly checked delivery slips against the parade of arriving supplies. Her eyes traveled around the dock and saw Chef Michèle making dramatic gestures to his sous chef, Ano, as he inspected a crate of cantaloupes. Rosemary, the executive housekeeper, was busy counting pallets of toilet paper before a forklift loaded them onto

3

the ship, and Franklin Blaas, the chief engineer, walked jauntily down the pier with a bundle of PVC pipe hoisted on his shoulder. In the distance, Kennedy saw Omar Meier, the *Helio's* director of security, walking briskly toward the ship, and her heart did a little flip-flop. Over the last nine months, their friendship had blossomed into something more. A few days ago, however, moments before the *Helio* left Port Canaveral for Mexico, Omar had received a phone call that caused him to become distant and moody on the cruise, leaving Kennedy perplexed and uneasy.

Omar was irritated this morning as he walked back to the ship. Having spent several hours with the local authorities, he now needed to address a more personal matter, one he hadn't wanted to confront, but it would have to wait until he had time to deal with it.

Kennedy began to raise her hand to wave to Omar and call out to him, but she stopped when she saw a woman with long dark hair walking purposefully down the pier, trying to get Omar's attention.

"OMAR!" the woman cried out in frustration, and he stopped in his tracks and slowly turned around.

"What are you doing here?" Kennedy heard him shout over the wind. "I tried to call you several times, but you didn't answer. There was an urgent matter I had to deal with this morning." He scowled at the woman and looked down at his

4

watch. "And I have a meeting in an hour. You were always so impatient, even as a little girl."

The wind died down, and the woman brushed strands of hair away from her face with one hand. "Matters more important than this?" she hollered angrily, not realizing she no longer needed to yell over the roar of the wind to be heard. She held up a sheaf of papers wrapped in light blue paper. "Omar, would you please sign the divorce papers? I want to get on with my life."

It was as if a vacuum had sucked up every noise on the pier, and heads turned to watch and listen to the conversation unfolding between Omar and the woman standing before him. Omar fished his reading glasses from the inside pocket of his suit and put them on. He made an impatient gesture for the pale blue bundle, and the woman handed it to him. Kennedy could see him flip angrily through the pages. When he got to the last one, his eyes snapped up at the woman in front of him for a split-second, and then he abruptly began walking back toward the cruise terminal, forcing the dark-haired woman to take two steps for each one of his to keep up.

That was the last Kennedy or any of the others saw of Omar. The staff meeting that was supposed to occur never happened, and those in the conference room sat in silence as they struggled to understand what they had seen and heard on the pier. Later that evening, they each received a note from Alfred, their boss, informing them that a temporary security director would be found to take Omar's place until further notice.

A few months later, Kennedy was sitting in the conference room when Mila walked in. "What do you think about Alaska?" she asked Mila point-blank before the spa director could get through the door and take a seat.

Mila lifted an eyebrow. "As in bears, ice, and lumberjacks?" She threw her notepad on the table and bent over to gather her long ash-brown hair in her hands. "You know we had bears in our circus." She stood up and pulled her hair into a top knot as a broad smile came across her face at the memory. "One rode a bicycle around the ring, another did the hula-hoop on a platform, and we had one that lifted weights." As she took her seat at the table, she saw Kennedy's open-mouthed look and waved her hand at her. "The weights weren't real. It was just two large rubber balls and a plastic pipe painted to look like a barbell," she explained.

Kennedy's brows knit together. "Excuse me? How did I not know about this?"

"Probably never told you about my fortune-telling gig either, huh." Waving her hands around an imaginary crystal ball, she said in an exaggerated Polish accent, "I am a woman of mystery."

Kennedy rolled her eyes and let out a silent chuckle. "When Alfred asks today about helping on the *Malina* test cruise, I'm going to say yes." She rested her head on the back of the chair and looked at the ceiling. "I need a change of scenery, even if it is only for a few days."

"Great! And I hear the ratio of men to women is high. So that could be a plus."

"True." Kennedy tilted her head and looked thoughtful. "As they say, the odds are good, *but*…the goods are also odd," she winked at her friend, and they both began laughing hysterically.

Franklin, Rosemary, Tony, Luke, and Chef Michèle entered the room noisily but fell into stunned silence when they heard laughter. It was a sound they had not heard lately in this room. Taking their seats around the long conference table, they exchanged curious looks as Kennedy and Mila tried hard to suppress their fits of giggles. However, before anyone could comment or ask a question, a forehead followed by a shock of fluffy white hair appeared on the video screen at the end of the table. "Can you see me okay?" a man's voice came through the speakers.

"Well, Alfred, I can see that the wrinkle-reducing cream and the new hair products I gave you are working. The wrinkles on your forehead have smoothed out, and your hair is white and shiny," Mila snickered.

"I will never get used to these things," Alfred grumbled as he sat back in his chair. "Is this any better?" The camera jiggled, and a larger-than-life Alfred Dawes, corporate director of operations for the Sunny Dayz Cruise Line, appeared on the screen, offering the group a view of their boss and his office. It was always hard for those around the conference table to connect Alfred with his office. While Alfred was a stickler for details and dressed impeccably, his office told a different story. Mounds of papers and binders covered every available space, and the framed photos on the wall behind him hung slightly askew. If you concentrated too hard on the pictures, you would begin to feel dizzy. "Well," he said, rubbing his hands together, "I know there is only one more cruise until you leave for your break, and I wondered if any of you had reconsidered my request for help with the Alaskan cruise. I know it is in the middle of your time off, but it's only a one-week trip as we explore bringing the *Malina* back online. Passengers will be by invitation-only: select travel agents, some of our favored recurring cruisers, and a few friends of the board of directors."

Franklin shook his head. "Sorry, Alfred, Rosemary and I are not available. We leave for our trip out west after this cruise and will be gone the entire time."

"I'm not either," said Tony Gano, the dining room

manager. "I'll be in Puerto Rico." He grimaced and pulled a roll of antacids out of his coat pocket. "If I make it that long." He pinched his waist as a pain shot through him.

"Are you already stressing about going home?" Luke, the bar manager, laughed. "Buddy, by the time you get back from your mother's, you'll have turned from a lump of coal into a diamond." The group burst into laughter. It was a well-known fact that if you looked up the word stress, Tony's photo would be beside the definition.

"I'm out as well, Alfred," Luke continued. "There is a tiki bar, a bottle of tequila, a hammock, and a beautiful young lady I plan to spend all my time with."

"Tequila," Mila looked at Luke with a simpering smile, "helping women lower their standards and expectations for years."

Chef Michèle laughed so hard at Mila's cutting remark that tears coursed down his face. As he wiped them away, he told Alfred he was also unavailable. He was making a guest appearance on the Classic Style Network's new hit show as they continued their search for a host chef. Michèle was appearing as a favor to the show's producer, Deuce Dawson.

"They still haven't found anyone?" Franklin asked.

Bert, the ship's photographer who was not generally in these meetings, shook his head. He was good friends with

Deuce's right hand, a fiery redhead named Art. Alfred had requested that he attend this meeting, and he was curious why he was there. "According to Art, the ratings are through the roof with the various locations they go to," Bert said.

"Kennedy and I are in," Mila replied.

"You are?" Franklin looked at Kennedy in surprise, and she nodded.

"I was already going to look at the spa for a potential facelift," Mila explained, "but now my partner in crime wants to go too."

Alfred clapped his hands together. "This is wonderful news! Now, Mila, remember, this is only to see if a renovation is feasible. *If* you get the go-ahead, you will have to adhere to a reasonable plan this time." He peered over his reading glasses at the camera. "You blew the budget on Oaza."

Mila batted her eyelashes. "Really? I thought I was helping to stimulate the economy." Alfred began to sputter, and Mila let out a laugh. "Relax. Let me see what it looks like before you start putting the brakes on the project."

"I'm told it's in excellent shape. So, you may only need to make a few tweaks," Alfred offered weakly.

"I'll be the judge of that, and don't forget I have Emily Abbott and Vera Jameson on my side."

Alfred wisely changed gears sensing he was already losing the battle on the spa renovation budget. "And Kennedy, you will only need to be a guiding hand. The *Malina* has a crackerjack team in place. The cruise director, J. Mitchell, was on the ship previously as an assistant cruise director, so he has a handle on what to do. Think of this as a working vacation. You don't need to take on any special duties. Just help out when and where you see fit."

"Happy for the change of scenery, Alfred," Kennedy smiled. "I've never been on an Alaskan cruise. Seeing snowcapped mountains and a shoreline of evergreens will be a nice change from palm trees and sand."

"Bert?" Alfred said slowly, and Bert could feel his face turn red at being singled out. "I could use a ship's photographer for this cruise. And, unfortunately, we don't have anyone booked."

"Actually, I have plans," Bert said, and Mila kicked him hard under the table. "OUCH!" he bent down to rub his shin and gave Mila a strange look. "What was—" he whispered, but she cut him off.

"Unplan them," she hissed and darted her eyes at Kennedy, then she turned and smiled at the camera, "Alfred, Bert would love to go. He was just telling me how much he wanted to see Alaska."

Bert turned toward her with a look of astonishment on his face. "I did?" Mila glared at him, and he shrugged his shoulders and sighed dramatically. "I suppose I'm going to the forty-ninth state," he said dejectedly.

"Fantastic!" Alfred clapped his hands together. "I'll send the three of you a note with the details and alert J. Mitchell. Thank you for doing this. Having part of the dream team on board gives me a feeling of comfort, although it's not like much could go wrong on one six-day cruise."

Weeks later, Kennedy and Mila pulled up to a red brick Victorian house with white lacy gingerbread trim. They had flown into Little Rock, Arkansas, an hour before and picked up the rental car they would drive to Seattle. The girls had convinced Bert that a road trip would be fun, but in his experience, the words fun and road trip didn't go together. Road trips meant endless miles of boredom, indigestion, and ticking away the mile markers until you reached your destination.

Bert pushed open the Victorian's white screen door and walked quickly down the front walk with his bags. "Wow, it's like the set for a family television show," Mila remarked as she got out of the bright red car and unlocked the trunk. Kennedy opened the passenger door and stretched. She held her hand up to her forehead to shield her eyes from the sun's glare.

"New backpack?" Kennedy pointed to the large bag on Bert's back.

"Yep, I just got it. Much bigger than my old camera bag. I can put tons of stuff in here."

"Don't we get to meet your mom?"

Bert threw his duffel bag and backpack in the open trunk. "Nope."

A matronly figure came out and stood on the porch waving for them to come inside. Wearing a yellow floral print dress and black lace-up shoes, she looked like a female version of Bert. "Bye, Mom!" he called out, turning around to face his mother. "I'll send you a postcard from Alaska!" Then, he turned back to Mila and Kennedy. "Quick, let's get out of here before she drags you inside and brings out the photo albums," he said with urgency and quickly opened the door to the backseat. Mila and Kennedy waved to the woman on the porch and got in.

"Welcome to the Flying Tomato," Kennedy turned around to face Bert as he slid into the backseat. "You are in charge of keeping Mila and me in snacks. I am riding shotgun, which means watching for speed traps and selecting the music."

"She's terrible at both jobs, Bert," Mila sighed, looking at him through the rearview mirror. "All she wants to listen to are

13

show tunes, and she completely missed the speed trap." She turned to Kennedy. "Maybe you two should switch jobs and let Bert sit up front."

"Wait…you named the car the Flying Tomato?" Bert asked, trying to catch up. "Why?"

"The car is red like a tomato and…well, Mila likes to push the limits," Kennedy held up a piece of paper. "She already owes the state of Arkansas one hundred dollars."

Mila turned her head over her shoulder. "Look," she protested, "if they didn't want you to use all of the numbers on the speedometer, they wouldn't have designed it to go that high. And *you* were supposed to be watching out for the highway patrol."

"It's a little hard when things are going by in a blur," Kennedy shot back.

Bert felt like a ping-pong ball as he listened to the two women and wondered again if taking the road trip was a good idea.

"Let's start this adventure!" Kennedy called out, turning around to face the windshield. "We are officially the three musketeers on this trip. One for all and all for one!" she hollered.

As Bert pulled his seatbelt on, the car took off with a jerk, and the locks clicked into place. "Are we there yet?" he whined, looking out the window.

Sunny Dayz Cruise Line

THE MALINA

DAY ONE

DEPARTURE FROM SEATTLE, WASHINGTON, USA

BOARDING BEGINS AT 4:00 P.M.

Kennedy, Bert, and Mila stood on the pier looking at the *Malina*. The ship was navy blue and white, with a three-foot-wide golden-yellow accent between the two colors. "The *Malina* is the smallest of the Sunny Dayz fleet and doesn't go out much," Kennedy explained. "As Alfred said in his message, the cruise season is only May through September."

"That's my kind of work schedule," Bert piped up. "I could get used to only working five months a year."

"Just remember, that also comes with a five-month paycheck," Mila chided, and she turned her attention back to Kennedy. "Where does the name *Malina* come from?"

"Like all of our ships, the name means sun. *Malina* is the sun deity of the Inuit people of Greenland, Alaska, and other Arctic regions."

"Sounds like another fine job by our crack marketing team," Mila offered dryly.

They had almost reached the top of the gangway when a portly man with a drooping salt-and-pepper mustache and matching comb-over held up his hands to stop them and began backing them down the gangway. Dressed from head to toe in khaki, with each step the man took, a ring of keys on his belt loop would jingle while a large flashlight and can of pepper spray bounced on his other hip. "Sorry, folks, no admittance. You can't be here." He tapped on his watch. "Passengers will

16

begin boarding the ship at four. You can come back then."

Kennedy extended her hand. "We aren't passengers. I'm Kennedy Reeves, and this is Mila Casimir and Bert Benson from the—"

The man interrupted her and pointed to the nametag on his tan long-sleeve shirt. "That's very nice, and I'm Mr. Phyfe," he said impatiently, "the director of security. "Now, if you are looking for a job with the cruise ship, I suggest you contact the corporate office in Florida, which is a long way from here."

"But sir, we are from the *Helio*," Kennedy tried to explain.

"The *Helio* is probably over there." He pointed at several other cruise ships docked further away. "This is the *Malina*, M-A-L-I-N-A," he spelled out slowly. "You'll have to go back to the cruise terminal to sort this out. Goodbye." He gave them a dismissive wave and frowned when they didn't move.

Kennedy was puzzled. This was not the way she had expected to be greeted. So, she decided to try another tactic. "Sir," she smiled sweetly, "the corporate office sent us to help. If you have a manifest, we would be on it."

"Who is or isn't on the manifest is not my problem." He jerked a thumb over his shoulder. "The cruise director and the folks at the guest services desk take care of that. My job is to take care of security, and as such, I need to ask you, *people*," he let out an exaggerated sigh, "to leave." He shooed at them with his hands, and the keys on his belt loop jangled like a flat bell. "Now, off you go to Florida, or the *Helio*, or the cruise terminal. I don't care. Just get off my gangway."

Kennedy was aggravated. "*Sir*, we've been sent by the corporate office to help on the test cruise. If you would call the cruise director, I'm sure he will straighten this out," Kennedy smiled at him through her clenched teeth.

The man crossed his arms. "I don't need to call anyone, and we certainly don't need any help. Now, off you go." He waved his fingers and walked toward them, making Kennedy, Bert, and Mila shuffle backward until they stood back on the pier.

"Tell you what, friend," Mila said with exasperation.

"Oh boy," Bert sighed.

Mila pointed her finger at the security director's waist. "How about you use that little radio on your belt and call the cruise director." She turned to Kennedy. "What's his name?"

"J. Mitchell Templeton."

Mila turned back to the khakied man. "J. Mitchell Templeton. Tell him Kennedy, Bert, and Mila are here from the *Helio*." She crossed her arms. "While *you* may not be expecting us, he is."

Mr. Phyfe glared at them. "Fine. I'll call J. Mitchell and see what he says, but if there were people from corporate coming, someone would have told me. There have only been a thousand messages sent about this cruise," he groused and pointed at them. "Don't move. Stay right there." He took a few steps up the gangway and pulled the radio from his belt. He whipped his head around quickly to ensure they weren't trying to sneak up behind him.

"Do we get a treat for staying like good dogs?" Mila snarled, and Bert pretended to pant.

After a few moments, Mr. Phyfe put the radio back on his belt and marched down to them. "J. Mitchell isn't answering, and that tells me he wasn't expecting you because if he were, he would have been down here ready for you, or he'd be waiting for my call to tell him you were here. And he never told me you were coming, so that's that," he brushed his hands together, "off you go."

Kennedy smiled through gritted teeth. "Why don't we call the corporate office? I am sure they can verify our presence. I can dial the number for you, so you don't have to look it up." She pulled out her phone and searched for Alfred's contact card.

"Put that away," the man sputtered. "You could be dialing anyone!"

"Then you'll call the corporate office? We aren't leaving

until we are admitted onto this ship."

Mr. Phyfe glared at them and pointed a finger at Kennedy. "I'll call the corporate office, but only to get rid of you. Stay here. I'll be watching you from my cameras." He walked heavily up the gangway, the keys on his hip rattling with each plodding step.

"I don't think global warming has hit out here," Mila shivered and ran her hand up and down her upper arm. "There are glaciers warmer than the greeting we just received."

"However, he would make an excellent security guard at the mall," Bert chuckled. "He's already got the khaki uniform, the ring of keys, flashlight, and pepper spray."

Kennedy began to giggle. "Can you imagine if Vera Jameson were on this cruise? If she assumed the director of security was like Omar and demanded he escort her for dinner, her face would be priceless when Officer Friendly knocked on her door." The three of them chuckled at the mental image of Vera Jameson's patrician face as she opened the door to find the short, pudgy, khakied security director standing there.

"Shhhh, here he comes," Kennedy whispered.

"I feel safer already," Mila mumbled.

The man in the tan uniform marched down the gangway wearing a scowl. "Well, you check out. Follow me. You can go into the lobby, but no further. J. Mitchell will be down shortly to sort this out."

"So, keep your hands at your sides, your eyes straight ahead, and try not to take up any available oxygen," Mila whispered. Bert snorted and quickly covered his reddening face behind his hands.

"Is something funny?" Mr. Phyfe turned around and narrowed his eyes at them. "I'm not sure how you folks do things in Florida, but I assure you the security of this ship is not a laughing matter."

"No, sir," Mila said, feigning seriousness. "I feel so much better knowing that you are around."

When they got to the top of the gangway, he led them inside. "Stay here," he barked, giving them a last glare before leaving.

Kennedy's eyes darted around the space as they entered. In the center of the lobby was a large square slate fountain with two stainless-steel tails sticking out of the dark water. On the far wall, opposite the fountain, was a seating area that featured a massive black-and-white mural of a 1920s seaplane flying over a glacier. The mural was flanked by enormous blonde cedar columns that rose to the ceiling, and the column at the far left stood on one side of a grand double staircase. Black leather upholstered wingback chairs with nail head trim, small brass tables, globes, and tripod floor lamps made from searchlights and old diving helmets were scattered throughout the seating area. The lobby gave the feeling of a time when ocean voyages were synonymous with grace and elegance. Turning around, Kennedy saw the guest services desk opposite the curved double staircase. The blonde cedar desk resembled a canoe for a giant.

"Why doesn't our lobby look like this?" Bert let out a series of loud sneezes. "It doesn't seem fair. They only work five months out of the year."

"Would you like some cheese to go with that whine, Bert?" Mila asked and then wrinkled her nose. "What is that smell? I can't place it, but it's awful. It reminds me of something old and dated."

"Maybe it's you," Kennedy quipped. "Have you looked in the mirror lately?"

Bert started sneezing again and pulled out a handkerchief. "I need to find my allergy medicine," he said with a stuffy nose. "I hope I brought enough."

Mila wrinkled her nose. "Oh, good grief, there it is." She pointed at the double staircase where an enormous lily and rose flower arrangement sat on a wood table. "Is this a cruise ship or a funeral barge?"

"Isn't that just *fantabulous*[1]?" a singsong voice called out, and a young man came bounding down the stairs. "Hi, I'm J.

---

[1] fantabulous: to be both fantastic and fabulous.

Mitchell, the cruise director, and you are?"

J. Mitchell had a slender build and was of medium height with baby-fine light-brown hair that formed an unflattering widow's peak on his high forehead. Kennedy extended her hand when he got to the bottom of the stairs, and he looked at it curiously, causing her to pull her hand back quickly. "I'm Kennedy Reeves," she pointed to Mila and Bert, "and this is Mila Casimir and Bert Benson from the *Helio*. Alfred sent us."

J. Mitchell waved both hands in front of his face as if fanning himself and made a staccato laugh that reminded Kennedy of a woodpecker. He gently slapped the handrail of the stairs. "Oh, that Alfred, such a kidder. I thought he was joking when he said he was sending a part of his *dream team* to help us on the cruise." He waved his hand again. "I'm so sorry you came all this way. I don't know what Alfred was thinking. It's one cruise for a few days with a limited number of passengers, and we have perfect weather. What could go wrong? But I guess since you are here—"

Bert sneezed again. "Sorry, I'm allergic to your flowers."

J. Mitchell looked lovingly at the arrangement. "It is *fantabulous*, isn't it? I picked it out myself." He inhaled deeply. "The scent reminds me of my mom and her seven sisters. They live in a big old house together."

The heavy silence that hung in the air was broken by

23

more sneezes from Bert. "How lovely," Kennedy said awkwardly.

"Well, I was just on my way out," J. Mitchell yammered. "I have some last-minute errands to do before we sail, but since you are here, you might as well stay. I'm sure we can find *something* for you to do." His eyes came back and rested on Kennedy. "So, you are *the* Kennedy Reeves. To hear Alfred talk, you practically walk on water. I suppose I should genuflect?" He wrinkled his nose. "Maybe not." He let out another machine gun laugh and offered her a smile that did not seem genuine. "Now, I'm sure you are tired. Traveling can *really* age some people."

Kennedy blinked. She wasn't sure, but she thought J. Mitchell had just inferred that she looked old. "I'm sure we look a little bedraggled," she tucked a piece of hair behind her ear. "Is there a formal meeting with the senior staff before the passengers arrive? We'd like to have time to freshen up before we meet everyone."

J. Mitchell let out another staccato laugh and waved his hand forward. "We aren't as formal as you guys on the East Coast. I would suggest you go down to the mess hall or the crew bar if you want to meet people." He looked at his watch. "Although it's a little early for The Wreck. They are probably still cleaning up from last night. It got a little crazy in there."

Kennedy persisted. "Perhaps you could help us with a tour of the ship? We should know where things are before we do

24

the muster drill." She gave him a tight smile. "We can't exactly call anyone if there is an emergency."

"Oh, Kennedy," he trilled, "you make me laugh. You are so by the book. This is a soft cruise. It's not a big deal, and besides, if there were an emergency, those dreamy Coast Guard boys are always close by." He clasped his hands to his chest and looked up at the ceiling. "Now, I simply must scoot." He tilted his head from side to side and twittered, "Busy, busy, busy."

Kennedy was frustrated at J. Mitchell's flip answers, and as he began to walk past her, she reached out and touched his sleeve. "But safety is important, J. Mitchell. The guests are putting their lives in our hands."

J. Mitchell stopped and looked at Kennedy's hand on his dark blue cardigan. He blinked his eyes rapidly. "And as *I said*, I have things to do," he said with false patience, removing her hand from his arm. "When you go down to the mess hall, ask someone to show you around." He placed his hands on his hips and rolled his eyes. "Now, I have to go before they start loading the ark with the *tourons²*."

Kennedy realized she wasn't getting anywhere with the young man regarding safety measures, so she changed tactics. "Perhaps you could give me a copy of the manifest to look over while you are in town?" she asked sweetly.

---

² touron: a tourist with moronic tendencies.

25

"Manifest?" he giggled. "Why on earth would you want to look at that?" He pointed at the canoe-shaped desk. "*They* take care of anything like that. I'm here to entertain the passengers, not babysit them." He shook his head. "I didn't realize how differently you guys do things. We aren't that formal out here."

"One last question?" Kennedy asked. J. Mitchell sighed dramatically and shifted his weight from one leg to another like an impatient toddler. "Where do you keep your office supplies? I need to find a clipboard."

"A clipboard?" he asked as if the word were foreign.

Mila had had enough. "A board with a clip," she snapped. "Kennedy puts her manifest with her notes on it and the daily schedule. If a passenger asks a question, she has the information at her fingertips."

"Wow," he looked at Mila, "it's pretty easy to figure out which of the seven dwarves you are today, and I don't mean *Happy*." He cocked his hip and rolled his eyes at them. "Look, whatever the passengers need, they can see on the reader boards. *If*, heaven forbid, they ask a question, put on your traffic cop hat and point them to the guest services desk, the reader boards, or the elevator, and explain that the signs will take them where they want to go," he huffed. "Honestly, it's painfully clear that the Alaskan cruisers are a smarter clientele than your Caribbean boozers. It must have something to do with alcohol, being a senior citizen, or that tropical heat you have." He let out a short, little laugh. "Now as to the," and he made air quotes with his fingers, "magic clipboard, I'm sure there is one around here somewhere. The old cruise director loved antiques, but then again, she was old, like almost forty," he smirked and looked Mila in the eye as he said the words.

"Easy girl," Bert whispered. If J. Mitchell went much further with his sly insults, he might end up as fish bait.

J. Mitchell turned to Kennedy. "Mr. Phyfe can let you into the old cruise director's office." He looked at his watch. "Now, I really have to go. Toodles." He waved his fingers and was halfway through the lobby before they could ask about their cabins.

"Well, that was a bowl of fun!" Mila blew her bangs up in the air. "I suppose we should check in with someone at the guest services desk. Hopefully, they are a little friendlier than the other two."

They walked over to the empty canoe-shaped desk and stood there patiently for a few minutes. "Hello?" Kennedy called out. "Is anyone back there? Hello?"

"Hold your pants on," a harried voice said, and a door on the wall behind the desk opened. "Oh, it's you again," the security director groused. "What's the problem now?" He hitched up his pants, making his keys jangle.

"Well, gosh," Mila said cloyingly in a breathy voice, "J.

Mitchell, bless his heart, forgot to tell us what cabins we had been assigned to, and as this is a matter of the highest level of security, I was wondering if you could help us." She batted her eyelashes while Bert and Kennedy looked at the ground, their noses hurting from stifling the laughter they were holding back.

"Wait here," he growled, and a moment later, a tall, thin young woman with straight, lank brown hair tucked behind her ears and enormous eyeglasses appeared at the counter. She began typing on her computer.

"Name?" she asked in a clipped monotone, never bothering to look at the three people standing before her.

"Kennedy Reeves, Mila Casimir, and Bert Benson," Kennedy answered with what she hoped was a pleasant voice.

The woman clicked the keys on the keyboard, and after a few minutes, she grabbed three plastic cards and laid each on top of a machine. "Staff accommodations. Deck three, Cabins 365 and 367," she said flatly and pointed a finger at Bert without looking at him, "and Cabin 314. Here are your keys. Don't lose them and turn them in on the last day, or you will be charged twenty-five dollars."

"Are you sure?" Kennedy looked perplexed.

"Sure about what?" the woman asked, still looking at her computer screen.

"About our cabin numbers. Are you certain we are on

28

deck three?"

"That's what the computer says," the woman said flatly.

"Would you pull a manifest for me?" Kennedy asked.

The woman shook her head and stared ahead at the terminal. "Sorry, you don't have the credentials for that. Other than those of us at the services desk, only Mr. Phyfe and J. Mitchell have access to the manifests."

Kennedy hesitated. "Okay, is there anything else we should know?"

"The elevators you are to use are that way," she pointed her finger to the right. During their entire interaction, she had never looked up from the screen in front of her.

"Thank you, you've been most helpful," Bert said quickly. He could tell from the look in Mila's eyes that she was at a point where she might begin to colorfully express her frustrations in Polish. He gently pulled their arms and led them away from the desk. "Well, now you will see how the rest of us live in the servant's quarters. Not as plush as your normal accommodations, ladies, but please allow your humble servant to show you the way," he lisped and began walking like a hunchback.

"Really, Bert? Really?" Mila asked. "Is that the best you can do?"

"Yes, master," he uttered, and Kennedy bit her lips to hold her laughter back.

"Before we get below decks," Kennedy said, "I need to talk to Alfred." Mila and Bert sighed, and Kennedy held up a hand. "I promise it will only take a second. Maybe he can pull a manifest for me since I evidently don't have the proper credentials."

"Kennedy, could we just go find our cabins and put our stuff up?" Bert whined.

"Hungry, Bert?" Mila asked. "I can ask our extremely helpful guest services agent to find some cheese." She motioned at the woman they had just left, who was staring intensely at her computer. Mila gave Kennedy a knowing look. "And it will be a quick call to Alfred because if it isn't, I will personally remove the phone from her hand."

"Good luck with that," Kennedy snorted, pulling her phone from her bag. She walked over to the seating area, dialed the number, and put the phone on speaker. "Alfred," she said and relayed their strange welcome. "I know we are only here to help, but—"

"Kennedy," Alfred interrupted, "J. Mitchell is a delightful young man. He knows the ship, and as I told you earlier, he was the assistant cruise director for a year on the *Malina*. He's probably just nervous. You have quite the reputation of being the best in the industry. Just keep an eye on things for me."

"Yes, but—" Alfred interrupted her again, and Mila and Bert began to pantomime Kennedy's call to her boss.

Mila made dramatic hand gestures mimicking Alfred. "Now, before I forget, there has been a slight change with the entertainment lineup. We didn't book our normal number of acts, and the three-piece group we contracted won't get on the ship until you reach Juneau. So, I need you to do your one-woman show in the theater tomorrow night. I've already messaged J. Mitchell with the change. We always get tons of comment cards about your show, and it would let our special VIPs know the caliber of entertainment we will have on future cruises. We need some of that Kennedy magic."

Kennedy sighed, and Bert made an exasperated face at Mila as he pretended to be Kennedy. "Alfred, do you realize how often I perform magic on our cruises? I'm beginning to wonder if I need to wear a top hat and carry a wand?" Mila had to stifle a giggle as Bert made a gesture like a magician pulling something out of his hat.

"Well, if you could work that into another act…oh, and make sure you see the totem poles in the pool and the Owner's Suite. I hear it's very Alaska-like. The wife of one of the board members, the same one who did the Owner's Suite on the *Helio*, designed it. We didn't have much time or a budget, but I'm told she did some interesting things. I can't wait to hear what you think. I'll get that manifest over to you, and remember, Kennedy, it's a six-day cruise. So, relax, have fun, and let J. Mitchell and the team there handle things. Now, I've got to go, there is a meeting with the marketing team, and I need to head off whatever insane idea they had this week. Goodbye!"

Kennedy rolled her eyes at Bert and Mila. "Thank you both for such a wonderful performance." She sighed and stood up. "I suppose it's down to the dungeon for us."

"Yes, master," Bert lisped, getting up and hunching his shoulders. He swung his backpack over one arm and picked up his duffle bag. Then, as he walked toward the staff elevator, he theatrically drug his left foot behind him.

A few minutes later, they arrived on deck three. "You guys are that way," Bert pointed. "I'll come by in a few minutes." He turned to Mila. "This may come as a shock for someone not used to staff and crew quarters. If you have any wine in your bag, now may be the time to find it."

Kennedy and Mila walked down the corridor and stood before their cabins. "One, two, three," they said and placed their keys against the locks and depressed the door levers.

"Ummm…" Kennedy swallowed hard as she stood in the doorway and looked in at the narrow room.

"It's only for six days," Mila said hesitantly, stepping

inside her cabin.

"It's not so bad, cozy and snug," Kennedy called out, taking in the twin bunk beds and desk-and-dresser combo that sat across from it. She opened a door and found a closet that was only large enough for the five security clothes hangers hanging on the rod. She had initially been taken aback by the bunk beds but quickly realized, after seeing the minimal storage space, that she could put her suitcase and backpack on the upper bunk. "It's not so bad," she repeated to herself. "I can do this."

Mila stood in Kennedy's doorway holding a flattened bed pillow. "Cozy is one thing, but I think these cabins are smaller than the security cells on the *Helio*."

"Missing your former dwelling?"

Mila threw the pillow she was holding at Kennedy. "I'll remind you that I was not held in one of our cells but confined to my comfortable quarters."

The pillow hit Kennedy in the shoulder. "Ouch!" She stooped to pick it up and tossed it back to Mila. "That thing is rock hard."

"Make sure to check out your luxurious bathroom. It gives a whole new meaning to time efficiency," Mila eyed the bathroom door and left Kennedy's cabin for her own.

Kennedy pulled her computer out of her bag and set it on the dresser-desk combination. She began to pull the chair out

33

from under the desk only to find she would have to straddle the seat to sit down. Putting the chair back in place, Kennedy braced her hands on either side of the desk to scan the list of messages on her computer. She spied the one from Alfred and clicked on it. As she skimmed the list he had sent, she sucked in her breath when she saw Vera Jameson's name on the manifest. "Great, no stress at all," and an image of Vera with her laser-like eyes came to mind.

Three words could be used to describe Vera Jameson: wealthy, opinionated, and imperious. Vera could insult someone with such sweet venom that it was not until afterward that one would realize they had received a cutting insult, not a compliment. Over the years, Kennedy had culled a unique friendship with Mrs. Jameson. She would make sure to pay attention to the formidable woman on the cruise to ensure things went smoothly.

Kennedy went back to the list and saw that a travel agent she often worked with, Ronnee Barrett, would also be on the cruise. Ronnee was a fun-loving, organized person who booked group tours and conferences on the ships. There was another name she recognized but could not place a face: LaVonda Taylor. She tapped her chin. "LaVonda, LaVonda…" Suddenly, Kennedy's stomach dropped to her knees as a queasy feeling wound around her insides." She let out a long groan as recollections of a disastrous cruise returned in a rush to haunt her.

Her trip down memory lane was interrupted by the bleat of the telephone on the desk. "Captain Volare wants to see you on the bridge," said the flat voice of the woman from the guest services desk through a staticky line.

"I'm sorry? Who?" Kennedy couldn't understand the voice on the other end.

"The captain," the voice said with exasperation, "and it's not a request. He wants to see you on the bridge ASAP, which means now!"

Kennedy replaced the receiver and went into the bathroom to check her appearance. She laughed at the image of a figure with a humungous forehead and tiny chin staring back at her. "Well, now we know where the funhouse mirrors go when the carnival is over," she said to her reflection. She poked her head into Mila's cabin, "I've been summoned to meet the captain. I'll be back as soon as possible."

Kennedy swallowed her nervousness and put on a winning smile as she opened the door to the bridge. "Hi, I'm Kennedy Reeves from the *Helio*," she said, walking into the room.

"And *I* am Captain Volare," a deep voice said. A handsome man with dark gray penetrating eyes, black hair threaded with strands of silver, and a neatly clipped goatee and mustache turned around. "I've heard a great deal about you, Ms. Reeves." He extended his hand to shake hers. "Word travels amongst the captains, and my colleague on the *Helio* sings your praises. He also told me I should say no if I am asked to introduce you at your after-hours show." He wrinkled his brow. "Something about being called Captain Foghorn, which I shall keep in my pocket for the next captain's get-together."

Kennedy had the grace to blush. "I see my reputation proceeds me."

"He also said that you have a knack for problem-solving and can get him to perform manual labor when the need arises. I hope we won't need your unique skill set on this cruise." He winked at her. "And you should know that I *don't* do manual labor." The captain began to walk in slow circles with his hands behind his back. "He mentioned you are a hostess extraordinaire, and I should rely on you for the welcome cocktail party this evening."

"But sir, J. Mitchell should be the—"

He cut her off and sighed. The circles he was walking were getting closer and closer to her. "J. Mitchell is a nice young man; however, he lacks your grace and elegance." He picked up her hand and kissed it. "I'm afraid my colleague failed to mention how incredibly beautiful you are. I consider it my good fortune to have your presence on the *Malina*."

Kennedy was astonished at the captain's forwardness. She took a step back and stuttered. "I would be pleased to help out tonight, sir."

His eyes drilled into hers, and Kennedy finally understood how a mouse felt when it fell under the hypnotic stare of a cobra. "And your accommodations, do you find your room comfortable?" he asked smoothly. "As captain, I have the most luxurious stateroom on the ship. Perhaps you'd like to see it?"

Kennedy smiled awkwardly and slid closer to the door, putting her hand on the knob. "Captain, I really should be going," she said hurriedly, "especially if I will be hostessing your event tonight. I need to make myself familiar with the ship, check the space for your party, and meet the staff," she rambled and looked at her watch. "Gosh, only a few hours until the guests arrive." She had her hand on the door and opened it, backing out of the room.

"Consider it an open invitation, Ms. Reeves," and he stared intently at Kennedy.

"Thank you, sir," she said, closing the door. She descended the stairs rapidly, and when she got to the landing, she looked back up at the entrance to the bridge. "Wow! I *did not* see that coming."

While Kennedy was using her skills to tap dance away

from the captain, Bert and Mila decided to take a quick walk around the ship. "That doesn't look good," Mila pointed at a column with rust and peeling paint.

Bert nodded. "I would have thought repairs to the ship would have been made before this cruise, especially with the amount of downtime they've had and the need to impress people. Franklin would have never allowed something like this to be visible."

"No," Mila sighed, "our friend lives and breathes for the *Helio*."

"I don't think he sleeps. He's usually tackled three projects before I've hung up the photos from the previous day, and he's still going at it when I'm taking the dinner shots."

Mila nodded. "He is a bit superhuman. Let's go up to deck six. I want to poke my head into the spa."

"You just can't wait, can you?" Bert snickered.

They found heavy wooden doors barring the entry to the spa. There was a small gap between them, and Mila tried to peer between the opening but could not see anything. Giving up, she sighed and rested her back against the doors. "Rats, I wanted to see—"

"Mila, you aren't going to believe this," Bert whispered urgently, motioning to her. Bert had taken a few more steps and found a short hallway leading to the gym. He pointed at a narrow window that looked into the spa. "I'm doing before and after shots if you get to renovate this place. No one will believe the before without physical proof staring back at them.

Mila peered in, and the first thing she saw was the red velvet and gold-flocked damask wallpaper. "Bert...this is...I want to stop looking, but I can't."

"I know," Bert said in amazement. "And I can't believe I don't have my good camera with me. It's in my cabin."

"Do you have *anything*?" Mila exclaimed, tearing her eyes away from the window. She clutched his arms. "Bert, I have to have photos!"

"I only have this," he held up a small pocket camera.

"Then start snapping. This place is in a time warp."

They took turns looking in the window, and the small camera lens captured the details of the dimly lit space. A curved banquette, upholstered in crushed red velvet, anchored the room, and a row of bonnet-style hair dryers sat like sentries behind it. An enormous white oval coffee table went from one end of the banquette to the other, and a large artificial floral arrangement sat in the center of the table. Behind the drying area, a wall of large white oval mirrors with round lightbulbs and red and white striped vinyl barber chairs indicated where stylists would perform their magic.

Mila poked Bert's arm. "Fifty bucks says the chairs have

an ashtray on the arm," she was breathing hard with excitement. "How much do you want to bet the stylists wear matching pink smocks."

"Smocks?" Bert snapped another photo, looked at Mila, and shuddered.

They heard the rattling of keys. "Excuse me!" a loud voice called out.

"Perfect, we've been discovered by the king of khaki. He'll probably want to frisk us!" Mila muttered, and Bert slipped the camera into his jacket pocket.

"What are you doing here?" Mr. Phyfe demanded. "You aren't supposed to be in this area!"

Mila turned around and gave him a radiant smile as she placed her hands on her cheeks. "Oh, my goodness, Mr. Phyfe," she said in a sugary voice. "I am so sorry! We were just so excited about being here, and I wanted to see what the gym looked like, so we took a little walk. I guess we got turned around. I'm sorry we took you away from your important security duties."

Mr. Phyfe narrowed his eyes at Mila. "I saw you on the cameras, and it looked more like you were snooping." He pointed to the camera in the corner of the ceiling at the fitness center entry and then put his hands on his hips. "I'm not sure how things work on the *Helio*, but on this ship, workers use the gym by the mess hall, and I suggest the two of you acquaint yourselves with the staff and crew areas, not the passenger ones." He beckoned for them to step into the corridor where he stood and returned his attention to Mila. "I looked you up and know you run the fancy-schmancy beauty shop on the *Helio*, but around here, Ms. Fischer runs things. So, if you want to see this place," he jutted his chin at the double doors of the spa and salon, "you'll have to clear it with her." He extended his arm, pointing a stubby finger down the corridor. "Now, I suggest you two move along that way."

"Yes, sir," they said in mock meekness.

Mr. Phyfe's eyes followed Bert and Mila as they walked down the hallway. "And use the associate elevators," he barked, "the passenger ones are off-limits to you. You need to remember that this isn't a pleasure cruise for the three of you. You were sent here to work."

Mila turned around and saluted, then she and Bert walked quickly down the hallway, trying hard to stifle the giggles bubbling up inside them. When they opened the doors to the employee elevator vestibule, the laughter they had been holding back exploded. They were still giggling when the doors to the elevator opened, and Bert and Mila exclaimed in unison, "Jordan?"

Chef Jordan Nima looked at them, equally astonished. "Bert? Mila? What are you doing here?"

41

"The better question is, what are *you* doing here?" Bert asked. The elevator doors began to close, and Mila put out an arm to hold them open so they could get on. "Does Kennedy know you are on board?"

Jordan shook her head. "No, is she here too? Is Ano? Michèle didn't mention anyone from the *Helio* coming on the *Malina* when he visited. After helping when Ano got hurt, I saw a new career path. Then, when Mrs. Abbott contacted me and said there was a temporary opening on the *Malina*, I jumped. Michèle gave me a good recommendation—"

"Oh, Michèle gave you a good recommendation, did he," Mila smirked.

Jordan blushed and ignored Mila's pointed innuendo. "So, I took a temporary leave of absence from my job at the restaurant, and here I am." The elevator doors opened, and the three stepped out. "But why are you guys here?"

"Bert is helping out since they don't have a photographer, and I'm looking at the spa and salon for a potential renovation," Mila answered.

"Have you seen it?" Jordan chuckled.

"Yeah, we saw the time warp through the window. I'm told a Ms. Fischer runs it, and I have to get permission from her to see anything more. Is there something I should know?" Mila asked slowly.

42

Jordan's eyes danced. "I hope you packed a suit of armor." Jordan then lowered her voice, "What about Kennedy? Michèle told me about Omar leaving without a word to anyone."

"She's helping out as well, change of scenery," Mila answered.

Jordan sighed and looked away. She, too, had once needed a change of scenery. "I can understand," she said quietly. "Have you met J. Mitchell, the cruise director?" Bert and Mila nodded.

"We also had the pleasure of meeting Officer Friendly twice," Mila interjected.

"Mr. Phyfe?"

"Yep," Bert answered, "and he was not happy to find us walking around the ship. He said we were snooping." Bert turned to Mila, "Do you realize that's twice now I've been accused of being snoopy?"

"It's probably because you look like a delinquent," Mila said dryly.

Jordan let out a sigh. "Don't take it personally. He thinks everyone but Tammy, J. Mitchell, and the chief engineer are criminals. His first name is Barnabas. I'll let you put that together."

Mila looked at Jordan, and the corners of her mouth

began to twitch. "You aren't serious," she said, and Jordan nodded. "Oh, that's perfect."

Bert looked confused. "What does that mean?"

"Bert," Mila turned to him, "Barnabas Phyfe, now shorten the first name," she saw the light come on in Bert's eyes as he began to put Mila's words together, "wears khaki, is in charge of security, and thinks we are all potential felons."

Bert began to chuckle. "Please tell me he's from North Carolina."

"What else do we need to know?" Mila asked.

Several people crowded the corridor, and Jordan tugged on Mila's arm. "Let's go to your cabin."

Once inside, Jordan shared what she knew about the staff and crew of the *Malina*. "I would probably know more if I went to The Wreck, but I thought I was at a college fraternity party the only time I was there."

Suddenly, there was rapid knocking on Mila's cabin door, and Kennedy burst in. "Mila, you aren't going to believe…" she trailed off when she saw the woman leaning against the desk. "Jordan? How? What are you doing here?" she asked in a rush and hugged the dark-haired chef.

Jordan gave Kennedy a quick recap of why she was on the *Malina*. "It's nice to see some friendly faces. I was worried I had made a mistake."

"How's the kitchen?" Kennedy asked.

Jordan lit up like a Christmas tree. "The kitchen is great! And I can't wait for you to meet Chef Sha." She looked at her watch. "Let's go to the mess hall, and you can meet everyone! I've told them a few stories about the competition and stories Michèle shared with me, but they don't believe me." She paused and looked kindly at Bert. "Bert, I am so sorry; I have been talking a mile a minute and have not stopped to ask about Art. How is she?"

Bert's face flushed in embarrassment. "S-s-she's good. It's a shame you couldn't have become the host chef. You would have been great."

Jordan gave a little shrug. "It's okay; it wasn't meant to be. Who knows? Maybe this is." She pushed herself off the desk. "Let's go, and I'll introduce you to everyone."

As Jordan led the way down the corridor, Mila leaned in and whispered to Kennedy, "What happened? You came in the room rather dramatically, even for you."

Kennedy stopped and turned. "The captain hit on me and invited me to see his cabin…up close and personal. I couldn't get out of there fast enough." She started walking again.

Mila stood in the hallway, one hand on her hip, and pointed a finger at Kennedy. "Now, hold on, is he cute?"

Kennedy whipped her head around. "Mila!"

"I'm just asking, and it wouldn't hurt for you to put your toe back in the dating pool. It's been several months."

Kennedy stared at her best friend. "You're starting to sound a lot like my mother, which I assure you is *not* a compliment. Lolly believes putting your toe back in the pool involves her giving you an aggressive hip check into the swamp on a moonless night only to find out that the water is teeming with starving alligators. So, thank you, but I will pass on your suggestion."

Mila waved her hand at Kennedy. "Meh, there you go being overly dramatic again."

"Don't you have a circus animal to train or someone's fortune to tell?"

"My crystal ball is on the fritz."

Kennedy began poking Mila on the arm.

"What are you doing?" Mila slapped Kennedy's hand away.

"Looking for a button to turn you off."

They followed Jordan into the mess hall, and Bert whistled as they entered. "Wow, it doesn't matter what ship you are on. They all look the same, don't they? High school cafeteria meets sad buffet restaurant." Dark yellow vinyl banquettes with matching chairs sat around metal tables with plastic wood tops. Stripes in mustard, burnt orange, and brown went around the room, and above the colored bars were framed posters of vintage fast-food images. Jordan walked toward a table in the back where a small group was seated.

"Jordan!" a woman with a New Zealand accent called out. "Who do you have there?" The woman's thick, wavy, raven-black hair was pulled into a ponytail, and she wore a purple paisley bandanna around her forehead.

"Chef Finch, do you remember me telling you about some of the staff on the *Helio*?"

Sha rolled her eyes. "Yes, and they seem too good to be true."

Jordan grinned. "May I introduce Kennedy Reeves, Mila Casimir, and Bert Benson. This is Chef Sha Finch, executive chef for the *Malina*, culinarian extraordinaire, and my boss."

"Nice bit of brown-nosing there, Jordan," Sha chuckled and began to stand up, extending her hand. "Welcome to the

Malina." The eyes of the three newcomers went up as she stood to her full six-and-a-half feet. She grinned. "I know, it's like having pieces from different puzzles that shouldn't go together but fit. My dad was in the Navy and fell in love with my mum when he was in Polynesia. I got her looks, his height, and this outrageous accent compliments of growing up in New Zealand."

She gestured for them to sit down. "So, before we find out why you are here, I have a question. Please describe Chef Michèle Josèf. I have heard over the years that he is a raging tyrant with bulging eyes and nostrils that flare to the size of omelet pans. That he breathes fire and takes out his aggression on whatever piece of meat is nearby, pounding it with a mallet until a person can read through it. However, Jordan paints a different picture of a kind chef who speaks softly to those around him and spends hours patiently teaching his staff, gently correcting their mistakes."

"Well, if you mean gently, like being hit with a sledgehammer," Bert muttered, "yeah, that's him."

Kennedy and Mila exchanged looks, and the corners of their mouths turned up into smiles. Kennedy cleared her throat. "Chef Finch," she said diplomatically, "all I can tell you is Chef Nima either brought out a side of Chef Michèle we've never seen...or an imposter wearing a Chef Michèle disguise was in our galley when she was on board."

"Hi, I'm Chuckie McDermott," said a ruddy-faced man

with a high-pitched nasal voice. He wiped a greasy hand on his shirt. "Chief Engineer." Kennedy shook his hand, noticing how smooth it was. It was the opposite of the *Helio's* chief engineer, Franklin Blaas, whose hands were rough and callused. Chuckie pulled off his gray baseball cap and ran a hand through his thinning reddish-blonde hair. "Sorry about the grease on my hands. I was working on the ship's fire system and came in for a drink of water. We've got a glitch, but I'll fix it one way or another, even if I have to disable it." He rubbed his baseball cap up and down on his forehead, not noticing the alarmed looks on the faces of everyone at the table. "So, how is old Eye Candy Handy?"

Kennedy looked at him blankly. "Eye Candy Handy? I'm sorry, I don't know that name. Perhaps it's someone on another ship?"

Chuckie's laugh sounded like a braying donkey, and he slapped his knee. "Franklin Blaas is still on the *Helio*, isn't he?" Kennedy nodded. "Well, back in the day, we called him Eye Candy Handy because he was so handsome. We came up together in the ranks, but because of his good looks, he got the cushy job on the fancy Caribbean ship."

"I didn't know you knew Franklin," Kennedy said hesitantly, "he's never mentioned you."

Chuckie let out another braying laugh. "That's because he'd be embarrassed to admit I had to teach him everything.

When I met him, he was green, walking around toting tools and getting in the way. He didn't even know how to hold a hammer." He sat up straighter and gave the assembled group a knowing look. "I was the more experienced of the two of us."

Mila and Bert shared a glance, remembering their earlier walk and seeing evidence of the ship's disrepair. Kennedy smiled at Chuckie. "It's a pleasure to meet you, Chuckie, and I'll tell Eye Candy Handy we met you."

"Yep, that was us. The dynamic duo, like Batman and Robin, joined at the hip. You know this one time—"

A pale, thin man with a dark receding hairline stuck his hand out and cut Chuckie off. "Hi guys, I'm Ismaeel Suarez, the beverage director for the *Malina*." He looked at the ruddy-faced man. "Sorry to have cut you off, Chuckie, but we'll be in Vancouver before you finish your story." He turned back to Bert, Mila, and Kennedy. "It's a pleasure to meet all of you. Jordan has told us some interesting stories."

"And I'm Cormac O'Shea, the executive housekeeper," a lilting Scottish voice piped up. "Welcome to the *Malina*."

They sat around the table the way people who work in any industry do—sharing war stories and discovering people they had in common.

"Do you remember when the dining room flooded?" Cormac chuckled. "It was the only time I ever saw Joy panic."

He held up a finger. "But it was only for a split second. She had us carry the dining room tables and chairs onto the pool deck and told the passengers it was an impromptu northern lights dinner."

"She sounds like you," Mila said to Kennedy.

Kennedy grinned. "Cruise Director 101: turn disasters into memorable events and make it seem like it was planned all along."

"This one," Mila nodded at Kennedy, "held a last-minute diva show on our pool deck. We still get asked on each cruise what time the show will take place."

Chuckie piped up excitedly in his high-pitched voice. "Remember the time the whale got lodged on the bow? We weren't sure if it had already died and we just picked it up or if we had killed it." The room was silent as four sets of eyes turned to him in shock while the others looked down at the table uncomfortably.

After a few moments of awkward silence, Chuckie pushed himself away from the table and stood up. "Well, I have to go. I need to check on some things before the passengers arrive."

"Any chance my requests will get fixed before they get here?" Cormac asked. "Some of them have been on the list for a few weeks, and we found a few lightbulbs out in the Owner's Suite."

Chuckie held up a hand and waved it dismissively. "Yeah, yeah, yeah. If it's on the clipboard, it will get fixed."

"And the tear in the carpet in the dining room?" Sha asked hopefully.

"Like I said," Chuckie's voice squeaked, "if it's on the clipboard, I'll get to it," he said irritably and walked out, muttering.

"Is there coffee down here?" Mila looked around.

Cormac pointed to the large urn at the opposite end of the room. "I'll warn you, it's awful. It will make you want to give up drinking coffee, at least while you are on this cruise."

Bert piped up, "Mila tried to give up coffee once. Her court date is still pending."

"Touché, Bert," Mila said as the group's camaraderie returned. "You must have found a snack-size pack of boldness on one of our stops across the country."

While Mila was at the coffee urn, Kennedy and Bert filled the others in on their drive from Arkansas to Seattle.

Mila sat down and sipped the dark brew, screwing up her face in disgust. "Oh, this is awful. It tastes like battery acid."

Sha cocked her head to the side. "You know what they say about bad coffee, Mila. It's like bad wine. After the first few sips, you're just happy it's taking the edge off." The group laughed and settled in around the table. "Tell us what you will be doing on the *Malina*. We didn't know any of you were coming."

"That's what is so strange. Alfred in the corporate office told J. Mitchell we were coming, but J. Mitchell thought it was a joke. It's odd."

Sha exhaled, placed her elbows on the table, and steepled her fingers at her lips. "J. Mitchell is odd and was a strange choice for this cruise. Granted, he was the number two under Joy, our old cruise director, and when Joy didn't come back, they offered him the job because he was already familiar with the ship and the route. But it was a bad choice, in my opinion. He spent more time in the spa with Tammy than with the passengers. We're hoping that if the corporate office decides to restart the cruises, we will get someone different, but we're stuck with J. Mitchell for this trip. Have you met anyone else other than us?" Sha asked.

"They met our very vigilant director of security," Jordan piped up, and Mila recounted their arrival, starting with the incident on the gangway and then admonished for being somewhere they shouldn't have been.

"Kennedy, we have to show you the pictures!" Bert began to pull out his camera. "The spa—"

"What *about* the spa?" a high, thin voice interrupted. The voice belonged to a woman wearing a skin-tight black skirt and leopard print blouse. Her chocolate brown hair had thick blonde streaks and was piled on top of her head in a teased bouffant. She walked up and placed both hands on the table, drumming her long red fingernails.

"I believe we now know who runs the spa," Mila whispered behind her hand to Bert.

"I'm Tammy Fischer," she said smiling, although her frosty tone was anything but friendly, "and while we haven't been properly introduced, I have learned that the two of you," she pointed a lacquered finger at Bert and Mila, "were caught snooping by the spa. So, I came down to see if there was something I could help you with."

A muscle in Mila's jaw twitched as she lowered her coffee cup. "I think the word snooping is out of context. Bert and I were taking a walk around the ship when Barney—"

"That's Mr. Phyfe to you, friend," Tammy snapped, and Sha snorted. She glared at the tall chef but didn't say a word. Tammy cut her eyes back over to Mila. "Mr. Phyfe said you were trying to peek into the salon and spa, but you told him you were looking for the gym." She narrowed her eyes. "So, which is it?"

The room crackled with electricity as Mila and Tammy stared at each other. Mila gave her an ingratiating smile. "As the gym shares space with the salon and spa as it does on the *Helio*, we wanted to look at both."

Tammy straightened and crossed her arms over her tight-fitting, button-down shirt. She paced the length of the table, and the only noise was the click of her high heels on the tile floor. "It's interesting that none of us knew of your impending arrival and even more surprising that corporate felt this cruise needed," she turned around and walked the opposite way, "assistance," she spat out. "We did these cruises for a long time without any additional support." She turned to Mila and gave her a forced smile. "So, may I ask why *you* are here? I certainly don't need any assistance."

Mila smiled. "I'm sure you don't. The corporate office asked me to see if a renovation would help boost future sales for the *Malina* as there are at minimum two full sea days on each cruise, which in their eyes means additional dollars."

Tammy placed her hands on her hips and narrowed her eyes at Mila. "We've never had any complaints about how the spa looked, and I *always* met my goals."

Trying to figure out a way to change the subject, Kennedy quickly spoke up, "Ismaeel, do you have something special planned for the captain's cocktail party tonight? I've been asked to hostess the event."

Tammy's brown eyes whipped from Mila to Kennedy. "Does J. Mitchell know this?"

"I'm not sure. The captain called me up to the bridge and asked me to host it."

"Well, we'll see about that! He's obviously forgotten the pecking order around here, but I'll make sure to remind him." She turned abruptly and stormed out of the room. There was a loud whoosh as she pushed the doors open. "Get out of my way," they heard her yell, and there was a clatter of dishes.

Sha and the others looked at each other. "The captain really asked you to host his cocktail party?"

"Among other things," Mila muttered.

Hearing Mila's comment, the tall, dark-haired chef looked at Kennedy. "Tell me he didn't." She let out a sigh. "He already hit on you?" Kennedy nodded, and Sha looked at Jordan. "It took a week before he offered to give you a personal tour of his lair."

Jordan winked. "There are benefits to being the lowly kitchen help and not a young, beautiful cruise director."

"Am I going to have trouble tonight?" Kennedy nodded at the doors, still swinging violently from Tammy's abrupt departure through them. "I don't want to step on J. Mitchell's toes, he is the cruise director, but the captain did request it."

Cormac, who had remained quiet for some time, spoke up with a twinkle in his green eyes. "Well, lass, we will find out soon enough. Ismaeel, why don't you tell Kennedy about your signature cocktails for tonight." He nodded at Sha and Jordan. "We were the official taste testers a few nights ago, and my friend here has some interesting options for our guests."

Ismaeel blushed. "You guys were easy. You just needed a few drinks after a long day." He turned to Kennedy. "I hope the ones I am serving tonight become permanent on our cocktail list. I think they complement our cruises. First, there is The Snowfall, a twist on a chocolate martini."

"It's pretty sexy," Jordan remarked. "What was in it again? After the second one, I was not feeling any pain, and it took care of my chocolate craving."

Ismaeel's eyes lit up, and he relayed the ingredients for the decadent cocktail.

THE SNOWFALL

CHOCOLATE SYRUP

1 OZ. BAILEYS IRISH CREAM

1 OZ. FRANGELICO

1 OZ. KAHLUA

WHIPPED CREAM

DARK CHOCOLATE SHAVINGS

POUR CHOCOLATE SYRUP ONTO A SHALLOW PLATE AND DIP THE RIM OF A MARTINI GLASS INTO THE SYRUP. DRIZZLE THE INSIDE OF THE GLASS WITH

ADDITIONAL CHOCOLATE SYRUP. ADD BAILEYS, FRANGELICO, AND KAHLUA TO A COCKTAIL SHAKER FILLED WITH ICE. SHAKE WELL AND STRAIN INTO THE GLASS. ADD WHIPPED CREAM AND GARNISH WITH DARK CHOCOLATE SHAVINGS.

"I've got several others, too—the Alaska Cocktail, which I learned about while reading an obscure book written in 1913 about cocktail recipes, but I still haven't learned why it got the name. The only thing I can come up with is that it has a golden color, and it was close to the time of the gold rush in Alaska. The final drink for tonight is a mixture of burgundy wine and champagne, but I don't have a name for it yet."

"Ismaeel has been working hard to get the right mix of drinks. But, what he won't tell you is that besides being a mixologist who likes to read cocktail recipe books, he's also a master cicerone," Sha said proudly.

Ismaeel blushed. "Sha, they don't need to know about this." He looked at Mila, Bert, and Kennedy and shrugged. "It's nothing."

"What's a master cicerone?" Kennedy asked.

"It's like a sommelier for beer," he answered. "There are four levels, the last being a master cicerone, which by the time you get to that point, you know more about beer than you ever wanted to. How to brew it, pair it with food, and the technical sides."

Bert was intrigued. "There's a technical side to beer? I'll have to give the next one I have more respect."

A young man walked into the mess hall and began talking loudly. "Which one of you ticked Tammy off? She bit my head off and looked like a tornado heading to the bridge." He threw himself into a chair. "Have you heard the latest? Corporate sent some cruise director to help, but I heard she's here because she was on the verge of a mental breakdown."

Seven sets of eyes stared at him.

"What?" he threw out his arms, looking at them stupefied.

Sha let out a deep sigh. "Kennedy, Mila, Bert, please forgive Mr. Allen. He is a toddler and speaks before he reads the room." She turned to Kennedy. "You don't look like you are having a mental breakdown. Are you?"

Kennedy bit her lips together and cocked her head to the side. "No," she said slowly, "it wasn't on my list of things to do today, but the day is still young, and there is plenty of time to be carted off in a straitjacket before the ship departs." She turned to the young man and gave him a winning smile. "Good afternoon, Mr. Allen. What do you do on the ship?"

"It's Jonny, and I'm the dining room manager," he mumbled, embarrassed.

"Wow!" she said, taken aback.

"What's *that* supposed to mean?"

"Nothing," Kennedy stammered, "I'm impressed. You are rather young for a position of such responsibility."

Jonny lifted his chin. "My Uncle Barry helped me out. He has a friend in the corporate office and made a call. I've been practically running his restaurant for the last year, and he thought I might want to try this. So, I figured, why not? It's a free trip to see Alaska, and there's a chance they'll offer me the job."

Kennedy wanted to say more but didn't think it was her place, remembering Alfred's words about allowing the team on the *Malina* to handle things. She hoped the young man had a seating chart. "I'm happy to help if you need anything. My friend Tony—"

"I won't," Jonny said smugly. "It isn't exactly rocket science."

Kennedy bit her lips together and looked at the others. "What time is the pre-arrival staff meeting."

Sha, Ismaeel, and Cormac exchanged looks. "We used to do those when Joy was here, but J. Mitchell didn't feel it was necessary," Cormac said.

"Have any of you seen the manifest?" she asked.

"Have you?" Sha demanded. "Are there any food allergies I need to be aware of? J. Mitchell told us that there was

60

nothing we needed to worry about. That it was, and I quote, 'A cruise for a bunch of old biddy travel agents.' "

"Kennedy, you need to tell them who is on the ship," Mila said earnestly.

Kennedy took a breath. "Well, first, there is Vera Jameson. She's a bit high maintenance and occasionally has some unusual requests," causing Bert and Mil to roll their eyes at the comment. "But she books many cruises with the company, and her best friend is one of the family board members." She looked at Ismaeel. "She likes old-fashioneds, and she likes them in a champagne glass." Ismaeel wrinkled his brow, and Kennedy held up her hand. "Oh, and she hates cocktail napkins. She finds them vulgar because she says they disintegrate in her hand."

"Could be her acidic disposition," Bert added, and Mila giggled.

"Is there a smoking lounge? I haven't been on a tour of the ship yet."

Cormac nodded and said hesitantly, "It's on deck ten—" Before he could finish his sentence, Kennedy moved on.

"Fantastic. Vera loves to smoke cigars, and if we didn't have a smoking lounge, she would simply smoke on the balcony of her stateroom, which causes its own set of problems with the guests around her. On the *Helio*, we got her to use the smoker's lounge, but only after we updated it."

Bert sighed dramatically and rolled his eyes at the group. "No, it was because—"

Mila kicked him under the table.

He clapped his hand over his mouth. "Sorry," he murmured.

"It's okay," Kennedy gave Bert a wink, "no straitjacket required." Then, she turned her attention back to the *Malina* staff. "Will we see any of the senior officers soon? Mrs. Jameson requires a different senior officer to take her for drinks and dinner each night. It's one of those special perks some of our frequent cruisers get. Especially the ones who book the most expensive staterooms and throw private parties." As she shared this information, two men in crisp uniforms walked in.

Sha motioned for them to come over. "Ask, and ye shall receive." When the two men reached the table, she made the introductions. "Kennedy, Mila, Bert, please meet Otto Armitage, our safety officer, and First Officer Andreas Pritchard. Gentlemen, *if* I can call you that after seeing you in The Wreck last night wearing your jockey shorts over your pants, please meet Kennedy, Bert, and Mila from the *Helio*."

Otto looked like he had come from a central casting call for an all-American man. Kennedy was confident that the tall, slender man with his clean-shaven jaw, wire-rim glasses, and winning smile made many hearts flutter when he was out on the

62

town. "Hi," he said with a midwestern twang, extending his hand. "Pleased to meet you. Welcome to the *Malina*."

Where Otto exuded a boyish charm, the dark-haired man with a neatly clipped beard beside him was staring at Mila.

"Have we met before?" he asked as he took Mila's proffered hand and lifted it to his lips.

"I don't believe so but play your cards right, and you'll always remember me," she said, speaking in a soft, husky voice neither Bert nor Kennedy had ever heard. They exchanged a quizzical look over her head while the others at the table rolled their eyes at Andreas.

Kennedy cleared her throat. "Otto, you are the safety officer?" He nodded. "I was wondering if you could take us on a quick tour. I don't like being on a ship I'm unfamiliar with. It's like sitting in a plane and not checking to see where the emergency exits are located."

Otto looked at the group sitting at the table and smirked. "Ha-ha-ha, did one of you put her up to this? Good joke." He removed his glasses, looked at the lenses in the light, and began cleaning them.

"Otto, Andreas, join us," Cormac smiled. "Kennedy was just going over who would be on the ship."

"That's great, Cormac, but we don't have much to do with the passengers."

"That's about to change, laddie," Cormac chuckled jovially.

"I was sharing that one of our VIPs is always escorted for drinks and dinner by a senior staff member or one of the ship's officers. Dinner is either at the captain's table or a table for two."

Otto and Andreas exchanged a look and gulped noticeably. Then, Otto began to speak but was cut off.

"Wait a minute," Jonny said, "the captain has a table?"

Kennedy wrinkled her brow at him. "Of course he does, and different people are seated at it each night. It is an honor to be asked to dine with the captain and the senior officers."

"Ma'am," Otto said, "no disrespect, but I'm not sure we'll be able to accommodate the guest's request. We are rather busy helping the captain, and we've never had to do this before. We'll have to check with him."

"It's not unusual, and I'm sure the captain has had to do it once or twice in his career. Just be the charming gentlemen your mothers raised you to be."

"That's where we might have a problem, ma'am. You see, Andreas was raised by wolves," Otto cupped Andreas's chin. "I've eaten across from him many times, and it isn't for the faint-hearted. Once, he mistook my finger for a Vienna sausage." He held up his hand to show a missing fingertip from his little finger. "He said it was tasty."

"Ketchup makes everything better," Andreas smacked his lips together and grinned. "Don't worry, Kennedy, we will be dashing officers and will take good care of your special guest."

The group laughed but quickly sobered when they heard the echoed clack of high heels.

"That noise can only mean one thing. The Queen of Mean is about to arrive," Otto said under his breath, and Andreas covered his grinning face with a hand.

Tammy marched up to the table. "Well, I spoke with the captain, and somehow *you*," she pointed at Kennedy, "*are hosting* the cocktail party tonight because he thinks J. Mitchell has too much on his plate." She placed a hand on her hip and looked at Andreas and Otto. "What are the two of you doing down here? Don't you have things to do?" she snapped.

Andreas smiled. "No, ma'am, nothing at all. Just listening to Kennedy tell us about the special VIPs and their requests."

"You know it is odd that J. Mitchell had this information but didn't choose to share it," Sha looked directly at Tammy.

Cormac quickly spoke up, "Kennedy, is there anyone else we should be aware of? Any housekeeping requests that I need to know about?"

"And that's our cue to go," Otto said to Andreas and stood up. "Not that this isn't fascinating, but it makes me like my job a lot more."

"Bye, Andreas," Mila waved her fingers. "Perhaps you could give me a personal tour of the ship later?"

"I'll look for a leash and a muzzle," Otto chuckled.

"Find two! I think we might need them." Kennedy shook her head and looked at her friend in astonishment.

"Ma'am, if you are serious, we can meet in twenty minutes in the lobby for your tour of the ship's safety areas," Otto said.

"That would be great, Otto, but could you stop calling me ma'am?"

"I'll work on that," he grinned and paused, "ma'am," and he and the first officer left the mess hall.

Mila pushed Kennedy's shoulder with her own. "I'm so proud of you. That was a nice bit of flirting," she whispered.

"It wasn't flirting, I assure you. You, on the other hand…"

Cormac cleared his throat, "Kennedy, you were telling us about the VIPs."

"Finishing up with Mrs. Jameson. If she chooses to smoke on her balcony, she may take the lilies out of the lobby arrangement. She believes it masks the smell of her cigar smoke."

"But doesn't—"

Bert piped up, "She's nose blind because she owns a chain of designer funeral homes, and most funeral arrangements have lilies."

"Wait a minute," Sha said, "designer funeral homes?"

Kennedy gave Bert an annoyed look, "And moving right along. Another VIP I saw noted is a woman named Ronnee Barrett. She books some conventions on the ships and takes her repeat high-dollar clients on a yearly cruise on the *Helio*. Ronnee is low-key, but if one of her 'dears' needs something, she becomes hyper-vigilant."

"A.K.A. annoying," Mila said.

"Has the Owner's Suite been checked?" Kennedy looked at Cormac. "There is a guest named Diamond Jim who has it booked. I remember seeing in the notes that he is a friend of one of the board members, so we will need to take good care of him, especially as he is getting married."

"Inspected and awaiting a re-inspection as soon as Chuckie reads the clipboard and replaces the light bulbs," Cormac said.

Kennedy turned to Jordan and Sha. "And you guys are ready for the wedding reception, right?"

"What wedding reception?" Sha, Jordan, and Jonny asked in unison.

"Diamond Jim's," Kennedy said slowly. She felt a wave of anxiety course through her body. "He's getting married on a glacier in Juneau. The manifest notes said there is a reception for the passengers that night to celebrate the wedding."

"*What?*" Sha exclaimed. "And J. Mitchell neglected to tell me about this? How am I supposed to pull this off? We leave in three hours." Her face was beginning to turn the color of her purple bandanna.

Kennedy pondered for a moment. "The dinner menus are set, right?" Sha and Jordan nodded. "So that takes care of the food. Ismaeel, how are we on champagne?"

"I can get more in Juneau if we need to," he answered.

"It doesn't sound like it will be too complicated from a dining room standpoint, but it would have been nice to know," Jonny said. "But what about the wedding cake?"

"Cake?" Sha's eyes bugged out. "A wedding cake! How am I supposed to whip up a wedding cake in the middle of the ocean? I'm going to kill J. Mitchell when I see him." She violently hammered her hand on the table. "I'm going to be like Chef Michèle and pound him with a meat mallet until he's translucent."

Jordan spoke up. "I could make a small, white three-tier

cake, and when we are in Juneau, we can send someone to pick up some flowers to decorate it. Then, we can wheel it out to the couple to cut and have a pre-plated sheet cake in the back for the servers to bring out to the passengers."

"I can take photos," Bert volunteered, and Kennedy and Mila looked at him in shock. He shrugged. "It's a couple of photos during dinner. It's not like I'll be photographing them all day."

"Anyone or anything else we should know about before the ship leaves?" Sha asked, standing up. "Jordan, we've got to get to the kitchen to make certain we have everything ready for this surprise wedding reception."

"No," Kennedy answered, "just one other guest, LaVonda Taylor. She's another travel agent who books a lot of groups and clients on the Sunny Dayz ships. She can be a handful."

"Kennedy, was she the one on the Mediterranean cruise with you years ago?" Mila asked, and Kennedy nodded. Mila looked at the others. "Ms. Taylor gave the cruise and Kennedy a terrible review. It was so bad that Alfred had to do damage control."

Sha sat down heavily and pulled Jordan down with her. "You can't leave us hanging with, 'she can be a handful.' Spill it."

Tammy's ears perked up. "Well, it couldn't have been that bad. You are still here and the darling of the corporate office."

Kennedy closed her eyes and sighed. "It was a terrible cruise from the start. I had just been promoted and was flown out to fill in for the regular cruise director on the *Oriana*, who had to go home to deal with a family emergency. It was a full cruise, and every cabin was occupied. The weather was rotten, and several ports of call had to be canceled, and because of this, we had to find additional activities for the passengers, who were not happy about the closed ports. On top of this, Vera Jameson was on board and was being particularly demanding."

"The same woman who owns the designer funeral home company?" Cormac asked.

Kennedy nodded.

"Vera and Kennedy had not had their kumbaya moment yet," Mila whispered theatrically from behind her hand.

Kennedy continued, "The regular cruise director had been given the key information about Ms. Taylor and Mrs. Jameson; however, she forgot to share the details with me in her hurry to get off the ship. When Ms. Taylor joined the cruise at a later port, she decided at the last minute to bring her dog but neglected to tell anyone." She looked at each of them. "It was a perfect storm: a green cruise director on an unfamiliar ship, the pouring rain, grumpy passengers unable to enjoy the sun and the ports of call, and a stressed-out staff and crew. But it wasn't until the next morning that everything erupted."

"It shouldn't have been anything you couldn't handle," Tammy said in a bored tone.

Kennedy gave her a tight smile. "You're right, but I didn't."

"Go on, finish the story," Sha said urgently.

Kennedy took a breath. "Several of LaVonda Taylor's cabin neighbors found me in the lobby and complained about her dog, who had barked all night. I apologized and offered them vouchers for the spa, which placated them, but before I could get to the services desk to alert the spa, I was accosted by Vera Jameson, who had come down to the lobby with another outlandish request."

"My word, lass, you were getting it from all sides, weren't you?" Cormac said sympathetically.

Kennedy nodded. "While I was trying to come up with a satisfactory compromise for Mrs. Jameson, LaVonda Taylor marched up and began berating me for not upgrading her to a stateroom or putting the dog in an adjoining cabin. She then proceeded to tell everyone within earshot that because the company was trying to get her to book all of her business with them, I would find a way to upgrade her, even if it meant bumping someone from the cruise. She kept getting louder and louder, and the dog, excited by LaVonda's agitation, began to yap incessantly. Finally, I closed my eyes, counted to five, and told Ms. Taylor I could not accommodate her requests, and she was free to take the dog and leave at the next port."

"Whoa!" Sha said.

"Yeah, not my finest moment."

"You don't think she's going to bring her dog on this cruise, do you?" Cormac asked.

Kennedy shook her head. "There was nothing in the notes, and the dog was old. I'm sure he's not around anymore."

Tammy stood up and smiled. She had already received information about the wedding as the bride had booked services in the spa for her wedding day, but now she had some interesting information to share with J. Mitchell when he returned from wherever he was. She was a little miffed at him, and she'd extract some form of punishment for his running off without inviting her. "Well, this was fun, but I need to go."

"Before you leave, Tammy," Cormac said, "don't you think we should meet every day like we used to? We can meet here. There's plenty of coffee and space."

Tammy gave him a tight smile. "I don't think so. I think we've learned everything we need to know," and she waved her long red nails in the air and left the room.

Kennedy, Bert, and Mila met the ship's safety officer in the main lobby. "I'll admit I was shocked that you wanted this tour," Otto said. "I honestly thought the others were playing a joke on me. So, first things first, did you find your life jackets on top of the closet in your quarters?" They nodded. "Great! I wasn't sure if some of them went home as souvenirs during the shutdown. We have them in each cabin and at the muster stations, so we are doubly covered if we have to evacuate. You've all been to fire school, correct?" Mila and Kennedy nodded. Otto did not see Bert looking away when he asked the question. "And are you comfortable with helping to fight a fire if necessary?"

"As long as the hose doesn't dance out of my hands," Mila quipped. During her last fire safety class, she had been daydreaming while holding the nozzle, and when the water shot out, it jumped out of her hands and drenched everyone around her. "I wasn't the most popular person that day."

They toured the ship, and Otto pointed out the locations of the lifeboats, life preservers, flare guns, and the designated muster stations for the passengers. When they got back to deck five, he rubbed his hands together. "Well, that concludes our tour. Do you feel better, ma'am?" he asked, looking at Kennedy.

"Otto, this is going to be a long trip if you continue to call me *ma'am*," Kennedy held out her hand. "Thank you for taking the time to show us around. I do feel better knowing where things are now."

"Well, I wouldn't worry. It's a short cruise, and the weather looks good. I'll see you around," he winked at her, "ma'am." Otto departed, leaving the three of them standing in the lobby.

"Should we explore the rest of the ship?" Mila asked. "I think there is a lot we need to see before the passengers arrive."

They took the elevator to the promenade deck and saw the library and golf area. Then, they took the stairs down to the pool deck to see the totem poles in the pool that Alfred had mentioned. They were near the back of the pool bar when they heard J. Mitchell and Tammy standing at the bar counter, talking. Mila put her hand to her lips and motioned for them to step back into the service entrance.

"You are about as useless as the letter 'g' in the word lasagna," they heard Tammy spit out. "Kennedy has only been here for a few hours, and she's already making you look bad. What was so important that you had to leave?"

"I had things to do," J. Mitchell whined.

"Like what?" Tammy looked at him closely and grabbed his chin, turning his face to one side and then another. "You look different. Did you get a facial? Your skin is all pink and swollen."

"I saw some wrinkles around my mouth, and my skin was losing its luster," he moaned, stroking his cheeks gently, "and I have such a beautiful baby face."

"You should be more concerned with saving your skin than pampering it. Chef Sha didn't know about the wedding reception and is ready to put you through a meat grinder." She grasped his chin between her thumb and forefinger and scrutinized his face. "I can't believe you went to some stranger instead of me. I'm the reason you have good skin now. Two years ago, you thought a facial was putting your face over a pot of water on spaghetti night."

J. Mitchell waved his hand. "Why was she upset? There's nothing to the reception. It's just some cake and a few glasses of champagne. She's blowing it way out of proportion."

"Yes, but sweetie, Sha has to make the cake," she said with feigned patience. "You are lucky the new sous chef figured something out quickly." Tammy had her hands on her hips. "Did you even consider the extra champagne we might need for the wedding reception?"

"No," J. Mitchell said petulantly, looking at his shoe.

She looked at him and shook her head. "Now, what do you know about the bride and groom?"

J. Mitchell sighed. "Why are you nagging me? This reception is nothing. I've exchanged a few messages with the maid of honor, and everything is worked out."

Tammy closed her eyes and pinched the bridge of her nose. Finally, she looked up at him. "Because this isn't just *any* reception. The groom is the friend of a board member. So, any glitch will get reported back to corporate. And if the bride is unhappy, you can be sure the groom will be even more unhappy, and he will be looking for someone to blame, and that someone is you, the cruise director who was supposed to be handling things. Got it?" She poked his chest. "So, when the bride- and groom-to-be arrive, you need to go over the top and act like the little suck-up we both know you to be."

He held up his hands defensively. "Okay, okay, I get it, be myself."

"Did you even read the notes on the manifest?"

"I looked at the names. There's no one famous, just a bunch of old biddies." J. Mitchell crossed his arms and kicked the wall holding up the counter. "This cruise is nothing more than glorified babysitting for six days." He held up his fingers. "Feed them, give them some activities to do, send them off to port, and feign interest in their dull little lives if you get stuck talking to one of them." He brushed his hands together. "And then it starts all over again. Rinse and repeat. Honestly, I could do it in my sleep."

Tammy poked a finger again at J. Mitchell. "That's where you are wrong. There were all sorts of notes you should have read. One of the VIPs is some bigwig named Vera something. She owns a chain of funeral parlors."

"Gross! Dead people."

"It may be gross, but Kennedy has taken care of her in the past. One thing you should know about, though, is that she is known for removing lilies from flower arrangements to hide the smell of her cigars."

J. Mitchell's eyes bugged out. "My lilies? I designed that arrangement. I'll smack her hands myself if I catch her taking one."

Tammy sighed. "Well, that would be a sure way to get fired, you idiot. Just let Kennedy handle her."

"What else?" he asked impatiently, fanning his face. "I need to get out of the sun."

"You need to listen to me if you want to keep this job!" Tammy snarled. "A travel agent is coming on board whose name is Ronnee. From what I can gather, this woman frequently brings wealthy guests whom she calls her 'dears.' "

"Dears?" J. Mitchell scoffed. "That sounds like a dreadful 1960s girl band." He turned the name over in his head again. "Ronnee and the Dears. Ugh, how pathetic."

Tammy crossed her arms. "I may have one little tidbit for you," and a smile peeked from the corners of her lips. "The person who gave Kennedy her first and only black mark will be on this trip."

J. Mitchell's eyes slid over to Tammy in intrigue. "Ohhh?"

"LaVonda somebody or other. Look her up on the manifest. Find out who she is and what she looks like before the passengers arrive. Then, when she gets here, you need to suck up to her and shine like a beacon in the night whenever you are around her and casually remind her of Kennedy's terrible customer service."

"Okay, okay. I've got it. LaVonda somebody or other. Can I leave now?" J. Mitchell asked in a whiney voice.

"Not yet. I have a few more things to share, which, if you had been here and not running off to some cheap salon to make yourself pretty, you'd know about."

"I don't have to take this," J. Mitchell said sullenly. "I think I'll go to my room and lie down before we load the ark." He began to turn to leave, and as he did, Tammy spoke up.

"Did you know the captain asked Kennedy to hostess his cocktail party tonight?" J. Mitchell whipped around, and Tammy watched his emotions play across his face. She enjoyed taunting him, like a cat with a mouse in the corner, and he played into her hand every time.

"*What?*" he spluttered. "How could he? It's my ship. I'm the cruise director! I'm more fabulous, more talented, better looking, *and younger*! She's closer to your age than mine, making her practically ancient."

Tammy narrowed her eyes at J. Mitchell. "Watch it, bub," she said sharply.

"I'm sorry, I'm sorry, I'm sorry," he began jumping up and down. "I'm just so upset now." He fanned his face with his hands. "When I get upset, I get hot." He touched his brow. "And now my face is sweating, which can't be good after my facial. I did the microdermabrasion one," he chattered. Then, seeing Tammy's irritated face, he reached out and took her hands, holding them in front of him. "You will never get old, Tammy. Because of your facelifts and filler regimens, you are practically immortal."

"Thank you," she nodded, "you may continue digging yourself out of the hole you are in."

"Your panache, your quick wit, your chic clothing sense. You, my darling, are a dazzling jewel. And that woman they sent from the *Helio's* spa," he coughed. "Have you seen her? She looks like an Afghan hound that's never been brushed. And those clothes? Ugh, *someone* should explain to her that it's the boho look, not the hobo look. She clearly doesn't know the first

79

thing about style, whereas you are a fashionista."

Tammy waved her hand. "Okay, that's enough. You are forgiven. Now, let's go for a walk so I can explain how you will handle things on this cruise with Miss Perfect Cruise Director on board."

J. Mitchell took Tammy's arm, and they began to stroll away from the pool bar. "So, where are they now?"

"Otto took them on a safety walk." Tammy rolled her eyes. "Kennedy made a big deal about safety drills and knowing where everything was. She said," Tammy spoke in a false breathy voice, "I feel so much better when I know where things are in case of an emergency."

"B-O-R-I-N-G," J. Mitchell yawned. "Like anything bad is going to happen."

Kennedy stopped by the canoe-shaped services desk after she, Bert, and Mila completed their tour of the ship. She turned over the conversation she had overheard on the pool deck in her mind. There was a strange dynamic between the spa manager and the cruise director. One minute, J. Mitchell would fawn over Tammy; the next, he acted like a petulant child in trouble with his mother. It bothered her that J. Mitchell knew about her

80

unfortunate encounter with LaVonda Taylor, but she had been the one to share what had happened on that cruise with the group, including Tammy. When J. Mitchell made his quip about Mila's appearance, Bert and Kennedy had to hold Mila back to prevent her from throwing J. Mitchell over the railing and into the ocean. Kennedy reminded herself for the tenth time today that she had taken this assignment to put some distance between herself and the *Helio* and to help Alfred. She knew the best way to do that would be to get organized before the passengers arrived, and to do *that*, she needed a clipboard. When she reached the services desk, the same woman who had given them their cabin keys was standing at her computer terminal, her eyes glued to the screen. "You again?" she asked without looking up. "What is it this time?"

Kennedy smiled. "I need to get into the previous cruise director's office to look for a clipboard. Could someone from security let me in?"

"The only person who can do that is Mr. Phyfe, and he's unavailable," the woman scowled at the computer screen.

"Oh." Kennedy could hear laughter coming from the office Mr. Phyfe had stepped out of earlier when she, Bert, and Mila were trying to find someone to help them with their cabin assignments. "How do you know?"

The woman jerked her thumb over her shoulder. "His door is shut. If the door is shut, he's either not there or not to be disturbed."

Kennedy now heard what sounded like Chuckie's high-pitched braying on the other side of the door. "It sounds like he is in there. If you could—"

"Look, the door is shut, which means he's not to be disturbed. He's probably doing important security work to get ready for the passengers, which is what I am trying to do," she said with exasperation. The phone beside her computer rang, and she picked up the handset and held it to her ear. "Uh-huh, uh-huh. Okay, I'll send someone down." She hung up the handset and, for the first time, looked directly at Kennedy. "Since it doesn't look like you are busy, I need you to go down to the pier and sign for something."

"What is it?"

"How should I know?"

"Didn't the person on the phone say what it was?"

"No."

Kennedy blinked. "Okay," she said slowly, marveling at the woman's attitude. Kennedy went down to the pier and was back a few minutes later. "I believe this is for the bride and groom."

"What gave you that idea?" the woman asked in a monotone as she looked at the oversized ball and chain made

82

from black carnations Kennedy held. A red satin sash was draped across the ball and said in gold letters, "Good Luck with the New Ball and Chain, Diamond Jim!"

"What am I supposed to do with that?" she asked.

"I believe we are to deliver it to someone's cabin," Kennedy said patiently, pointing at the red sash. "I would be willing to bet his name is Diamond Jim, and he's on the manifest. Perhaps he is the groom? The one having his reception on the ship?" She couldn't believe the conversation she was having. It was surreal.

The woman blew a large puff of air out of her mouth, making her eyeglasses fog up and her bangs flutter. "Fine." She opened the drawer below her computer and handed Kennedy a plastic card on a lanyard. "Here is a master key. Take this *thing* to the room and come right back. Do you know which one it is?"

Kennedy couldn't help herself. She looked at the woman with mock surprise. "How would I know what room they are in? I wasn't allowed to have a manifest, remember? I guess you'll have to look it up for me." She was fighting the urge to laugh.

The woman let out an irritated sigh. "Fine." She tapped a few keys on the keyboard. "Cabin 1002, that's on deck ten. It's the Owner's Suite, so don't touch anything inside, and since you are taking that to the cabin, there are a few more things to go." She pointed to a mound of gift baskets in the corner. "Are you going to need help?" she sighed.

"No, I'll handle this. I don't want to take you away from your work." Kennedy pulled her phone out of her pocket and dialed a number. When the person on the other end answered, she said, "I have a special delivery for the Owner's Suite, any interest in helping me?"

It took Mila and Bert precisely five minutes to get from their cabins to the main lobby, and both burst into laughter when they saw the black floral ball and chain arrangement and several baskets in front of Kennedy. As they picked up the items and began walking, they heard the flat voice of the woman call out to them, "Don't touch anything in there, and bring me back the key!"

Getting off the service elevator when it reached deck ten, the three friends walked down the long corridor and stopped at Cabin 1002. They wondered what they would find on the other side. "It can't be worse than the *Helio*," Mila commented.

Kennedy cocked her head and looked at Mila as she put the key to the lock on the door. "Are you sure? May I remind you about the *Helio's* Owner's Suite?"

"Good point." Mila shifted the baskets she was holding in her arms. "Now we have to see it."

Kennedy opened the door and entered the foyer carrying the black carnation ball and chain. Bert and Mila followed, and

84

no one spoke for several moments. "When I was taking classes for interior design, I had a professor who said a room's style should be able to carry a conversation," Kennedy breathed.

"Then this one needs some serious therapy," Bert replied, setting down his packages.

Mila was stunned. "I'm just going to say what we are all thinking. The suite on the *Helio* may be tacky, but this is downright creepy."

They ambled into the living room, speechless. A low-slung artic blue sectional sat across from a fake fireplace. The fabric on the back of the couch got lighter as it reached the top, reminding Kennedy of the crest of a wave as it curled. A glass coffee table held up by eight animal horns sat in front of the sectional, and underneath the table lay a chocolate brown bearskin rug trimmed in gray fur. The bear's face appeared to be staring and growling at the fireplace. "I hope this is fake," Mila said as she stooped down and ran her fingers over the rug. "It is," she sighed with relief. "I bet Cormac has to use a rake on this thing. It is so thick you couldn't use a vacuum; it would get tangled as it got sucked up."

"Mila, look at the size of the rug. The bear would have been almost twenty feet tall," Bert said distractedly.

Faux animal heads made from resin hung on the walls, including a slate-colored moose with gold antlers, a narwhal with a glittering horn, and a deer proudly displaying an arctic blue rack. Mila pointed at them. "Well, those are obviously fake but quite odd."

Bert was staring at the massive fireplace. "I've never been afraid of a fireplace before, but this one looks like it has been used for human sacrifices." Kennedy and Mila walked closer. "Be careful!" he whispered. "It looks hungry."

The fireplace was a four-foot by six-foot stone relief of the god Pan. Detailed stonework captured the individual strands of wavy hair and thick bushy eyebrows that begged to be combed. Large upper teeth that looked like they could snap a branch in half sat at the top of the fireplace opening while the lower teeth held the glow of embers, and the god's long, tangled mustache ran down the sides of the fireplace to the hearth.

Kennedy began to walk around the room and suddenly turned back to look at the fireplace. "Okay, that's creepy. It feels like the eyes are staring at you."

"Let's check out the bedrooms," Mila said, pulling Bert away from where he stood still rooted in front of the fireplace.

She opened the door to the first bedroom. "A bit rustic, but not terrible. I've seen furniture like this in a magazine. Not my style, but it wouldn't give me nightmares."

"Until you look up," Bert pointed to a lifelike painting of the underside of a whale.

"So many questions," Kennedy said slowly, and her eyes darted around the room. "Do you think anyone from corporate saw the final product?"

Mila walked over to the window. "I doubt it. Would we call these furkins?" she asked, running her hand down the artificial fur curtains that hung from a curtain rod made from a tree branch.

"I wish we had turned this into a bingo game," Bert mused.

Mila agreed and grinned. "There has got to be a polar bear rug in here somewhere," and she brushed past Kennedy and Bert. "I'm going to see what is in the next bedroom." It was quiet for a moment, and then they heard her cry, "BINGO!"

"You're right. He's following us," Bert uttered as he and Kennedy walked back through the living room to the bedroom on the other side of the cabin where Mila was.

"Who?"

"Him," Bert pointed at the fireplace.

"He might need a snack," she whispered back. "Maybe we could feed J. Mitchell to him."

"Too skinny," Bert replied. "What about Officer Khaki?"

"Might give him indigestion."

"*That* will definitely make him grumpier."

Mila was leaning against the doorway to the second bedroom. She had a look of amusement on her face. "I'm almost glad we saved this room for last."

"Why?" Kennedy pushed past her. "Oh my…"

The second bedroom's bathroom was directly on the right, and a white marble tub, placed on a dais and surrounded by white carpeting, begged Kennedy to enter. A life-size photo mural of a snow-encrusted forest covered two of the bathroom's walls, while a third featured a wall-sized mirror with glass sinks and icicle sconces.

Bert tapped Kennedy on the shoulder. "How do you fill the tub?" Kennedy looked around and spied a circle of acrylic icicles on the ceiling that disguised the spout. She pointed to them. "Wow, sort of like a waterfall,' he said in amazement.

"It gets better, ladies and gentlemen," Mila called out. "Come into the bedroom, but first, let me set the mood. Still in shock, Bert and Kennedy walked out of the bathroom and entered the darkened bedroom. Mila flipped a switch, and green, blue, and rose lighting that the designer had artfully hidden in the crown molding undulated on the ceiling and walls. "Your own private northern lights show with your darling friend, Chilly Willy." She had draped a fake polar bear blanket over her head.

"You are sick," Kennedy laughed. "Does he make you

long for your former playmates at the circus?"

"They were wonderful friends and, unlike some people, never make snarky comments," Mila answered, reaching up to pat the polar bear's head.

Kennedy suddenly looked from Mila to Bert. "I just had a thought. We have to make sure that Jones and Terri Butler do not take a cruise on this ship any time soon. Seeing this cabin might push their renovation back."

"Wait, isn't this the same designer who is working with them on their house?" Bert asked. "When they left after their last cruise, Mr. Butler wanted his office to have a safari theme. Can you imagine the design if he saw the fireplace monster?"

They were laughing as they left the stateroom, and Kennedy pulled the door shut, listening for the click to ensure it had latched.

"I thought it was you three! Exactly what are you doing in there? This area is off-limits to you!" the gruff voice of the director of security called from the corridor. "Stop right there!" He was panting hard when he waddled up to them.

"Honest, Barney, we were just dropping off some welcome baskets and flowers for one of the VIPs," Mila said sweetly.

"It's Mr. Phyfe to you," he roared, pointing at his nametag. "P-H-Y-F-E, and you have no business being in that room." He pointed at the cabin door. "How did you get a key? Did you steal it?"

Mila gave the security director what she hoped was an earnest look. "Why, Officer Barney," she began, and Bert tried hard to stifle a snort, and it came out like a honk. "We got it from the very helpful lady at the services desk. She asked us to deliver some items to the room. You know she's super busy, and we *are* here to help."

"I'm going to check that room, missy. That's twice now that I've found the two of you," he pointed at Bert, "in places you don't belong." He made a "V" with his fingers and moved them from his eyes to theirs. "I'm watching you."

"Gosh, that makes me feel—"

Kennedy cut Mila off before she could finish her sentence and smiled at the man. "Mr. Phyfe, please feel free to check the room. We dropped off the items as requested. I am sorry to have caused you concern," she said graciously.

He glared at her and then hitched up his pants. "See that you keep an eye on these two, so I don't have to. And I'll take this," he snatched the keycard from her hands. As they walked away from the pudgy man, they made sure not to make eye contact, as any sudden glance would cause them to break out into gales of laughter.

It was almost time for the passengers to board the ship, and Kennedy was walking through the lobby when she saw Bert setting up his photo area. "Have you seen this?" he pointed to the photo backdrop of a ship's prow with a glacier in the background. A large captain's wheel prop stood nearby. "Could this be a little cheesier?"

Kennedy grinned. "I'm sure it could be. Do you want me to hold your camera while you do that?"

"No, it's fine; this will only take a second," he grunted as he picked up the heavy wheel and duckwalked to position it in front of the backdrop, not noticing that his camera strap had looped around one of the handles. "Wow, it was heavier than I thought." Then, as he began to move away, the strap, still hooked on the handle, pulled the wheel, and it toppled to the floor, taking Bert with it.

"Ah, it feels like old times," Kennedy bent down to unhook the camera strap from the wheel and held out a hand to help Bert to his feet.

"At least I wasn't purple from oxygen deprivation this time. Thank goodness no one saw—"

They heard the staccato laughter of J. Mitchell as he came out of a door behind the guest services desk. "Now *that* was *sadlarious*[3]!" he pointed at Bert. Bert huffed and took off his camera to pick up the ship's wheel and reposition it.

"Will you be in the lobby to greet the passengers, J. Mitchell?" Kennedy asked. "There are a few people I'd like to introduce you to."

J. Mitchell wrinkled his nose. "Not my thing but have fun. Toodles!" He waved his fingers at Kennedy and walked up the grand staircase.

The passengers began to arrive, and Kennedy was pointing one couple to the elevators when she saw a commotion from the corner of her eye. An impeccably dressed woman in a black suit and a gray silk turtleneck was marching through the lobby. Her silver, shoulder-length hair bounced with each purposeful step, and she scowled as she looked left and right with her laser eyes. Sensing the woman's body language, staff members on the floor made sure not to make eye contact. Kennedy wasted no time walking up to her as members at the service desk looked on in terror, wondering who the woman was and why Kennedy was seeking her out. The hardened features on the woman's face instantly softened when she saw Kennedy. "Thank goodness!" she said.

"Good afternoon, Mrs. Jameson, and welcome to the *Malina*."

---

[3] sadlarious: an act that is both sad and hilarious.

"I assure you that seeing your face is the only good thing about being in this gray, depressing city," Vera said in her clipped tone, waving her hand in the air. The movement caused her large teardrop pearl earrings to sway back and forth. "How do these people deal with this dismal weather and the horrendous traffic?"

"It sounds like you are falling in love with the city and might consider moving here."

"You are turning into an insolent young lady," and there was a smile in Vera's eyes as she spoke. She whipped her head around and snapped her fingers at the porters who had entered the lobby and were struggling with her bags. "Speed it up, gentlemen." Flustered, the men handling her baggage collided with one another. "Good grief," she muttered.

A man of medium build with wavy brown hair eyed the two men with sympathy. "You know you could have just had it brought on board like a regular person's luggage," he said in a bored tone as he walked up to Vera. He was dressed casually, wearing a blue oxford cloth button-down shirt, jeans, and a brown leather jacket.

Vera gave the man a look of disdain. "And I, young man, am not a *regular* person." Unafraid of Vera's tone, the man wiped his sunglasses with a cloth. She narrowed her eyes at him. "I do hope you have something more suitable to wear while we are on this cruise. Had I known Kennedy would be here, I would

93

have insisted that you wear something more presentable."
Kennedy stood awkwardly during the exchange. While she knew
Vera well, she was unsure who the man with her was. He
continued to polish his sunglasses.

"Kennedy," Vera sighed heavily, "this poorly dressed
irritant is my nephew, Justin Jameson. Justin, please meet
Kennedy Reeves."

"Ah, the infamous Ms. Reeves." Justin placed his
sunglasses inside his coat pocket and turned his attention to
Kennedy. "I've heard a great deal about you from my aunt. I
checked the cruise line's website to see if there was a halo over
your head in your photo. No halo, but there were some amusing
ones of you in a sequined top hat and pirate jacket. Interesting
choice for a uniform."

Kennedy smiled at Justin and held out her hand to shake
his. "It's a pleasure to meet you, Justin. Your aunt is one of my
favorite people."

A hearty laugh escaped Vera, and Kennedy and Justin
turned to look at her. "You wouldn't have said that a few years
ago."

"Neither would you about me," Kennedy grinned. "I was
surprised to see your name on the manifest. What brings you on
an Alaskan cruise? Usually, your trips with us coincide with
checking on your business interests in the Caribbean."

"My good friend, Emily, made certain I was invited to experience this cruise as their guest. As a discerning traveler, the corporate office values my opinion, and you know me, I *always* have an opinion."

"And you make sure everyone knows it," Justin muttered.

Vera's head turned quickly to face Justin, and her lips made a thin red line. "I'm sorry. Did you say something we needed to hear?" He shook his head. "I didn't think so." She turned back to Kennedy. "Now, on to other things. Since you are here, I am slightly more confident about this cruise. I despise going on any of the other ships because no one reads the notes regarding my special requests, and I spend most of my valuable time explaining what is expected while I am on board."

Kennedy nodded. "As soon as I saw your name, I selected two of the ship's officers to be at your beck and call. One of the gentlemen will pick you up at your stateroom at six o'clock to escort you to the captain's cocktail party and then to dinner."

Vera arched an eyebrow. "And do we know the name of this charming officer?"

Kennedy smiled slyly. "Not yet. Both officers were vying for the honor. There was mention of a duel on the promenade deck."

"I think I liked things better when you were terrified of

me," Vera sniffed. She was momentarily distracted when a distinguished-looking gentleman strolled past her and nodded when they made eye contact. "Who is that?" she asked, pointing her head at the man being helped by one of the agents on the floor.

"I'm not sure, but I can find out," Kennedy offered.

"Please do," she said, still looking at the man. Then, she turned her attention back to Kennedy. "And before I forget, thank you for helping Emily. The cruise she went on put her in a completely different frame of mind. She suddenly has the desire to best me in business."

Kennedy cleared her throat. "I understand from Mrs. Abbott that you are taking your company in a new direction. And if you are here, who is managing things at the office?"

Vera nodded. "Destination funerals: the wave of the future and a way to lighten up a somber affair. They are doing quite well. I just finished one in Napa. The deceased wanted to be scattered over a vineyard where he was part owner." She made a face. "Sour man, I hope his disposition doesn't ruin the wine."

"And I'm—" Justin began, but Vera spoke over him to finish answering Kennedy's question.

"Inez, my niece, is handling things at the office while Justin and I get to know each other. She is the only person I completely trust other than you."

Irritated by his aunt's interruption, Justin put his hands out in front of him. "Look, I understand the two of you want to play catch up, but at this rate, we could be in Juneau before we get to our cabins." He pointed at the two bellmen. "And I'm sure they have other passengers to take care of. Could you tell us what cabins we are in and how to get there? I'd also like a second keycard for Aunt Vera's room. We had a slight problem in Napa."

"Justin!" Vera snapped and glared at her nephew, "Please stop treating me like some forgetful old woman."

"It was a pain in the neck to get you a new one, Aunt Vera. Especially because you neglected to have my name on our reservations, and this is for *my* convenience in case you have another…forgetful moment."

Vera sucked in a breath and closed her eyes in aggravation. "Fine. Kennedy, please have a second key for my stateroom made," Vera said through clenched teeth.

Kennedy watched as Vera struggled to keep her composure. Vera was anything but a forgetful old woman. On the contrary, as a savvy businesswoman, she had taken her husband's modest and old-fashioned funeral business and turned it into a modern empire. So, it surprised Kennedy that Vera was going along with the request to appease her nephew.

"My pleasure, Mrs. Jameson. Justin, I apologize for taking so much of your time, your aunt is a very dear person to me, and I'm afraid I was a chatterbox. If you will excuse me, I'll see to that additional key." Kennedy left them and walked behind the services desk.

"Why didn't you tell her I was head of the destination funeral division? That *is* the plan, isn't it?" Justin demanded in a childish tone. "And why did you say that about Inez? It's bad enough that all I hear about is Kennedy this and Kennedy that, but now Inez and Kennedy are the only people you can trust? As the person who will eventually take over the family business, I should be the one you trust completely."

Before Vera could respond, Kennedy rejoined them holding out the keys. "Mrs. Jameson, you are in Cabin 902, one of our more luxurious staterooms, and Justin, you are in Cabin 906." Justin took the keys from her hand, handed one to Vera, and stuffed the other two in his jacket pocket, and Kennedy saw a look of irritation cross Vera's face.

"Thank you, Kennedy," Vera said flatly. "I'm looking forward to the cocktail party this evening. I purchased a few pieces of jewelry in San Francisco, and now I have a reason to wear them."

"When did you buy jewelry?" Justin looked at his aunt in surprise. "Where was I?"

"When I realized you don't rise before noon, I called and made an appointment with a renowned estate jeweler in San Francisco." She turned back to Kennedy. "I was quite pleased with the number of things I purchased, including a one-of-a-kind jade set I plan to wear to the Captain's Dinner."

"Aunt Vera, I don't think you should discuss what you brought," Justin chided. "You don't even know if the safes in the cabins are secure. Everyone who works on this ship probably knows how to open them."

Vera laughed at her nephew's sudden concern and pulled an ordinary-looking cigar box out of her large leather tote bag. "You are right. I don't trust in-room safes for that very reason. Which is why this box has been my safe for longer than you have been alive." She gave Kennedy a knowing look. "And as every place I travel is aware that I smoke cigars, the box is inconspicuous."

Vera saw the two bellmen slouching against the carts. She snapped her fingers at them. "You two, let's go. I assume you can find Cabins 902 and 906?"

As they began to walk toward the elevators, Bert stepped out, not looking up but down at his camera. "Would you like—" he clammed up when he saw Vera Jameson standing across from him.

"Oh, not you," she said with aggravation. "Although I

suppose I should be grateful it's you and not some other parasite. I'll remind you there will be no photos taken of me during this cruise."

Bert gave her an ingratiating smile. "Of course not, Mrs. Jameson. I am only here to take photos of happy people." Vera glared at Bert for a moment longer and stalked away with her nose in the air.

Justin snickered and handed Bert a five-dollar bill. "I think you are my favorite person on this ship, friend."

Kennedy walked over to Bert. "I'm sorry she was so awful," she apologized.

Bert shrugged. "It's okay. She's always like that when she sees me. It was nice to get the last word in for a change, and I even got a tip!" He held up the money Justin had given him.

"Who was the single man who had his photo taken a few minutes ago?"

Bert looked at his notepad. "Oliver Parsons, why?"

"No reason." Kennedy flipped through her manifest, and she was pleased to see that Mr. Parsons was traveling alone and had also been invited to the captain's cocktail party.

"No clipboard?" Bert asked. "I don't think I've ever seen you with stapled papers."

"No, and I hate this. It feels so unprofessional. All right,

100

enough whining, back to meeting and greeting."

The flow of passengers continued, and Kennedy saw another friendly face in the crowd.

"Ronnee Barrett, it is so good to see you," she walked up to greet a woman wearing a black-and-white houndstooth suit.

"Kennedy? What are you doing here?" The two women embraced.

"Helping out, making sure everything goes smoothly for our VIPs."

"Well, thank goodness you are here." She tucked a lock of caramel-colored hair behind her ear. "I've got five of my dears on this cruise, and I might need some help." She motioned to the five older ladies standing in front of the seaplane mural to join her. "Kennedy, please meet Estelle, Mary Margaret, Helen, Marge, and Irene."

"It's a pleasure to meet all of you," Kennedy said. "Welcome to the *Malina*."

"Kennedy is normally on the *Helio*," Ronnee explained, and a look of comprehension came across the five faces.

Mary Margaret pointed at Kennedy. "So, she's the one the hottie chef kept talking about."

Ronnee nodded, and Kennedy looked at her in confusion. "The hottie chef?"

Ronnee chuckled and explained they had met Deuce Dawson when she had taken the ladies on a tour of the Casual Living Network. Ronnee had been at the network to meet with the travel producer and had brought the ladies along as they were avid fans of the network. "When I mentioned we were going on a Sunny Dayz cruise, your name came up, and Deuce sang your praises."

The two women chatted briefly as Kennedy caught Ronnee up on everyone from the *Helio*. "Bert and Mila are on this cruise, too," she said.

"Bert's here? How wonderful. Let me get the dears over to him for some photos, and I'll be right back, don't move. I need to tell you about a group I want to book on the Helio." Ronnee walked the ladies over to Bert and introduced them, and then she came back to stand by Kennedy. "They'll be busy for a little while. Now this group…" Ronnee's voice trailed off, and Kennedy saw that Ronnee was looking past her with a look of aggravation on her ordinarily cheerful face. Kennedy turned around, curious about what had caused such a look.

"Ugh! Had I known that woman would be on this ship, I might have reconsidered the invitation." A stocky, black-haired woman in a red and black houndstooth suit similar to Ronnee's was approaching them like a tank barreling through a battlefield. The two women squared off like wrestlers.

"Ronnee Barrett, how interesting to find you on this

102

cruise," the woman's tone went from snide to saccharine in a split second," but isn't it a bit far for your...what is it you call your little band of octogenarians? It's something cute." She tapped her chin with a bejeweled finger, pondering. "Now, what is it? Pets? Loves? Dears? It's dears, isn't it?" She clapped her hands together so that only the palms touched. "At their ages, I didn't think they would be allowed to go further than ten miles from their doctors' offices," she said with lilting amusement.

"I'm just as surprised to see you here, LaVonda. I wasn't aware your broom would fly this far," Ronnee smiled, although her tone was glacial.

"Oh, aren't you funny," LaVonda let out a little laugh. "I flew private, of course. Just one of the perks of having important clients who can't do enough for me." She cocked her head to the side. "Poor thing, I assume you had to fly coach. It must have felt like being a sardine in a can, but then again, you are just skin and bone. You could have saved some money and had them fold you up and put you in the overhead compartment." She licked her lips like a cat who had just lapped a bowl of cream. "I'm actually a little surprised to see you here. I heard this was for *top-level* VIPs of the cruise line." She held her hands out and admired the rings on her fingers. "I, of course, couldn't decide whether I would come as a guest of the cruise line or as a guest of Casual Living Network. They practically begged me to author an article about cruises to Alaska, and you know Sunny Dayz wants all of my business."

Kennedy's neck was beginning to hurt as she ping-ponged back and forth between the two women.

Ronnee leveled her gaze at LaVonda and gave her a forced smile. "I am here as a guest of the cruise line, and I'm working with the network as well," Ronnee said coolly. "They've asked me to do some on-air travel segments for their morning talk show. So, when the cruise line invited me, I decided it would be a perfect travel segment." Ronnee placed a hand on her hip. "And it's a good thing I'm skin and bone, LaVonda. I hear the camera can add ten pounds," she winked.

LaVonda glared at Ronnee, and Kennedy looked down at the papers in her hand to hide her smile. Ronnee turned to Kennedy and placed a hand on her forearm. "Darling, I simply must go, I want to get my dears settled into their cabins, but we'll catch up soon, I promise."

Ronnee walked over to Bert and opened her arms to the five ladies who were having their photos taken. "Now, how are my dears?" she called out with gusto. "Bert, I want doubles of every photo the dears are in during this cruise. One for me and one for them."

Kennedy was left standing with the black-haired woman. While she and Ronnee had been exchanging barbs, Kennedy realized it was the same LaVonda Taylor from the ill-fated Mediterranean cruise many years ago. When she turned around, Kennedy took a breath. She had forgotten about LaVonda's eyebrows. Thick, painted-on, cartoon-like commas sat high above her violet eyes.

"*That woman*," LaVonda spat out. "To think I traveled three thousand miles only to be stuck on this ship with that bag of bones. I wish society would bring back the days of burning witches at the stake. I'd start a lovely bonfire with her in the center." LaVonda finally noticed Kennedy standing there. "I'm LaVonda Taylor." She tapped a long red fingernail onto Kennedy's sheaf of papers. "I'm on the VIP VIP list." She gave an exaggerated sigh. "You know it would be much better if you had a clipboard. Walking around with papers stapled together looks rather unprofessional." Kennedy smiled tightly. "I hope the cruise line had the foresight to book me in one of the larger staterooms. It would be in their best interest, especially if they want me to recommend this cruise." She looked around the lobby and smiled. "I'm sure they did, especially after the dreadful customer service I received a few years ago. They were practically on their knees begging for my forgiveness and business."

Suddenly, three yapping dogs ran through the lobby, followed by a harried terminal agent. The dogs ran straight to LaVonda, tangling their leashes between her legs, and jumped up and down. Kennedy, a dog lover, looked at the three tan canines with black faces and thought that, like LaVonda, the dogs had a look of perpetual irritation. "Are those Brussels griffons?" she asked.

"Yes," LaVonda pointed at the three dogs, "this is Bailey, Banks, and Biddle. I named them after my favorite jewelry store."

"We were unaware they would be traveling with you on the cruise."

LaVonda gave Kennedy an icy smile. "And if your corporate office wants my business, you'll find a way to make it work."

"Of course," Kennedy smiled, "I'm sure your dogs will have a lovely time with us. We'll have to see about—"

But before Kennedy could finish her sentence, Lavonda steamrolled over her. "I'd like a cabin adjoining my stateroom for the dogs. My sweeties like their own space, and since this is a trial cruise, I'm sure there are more than enough empty cabins." She waved her hand dismissively. "So, move whoever is next to my stateroom somewhere else. I'd also like to meet with your executive chef. I have a list of dishes I would like the kitchen to prepare for the dogs, and someone must walk them four times a day." She held up her hand and pointed to her fingers, "Breakfast, lunch, dinner, and before bedtime. There should also be a television channel for them to watch. They like nature shows, but nothing graphic."

Kennedy looked from LaVonda to the three dogs sitting at her feet, and they looked back at her as if to say, "Lady, do what she says, or you'll look as miserable as we do."

"Ms. Taylor, I—"

LaVonda cut her off with a wave of her hand. "Young lady, I am very important to your company, and they want me to experience this cruise and recommend it to others. To do that, I need to know that my sweeties are being taken care of in the manner to which they are accustomed." She raised her eyes at Kennedy and added, "and by someone above a junior level." LaVonda tapped on the papers Kennedy held in her hands and let out an irritated sigh. "Are you going to write this down?" LaVonda stopped speaking and peered at Kennedy curiously. "You look familiar, but you do have one of those ordinary faces."

Kennedy stayed silent, praying LaVonda would not remember the disastrous cruise through the Mediterranean. However, as Vera was on board, there was the distinct possibility that she would put the pieces together. "Ms. Taylor, I'll see what we can do about arranging an adjoining cabin for your dogs and your other requests, but it may take some time."

LaVonda sniffed and looked around the lobby. "I suppose that will be fine, but don't take too long. The dogs and I need our space."

"Ms. Taylor!" J. Mitchell called out and waved from the main staircase. He raced down the steps and power-walked through the crowd. When he reached a curious LaVonda, he took both of her hands in his. "I'm J. Mitchell Templeton, the cruise director. I'm sorry I wasn't here right away." He rolled his eyes and fanned himself with his hand. "There has been so much to do. I hope we have been taking care of you and your precious little ones." He stooped down, put his face near the dogs, and made kissing noises. One of the dogs snapped at him. "Goodness, it looks like someone might have a *bratitude*[4]," he said in a singsong voice, and LaVonda giggled. He stood and guided LaVonda to the photo area, leaving Kennedy with the three dogs. "We are so fortunate to have someone of your caliber on this cruise," he gushed. "When I saw the manifest, I thought I would just die! I would consider it an honor to give you a tour of the ship." He looked over his shoulder at Kennedy and gave her a sick smile. "Be a dear and bring the little ones to the photo area."

"But I was—"

"Ms. Taylor needs to have some photos taken with her sweeties. And let's get some champagne sent up to her room. After all, *she is* a very important guest. I can't believe you didn't see it in the manifest notes."

"Five more days," Kennedy muttered as she untangled the rhinestone-studded leashes.

When Kennedy and the dogs arrived at the photo area,

---

[4] bratitude: having an ill-mannered attitude.

Bert looked from Kennedy to the grumpy-faced dogs and then back at Kennedy. She shrugged, and they watched as the dogs made a beeline for the ship's wheel, and Kennedy worried for a moment that they might decide to use it as their personal fire hydrant.

LaVonda picked up the dogs and hugged them to her bosom. "Smile for the camera, sweeties," she cooed at them, and Bert snapped as many photos as he could of the wiggling dogs in LaVonda's embrace.

When Bert finished taking photos, J. Mitchell escorted LaVonda toward the elevator while she filled him in on her requests. He nodded sagely and then turned around and motioned impatiently for Kennedy to join them with the dogs who had returned to sniffing the ship's wheel. J. Mitchell pressed the up button and patted LaVonda's hand. "Now, darling, I wish I could escort you and your precious pups to your stateroom, but I have to stay down here." He leaned in and whispered conspiratorially, nodding his head in Kennedy's direction, "The truth is I can't leave her for too long. She gets overwhelmed easily."

LaVonda turned back to look at Kennedy with pity. "I noticed that right away," she whispered. "You could tell by the stapled papers in her hands and the fact that she doesn't know when to take notes. She's lucky to have someone like you to learn from."

J. Mitchell gave her a sad but serious face. "Well,

anything to help the company. I don't know what they'll do with her after this cruise. I just hope she doesn't become my pet project." He motioned for Kennedy to hand him the leashes and pressed them and a keycard into LaVonda's hands as the elevator doors opened. "Now, take this to deck eight. You are in Cabin 801. I'll have some champagne sent up to give you a perfect bon voyage, and we'll get to your requests right away. Toodles!" He wiggled his fingers at LaVonda as the doors to the elevator closed.

"Wow, that one has a serious case of *dramatude*[5]. She puts the *queen* in drama queen," J Mitchell griped as he walked past Kennedy. "Well, someone needs to get that bottle of champagne sent up to her and call Chef Sha about her brats' meals. I'd do it, but I'm busy, so I guess that leaves," and he pointed at Kennedy, "Y-O-U."

Kennedy counted silently in her head to five. "Happy to help." She watched as J. Mitchell disappeared into the security director's office behind the guest services desk.

When Mila came down to the lobby a few minutes later, Kennedy was still counting in her head. She had gotten to five hundred and fifty-six and was thankful when she saw her best friend. "How's it going?" Mila whispered.

"Six days is going to feel like an eternity. I don't know what I was thinking."

---

[5] dramatude: an overly dramatic attitude.

Mila looked over her shoulder. "I believe you were thinking…" Mila's voice trailed off. "Wow, I didn't think it was possible, but there is a Terri Butler clone in the lobby."

"What?" Kennedy followed Mila's gaze. A suntanned young woman with silky blonde hair entered the lobby. Her tight, pale pink, long-sleeve tube dress stopped at mid-thigh and had rows of large ruffles that stopped at her knees. "It's like déjà vu," Kennedy whispered, watching the woman toddle on her high heels.

The woman suddenly stopped and looked around behind her anxiously. Then, finally, a short, older man at least fifty years her senior joined her, and the two embraced awkwardly. She lifted his black hat and kissed his bald head.

"Do you think that's Diamond Jim and his ball and chain?" Mila asked, and as the couple got closer, their jewelry sparkled in the lights. The bride wore a large diamond and gold necklace that spelled out T-R-I-X-I-E. "I guess that's in case she forgets?" Mila whispered from the side of her mouth.

"Stop it," Kennedy hissed and smiled at the approaching couple. "Good afternoon, and welcome to the *Malina*. How may we help you?"

The man stuck out his hand, and Kennedy noticed a thick gold bracelet and a diamond-encrusted watch on his wrist. "Good afternoon, young lady," he said with a Texas accent. "I'm

Diamond Jim, and this sweet thing," he put his arm around the waist of the woman beside him and hugged her to his side, "is my bride-to-be, Trixie Dubois." The gold chains around the open neck of his shirt flashed as he moved.

"Diamond Jim is an unusual name. Are you perhaps in the jewelry business?" Mila asked slyly.

"Nothing gets past you, does it?" he chuckled and tipped his hat. "If you are from anywhere in the South, you may have seen my commercials or been to one of my stores, The Little Black Box. I started with one store in an outlet mall in Texarkana and have been helping people sparkle for over forty years." He took a bow-legged cowboy stance, holding out both index fingers like guns, and sang, "A little black box, you won't go into hock when you just want to show off your sparkle!" He shot his forefingers in the air and pretended to holster them at his side.

Mila and Kennedy applauded. "I've never been to one of your stores, but now I feel like I must!" Mila exclaimed.

"You should. A pretty little filly like you needs lots of sparkles, and we have a sale every two weeks." He winked at her and whispered conspiratorially, "I did that because it coincides with most paydays. Pretty clever, huh?" He spoke louder this time so Kennedy could hear him. "We sell previously owned jewelry, watches, and pieces with minor flaws. Show them your rock, Trixie!" Trixie held her left hand out for the two women to

112

admire the sizable pear-shaped diamond on her finger.

"How did you two meet?" Kennedy asked.

"Funny you should ask. I picked her out of a book." Mila and Kennedy wrinkled their brows, trying to understand the man's comment. Diamond Jim continued, "I was going through a book of models for my new commercial and saw Trixie's photos. Her poses captivated me. Show them, honey," he urged. Trixie cocked her head to the side and then moved a slender hand to her pouted lips. Then she laid her other hand on her wrist. Jim pointed at Trixie's hands. "You see, with that pose, we capture the excitement and anticipation in her eyes as she shows off the rings and bracelets on both hands. Do the necklace one," and Trixie shook her blonde hair back and extended her long, elegant neck. Her hands went to the center of her collarbone and swept them across her shoulders. "Isn't she something?" he said breathlessly, staring at her. His phone rang, and looking at it with annoyance, he stepped away from the group to take the call.

"Oh, my goodness, the bride-to-be!" J. Mitchell threw his arms out straight as he sashayed over to Trixie. "Now, I don't want you to worry about a thing, dear. I'm overseeing everything personally. The chef has a *fantabulous* menu planned, and our pastry team is working around the clock to make the cake," he chattered. "Oh, and our ship's photographer is going to take photos of your big day, and you are all set up to have your hair and makeup done the morning of the wedding. Should I book a

113

massage for you and the groom the day before? Or maybe the day after?" he leered.

Kennedy noticed that the bride looked apprehensive and wondered if J. Mitchell's exuberance was overwhelming her. She began to say something, but before she could, J. Mitchell clapped his hands together and brought them to his chest. "This is just going to be *fantastical*[6]. A wedding on our cruise. I'm just over the moon." He pressed a finger on Trixie's nose. "The only thing you have to concern yourself with is being the gorgeous creature you are." Diamond Jim returned to the small circle, and J. Mitchell turned his attention to him. "Is this your father?" he asked Trixie and stuck out a limp hand to grab Jim's. "You must be so proud, sir." He shook Diamond Jim's hand enthusiastically while his eyes traveled around the lobby. "Now, where is that groom of yours?" He turned to Trixie. "Are you already training him to carry your bags? Good girl!"

"J. Mitchell," Kennedy had been trying hard to get his attention and finally made eye contact. "This is Diamond Jim." She made a motion with her eyes. " The *groom and* a friend of the corporate office," she said with emphasis.

"Of course you are!" J. Mitchell made a quick recovery and waved his hands. "The excitement about the cruise and your wedding has made my brain as foggy as a morning on Puget Sound. I'm so glad I have *my assistant*, Kennedy, here to keep

---

[6] fantastical: an event that is both fantastic and magical.

me on track." He put his hands on his hips. "Now, tons of welcome gifts have arrived for you two. I felt like Santa Claus each time I delivered something to your stateroom. And you are so fortunate to be in our Owner's Suite. It reminds me of a winter wonderland." He swayed back and forth and hugged himself. "I'd take you up there myself, but I'm simply swamped getting this tub of steel launched. No rest for the wicked cruise director!" He let out a short burst of laughter.

Mila coughed and looked down at her feet.

"Has my cousin arrived?" Trixie spoke for the first time as she looked around. "His name is—" She stopped talking and squealed and then ran across the lobby into the arms of a handsome man. Kennedy, Mila, and J. Mitchell stared at the couple while Diamond Jim looked at his phone.

"*Hunkalicious*[7]," J. Mitchell breathed dramatically, and both Mila and Kennedy had to agree with him.

Trixie led her cousin to Diamond Jim and the others. "This," she said, smiling widely, "is my cousin, Cameron."

Diamond Jim stuck out his hand and shook Cameron's. "Thank goodness you got here," he said and nodded at Trixie. "This one has been fretting that you wouldn't make it. She said at one point that if you weren't here, she didn't know if she could go through with the wedding. I was afraid I would have to

---

[7] hunkalicious: a delicious good-looking man.

115

send my plane back to Texas and drag you here in handcuffs."

"Just pre-wedding jitters, Jim," Cameron chuckled. Then, he smiled at Trixie and squeezed her hand. "She's going to marry you, I promise."

"Mr. ..." Kennedy spoke up, "I'm sorry Trixie didn't tell me your last name." Kennedy was having difficulty taking her eyes away from the bride and her cousin. They looked like a toothpaste ad: tan, leggy, blonde, and wholesomely good-looking.

"Allen. It's Cameron Allen," he said with a lazy drawl.

J. Mitchell cleared his throat and gave Cameron a weak handshake. "And I'm J. Mitchell, the cruise director. It's wonderful that you could be here to help celebrate your cousin's winter wonderland fairytale wedding," he gushed.

Cameron flashed the group a smile. "I should know. I've been helping her plan it, and I'm standing up for Trixie."

J. Mitchell clapped a hand to his forehead. "I thought I was exchanging messages with the maid of honor all this time, but it was you. I didn't think about Cameron being a boy or girl name. I guess that makes you the *bridesmate*[8]!" J. Mitchell's loud, staccato laughter rang out around the lobby causing several people to turn around. He quickly clapped a hand over his mouth. "I'm sorry. I told Diamond Jim right before you got here

---

[8] bridesmate: a male maid or matron of honor.

116

that I could just burst from excitement about this wedding!" He motioned to Kennedy for her manifest and made a face at the dog-eared papers. "Kennedy, do you have their keys? They are VIPs, after all."

Kennedy stiffened, and Mila put a hand on her shoulder. "Easy girl," she whispered.

"I'll be right back," Kennedy said, leaving the group.

J. Mitchell put his hands on his hips. "I'm sorry about this," he sighed. "She's new. But, while we are waiting, why don't I introduce you to your wedding photographer? He can take your welcome aboard photos." J. Mitchell waved at Bert. "Oh, Mr. Photographer," he sang out and bustled over to where Bert was set up. "I have some special passengers for you. Our very own bride and groom, and the *bridesmate*. Aren't you excited? These photos can be your warm-up for their big day."

Bert blinked at J. Mitchell. As far as he knew, he had only volunteered to take photos at the reception. He let out a heavy sigh and turned to Diamond Jim, Trixie, and Cameron. "We have the traditional background with the ship's bow, a glacier, and the ship's wheel, or I can use a solid one," he explained in a monotone. "Which would you like to use?"

Diamond Jim's phone rang again. "You kids go first," he said. "I need to take this call," and he stepped away from the photo area.

Trixie shrugged. "I guess we'll do the traditional background." She motioned for Cameron to join her at the ship's wheel. They stood beside each other, their shoulders touching, and as Bert snapped the shutter, they subtly changed poses from looking at the camera to looking at each other. For the next shot, Cameron had both hands on the wheel while Trixie moved behind him and placed one hand on his shoulder. For the last pose, Bert removed the ship's wheel, and the couple moved in closer to each other, and Trixie had one perfectly shaped leg turned out.

"Well, don't you two beat all. If I didn't know you were cousins, I would think you were trying to steal my bride away, Cameron," Diamond Jim said, walking up to the group. J. Mitchell and Mila shared a quick look as Trixie and Cameron had looked very cozy having their picture taken. "Okay, I'm next," Diamond Jim said and pointed at the backdrop. "But I want the solid background." Bert changed screens while Diamond Jim practiced his signature gunslinger pose.

Kennedy joined Mila and J. Mitchell. "Talk about a May-December wedding," J. Mitchell whispered behind his hand. "Although I think this is more like a May-Revolutionary War one."

An hour later, the ship's speakers crackled, and two long notes—made famous because they signified that a hungry, man-eating great white shark was nearby—came across the speakers. "Duuuuuuh Da… Duuuuuuh Da…" The notes began to play faster. "Duh Da Duh Da Duh Da Duh Da!" The passengers strolling on the decks looked around in confusion. Then they heard J. Mitchell's singsong voice. "Now that I have your attention, it's that time, so no *cruisitudes*[9]. Our bars and service areas will close for a few minutes, and we ask that you return to your cabins to review the safety guideline video and report to your designated muster station."

Kennedy took the steps up to her assigned station, the Starlight Lounge on deck seven, to wait for the passengers. The television over the bar showed colored bars and the words, "Please Stand By." Moments later, J. Mitchell appeared on the screen. An orange life ring encircled his waist, and he wore a bright yellow T-shirt with the caption, "Titanic Swim Team," a green scuba mask, snorkel, and bright blue flippers. He waved animatedly to the viewers as he got into a lifeboat. "There may be fifty ways to leave your lover," he let out a staccato laugh, "but there are only a few ways to leave this ship!"

Kennedy watched as the television then showed J.

---

[9] cruisitude: having a bad attitude while on a cruise.

Mitchell wearing a fireman's hat. He pointed a fire hose at an ashtray full of cigars and cigarettes. "There is no smoking in our cabins or public areas. However, for those who need to be fire-breathing dragons, our *smokequarium*[10] can be found on the pool deck."

In the next scene, J. Mitchell was standing outside a cabin door with clouds of smoke billowing out. "And remember, if we see smoke coming from your cabin, we will assume that *your flaming personality* is to blame." The video then cut to the former cruise director, who shared important safety instructions on what to do in an emergency.

Kennedy was standing at the entrance to the lounge marking off the names of the passengers who arrived at her muster station when LaVonda marched down the corridor. She stomped up to Kennedy. "You! I am absolutely furious! My bags never arrived, and you better hope they aren't still at the cruise terminal. One of them contains my jewelry which I assure you is expensive." Kennedy watched as LaVonda's brows climbed to her hairline with each shrilly spoken word. "Well? How do you intend to rectify this horrendous situation?"

Kennedy opened her mouth to apologize, but before she could say anything, LaVonda continued her tirade. "Secondly, my sweeties are still in my stateroom, which is completely unacceptable. I cannot believe *my requests* were not at the *top of*

---

[10] smokequarium: a smoking area usually resembling a fishbowl.

the list, and the chef has not been to my room to discuss the menus."

"Ms. Taylor, Chef Finch—"

LaVonda shook her finger in Kennedy's face. "Don't interrupt me! I'm not finished! After watching that little safety demonstration, I want some answers," she huffed. "How will my sweeties be taken to safety if we are forced to evacuate? Will the person who walks them have that responsibility? I'm sure you don't expect me to do it by myself. I am a VIP. And who will transport my jewelry? Of course, that is if we ever find it!" She put a hand on her hip and tapped her foot. "Hello? Have you heard me? You don't seem to be taking my complaints seriously."

J. Mitchell and Tammy were stationed at the entry to the dining room, which was nearby. "Wow, that is one serious case of *baggravation[11]*!" J. Mitchell said to Tammy as the two watched LaVonda harangue Kennedy.

Tammy saw the smile on J. Mitchell's face. "You know something," she said.

"I may have changed the cabin number in the system," he smirked, "and her bags might have gone to a different room."

Tammy playfully hit his shoulder. "You naughty boy."

---

[11] baggravation: feeling aggravated over an issue with one's luggage.

121

She sniffed theatrically and pretended to wipe away a tear. "I feel like a proud mother. Now, go play the hero."

"Ms. Taylor, if you will allow me a moment to speak," Kennedy said patiently. "If there is an emergency, we will do our utmost to get your dogs on a lifeboat; however, human passengers will be taken care of first. And I'm sorry, but personal belongings will not be allowed on the lifeboats."

J. Mitchell sauntered over. "Ms. Taylor, whatever is the matter? You look as if you will explode!"

LaVonda turned to him, and her snarling face was replaced by teary eyes. "Oh, J. Mitchell," she wailed, "thank goodness you are here. My luggage is missing, and one of the suitcases has my jewelry. Do you think someone at the cruise terminal took it? Those workers looked a little sketchy to me. And then my sweeties. They don't have a cabin, and no one has walked them, and," she exhaled, "I'm worried sick about what will happen if we have to evacuate. My dogs are such tiny, dear, helpless little creatures," she sniffled. Then she turned her attention back to Kennedy, and her wet eyes were replaced with fire. "And I'm getting nowhere with her. She is completely ignoring me!"

J. Mitchell smiled and took her hands in his. "LaVonda, I don't want you to fret. I'm here to take care of you. Now, I want you to go inside and sit and wait for the announcement that the drill is over. In the meantime, I'll personally lead the search for your bags. I am sure they are here. Did your champagne arrive?" LaVonda nodded. "Do I need to send up some more?"

"Well, that would be nice," LaVonda said in a small voice. "It would help calm my nerves."

J. Mitchell pointed at Kennedy. "My assistant is working with our chief engineer on the pet relief area." He cocked his head at Kennedy. "Would you be a dear and walk Ms. Taylor's dogs as soon as possible and again before they go to bed? Oh, and first thing in the morning? Of course, I would, but I have so much to do."

Kennedy gave J. Mitchell an annoyed smile.

"See, LaVonda? We are all working together to take care of you," J. Mitchell cooed. "Now, if I'm going to find your luggage, I need to go."

"Thank you, J. Mitchell," LaVonda said. "I feel better already. You truly are an expert at your job." She glared at Kennedy and brushed past her. "Unlike some people."

An hour later, the ship's horn made a loud blast signaling that it was leaving port and heading for open water. Kennedy walked up to the pool deck to watch the ship's departure. Leaving port was always a magical time for her. But, for some reason, today, it felt like a page was turning. She saw Vera standing at a nearby railing and approached her.

"Would you explain why the horn must be so loud?"

Vera shouted in her imperious tone, her hands cupping her ears. "I don't understand how all of you aren't deaf!"

"I'm glad I found you. The gentleman you inquired about is Oliver Parsons, and he is traveling alone." She gave Vera a grin. "He will be at the captain's party tonight. I would be happy to make an introduction."

"That won't be necessary," Vera sniffed and looked at the cuff of her jacket. "His name isn't familiar to me."

"Oh, okay. I'll leave you to your view of the departure." Kennedy began to walk away.

"Kennedy," Vera called out, and Kennedy turned around, "an introduction would be lovely, thank you." Vera turned her head to look back at the ocean.

Kennedy saw Ismaeel at the pool bar polishing glasses while his bartenders were busy serving passengers. "I have a question," she said, walking up to the bar. "If I were looking for Chuckie, where would I find him? I need a favor."

"Probably his office on deck four. As much as he likes to tell stories and be the center of attention, he avoids the passengers."

"Maybe that's a good thing," she chuckled. "Thank you!"

"Anytime."

Kennedy took the steps down several flights and luckily

saw Chuckie as he opened the door to go inside. "Chuckie!" she called out. "I need a favor." She saw Chuckie's shoulders sag at her words.

"What kind of favor?" he whined when she reached him.

"I know how busy you are, but I need a pet relief area. One of our passengers brought her dogs with her."

"What kind of person brings dogs on a cruise ship?" Chuckie asked irritably.

"A very special VIP."

Chuckie rolled his eyes. "Why can't you just pick a spot and have Cormac's team hose it down after they use it."

Kennedy scrunched up her face. "That would be unsightly, not to mention unsanitary. We want to impress these people so they will promote the cruise. Don't you want to restart the trips?"

Chuckie put one hand on his hip and scratched the back of his head, making the ballcap bob up and down. "I suppose," he said stubbornly. "How exactly do you propose I make this thing?"

Knowing the rivalry between Chuckie and Franklin, Kennedy tiptoed with her answer. She was going to use a little competition to inspire Chuckie. "Franklin made one for me a few years ago. I can sketch out what he did."

"And I suppose you know where you want this thing to go?"

"Not really. I wanted to rely on your advice. You know the ship better than anyone, but it should be somewhere near a hose and out of sight of the passengers. We put it under the stairs on the crew deck on the *Helio*."

Chuckie nodded and motioned for her to follow him. "Let's go to my office." He turned to her as they walked down the corridor. "How long did it take Franklin to make the one for the *Helio*? I bet I can make the one you need in half the time. I told you he isn't as good as I am. It's why I had to teach him so much when he first came to work on the ships. He might be good-looking, but he doesn't know what end of the hammer to hit the nail with."

At precisely six o'clock, Andreas knocked on Vera Jameson's stateroom door. "Mrs. Jameson?" he asked when she opened the door. "I'm First Officer Andreas Pritchard. I'm your escort for the evening."

"You must have won the duel," Vera said dryly, stepping out into the corridor. She wore a figure-hugging red dress, and the diamond and pearl earrings that graced her ears were part of her recent purchase in San Francisco.

"I'm sorry?"

She sighed. "It seems the company did not issue a sense of humor with your uniform." Andreas gave her an unsure smile, and Vera shook her head. "Never mind. I need to stop at my nephew's cabin to let him know we are making a stop before the cocktail party and will meet him there." Vera shut her door. "Do you smoke?"

"Ma'am?"

"This is like pulling teeth, Mr. Pritchard. It's a simple question, and if you are a first officer, I assume you have some brain cells. So, I will ask again. Do you smoke?"

"Yes, ma'am," Andreas answered slowly.

"Good, because I am dying for a cigar." She patted the red beaded purse under her arm. "And, according to the safety instructions given this afternoon, if they catch me smoking in my cabin, they reserve the right to turn a hose on me."

"W-w-well," Andreas stammered, "we wouldn't do that immediately. We'd ask you to put it out first."

"That's refreshing news. I'd hate to waste a good cigar." She knocked on Justin's door, and when he answered, she told him they would meet him at the cocktail party. "Don't be late," she gave him a meaningful look.

"But, Aunt Vera, if I am late, the time I am forced to be at this party will be that much shorter."

Vera gave her nephew an icy glare. "May I remind you that this trip is to see if you are the right man for the job you keep telling me you should have?"

Justin swallowed. "I'll be there, Aunt Vera, and on time."

"See that you are." Vera turned to Andreas and slipped her arm through his. "Now, I believe we are off to find a place where I can smoke my cigar without being doused by a fire hose."

Having known Vera for only a few minutes, Andreas dreaded showing her the smoking area. When they reached the aft end of the ship where the hot tubs were located, he stopped.

"You can't be serious," she looked first at the plastic igloo and then at Andreas.

"I'm sorry, ma'am."

"Is there another alternative?"

"I'm afraid to show it to you."

"It can't be any worse than that," she pointed at the igloo. "I may have been too harsh about the smoking area on the *Helio*. It may have looked like a very fancy birdcage, but it didn't resemble a playhouse for penguins." Andreas escorted Vera to the elevator and pressed the number eight on the panel. When the doors opened, he steered her outside and motioned to a bench. Vera looked from side to side. "It's a marginal improvement." Then she looked up and saw a yellow inflatable raft hanging above her. "Should I be worried?"

Andreas grinned. "I'll stand here to take the brunt of the fall. It's a part of our special VIP customer service package."

Vera looked at Andreas with amusement. "Oh look, you found your sense of humor."

"It was in my pocket, ma'am. I must have forgotten it was in there."

Vera pulled her cigar case and cutter from her purse and waved them in the air. "Would you care for one? I brought two cigars with me. I wasn't a Girl Scout, but I like their cookies and try to be prepared."

Andreas looked longingly at the silver cigar case Vera held out and shook his head. "I'm not supposed to," he answered.

"Yes, but this falls under the special VIP package." Vera winked and handed Andreas the cigar case and cutter while she fished around for her lighter. Soon, they were both inhaling the heady scent of their cigars in silence. A couple walked past and, smelling the cigar smoke, the woman gasped and waved her hand theatrically.

"Steerage, most likely," Vera whispered conspiratorially,

pointing her cigar at the couple. Andreas began to cough and covered his mouth with one hand while holding his cigar with the other. "Have a delightful walk," Vera called after the couple, and the woman turned her head over her shoulder and glared at Vera. "Yes, I'm sure there is a special place in hell for people like us. Those with hideous vices…and personalities, of which you don't appear to have either." The woman snapped her head forward and began walking quickly, pulling the man with her.

"You don't mince words, do you, ma'am?" Andreas chuckled.

"I'm afraid the doctor removed the thing that made me care what others think instead of my tonsils when I was a child."

Andreas looked at the orangey-red embers on the end of his cigar. "These remind me of my grandfather. He smoked one every night with his whiskey."

"He sounds like a good man."

Andreas nodded. "Yes, ma'am. He was a boat captain. I wish I had gotten the chance to sail with him. Unfortunately, I was in maritime school when he died suddenly at the helm." Andreas had a wistful look on his face.

"He died at the helm? How old was he?"

"Eighty. He loved the sea and hated being on land for more than a few days." Andreas chuckled. "He claimed he was born on a ship."

"He sounds fascinating. Tell me about him."

While Vera and Andreas were in the ship's less-than-luxurious smoking area, Kennedy was a few decks lower checking on the pet relief center Chuckie had made. She was delighted to see he had covered the top with artificial grass from the putting green. A red bucket in the center turned over to look like a fire hydrant was the perfect touch. She thanked him profusely and took a photo. "I can't wait to show this to Franklin," she said. "He's going to be jealous."

"You know, this one time—"

Kennedy looked at her watch. "Oh, gosh, Chuckie, I wish I could stay and hear your story, but I need to get upstairs for the captain's cocktail party. Can we catch up later?" After spending an hour with Chuckie in his office, she quickly learned that his stories were long-winded and meandered. If she stayed and listened to another tale, the cocktail party would be over by the time he finished.

Taking the stairs two at a time, Kennedy entered Sedna's View quietly and walked over to the bar, not wanting to disturb Chef Sha and Ismaeel as they explained the appetizers and signature cocktails to the serving staff. She eyed the space appreciatively. Near the observation window, cream-colored slipper chairs and saddle brown leather sofas sat in groupings with blonde cedar tables made from tree stumps. Blue-gray upholstered chairs with blonde cedar frames sat around gray

131

glass tables in the middle of the room. Ismaeel walked over to where she stood.

"It's beautiful in here." She nodded her head at the bartenders who were putting the finishing touches on their bars. "The team knows what to do if Andreas comes up to them for Mrs. Jameson's old-fashioned?"

Ismaeel nodded. "Champagne glasses and bourbon at each station. If they found the information odd, they didn't let on, but I would feel better if he came to me for the drink."

"Great, thank you." She blew out a breath.

"Are you okay?" he asked with some concern.

"It's been a challenging day. J. Mitchell went out of his way to make me look like an idiot in front of a passenger."

Ismaeel looked sympathetic. "The one you told us about?" Kennedy looked away and nodded. He wiped an imaginary spot from a glass. "Joy loved this party. She had a gift for connecting with the passengers, which is definitely lacking in J. Mitchell. He's too brittle and forced, and let's face it, he only cares about himself." He put the glass down, picked up another, and held it to the light. "There is a reason the captain asked you to hostess tonight. You have a warmth about you, and people notice it when they meet you."

Kennedy gave Ismaeel a grateful look. "Thanks." She glanced at her watch. "It's almost time."

"Then let's get this party started." He walked to a panel at the other end of the bar and pressed a few buttons on a keypad. The lights dimmed, and soft music filled the room.

A little while later, as the noise in the room got louder and the lines at the bars decreased, Kennedy decided it was time for the toast. She found the captain standing with his senior officers. "Captain Volare," she said quietly, and when he turned, she took a quick step backward and extended her arm straight out to hand him the microphone. "It's time for your toast."

He gave her an apologetic smile. "From the way you are holding the microphone, I take it I was inappropriate on the bridge."

"A little too forward, sir," Kennedy answered him honestly.

"Would you accept my apologies?"

"If you'll make the toast and stop hitting on the female members of the team, then the answer is yes."

The captain let out a laugh. "Well done, Ms. Reeves. Tactful and to the point." He took the microphone and walked to the center of the room. When Kennedy handed him the glass of champagne, he frowned. "Just one? It's a long toast."

"Take tiny sips," she responded, which brought a smile to the captain's face.

"I'm beginning to feel sorry for my friend on the *Helio*," he sighed and tapped on his champagne glass while Kennedy melted away into the crowd. "Welcome to the *Malina*," he said in a deep, rich voice. The room went quiet, and the only sound heard was the muffled clacking of plates as they were collected and placed on serving trays. "I only have this one glass of champagne, so I'll keep my toast short." The passengers chuckled. "We hope you enjoy your time with us on this voyage as we sail through the lands of arctic breezes and ice, of green fields and sun. For thousands of years, we have crafted vessels to carry us into the waters. We call these vessels *she* because they guide and protect us like the women in our lives. I offer a toast to the *Malina*."

The crowd raised their glasses. "To the *Malina*," they repeated solemnly.

Captain Volare took a sip of champagne. "The tempers of the sea are also like a woman," and there was a collective laugh from the audience. "She can be peaceful and calm or a violent tempest. But it is she who sets the tone. I offer a toast to the sea."

"To the sea," the passengers replied.

"To the goddess, Sedna, mistress of the sea and mother of all sea creatures, for whom this room is named, we ask your blessings as we travel your waters. To Sedna," he said, his voice carrying.

Captain Volare continued, and finally, he was at the end of his toast. "To the *Malina*!" he cried out passionately, holding his glass high in the air, and then he brought it down and drained the contents of the glass.

"To the *Malina*!" the crowd responded enthusiastically and began clapping.

Kennedy had taken the second microphone from the bar and began walking toward the captain. "Thank you, Captain Volare," she said into the microphone. However, the sound coming out of the speakers was not her voice. Instead, it was J. Mitchell's.

"Captain, my mother always told my sisters that a person's speech should be like a woman's skirt," J. Mitchell trilled, "long enough to cover the subject but short enough to create interest! We need to work on your skirt length!"

The passengers exploded into laughter as J. Mitchell walked to the center of the room wearing a silver sequined dinner jacket with black velvet lapels. "So, I have a question." He had a mischievous look on his face. "Are any of you feeling a little *nauti*?" The groans and guffaws from the passengers told Kennedy that J. Mitchell was in his element. "So, I've been asked many, many questions today. One of them was, is it easy to fall off the ship? The answer to that question is no." He paused for a second and tilted his head. "Unless the captain decides to make another toast, and then you may want to jump overboard."

As J. Mitchell held the audience's attention, Kennedy walked over to Ismaeel and handed him the microphone. She held up a hand, shaking her head to prevent him from offering an apology. She scanned the room and saw Vera standing with Andreas and her nephew, and she walked over to them.

"Good evening, Mrs. Jameson, Justin. Are you enjoying the party?" she asked.

"Honestly, Kennedy, I would have enjoyed it more if there had been a decent smoker's lounge. Have you seen it?" Kennedy shook her head. "I'll let you come to your own conclusion." She inclined her head toward Andreas. "First Officer Pritchard took me to another spot, although we were on guard in case one of the life rafts fell on top of us. With that said, please alert the fire brigade that I will take my cigars on my stateroom balcony, and I don't wish to be hosed down when I light up." She noticed Justin fidgeting. "Are you quite all right?"

"Bored," Justin yawned. "This party is as exciting as a cemetery. I'd rather be in the casino making money."

"Making money?" Vera scoffed. "I'm not sure, but I believe they call it gambling for a reason."

"Only if you lose, Aunt Vera, and besides, you are here with the perfect Ms. Reeves and Officer Handsome. You don't need me around."

Vera sighed. "Go. But please be in the main dining room at eight. And Justin, while I intend to see some whales on this trip, *you* are not one."

Justin gave his aunt a surprised smile. "Aunt Vera, I'm impressed."

"I know more than you think," she answered dryly. She presented her cheek to him for a kiss. "Now, please leave so I may enjoy myself. Your pouting like a three-year-old child is annoying."

Kennedy watched Justin's quick departure and, in doing so, saw that Oliver Parsons was standing alone nearby. "Mrs. Jameson, there is someone I would like to introduce you to." Kennedy led the way, and as she made the introductions, she could see there was an instant attraction between Vera and Oliver.

"Your name seems very familiar," Vera said. "Where would I have heard it? Do you do business in Alabama?"

Oliver, a tall, well-built man, looked at her with mournful brown eyes and ran his fingers through his thinning white hair. "No, ma'am," he said in a deep polite voice. "I'm just a simple horse trainer."

"If you are attending this party and this cruise, you are certainly more than that." She studied him. "I wish I could remember why your name is so familiar. Unfortunately, it will come to me at the most *inopportune* time. The vulgarities of age are annoying." Oliver chuckled silently at her quip.

Andreas was feeling like a third wheel. "Mrs. Jameson, may I get you a drink?

Vera nodded. "That would be lovely. An old-fashioned, and as Kennedy is on board, I'm certain she has briefed the staff on how I like them."

Kennedy grinned. "Yes, ma'am." Then she turned to Andreas. "Ask Ismaeel to make it."

"Is he my Luke on this cruise, Kennedy?" Vera queried. "I'd like to meet him and see if I like him better. I am very irritated with Luke now that Emily has a drink named after her."

"An old-fashioned," Oliver said. He was pleasantly surprised by her choice of cocktail. "Do you have a particular bourbon you prefer?"

Vera looked at him steadily. "Anything expensive." Kennedy and Andreas eased away from the conversation.

Andreas walked up to the bar. "I need an old-fashioned," he said to Ismaeel. "And Kennedy sent me over here to get it." The beverage director nodded and began to make the drink. When he was finished, he poured it into a champagne glass. "Are you sure?" Andreas looked warily at the long-stemmed glass. "I don't want her to throw it in my face."

"Does that happen often to you?" Ismaeel smirked. "Now, when you give it to her, present it with a flourish." Ismaeel pushed the drink forward.

"A flourish?"

Ismaeel rolled his eyes. "You are lucky you are handsome because sometimes you are as thick as a cement block. Dramatically bow to her as you present it, dummy!"

"If she throws it at me—"

Ismaeel sighed. "Just do it."

Andreas walked over to Vera and, bowing deeply from the waist, held the glass in the air. Vera chuckled as she took the drink and sought Kennedy out with her eyes. When they connected, she raised her glass and mouthed, "Thank you!"

Justin had gotten halfway to the exit when he noticed a beautiful blonde sitting at the bar. Her long hair cascaded down her back like a silky curtain. The pink off-the-shoulder satin dress she wore showed off her deep tan, and as he got closer, he noticed the diamond and gold necklace that spelled out her name. An open barstool sat beside the woman, and Justin stood in front of it and motioned for another beer.

"Trixie, this place is like a morgue," he said, trying to engage her.

Her blue eyes slid over to him. "How did you know my

name was Trixie?"

"Your necklace," he pointed. "Although I suppose you could have a different one for each night, depending on which name you wanted to be."

Trixie felt for her necklace. "Clever."

"Thanks. I'm Justin Jameson." He looked around the room and blew out a breath. "I'm glad I ran into you. I was afraid there wasn't anyone else under the age of fifty on this ship. If I had known this was a geriatric cruise, I would have told my Aunt Vera to find another escort." Trixie nodded but didn't say anything. He saw her eyes searching the room, and an awkward silence filled the space between them. He was about to leave when he noticed a short man wearing a black cowboy hat. The man was animatedly telling a story and was shooting his hands in the air like guns. Justin lifted his chin toward the man and took a long pull on his beer. "Who does that old geezer think he is?" He laughed. "'His hat is taller than he is."

Trixie's gaze followed Justin's glance. "That's my fiancé," she said quietly. "His name is Diamond Jim, and he owns a string of jewelry stores."

"You can't be serious!" Justin looked at her in disbelief.

"Oh, I'm quite serious." Trixie slowly turned her head toward Justin. "Diamonds really *can be* a girl's best friend. We're getting married in Juneau." She looked back at the crowd, and Justin noticed her eyes light up as a man walked toward them.

"Is everything okay, Trixie?" the man asked, standing protectively behind Trixie's barstool.

Trixie nodded and turned her long graceful neck back to look at him. "Yes, Cameron. This is Justin Jameson. Justin, my cousin Cameron. He's standing up for me at the wedding." Trixie lifted her hand to tuck a stray curl behind her ear, and her diamond tennis bracelet fell off. Justin quickly bent down and scooped it up. "It looks like I have a knight in shining armor," she said. "This was the first piece of jewelry Diamond Jim gave me. Thank you for catching it."

Cameron glared at Justin's bent head as he refastened the bracelet onto Trixie's slender wrist. "With all the jewelry he's given you, would he even notice if you lost it?" Cameron asked in a testy tone.

She shrugged. "Probably not. He'd just give me another one to replace it. He may even have one with him. He usually carries a few extra pieces on trips in case he can make a sale."

Diamond Jim came over to the bar and fanned himself with his hat. Then, he jumped up on the open stool and signaled for the bartender. "Can I have that Alaska thing they were passing around?"

THE ALASKA

2 OUNCES DRY GIN

3/4 OUNCE YELLOW CHARTREUSE

2 DASHES OF ORANGE BITTERS

ORANGE PEEL

IN A MIXING GLASS FILLED WITH ICE, ADD ALL
INGREDIENTS EXCEPT THE ORANGE PEEL. SHAKE OR
STIR FOR 30 – 45 SECONDS UNTIL WELL CHILLED.
STRAIN INTO A CHILLED MARTINI GLASS. TWIST
ORANGE PEEL OVER THE DRINK TO EXPRESS OILS
AND GARNISH.

Diamond Jim pointed at the large group he had just left.
"They may not have known who I was before we got on this
ship, but I assure you I'll make a few sales before this cruise is
over." He rubbed his hands together. "Plenty of women on board
with money to burn on jewelry." He turned to face Justin and
held out his hand. "I apologize. I didn't introduce myself. Too
busy thinking about making some sales on this trip. I'm
Diamond Jim." Justin took Jim's hand in both of his as they
shook hands.

"Justin," Cameron said, "what is it you do? Are you a
travel agent?"

"No, not at all. I'm in the funeral business. Destination funerals, to be exact. It's the wave of the future," he boasted.

Diamond Jim let out a hearty chuckle. "The funeral business. Well, ain't that a hoot. You don't meet someone who admits to being in that line of work every day. So, what is a destination funeral?"

Justin explained the concept. "I'll be taking over the company soon. In addition to destination funerals, we offer custom services, handling things the way the departed wants versus what the family requests. We did one a few months ago where the deceased was buried with his golf cart and clubs. When his wife found out, she was pretty unhappy, but he had paid for it, and she decided she didn't want to spend the money twice."

Diamond Jim began to laugh and slapped his knee. "That reminds me of a friend of mine who looked in his mother's casket at the funeral only to find a stranger wearing his mother's clothes and jewelry. There was some mix-up at the funeral home."

"How horrible!" Trixie held her hand up to her mouth. "No more talk about morbid funerals. I'm on this cruise to get married," she said, petting Diamond Jim's head, "not talk about dead people."

The bartender brought Diamond Jim his drink, and as Jim

lifted his arm to pull the glass in front of him, Cameron noticed that Diamond Jim's watch strap had come out of the buckle. "Jim, you are about to lose your watch!"

Jim set the glass back down and looked at the watch. "Wouldn't want to lose that!" He chuckled as he resecured the band and held his arm toward Justin and Cameron. "There are over a hundred diamonds on here," and he tapped the face of the watch.

Justin and Cameron both eyed the beautiful watch hungrily. "If I can be rude, how much would something like that set you back?" Cameron asked.

"Retail price is seventy-nine thousand smackaroos," Diamond Jim said. "But I got a steal on this one. The guy had to unload it because he was getting ready to divorce his wife and needed to hide some cash. I know the feeling firsthand. Ex-wives can squeeze blood out of a turnip. I made him an offer, and he walked away a happy man with cash in his pocket. He told everyone he had lost the watch so he wouldn't have to declare the sale on the settlement paperwork."

Justin whistled appreciatively at the story and then pointed to Diamond Jim's little finger. "That's a heck of a ring, Jim. I think I am in the wrong line of work."

Diamond Jim pulled the ring off and held it between his thumb and forefinger. Off the center of the gold nugget was an arresting blue gemstone surrounded by diamonds. "Trixie picked that out for me. It started this whole idea of a wedding in Alaska." He pointed at the dark jewel nestled against the gold metal. "That looks like the water in front of the glacier we will be married on. I'm sure Trixie told you all about what we have planned when we get to Juneau." He put the ring back on his pinkie.

Justin took another pull on his beer. "She did, but where are my manners? I have not asked to see the bride's engagement ring." He gave Diamond Jim a knowing look. "As a man in the business, I am sure the ring is as exquisite as the bride."

Trixie held up her hand and placed it on Justin's outstretched one. He looked intently at the ring on her finger. "That's a big rock!" he said appreciatively. "Three carats?"

Diamond Jim nodded at Justin. "Good eye. I'm tempted to hire someone just to stand around and watch her hand all day." He pointed at Cameron. "But as this one hasn't left her side since we got engaged, I've put him on security detail."

Justin placed Trixie's hand onto Diamond Jim's and put his hand in his coat pocket. "It's almost as dazzling as she is, sir." He put his beer on the counter. "It was a pleasure meeting you and Trixie." He shook Jim's hand. "You are a fortunate man." He turned and looked at Cameron. "Pleasure meeting you. I'm sure we'll see each other around on the ship. I'm going to get a breath of air before I am on Aunt Vera duty again."

"I want to meet the captain," Diamond Jim said, jamming his black hat onto his head and jumping from the barstool. "Come on, you two." Cameron and Trixie reluctantly slid off their barstools to follow him.

LaVonda had entered Sedna's View with the confidence of a queen. She glided through the lounge, pleased to see the number of heads that turned and the whispers that followed as she walked by. LaVonda knew she looked good. She had carefully searched for a dress that would complement the gold and sapphire hair comb she wore like a tiara in her upswept hair, and the flecks of gold on her dress popped against the deep blue and black swirls.

She found an empty table in the center of the room and looked around delighted. She could see everything happening in the room and felt sure everyone could see her. Although she had a slight buzz from the champagne she had drunk earlier in her cabin, she happily accepted a glass of the red wine and champagne concoction from one of the servers. LaVonda had thought it curious when the young man stared at her and then tried to stifle a smirk, but she dismissed it as immaturity.

A breeze caused by someone brushing past her table

made her cocktail napkin slide off and float to the floor, and as LaVonda bent down to retrieve it, she discovered, to her horror, that the carpet pattern was identical to her dress. She sat up slowly, now understanding the reason for the head turns, whispers, and the smirk on the server's face. LaVonda felt her stomach cramp, and her forehead and cheeks felt hot. She wondered if the sudden illness was the alcohol she had consumed or the humiliation of knowing that if she lay down on the floor, she would probably get stepped on, as no one would be able to tell the difference between her dress and the carpet.

Her eyes scanned the room, desperately seeking a way to exit the party inconspicuously. The answer came a few moments later when the lights dimmed, and the captain began to make his toast, and LaVonda used the distraction to slip outside. She stood at the railing for a few minutes hoping the chill night air would cool her skin and calm her stomach. When the door to the lounge opened, the sounds of the cocktail party flowed out, and LaVonda turned her head in the direction of the noise and saw a youngish man make his way to the railing a few feet away. Suddenly the ship heaved, and LaVonda, white-knuckled, clutched the white metal as her stomach rolled.

"Nice out here," he remarked.

LaVonda could only nod. The queasiness in her stomach was growing.

He gestured at the door. "I needed some air. It was

147

getting pretty crowded and noisy in there." He looked at her curiously for a moment, and LaVonda felt her cheeks flush as she wondered if he had realized her dress and the flooring in the lounge had the same pattern.

"I'm Justin Jameson." He held out his hand to her.

"LaVonda Taylor," she said, and as she leaned over to shake his hand, the ship dipped again, and LaVonda fell against Justin. "I'm so sorry. Perhaps we should sit down," she said shakily, motioning to the chairs.

As they settled themselves, he pointed at her dress. "Very few women could carry off that outfit. Your earrings and hair comb are an elegant touch."

LaVonda grimaced. "I felt pretty good about myself until I realized my dress and the carpet matched."

"Ouch," Justin said. They were both quiet for a few moments until Justin spoke again. "On the positive side, at the end of the night, your dress won't have spilled cocktails and ground in hors d'oeuvres on it unless you are attending some wild party in one of the cabins. And, honestly, most of the people inside would have to find their glasses to see anything more than the drink in their hand."

LaVonda let out a little laugh. "Thank you. I needed that."

They made small talk. LaVonda shared that she was a

148

travel agent and was on the cruise as a guest of the company, and he was surprised when she told him she was traveling with her dogs.

"So, let me get this straight. They are paying you to be on this cruise, and other people are paying for your excursions?" He let out a long whistle. "That's the second time tonight I have realized I am in the wrong business. Have you met Diamond Jim?" He twisted his torso and pointed at the glass wall. "He owns a string of jewelry stores."

The ship rolled again, and LaVonda suddenly looked green. She held a napkin to her mouth. "I suppose I haven't gotten my sea legs yet," she apologized.

"Can I get you something to drink?" he offered. "Some champagne or ginger ale? And maybe a wet cloth?"

She clutched the napkin to her lips and nodded quickly.

"I'll be right back." He jumped up and went inside. When he returned, he found LaVonda leaning over the railing. He helped to hold her steady and wiped her forehead with the cool cloth while she was sick, and when she felt better, he guided her to one of the deck chairs.

Inside Sedna's View, Kennedy looked around with satisfaction. Those invited to the captain's cocktail party seemed to be enjoying themselves, except for the captain, who looked like he would prefer being stranded on an iceberg than chatting with Diamond Jim.

She turned her head the other way and saw that Ronnee and her dears had cornered Andreas and the ship's safety officer, and she walked over to where they were gathered. "How is everything? Are you enjoying the party?"

Ronnee was trying valiantly to hide a smile. "I'm afraid the dears have latched onto these two fine gentlemen and have been peppering them with questions."

Estelle, the shortest of the five, peered up at Otto. "So, is this a ship or a boat? We've heard it called both."

Otto grinned at the tiny woman with piercing blue eyes. She reminded him of his grandmother. "Rule of thumb is that you can put a boat on a ship, but you can't put a ship on a boat."

"Okay, I have one," said Mary Margaret, who was tall and thin. "What time will we see the whales?"

Andreas chuckled. "I'll check the sonar in the morning. Sometimes we have them booked for noon on the ship's port side."

Suddenly there was a commotion behind the bar, and Kennedy saw Ismaeel clap a bar towel over his nose as he ran through the service doors. She excused herself and walked to the bar to see if she could help.

"I hope he didn't break it," Bert said, approaching

Kennedy.

"What happened?"

"From what I could see, the bartender was showing off and threw his shaker in the air, and Ismaeel got clonked on the nose."

"Well, that's one way to end the cocktail party," Kennedy replied as the passengers began to leave. Then she looked at Bert. "Aren't you—"

"Already set up to take photos outside of the dining room. I was on my way to tell you when I saw Ismaeel get clobbered." He let out a little huff. "Oh, and apparently, I am the official wedding photographer. Which means I won't be able to go sightseeing with you and Mila in Juneau. J. Mitchell found me a little while ago and gave me the orders," he said irritably. "He could have asked instead of making a big deal about telling me how we were sent here to help."

"I'm sorry. Maybe we can find something to do after the wedding. And speaking of helping, I'll see you in a few minutes. I thought I would poke my head into the dining room."

Bert grinned. "Face it. You're worried that the dining room manager is too green."

"Well…"

J. Mitchell, Tammy, Mr. Phyfe, and Jonny stood at the

back of the room. "Well, that was the perfect ending to the cocktail party," J. Mitchell snickered.

"Did you see the woman wearing the dress that matched the carpet?" Tammy asked. "How humiliating. The carpet looked better than she did."

A round of staccato laughter erupted from J. Mitchell, and when he had composed himself, he pointed at Kennedy. "Speaking of unattractive dresses, did you notice the black-and-white dress our corporate help was wearing? Most unflattering, and I hear the orcas are upset."

"Those aren't the only fashion disasters on this ship." Tammy turned to the dining room manager, "did you accidentally bring your little brother's suit on this cruise, Mr. Allen? Your pants are above your ankles."

"It's stylish, and I look better than him," he pointed at Mr. Phyfe. "Do you own any other color? You look like you are on safari."

Mr. Phyfe bristled and glared at Jonny, but Tammy snapped her fingers to get Jonny's attention before he could say anything. "Sweetie, let's get back to what *you* are wearing. Fashion should be a statement, not a question."

"Check out my socks," Jonny said, clearly not understanding what Tammy was trying to say. He pulled his pant leg higher to reveal a pair of bright yellow socks with donkeys on them.

"Well, if those are to tell people you are an ass, you've hit the nail on the head."

Kennedy heard the loud grumbling before she reached the main dining room on deck seven, and as she got closer, she could see a lengthy line had formed outside of Siku's doors. Bert motioned for her as she walked by the photo area. "The doors aren't open, and people are frustrated," he warned. Kennedy slipped inside and headed to the podium, where a group of nervous servers stood.

"Hi," Kennedy said. "Is there a reason we aren't seating people?"

"We don't know what to do," one of the servers said.

Kennedy looked puzzled. "Is there a seating chart?" The servers met her curious eyes with shaking heads, and Kennedy let out a breath. "Okay, is Jonny around? Or J. Mitchell?"

One of the servers pointed to the back of the dining room. "Jonny opened the door, saw the line, and ran back to his office," she whispered. "And we don't know who J. Mitchell is."

Kennedy smiled and began talking through her teeth.

"Okay, so here is what we are going to do. I'll stay at the host stand, greet the passengers, and tell you where to seat them. Pass the word to those not seating passengers to begin putting salads at each table, and then we'll start the dinner service."

The long line of grumpy passengers dwindled, and most were forgiving and accepted Kennedy's explanation that the delay had been due to first-night jitters. She walked around the dining room visiting with the passengers, and when she passed the captain's table, she saw that it was full, except for one empty chair. She sidled over to Otto. "Where is he?" she whispered, pointing to the vacant seat.

Otto gulped and stumbled for an answer. "He told me he—"

A loud crash drowned out Otto's explanation for Captain Volare's absence. Kennedy looked in the direction of the noise and took a deep breath. "It's going to be fine, it's going to be fine," she whispered. She walked quickly toward the back, where she found one of the servers on the floor, surrounded by broken dishes and food.

"My foot got caught in this tear in the carpet," he said, pointing at the large rip.

After helping to clean up the mess and reassuring the server that it had been an accident, Kennedy went to find Jonny. She knocked on the office door, but there was no sound on the other side. Kennedy became both irritated and concerned. For all of his earlier bravado, it was clear that the young man was in over his head.

Kennedy cringed when she heard another crash and looked around. Another server had tripped in the same area, and broken plates, glasses, and silverware surrounded the young man like confetti.

Vera, Justin, and Andreas arrived at the host stand just as the second server spilled their tray of dishes. Andreas leaned over to Vera. "May I suggest we return to Sedna's View for dinner?"

Two hours later, Kennedy, Bert, and Mila were walking LaVonda's dogs on their special deck, where the wind could carry their sharp barks out to sea. Unfortunately, there had already been noise complaints, but as the ship was not full, Kennedy would upgrade the guests near LaVonda's stateroom to new rooms in the morning and send an amenity.

"I'm exhausted," Kennedy yawned. She tugged on the leashes she was holding and received vicious looks from the three dogs.

"I think today has been the longest day of my life," Bert grumbled. "To think we started the day with Officer Friendly not wanting to let us onto the ship."

"Was that only this morning?" Mila asked.

"Maybe we should have taken that as a sign," Kennedy sighed. "I'm terrified of what may happen tomorrow."

"A little late now," Mila said wryly. "Other than absconding with one of the life rafts and a couple of paddles, we're stuck."

"Well..."

"And on that note, I'm leaving," Bert said. "Knowing how you two talk me into things, I'll be lowering one of the rafts in a few minutes." Bert looked at Mila from the side of his eye. "Are you going to do it?"

Mila gave him a smirk. "Yep."

Kennedy looked curiously at Mila. "Do what?"

"Let me get out of here before you do it," Bert said. "For once, I'm glad I've got photos to edit and hang in the lobby." He left them standing on the deck with the three bug-eyed dogs.

"Kennedy, you know I love you, right?"

"Yes..." Kennedy answered, wondering where Mila was going with this conversation.

"Then, can I ask where that dress came from?" Kennedy looked at the long-sleeve black dress with a white panel that ran down the front.

"Why?"

"Well, I was just wondering what possessed you to put it on. Did you look in the mirror?" Mila was biting her lips together hard, but there was laughter in her eyes.

"I don't have a mirror. I have something from a carnival funhouse that I refuse to use. I've been using my computer to see my face and hair." Kennedy gave Mila a strange look. "What is it?"

"I want you to promise me that you will either throw that dress away tonight or put it in the costume room on the *Helio*." Kennedy furrowed her brow. "And you can only bring it out if we have a costume party or you are reenacting the first Thanksgiving."

"What? Why?" Kennedy's face was wrinkled in confusion.

Mila held up a piece of paper with a picture of Kennedy on the left and two other images on the right. "Because I can't decide if you look like a penguin or a puritan." Mila's laughter escaped her lips in hearty chuckles.

Kennedy snatched the paper from Mila's hand. "You know, best friends are supposed to be the universe's way of making up for not being around family."

"And after hearing about yours, aren't you lucky to have me?" Mila linked her arm into Kennedy's as they made their way to the stairs. "It could be worse," she said.

"How?"

"I'm not sure, but give me some time." She snatched the paper from Kennedy's hand and stuffed it into her pocket.

Sunny Dayz Cruise Line

THE MALINA

DAY TWO

AT SEA

When Kennedy's alarm chirped, she opened her eyes in momentary confusion at the sight of the wood slats above her. She reminded herself she was on the *Malina*, and the slats were the bottom of the bunk bed above her. Turning her head to look at the porthole, Kennedy saw a few dim rays of gray light highlighting the water beads on the glass. She blew out a long breath and contemplated lying in bed for another fifteen minutes, but her practical side, who sounded a lot like her mother, Lolly, insisted she get up and get moving. Kennedy rolled over on her side to face the wall and pulled the blanket over her head, trying to ignore the voice. She had not slept well and wondered if the cheap carpeting on the floor would be more comfortable than the paper-thin mattress under her.

Giving up on the notion of extra sleep, she threw off the covers and began to sit up until she smacked her head on the upper bunk. She dropped back down on the bed and rubbed the tender spot. "Five more days," she groaned and held a hand to cushion her head as she got up and went into the closet-like bathroom. She decided the first order of the day would be to get coffee in the mess hall and walk LaVonda's dogs. She knew that if she did not talk to J. Mitchell about the dog duties, she would spend the entire cruise taking care of them. Although, walking them four times a day would keep her from being J. Mitchell's lackey. She got ready quickly, brushed her chestnut hair into a chignon, and wrestled a blue pencil dress from the tiny closet. Kennedy fastened her pearl earrings onto her ears, gave the image on the computer screen one last look, and left her cabin.

She walked into the brightly lit mess hall to the coffee urn, thankful there were paper cups. She could drink her coffee while she walked the dogs. Kennedy watched the dark brew fill her cup and placed a lid on top. As she made her way to the exit, she heard several people snicker. "Five more days," she whispered to herself. The team on the *Malina* seemed less friendly than her *Helio* coworkers, and she wondered if it was because the corporate office had pulled them from various places for the temporary duty. She stood at the elevator landing, waiting with several others for the doors to open, and heard quiet tittering. She carefully patted her dress. Nothing felt out of place, and there was no draft on her upper legs to indicate she had tucked her dress into her pantyhose. She told herself she was being paranoid and took a sip of coffee. When the elevator doors dinged, she waited for her turn to get in the cab and pressed the number for deck eight. The elevator made several stops, and when it reached her destination, she stepped off, but not before she heard giggles as the doors closed.

Kennedy stopped at the cabin beside LaVonda's and put the keycard on the lock. As she began to open the door as she had the previous night, the door struck the night latch causing a loud bang which made the dogs inside bark frantically in alarm. The yapping continued, and a very disheveled LaVonda yanked open the door to her stateroom. "What time is it?" she snarled, holding a hand out to shield her eyes from the brightly lit corridor. Kennedy noticed LaVonda's eye makeup resting under her lower lashes, making her look like a baseball player wearing grease paint to cut down on the sun's glare.

Kennedy gave her an apologetic smile. "Good morning, Ms. Taylor. I'm sorry I disturbed you. I've come to take the dogs out."

"Good?" LaVonda barked. "The word *good* does not belong with the word morning in my dictionary. I don't like morning people…or mornings…or people in the morning for that matter," she snarled.

"If you could unlatch the door to the dogs' cabin, I can take them out and get out of your way," Kennedy said, trying to be cheerful.

LaVonda's response was to slam the door in Kennedy's face, and Kennedy could hear her clomping angrily through her stateroom and into the adjoining one. Suddenly the door opened, and Kennedy saw three leashes tossed into the hallway, followed by two bewildered dogs who looked over their shoulders as they scampered out. A third dog was pushed out by the toe of LaVonda's feathered slipper, and it turned around to glare at her when the door slammed shut.

Kennedy looked at the three perplexed dogs. "Do you ever wonder why it's called beauty sleep?" The dog LaVonda had pushed out of the cabin bared its teeth at her and uttered a low growl. "I assume you don't like mornings either?" The dogs began yelping and snapping, causing a ruckus as they ran in circles while Kennedy attempted to clip the leashes onto their collars. Finally, after several moments of chaos, they began walking down the corridor, but not before the sound of quiet snickers reached Kennedy's ears when a few heads popped out of their cabins to follow the noisy parade.

Pushing the door to the deck open, Kennedy immediately wished she had thought to bring her jacket as the damp chill air immediately cloaked her. She noticed the clouds were hanging low, but thankfully, the rain was holding off, and she prayed it would stay that way until they got back inside. Kennedy didn't relish the idea of returning three dripping dogs to their owner—especially in her present state of mind.

She led the dogs down several flights of steps, and she saw Otto and Captain Volare. "After you," Otto said, looking at the three gremlin-like dogs who gave him an irritated stare. "Not morning people, I take it?" he asked, and the two men began to follow Kennedy down the steps.

"I don't even think coffee would help these charming canines," she said brightly and bounced down the steps after the dogs.

When they reached the next deck, Otto looked at her awkwardly, and the captain stifled a grin. "What?" she asked, puzzled and a little frustrated.

Otto looked visibly uncomfortable. "Ma'am, Kennedy, I…" But the dogs, knowing that relief was nearby, took off, pulling Kennedy along with them.

"What is wrong?" she called out over her shoulder. "I've been getting funny looks from people all morning!"

The dogs reached their area, and Kennedy bent down to unclip their leashes. When she stood up, Captain Volare motioned for her. "I'm going to be inappropriate, Ms. Reeves. Would you turn around, please?" Kennedy did as he asked but was perplexed. He pulled a sticker from the back of her dress and handed it to her, smiling. "I believe you are getting noticed due to your advertising." Otto looked the other way, red-faced.

"Oh no," she moaned, reading the words "Irresistibly Soft and Snuggly" on the cloud-like label. She realized it had come from the blanket she had bought on their road trip, and it had somehow attached itself to the dress.

"Ms. Reeves, you have given us something amusing to think about on this dreary morning." He waved to her as he and Otto walked on, leaving Kennedy with the three dogs, now giving her the same disapproving look her mother often gave her.

Minutes after dropping off the dogs, Kennedy heard a loud drumming outside. The heavy clouds had finally let loose, and rain was hammering the decks. She made her way to the mess hall, hoping no one had been alerted to her fashion faux pas.

"Good morning, Kennedy," Mila sang out, waving from the back table where the others sat. Seeing Mila's smirk, Kennedy groaned inwardly and walked over to the table. "I hear you are irresistibly soft and snuggly," she snickered and reached out to squeeze Kennedy's arm as she sat down. Mila nodded and looked at the others, who were trying hard to hide their laughter. "She is rather squishy, like a pillow."

Sha slid into the booth and placed two cups of coffee on the table. "It could have been worse."

"How?"

Sha cocked her head to the side. "It could have said, 'Recommended by Experts,' " and she took a drink of her coffee. The others burst into gales of laughter, and Kennedy chuckled along with them, realizing she was taking herself too seriously. "Here, we got you some coffee," Sha pushed the mug toward Kennedy. "It's dark and bitter like our spa manager."

Kennedy read the side of the cup, "Chaos Coordinator: Fueled by Caffeine." Then, she noticed that each of them had a mug with a saying on it.

"Joy got them for us a few years ago," Sha shared. "It lightened the mood in the morning." She pointed to her mug with a skull and crossbones on one side. She turned it so Kennedy could read the other side. "Annoying the chef will result in starvation."

Ismaeel came over carrying his cup of coffee. Those at the table winced when they saw the purplish-blue pockets under his eyes. "It's not as bad as it looks."

"What happened?" Cormac asked.

"A shaker full of ice, a heavy rocks glass, and an overzealous new bartender collided with my nose. I'll live. I just won't be very pretty."

"Funny, I don't remember you being pretty before," Cormac retorted, and Ismaeel grinned and lifted his mug to his lips. His cup read, "Adult Daycare Attendant A.K.A. Bartender."

Kennedy looked at her watch. "I know this is an informal meeting. Do you think anyone else is coming?" Sha, Ismaeel, and Cormac shrugged their shoulders. "Well, we should get started. It's pretty dreary outside, and I'm concerned the passengers will be frustrated because they won't be able to see much."

"Rule of thumb is that most will look out their window and roll back over in bed," Ismaeel offered. "They drank heavily last night, and my team is restocking the bars double for today. I have a feeling we will be making a lot of Bloody Marys."

Chuckie and Tammy entered the mess hall, laughing loudly. They stopped at the coffee urn and walked to the table, still talking. Tammy cut her eyes at Kennedy. "Oh, look, it's the meeting before the meeting," she said mockingly and pulled up a chair. She placed her mug on the table and turned it so the words faced Mila, who sat opposite her. "The difference between your opinion and coffee is that I asked for coffee," it read.

"Cormac, would you like to lead us off?" Kennedy asked.

"Happy to," he said merrily. "The first thing on my list is to notify everyone that several flower stems are missing from the arrangement by the stairs, lilies mainly. Could it be the VIP you told us about? I spread things around as much as possible, but we'll need to get more in Juneau."

"I'll speak with Mrs. Jameson. Perhaps I can talk her into an ionizer," Kennedy said. "I'll also gently remind her that she cannot remove the lilies from the flower arrangements."

"Chuckie," Sha spoke up, "would you please fix the tear in the dining room carpet? Several of the servers tripped last night and lost their trays of food. Not that our dining room manager would have known since he locked himself in his office. If you aren't going to fix it, could you at least tape it down? It's not safe."

"Don't get your knives in a twist." Chuckie banged his coffee cup on the table. "I don't tell you how to cook the food, and I don't need you to tell me how to do my job, especially in front of *them*." He darted his eyes at Kennedy, Bert, and Mila. The table became awkwardly silent, and Kennedy noticed Tammy was smiling at the exchange.

Jonny walked into the room wearing lime green plaid pants and a pink shirt. He held a golf club and took practice swings as he walked to the table.

"Whoa!" Tammy held her hand over her eyes. "Your outfit is scorching my eyeballs. Didn't we talk last night about fashion being a statement and not a question?"

"Pretty great combo, isn't it? And I have another pair of neat socks today. See?" He propped his golf club against the table, raised his pant leg, and showed off his pink socks with golf balls. "My Uncle Barry says a bad day of golf is better than a good day at work." He picked up his golf club and pulled it back, pretending to make a long drive.

"You need to stop swinging that," Sha growled, "or I might pretend your head is a golf ball. I can't believe you hid in your office while the dining room was in an uproar last night."

"It all worked out," he said defensively and pulled back the golf club to take another swing; however, this time, Cormac grabbed the club in midair, startling Jonny.

Cormac looked meaningfully at Sha and Jonny. "That's enough. We need to remember we are one team, and I will remind everyone at this table that this cruise will determine if we have jobs, and quite frankly, I would like to get back to a normal schedule and stop going wherever the corporate office sends me to fill in."

"No big deal for me," Jonny sniffed, "I have a steady job with my Uncle Barry if this falls through."

"Not all of us are that lucky," Sha barked, "and I'm not going to allow some two-bit, wet behind the ears, who only got the job because of his uncle's friend in the corporate office, twit, undo my years of sacrifice and training." Sha was breathing hard as she stabbed the table with a finger. "Tonight is the Captain's Dinner, the most important dinner of the cruise, the one the passengers remember the most."

"Jonny," Kennedy said gently, "in addition to the seating chaos in the dining room last night, the servers couldn't explain the dishes." She looked at Sha for help. "Do you have time to review the menu with the staff today? It worked well at the captain's cocktail party."

Sha nodded. "If it will help, sure. I should have thought about that."

J. Mitchell sashayed up to the group. "Sorry I'm late." He shielded the top of his sunglasses against the glare of the overhead lights. Wearing a fedora in addition to the sunglasses, J. Mitchell threw a folder onto the table and fell into the empty chair. "Wow, I was in The Wreck way too late last night," he said, adjusting his hat. "After all the work getting ready for the passengers, the captain's cocktail party—which I rocked, by the way—I needed to unwind with a drink or two…or three. What a day!"

"We're glad you could join us, J. Mitchell; it would have been nice if you had been in the dining room last night to offer some assistance," Sha grumbled.

"I was busy." He pointed at Jonny. "And worrying about the dining room is his problem, not mine. I'm Mr. Entertainment." He bent forward and looked at Jonny, shaking his head. "I can't believe you locked yourself in your office." Jonny opened his mouth to retort, but J. Mitchell turned back to the group. "Well, *someone* sent me a message yesterday and told me about this little unofficial meeting and thought we should review today's itinerary because that is how *they* do it on *their* ship." He threw Kennedy a look and passed out the sheets of paper in the folder. "I'm sure *someone* will overanalyze it, and *someone*," he rolled his eyes, "will want to make changes."

Kennedy looked over the sheet. It was overcast, and the skies alternated between drizzling rain and heavy downpours, which meant the passengers would not spend the day taking in the views of the Alaskan coast from the deck chairs as the itinerary read. "J. Mitchell, watching for wildlife and shuffleboard contests are nice, but have you seen the weather today? We need things for the passengers to do inside."

"Didn't you just tell us you were Mr. Entertainment?" Mila asked with a saccharine smile.

J. Mitchell bristled. "I suppose I'm open to suggestions," he said huffily.

Everyone at the table stared at the piece of paper in front of them. "Just throw something out," Kennedy finally said. "Anything."

"How about ballroom dancing?" Cormac offered. "I was a competitor in my younger days." Everyone at the table turned to stare at him. "I was much slimmer then," he laughed, patting his ample stomach, "but I'm still light on my feet."

"What about a beer-tasting class, Ismaeel?" Sha asked, and he nodded. "Or you could teach the passengers how to make your signature cocktails." The group began to get excited. "I could do a cooking class."

"You are too busy getting ready for the dinner tonight," Kennedy said, "but could we offer the passengers a galley tour while you are working?" Sha nodded her head vigorously.

"We have some great artwork on the ship," Cormac shared. "My team can make a list of the pieces and create a scavenger hunt."

"I'm happy to teach a yoga class," Mila said, nudging Bert. "What about you, friend?"

Bert looked at her like a deer in the headlights. "W-w-what about m-m-me?" he stammered. "I'll be taking photos of the passengers while they do all this stuff."

Mila snapped her fingers. "I know! You could teach a class on how to take great wildlife photos."

"M-M-Mila, y-y-you know," Bert was turning bright red, and sweat began to bead on his forehead. "Ouch!" He bent down and grabbed his ankle, rubbing it where Mila had kicked him. This was becoming a habit lately when she wanted him to do something or he said something stupid. "Fine, I'll teach a class," he mumbled.

"Well, hasn't this been a special meeting," J. Mitchell rolled his eyes. "It looks like the problems of the world have been solved. Can we go now? I have things to do."

"You shouldn't," Kennedy said, "because we aren't done. This meeting allows each senior leader to share what is happening in their department and head off any potential issues."

J. Mitchell pulled his hat down over his eyes, tucked his chin on his chest, and let out a loud snore.

Chuckie spoke up first, rubbing his hands together. "Well, I have an easy day today."

"Good, maybe some of the work orders can get filled," Sha muttered.

"The spa will be busy," Tammy spoke up. She had been quiet during the meeting. "We are full, but our corporate guest," she gave Mila a sick smile, "will be sampling some of our services. It's inconvenient, but we want to make sure everyone is happy."

"Tammy, again, I'm just here to see if there is an opportunity to give your spa a little lift."

Tammy looked at her nails, which she had fanned in front of her. "Perhaps something was missing from the formula at *your* spa that made the company decide to do such a massive renovation on the *Helio*."

Mila dug her nails into her palm to prevent herself from saying more.

Kennedy broke in, "Is the theater available for rehearsal today, J. Mitchell? I need a few minutes with the audio-visual team for tonight's show. Could you introduce me to them?"

"Why? What?" J. Mitchell spluttered and sat up jerkily, causing his hat to fall on the floor. He pulled his sunglasses down. "I don't understand. You need to rehearse something?"

Kennedy nodded. "Alfred asked me to do my one-woman show tonight. He said he messaged you about the change."

"It's quite good," Mila said excitedly, looking at the group.

"It might be fine for your booze cruises," J. Mitchell snapped, pushing his sunglasses back up. "They are all probably so drunk you could put a monkey on the stage with cymbals, and they'd applaud." He crossed his arms and legs tightly. "It's strange that Alfred didn't ask me to do one, as *I am* the ship's cruise director and *exceptionally* talented," he paused, "some say Broadway-bound." He looked at Tammy so she could add to the conversation, but she had become fascinated watching the toe of her high heel as her leg bounced rapidly.

J. Mitchell's mind was spinning like a tornado. He should be the one entertaining the passengers, not Kennedy. He gave her a sarcastic half-smile and pointed at the list she had scribbled on her piece of paper. "It appears you have a little jigsaw puzzle to put together, and once you have figured that out, you'll know when the theater is available." He snatched the folder off the table and stood up. "I have announcements to make," he sniffed, glaring at Kennedy. "It's an Alaskan cruise director thing. You wouldn't know what to say. I'm just glad that none of these extra activities are my responsibility."

"But—" Kennedy began, and before she could say another word, J. Mitchell had flounced out of the room. "Great," she muttered.

"I'll help you find the AV guys, Kennedy," Ismaeel said.

"I'm known for nerding out with them. I was a disc jockey in college."

"You were?" Sha said incredulously. "Cormac was a dance competitor, and you were a disc jockey. The things I am learning after all of these years."

"We have to keep you on your toes," Ismaeel said.

"One last question," Kennedy said, which elicited a sigh from Chuckie, Jonny, and Tammy. "I'm surprised Mr. Phyfe wasn't here, and I haven't seen him out amongst the passengers."

"Probably starching his underwear," Jonny scoffed.

Tammy glared at Jonny as she stood and pushed her chair under the table noisily. "Mr. Phyfe has real work to do, Kennedy. He's not a lap dog at the beck and call of the cruise director, although I hear the one on the *Helio* isn't jumping around for you anymore." She threw her shoulders back. "Now, this was fun but unnecessary. Shall we?" She looked down at Chuckie, and he scrambled to his feet, causing the chair to squeak against the flooring.

The meeting broke up awkwardly after Tammy's comment. Ismaeel, Cormac, and Sha helped Kennedy decide on times for the additional activities, but they were quiet and left as quickly as possible. Finally, only Kennedy and Mila were left sitting at the table. "I'm not sure what to do first. Should I get a bucket to mop up the blood, find you some bandages, or let you borrow my suit of armor for the next meeting," Mila said.

"Armor," Kennedy sighed, "definitely the suit of armor."

While Kennedy and the team were meeting in the mess hall,
Vera, not confident that the perfume of the lilies was disguising
the odor of her cigar smoke, went to the lobby to select a few
more stems from the flower arrangement for her stateroom. Then
she went in search of the ship's library. Her friend Emily Abbott,
the great-granddaughter of the founder of the Sunny Dayz Cruise
Line, had asked her to look at the collection to see what it
needed.

She opened the glass entry door and walked into the
room, casting her eyes about as she took a mental inventory. The
books were housed in wooden cases behind glass doors, and
twelve dark walnut tables were placed around the room with one
or two comfortable-looking dark gray upholstered chairs at them.
The only things that told her the room was on a cruise ship were
the various images of nautical knots scattered across the indigo
carpet and the breathtaking view of the ocean from the wide
window. She perused the contents of the bookcases and saw an
array of popular hardbacks and books on Alaska. Other shelves
held Alaskan Native American art, including woven baskets,

carvings made from walrus tusks, wooden masks, and jade carvings. She was studying the beadwork on a pair of mukluks when she heard the rustle of a newspaper at the back of the room. Oliver Parsons peered over his newspaper, his reading glasses perched on the end of his nose, and looking at him, Vera felt a strange feeling as her heart suddenly skipped a beat.

"Good morning," she said briskly and walked toward him. "I still haven't remembered where I heard your name, but I am not giving up."

"I hope you don't," he beamed. "Would you care to join me?" he pointed to the chair opposite him, and Vera sat down. "We talked about many things last night at the cocktail party, and Kennedy mentioned you are a businesswoman, but I failed to ask. What is it that you do?"

"Funerals," Vera answered flatly and stared at Oliver to see his reaction.

"A solid business," he said, nonplussed. "Something everyone needs at some point in their life. You are obviously successful, but please tell me you don't offer coupons."

Vera cracked a smile. Usually, people were put off when she told them what she did and found ways to extricate themselves from the conversation. However, Oliver saw it as a normal business and was astute enough to make a clever joke. His directness reminded her a little of Omar, the director of security on the *Helio*. Vera shared how she had turned her husband's small southern family business into a successful national company and explained Justin's presence on the cruise. "The idea was that he would take on the destination funerals and grow into taking the company's reins in a few years."

"Was?" Oliver asked quietly.

Vera nodded. "Was," she said firmly. "The company has a solid reputation that I've worked hard to build, but Justin is not the right person to take over. He's very charming and good-looking," she sighed, "and he knows how to work a room, but Justin expects things to land in his lap, and unfortunately, they usually do. I'm sorry to say that hard work is a dirty word to my nephew."

"It isn't like the days when we were building our businesses, is it?" Oliver offered, but before Vera could answer, J. Mitchell's voice came across the speakers so loudly that Vera was forced to put her hands over her ears.

"Hello, my cruisers! I hope you all slept like babies in the ship's gentle rocking last night," he crooned. "We have a *funtastical* day at sea planned. We are on day two of our cruise, and I encourage you to sit on the deck and watch the scenery today as we glide past bald eagles, whales, and sea lions that will be sunning themselves on the small islands we pass."

"Has he seen the weather?" Vera pointed to the window

wet with rain causing Oliver to chuckle at her sarcastic remark.

J. Mitchell's abrasive announcement continued. "The Inside Passage was known for thousands of years to locals, and while our voyage is one of luxury, the first cruise to take this route took place in 1881 and was filled with miners seeking gold. A fun fact for you: in 1894, potatoes were so valued during the gold rush that miners would trade their gold for them. But don't worry," he trilled, "our culinary team has plenty of potatoes, so if you strike it rich in our casino, The Main Vein, you won't have to use it for trade in the dining room."

"Where did they get this guy?" Oliver asked, and Vera shook her head. "Was he the loser at a comedy club in Seattle?"

"Some fun facts about Alaska," J. Mitchell chattered. "Alaska means 'the great land' and is home to seventeen of North America's tallest mountains. For my friends from Florida, Alaska has more coastline than the rest of the United States combined and shorelines on three different seas. All the beaches and none of the crowds! And believe me, some of the bathing suits I have seen on this ship make me glad to know we can walk the beaches for miles without seeing anyone," he tittered.

"Is there a way to turn him off?" Vera looked around the room.

"I think we have to suffer for a few more minutes," Oliver said solemnly. "My mother used to say that some people brought joy when they entered a room and others when they left. I'm willing to bet we will feel immense joy when he is done."

"If he makes that woodpecker laugh again, I may see if I can borrow a sledgehammer to gently pat him on the head to put us out of our misery." Not prepared for Vera's unladylike and savage comment, Oliver let out a deep laugh.

After Kennedy and the others decided what additional activities they would offer to help fill the day, Kennedy made her way to Siku, the ship's main dining room, and found Jonny sitting at his desk, looking miserable. "I doubt I'll be on the ship much longer. I just got a message from my Uncle Barry." He pointed at the computer screen behind him. "He heard about dinner last night, and he's furious. One of the passengers is his travel agent, and I guess she gave him an earful. Especially the part where…well, you know, when there was a long, unmoving line and I wasn't around." He looked uncomfortably at Kennedy. "I freaked when everyone showed up at once. I guess I didn't think it would be that different from my uncle's restaurant."

Kennedy took a seat across from him. "I'm sorry."

Jonny sniffed and pinched his eyes closed. "My Uncle Barry said I embarrassed him and jeopardized his friendship with the guy in your corporate office. He's so mad he told me I could forget coming back to work at the restaurant," he said morosely, "even as a busboy. My uncle is one of the best in the business and taught me everything I know." He let out a defeated sigh. "Just not how to run a ship's dining room."

Kennedy chose her words carefully. "Jonny, if the company decides to restart the cruises, do you want this job?"

He furrowed his brow. "Why wouldn't I? It's a chance in a lifetime."

"Then you will have to work hard and fast to prove it. The dining room manager's job is critical for the success of a cruise. Passengers will not remember many of the people they encounter on the ships, but they remember their dinners because they get dressed up each night. To them, this is more than a night on the town or a special occasion celebration. This is glamour and style, class and sophistication, and the dining room becomes those things because of how you, the manager, set the tone and the mood."

"So, how do I save my job?"

"Lesson number one is to draw a floor plan. I'm willing to bet your Uncle Barry does one."

Jonny nodded. "Especially on Saturday night. There are usually a lot of VIPs that night."

"Then you need to treat each night on the ship like

Saturday night. Your Uncle Barry taught you about table touches, right?"

Jonny's dark hair fell forward as he stared at the top of his desk. "Yeah, he complained that I didn't do it enough," he admitted. "He used to get on my case and tell me that table touches are what made a great restaurant manager." Jonny looked up to meet her eyes. "But it's not a big deal on the ship, is it? These people are only here for a week."

"*The passengers*," she corrected him, "may only be here for a week, but visiting with them is how you leave an impression, especially the older ladies. A small act of kindness goes a long way, and when a comment card comes back with a glowing review, that review goes toward the goal that corporate sets for you and the ship. Meeting and exceeding those goals is a part of the bonus you receive at the end of your contract."

Jonny looked thoughtful as Kennedy's words turned in his head. "I think I could begin to love table touches and seating charts."

They spoke for thirty more minutes, discussing the staff training he would go over today, and when she left, the young dining room manager seemed to have a new perspective on his role.

She took the stairs from the seventh to the fifth floor, where the Aurora Theater was located. When they had first arrived and poked around the ship, Kennedy found it strange that the staff service corridor connected the main dining room and kitchen to the small Starlight Lounge and the casino. However, she had since realized connecting the three areas made sense as the *Malina* had fewer kitchens and a staff that pulled double duty in the various outlets. The setup was thankfully much different on the larger *Helio*. With a back passageway connecting the dining room to the Solstice Theater, Kennedy could mysteriously disappear and reappear between the two spaces as if by magic.

She walked through the theater's front doors and was surprised to see the coat check. "I guess I didn't think about that," she mused. "We certainly don't need jackets on our warm Caribbean nights." She walked down the aisle and took the side stairs to the center of the stage, quietly channeling her thoughts while she turned in place. The quiet stage was her sanctuary, devoid of people and problems to be solved. Kennedy wasn't necessarily superstitious, but she wondered if her lousy start on the *Malina* could have been because she hadn't taken the time to find the theater and perform her own little good luck charm. They all did something on the *Helio* before a cruise. Franklin threw a shoe overboard before every trip, and Rosemary always wore the same earrings on embarkation day. Luke would pour a shot of rum, walk over to the railing, and spill it into the ocean as a salute, and Omar—

"Hello?" a voice called out. It was Ismaeel, followed by another man. "We aren't disturbing you, are we?"

Kennedy smiled and came down the steps. "Not at all." She extended her hand. "Hi, I'm Kennedy, I'm with corporate, and we're here to help," she joked.

The man standing beside Ismaeel laughed and shook Kennedy's hand. "Hi, I'm Jimmy, and I'm here to make you look and sound good."

Kennedy followed Jimmy to the sound booth and handed him her computer file with the script, music, and lighting needs. He nodded as he looked over the script. "Looks pretty straightforward," he said, "and these songs are great. I'm sensing a theme here. Do you want to do a run-through?"

"If you don't mind."

Kennedy walked down the aisle again and took her place on the stage. She felt like someone was staring holes in her but was sure Jimmy was the only other person in the theater. "Paranoia will destroy you," she whispered to quell the feeling.

She heard the notes of the first song in her show come through the speakers. It was a rib-tickling song from a popular musical about the hilarious ways a date could go wrong. It was a good opening number for her show as it complemented her theme about the dating world. When she finished running through the songs, she gave Jimmy a thumbs up. Then, she walked down the steps and gathered her papers from a seat on the first row, not noticing the figure standing in the shadow of the stage's left wing, seething with jealousy.

Mila stood in front of the spa and salon's reception desk where a woman in a carnation pink smock with overly bleached hair and a tan resembling the skin on a Thanksgiving turkey held up a finger and mouthed, "I'll be with you in a minute." As the woman's gravelly voice flexed between whining and berating the person on the other end, Mila realized she would not be helping her anytime soon. She stepped away from the desk and turned around as her eyes took in every nook and cranny.

When Mila had looked through the window yesterday, she had not seen the dark walnut wainscoting on the lower third of the walls. The same dark walnut also formed the clunky reception desk that looked primitive compared to the sleek creamy stone she had used in Oaza. Her eyes searched for the retail area but only saw a set of cheap wooden bookcases tucked away in a corner. Alfred's comment about the spa and salon being in decent shape must have been one of his quirky jokes.

She turned as she heard one of the spa techs, dressed in wrinkled mint green scrubs, trying to sell face cream to a passenger. Instead of a sleek sales pitch crafted to make the passenger beg to buy the product, the tech's high-strung sales approach made the passenger anxious to leave. If done correctly, the foundation for the upsell was laid out early with a tantalizing written description of the treatment, highlighted in the retail area with product placement, and then casually discussed during the session where the product was discreetly placed in the passenger's sightline. The non-threatening approach almost always netted a sale.

Tammy had shared that the spa was full at the morning meeting, but Mila noticed only a few people in the space. She turned around and walked back over to the desk. The receptionist put her hand over the mouthpiece. "Go on over there," she mouthed, pointing a green sparkled fingernail to an alcove. "Then why don't you come up here and explain it to me," she hissed into the phone and slammed it down.

Mila walked into what she assumed was the waiting room, a place to transition and begin relaxation. What she saw was anything but soothing. On the *Helio*, after greeting the passenger warmly, her assistant, Anna Marie, would escort the guest to the locker room, where they would change into a soft robe and slippers. During the walk, Anna Marie took their beverage order and showed them the door that led from the locker room to the private relaxation lounge. As they sunk into a soft upholstered chair, Anna Marie would magically appear with their drink.

Mila looked inside the space the receptionist had pointed

186

to. The only thing that separated the small rectangular room from the rest of the salon and spa was a dark walnut half-wall with matching spindles that went to the ceiling. The spindles and the harsh overhead yellow lighting cast shadows, making the room feel like a jail cell. She shuddered at the cracked red leather chairs placed against the wall and the dark laminated wood tables beside them. The tables were either littered with magazines or had ceramic lamps with dusty plastic covers on the shades. Mila glanced at the magazines and wondered if they had been bought with the furniture several decades earlier. Cringing, she looked apologetically at the other women in the room when the hardened leather on the chair crinkled loudly as she sat down. She pulled a small notepad from her pocket and began jotting down ideas but stopped when she heard voices arguing. She picked out Chuckie McDermott's high-pitched whine and the raspy, hardened voice of the receptionist. The squabble, Mila would later tell Kennedy and Bert, was over the receptionist's belief that Chuckie was flirting with one of the housekeepers. "No one seemed to care that there were people only a few feet away who could hear everything!"

A few minutes later, the rumpled technician Mila had seen earlier walked into the reception area. "Come on," she motioned to Mila, and her eyes quickly darted to the notebook Mila was stuffing into her pocket.

"Hi," Mila extended her hand. "I'm Mila Casimir, from the *Helio*."

"I've heard," the woman sighed and began walking away.

Mila later shared the story with Kennedy and Bert while walking the promenade deck that night with LaVonda's dogs. "She handed me a pale pink polyester robe and showed me where to change. The locker room was as sad as the reception area. Five tiny changing rooms with swinging louvered doors and a linoleum floor that looked like cobblestones." She gave a little shake of her chin and shoulders.

"No!" Bert fanned his face with his hands and feigned distress. "Say it isn't so, a polyester blend robe *and* linoleum flooring?" he asked sarcastically. "I would have left on the spot!"

Mila playfully punched his arm and grinned. "It gets worse," and she continued her story. "I had to shuffle down the hallway in cheap paper slippers and poke my head into rooms, trying to find Miss Personality."

Bert shook his head. "Tsk, tsk, tsk."

Mila gave Bert a withering look. "Anyway, once I found her, I walked into the room, and my foot stepped on something that made a crunchy noise. Then, as I began to sit in the chair, I saw something gritty on the seat."

"Gross!" Kennedy and Bert exclaimed in unison.

"I mentioned it to Miss Personality, who still hadn't told me her name, and she said, 'Yeah, okay, thanks.' "

"That's it?" Kennedy asked.

"Yep."

"Mila, do you think they were pranking you?" Bert asked. "It's obvious that Tammy doesn't like you."

"I think it's the status quo. After I brushed off my chair, the technician began to bully me into getting a more expensive facial. She told me that my skin, *my skin*," she emphasized, "was in horrendous shape and the harsh Florida sun was giving me, and I quote, 'a chicken-like complexion.' "

"Tell me you didn't hit her," Kennedy breathed.

"I politely declined and tried to relax…until I heard the crinkle of her plastic gloves." She held up a hand, seeing that Kennedy and Bert both wanted to speak. "Plastic gloves! The kind people wear at the deli. When my facial was over, Miss Personality told me we were going to another room for my massage. I am so glad my technicians come to the guest when they book multiple treatments; it just ruins the relaxation when you have to go from one room to another. So, I followed her, and she handed me a towel." Mila put one hand on her chest and the other on her hip. "The towels were this big, and Chuckie should be using them as sandpaper." She shook her head. "The masseuse was horrible. She also wore plastic gloves, and now I know what a chicken breast must feel like when you rub olive oil over it before putting it in the oven. Her technique was rough, and she reeked of cigarette smoke and cheap perfume, and between the tick of her watch, which sounded like a grandfather clock in my head, and the thump of the music from the gym coming through the walls, I wanted to run out, but the size of my towel prevented it."

"It's a shame she didn't give you two," Bert said.

"Two what?"

"Towels. You could have used them together to flag a distress signal."

Although the day was overcast and rainy, the passengers stayed busy thanks to the extra activities the staff had planned. Vera had stopped at her cabin to change her shoes when she saw her nephew coming down the corridor. "I've looked all over the ship for you." Justin's tone was testy. "We were supposed to talk at lunch about my place in the company."

"Oh, Justin, I am terribly sorry. I went to the beer-tasting class with Oliver Parsons, and then we grabbed a bite to eat. I'm on my way to meet him at the ballroom dancing class now."

"I can't believe you have been drinking this early in the day and with someone you barely know. And beer? I didn't know you drank beer. The family would be a bit surprised to hear about your unusual behavior, Aunt Vera."

Vera, who had been unusually happy moments before, felt a cold wave wash over her. "It was a beer-tasting class, Justin, not a bar crawl, and it would behoove you to remember your place," she said slowly and evenly. "I met someone, and we have some common interests. Regarding your taking things over, we will discuss it, but only when I am ready to do so."

"Well, I think we should discuss it now since there are no distractions or interruptions like we have at the office."

"You do?" Vera asked coldly. "Fine. Let's go inside. I don't intend to discuss our private business matters in a common hallway." They entered Vera's cabin, and Justin was taken aback at her luxurious quarters while he had been given what he felt was a standard cabin. Vera sat down at the small glass dining table and motioned for Justin to take the seat across from her. She steepled her fingertips but did not speak right away. "At this point, Justin, I don't believe you are ready for that responsibility, as evidenced by the fiasco in Napa for Mr. Overcash. It was just short of a disaster, and your handling of it was sloppy, irresponsible, and lacked the attention to detail my company has become known for."

"*Your company?*" Justin looked at her incredulously.

"My company," Vera replied evenly. "And be assured

that it will be *my company* until I take my last breath. Do you realize that your sister, Inez, is refunding the hefty fee we were supposed to collect because of your carelessness? I can only pray that the family won't sue us. Would you care to discuss the matter further?"

Seeing the firm set of his aunt's jaw, Justin decided to take another tactic and softened his tone. "Aunt Vera, I'm sorry. I'm just worried about your new friend. We don't know anything about him. You are a very wealthy woman who has been alone for a long time and are suddenly doing things that are not normal for you, like drinking in the middle of the day. Have you looked into his background? We could do it from the ship's business center. The man could be a serial killer."

Vera stared icily at her nephew. "The cruise line did not invite serial killers on this cruise. For that matter, you would not have warranted an invitation, either. It's for guests of the corporate office and travel agents. Oliver has a friend in the corporate office."

"Yes, but—"

"Secondly," Vera interrupted him, and Justin wondered if the blood that ran through his aunt's veins was indeed ice water, as his father had inferred on more than one occasion. "Mr. Parsons is a businessman who trains racehorses at his farm in Kentucky. Kennedy introduced me to him because I asked her to. Now, before I decide to end your trip in Juneau, please find

192

something to do far away from me," she said frostily. "I will not allow you to ruin my good mood."

Justin stood up and looked down at his aunt. "I'm only looking out for you, Aunt Vera."

Vera softened. "My dearest nephew, I have met someone whom I find charming. It doesn't happen every day, and certainly not when we are home. There are too many people who would enjoy treating my private life as their personal soap opera. Now, I know we aren't used to being around each other much, and frankly, I am not used to having someone underfoot, or for that matter, someone who believes they can tell me what I can or cannot do." Seeing that Justin was fighting the urge to say more, she continued speaking, "Why don't we meet later today at the golf area? You can show me what you are really doing during the middle of the day when you are supposed to be working."

Justin gulped. He wasn't sure how his aunt knew about his afternoon excursions to the driving range. "That sounds good, Aunt Vera. I'll see you after your ballroom dancing class." He bent down and pecked her on the head. "I'm only looking out for our future," he said softly.

Justin left Vera's cabin and went directly to the ship's business center, where he fired off a message to his sister.

Inez,

I'm worried about Aunt Vera. She's met someone compliments of "Kennedy the Great," and I'm pretty sure he's one of those guys who prey on lonely older women, which is Aunt Vera to a tee. His name is Oliver Parsons, and he's from Kentucky. See what you can find out.

Justin

As Justin exited the business center, he saw LaVonda approaching it, dabbing her eyes. "Are you okay, LaVonda?"

"I'm fine, just sad. I lost my sapphire hair comb last night, and I am devastated. I need to send a message to my insurance agent. It was a one-of-a-kind piece, and I doubt I will ever be able to find another one."

"The piece you were wearing in your hair? Do you remember when?" LaVonda shook her head. Justin furrowed his brow. "I remember you had it on when we met. Have you checked with security to see if someone turned it in?"

"I checked but got the runaround. The man in charge of security was very unsympathetic. He gave me some lip service about the amount of paperwork involved in filing a security report."

"Would you like me to speak with him?" He gave her a dazzling smile. "In fact, why don't you meet me at the mixology class they are having in two hours, and I'll report back what I find out."

LaVonda's face lit up at the suggestion. "There you go again, being gallant."

"I'm working on my Boy Scout badge," he grinned.

"I'm due for a private tour of the ship, but I'd be delighted to meet you at the mixology class. Where is it?"

"It's in the whiskey bar on deck eight." He gave her a wink. "I'll see you then." He turned and walked down the corridor while LaVonda caught her breath at receiving such attention from the handsome young man.

Kennedy had just left LaVonda's cabin with the three dogs for their second walk of the day when she ran into Ronnee and her ladies, who had stopped at their cabins to freshen up after a late lunch. "Oh dear," Ronnee looked at the grumpy-faced dogs, "it looks like you pulled the short straw. I think I remember their names. Aren't they Crabby, Cranky, and Cantankerous?"

Kennedy had to stifle a giggle at Ronnee's comment.

"Just another part of my glamorous life."

"My dear," Irene, a diminutive woman with a head full of short red hair and large round tortoiseshell glasses, said in a warbly voice, "we were thrilled that there were more things to do today. I can only sit and stare at nature for so long. There is no remote control when you get bored with the scenery."

"The man with the black eyes who taught the beer class, was he in a fight? Does that happen a lot below decks where the crew lives?" Mary Margaret asked with a gleam in her eye. Kennedy shook her head and explained that Ismaeel had collided with a shaker at the captain's cocktail party when one of the bartenders was showing off.

"I think these ladies were too busy flirting with the ship's officers and missed the accident," Ronnee said with amusement.

The dogs began yapping and barking, and Kennedy hurried off before they became a nuisance. The weather had cleared, so Kennedy decided a walk around the promenade deck would tire them out after visiting their spot under the steps. After making the first turn, she saw Vera taking in the view.

"Why on earth are you walking these beasts?" she looked down her nose disdainfully at the three dogs, who had begun to snort in displeasure that someone had halted their walk.

"Keeping one of our VIPs happy," Kennedy replied. "She can be a handful, and if this keeps her in a pleasant mood, it's a small price to pay."

"I thought I was the only VIP you concerned yourself with, Kennedy," Vera said cooly. "And as we are speaking about VIPs and their needs, you may let Officer Armitage know that he and whomever he was dueling with are off the hook tonight."

"Oh dear, was there a problem? I didn't see you in the dining room last night."

"Not at all, but it isn't as fun as having dinner with Franklin or Omar." At the mention of Omar's name, Vera saw Kennedy's ordinarily cheerful face fall for a split second. "I'm having dinner with someone else tonight."

"Oh?"

Vera felt a rare smile come across her face. "Mr. Parsons, for your information. I find his company most refreshing. Now, I'd like to talk about something else." The dogs had tangled themselves around Kennedy's feet and were beginning to snarl at each other. Vera nodded at them. "Perhaps we should walk and talk."

"First, I spoke with Emily. She had a wonderful time as one of the judges for the chef's competition and shared the sordid details of what happened on the cruise, and she's suddenly developed a desire to cook. You probably don't know this, but Emily has never stepped foot in her kitchen in the many years I have known her, and now she believes she is Julia Child.

She boasted the other day that she had made mayonnaise from scratch. And I must tell you that Emily was very complimentary of your quick thinking, something about that dreadful trophy you feel compelled to give out."

"I understand she will be joining us for some cruises in the future as a guest lecturer," Kennedy said happily. "She's very well-versed in history. Her stories make events from the past come to life."

"Well, they should. She was there when most of them happened. She's as old as dirt," Vera said loftily.

Kennedy couldn't help herself. "Weren't the two of you college roommates, Mrs. Jameson?" she grinned.

"Emily is much older than I am," Vera sniffed. "As a child protégé, I was barely out of the nursery when I went to college." She tapped Kennedy on the arm. "Do you know you are the only person who gets away with such impertinence, young lady? Now, do we need to discuss the rather large elephant in front of us? I saw your face fall when I mentioned Omar's name, and Emily shared that he took a leave of absence as soon as the ship docked."

Kennedy groaned inwardly. The problem with dating anyone on the ship was that everyone in the company knew your business. "He had some family matters to attend to." She paused. "I completely forgot to ask if you wanted a spa appointment.

Mila is on the ship and can take care of you."

Vera shook her head. "Kennedy, *that* was a terrible deflection. Thank you, but no. Although I adore Mila and love being taken care of by her, I saw the spa. It's deplorable. I'll tell Emily that Mila must get a hold of that space and sooner rather than later."

The two women walked in silence. "Mrs. Jameson, please forgive me for overstepping, but we have known each other for many years. I've heard you speak of Inez but never Justin."

Vera sighed. "Justin is…" She searched for the right words and cleared her throat. "My brother-in-law has been pressuring me to bring Justin into the company to continue the family business. Unfortunately, Justin has not had a good track record with jobs, falling into them as quickly as he loses interest in them. Although somehow, he always has plenty of money to spend. I assume his parents are still giving him an allowance. He prefers to socialize more than work, has the attention span of a gnat, and cuts corners."

They had reached the putting green. "And now, my dear, I must leave you here." Vera waved at Justin, who was standing by the driving range. "We had words earlier today. I'm sure he meant well, but the subject matter rankled me. So, to make up, I promised I would hit a few balls with him."

Although she frequently played at home, Vera had never paid attention to the golf amenities offered on the other ships, preferring to play at the resorts near the ports of call. She saw a short man in the ten-foot by fifteen-foot netted box taking swings.

Justin brushed her cheek when she reached him. "Aunt Vera," Justin said amiably, "please meet Diamond Jim Adair, Diamond Jim, Vera Jameson." They shook hands, and Vera selected a driver.

"Ladies first," Diamond Jim held out his hand, and Vera took her place at the tee box and swung.

LaVonda and J. Mitchell had one last stop on their tour of the ship: the golfing area. "This is wonderful," she pointed at the putting green and tee box. "So many of my clients cannot be away from their golf clubs for a day, let alone a week."

"And the golf balls are biodegradable in case one makes it through the net and out to sea," J. Mitchell added. He was thankful this was the last stop of the tour. LaVonda had peppered him with questions, many of which he did not know the answer to but made up what he hoped were plausible responses.

They walked over to the driving range, and Justin made

the introductions. LaVonda stared at Vera. "You look familiar. Were you on the *Oriana* a few years ago in the Mediterranean? It rained the entire dreadful cruise."

"I may have been," Vera said dryly. "Why do you ask?"

"There was a horrible little cruise director, and I swear her twin is on this ship. I wanted to see if you recognized her."

"Kennedy?"

"That's her!" LaVonda's eyes flashed as pieces of the puzzle she had been trying to solve came together. "I knew she looked familiar." She looked at J. Mitchell and lowered her voice. "I guess she wasn't fired but demoted. It must be why she is your assistant. I hope you can teach her a few things about customer service on this cruise," she huffed. "Oh, she was so awful. I had one tiny little request, and she wouldn't help me." She looked at Justin and Diamond Jim for sympathy and, finding none, turned her gaze back to J. Mitchell.

Vera now vividly remembered the cruise, including how she and Kennedy had turned a corner on that trip. "If I remember correctly, I was in a conversation with Kennedy when you rudely and loudly made your demands for everyone to hear."

Diamond Jim, Justin, and J. Mitchell backed away, watching with comedic interest as the two women squared off. Both were formidable in their own right, but each man silently placed their bet on Vera in this skirmish.

"I don't think I was that loud," LaVonda said, annoyed at Vera's comment. "I was simply trying to get someone to help me." She batted her eyelashes and looked at the three men.

"You bawled like a cow separated from the herd. I believe you were trying to get anyone within earshot to listen to you, but they couldn't because your dog was barking as obnoxiously as you were complaining," Vera replied coolly.

LaVonda turned back to the three men to explain. "Kennedy had the nerve to tell me that I was welcome to leave at the next port. I only wanted a cabin for my sweet puppy, but Kennedy made some excuse about not having any unoccupied cabins."

"I believe you told her to bump someone from the cruise."

LaVonda ignored Vera's statement. "I fixed her, though. I wrote a scathing review and called the corporate office to complain about her in detail. I told them I couldn't recommend the cruise line if they allowed their cruise directors to treat people as horribly as Kennedy treated me, and I demanded that they fire her." Justin saw his aunt's nostrils flare, and Lavonda gave J. Mitchell, Diamond Jim, and Justin a sly smile. "Well, they fell all over themselves to make it up to me." She turned to J. Mitchell. "J. Mitchell, I cannot believe she is the person taking care of my sweeties. Will you take care of them from now on? I cannot bear the thought of Kennedy being around them. She might decide to retaliate by being mean to them. I'm sure that by now, she has realized who I am."

J. Mitchell gulped and looked at his watch. "I'll see what I can do, Ms. Taylor," he said, suddenly in a hurry to leave. He had no desire to take care of LaVonda's snarling dogs. "I apologize, but I have to leave. I need to make some announcements."

"Thanks for the warning," Vera said sarcastically, brushing past LaVonda as she stepped up to the tee box.

While Vera was taking her turn, Justin asked Diamond Jim where Trixie and Cameron were. "I have no idea," Diamond Jim answered. "The spa, the casino, shopping. Who knows? Those two are as thick as thieves." Vera walked back to the group, and Diamond Jim approached the tee. "I've never seen adult cousins as close as they are, but it makes my girl happy that he is on the cruise and keeps her busy so I can concentrate on this," and he smacked the ball hard. Diamond Jim took another golf ball from his pocket and placed it on the tee.

Justin cleared his throat. "Aunt Vera, LaVonda, Diamond Jim is in the jewelry business."

"I'm sure you've heard of my little store," Diamond Jim called out as he swung his golf club. "It's called The Little Black Box."

"That's you?" LaVonda's eyes opened wide in

recognition. "I've seen your commercials. You sing a song and then hold your fingers out like guns."

"A little black box, you won't go into hock," Diamond Jim crooned, and LaVonda joined him singing, "when you just want to show off your sparkle!"

"Justin, I do apologize, but I have another engagement," Vera announced. "I'll see you tonight. Let's have a drink in my cabin before dinner." She purposefully ignored LaVonda and nodded at Diamond Jim. "It was a pleasure meeting you, Mr. Adair."

"Since we're friends now, why don't you call me Diamond Jim?"

Vera smiled tightly. "Diamond Jim," she said through gritted teeth, and Justin had to look out to the horizon to keep from laughing out loud. To Vera, Diamond Jim's name was akin to that of a personal injury attorney or used car salesman. She pulled her shoulders back and looked down her nose at LaVonda. "And for your information, Kennedy is the best cruise director on the Sunny Dayz Cruise Line, and I hold her in very high regard," she said imperiously. "If she was unable to help you, I am certain it was because she could not meet your request, and any fawning by the corporate office was most likely to shut you up." She turned on her heel and marched off, leaving LaVonda blinking rapidly and screwing up her mouth to retort.

"Your aunt is a pistol," Diamond Jim chuckled and slapped his thigh. He leaned over to Justin and whispered, "If I ever need someone dressed down, I'm calling her. But I don't think she liked calling me Diamond Jim. Must rankle her somehow."

Desperate to change the subject, Justin searched for something to say. "Jim, LaVonda is a connoisseur of fine jewelry. Unfortunately, she lost a piece last night. It was rare, a sapphire hair comb that she wore as a tiara."

"You don't say." Diamond Jim now looked at LaVonda with renewed interest. "Well, that is a shame. If we were back home, I'd have you set up in no time. As it is, I brought a lot of jewelry with me but no tiaras. I can loan you a few pieces to get you through the cruise if you like."

LaVonda waved her hand. "Oh, I brought plenty of pieces, Diamond Jim. I just loved that one. But as they say, 'Que sera, sera.' " She raised one of her thickly crayoned eyebrows at him. "But, if I was interested in borrowing or buying something, what did you bring?"

The conversation continued as Diamond Jim and LaVonda talked about jewelry, and finally, Justin cleared his throat to tell LaVonda it was time for the mixology class. Diamond Jim sighed with relief when they left, thankful to have quiet again. The only noise he now heard was the whack of his club hitting the golf ball.

Kennedy had checked the various activities on the ship and stopped by the ship's whiskey lounge to see how the mixology class had gone over. Ismaeel was collecting glassware from the tables and looked up when she entered.

"Success?"

"I think so," he answered, taking the tub of glassware behind the bar to wash the dirty glasses. "Either they heard about the bartender with two black eyes, or they wanted to learn how to make some of the cocktails we have been offering. Interestingly, my spiked cider was the biggest hit of all the cocktails I taught them how to make." He chuckled. "And it's the easiest."

"Cider always makes me think of fall, which is something we don't see much of in Florida."

ISMAEEL'S MAPLE SYRUP CIDER

1 ½ OUNCES MAPLE SYRUP VODKA

10 OUNCES HOT APPLE CIDER

CINNAMON

COMBINE WARM CIDER AND VODKA IN A MUG. DUST WITH CINNAMON FOR GARNISH.

"I know it is too late now. We probably should have thought about—"

Ismaeel held up some stapled papers. "Already done," he chuckled and looked at the woman walking toward the counter. "It looks like someone could use a cup of coffee."

Kennedy turned around to see Mila sliding tiredly onto a barstool. "I would adore a cup of coffee as long as it isn't the sludge in the mess hall."

Ismaeel stooped down and brought out a thermos from the shelf below. He poured the contents into a mug and pushed it toward Mila. "From my personal stash, I get the beans from a roaster in Seattle."

Mila brought the mug up to her nose and inhaled the fragrant smell. She closed her eyes in appreciation. "Heaven," she sighed. Her eyes fluttered open. "It's been quite a day. Yoga class was interesting," she said as she sipped her coffee.

"Oh?" Kennedy asked, and Ismaeel leaned forward over the bar top.

"The bride-to-be and her very handsome cousin were in my class. He told her that the class would help reduce her stress about the wedding and asked me about tantric yoga poses to help his sex life."

"What did you say?"

"I mumbled something about it being time for class to start." Mila took another sip of coffee. "Then, halfway through the class, he got up and stood over her and," she rolled her eyes and held up her hand, "adjusted her hips during the bridge pose. There was a lot of giggling between them, and then he began doing handstands while I moved us into the next pose. I suddenly understood what a parent must feel like when their kids constantly say, 'watch me.' "

"What did you do?" Ismaeel asked.

"I pushed through the poses and ignored him, although his cousin certainly couldn't."

Kennedy hopped off her barstool. "I've got another stop to make. Oh, and I think I got through to Jonny."

"How?" Ismaeel coughed. "I thought he was a lost cause."

"Between a message from his uncle and my words of wisdom, he is more focused on running his dining room. I'm on my way there now."

It only took Kennedy a few minutes to get from the Quiet Distil on the eighth deck to Siku on the seventh. She slipped into the back of the room and stood beside Chef Sha and Chef Jordan while Jonny demonstrated the finer points of service etiquette to the staff.

"What did you do?" Sha asked. "Tell him we would tie

him to the ship's funnel? Or threaten him with walking the plank?"

Kennedy smiled at Sha's bloodthirsty ideas. "No, I just shared some advice."

Sha snorted and stared at Jonny. "We'll see. I'm hopeful but not convinced. We have to get back to the kitchen. But if tonight is as bad as last night, I'm tying him to the funnel until we arrive in Juneau. Then, I'm throwing him off the ship."

Kennedy walked up to the podium and was pleased to see the seating chart. She was reviewing it when Jonny walked up. "What do you think?"

She gave him a winning smile. "You've done a great job with this, Jonny," and she saw him bask in her praise.

Suddenly, J. Mitchell's voice came over the speakers. "Me, again, *your favorite* cruise director, J. Mitchell, with more fun facts about Alaska."

"I'm going to my cabin," Kennedy said quickly.

Jonny gave her a wry look. "If you are trying to escape the announcements, you can't. They play in our cabins as well. And his voice has a way of circumventing earplugs."

J. Mitchell's singsong voice crackled through the speakers. "As I said earlier, we will see some wildlife on this trip, and I'm not talking about any of you who choose to show off your dance moves in the disco tonight." His jerky laugh sounded harsh and forced. "The largest salmon ever caught weighed close to one hundred pounds. That's a lot of bagels and lox!" Kennedy and Jonny rolled their eyes, and J. Mitchell went on to talk about other wildlife in Alaska. "Okay, that's all for now! Signing off! This has been J. Mitchell, *your* cruise director!"

While J. Mitchell was making his announcements, Justin had stopped by the business center hoping his sister had done what she always did and dropped everything to help him out. As he read the message, a small smile lifted at the corners of his mouth, and he felt confident his aunt would now see him in a new light.

Justin tapped on his aunt's cabin door and placed his key against the lock. "Aunt Vera, I need to talk to you," he said, walking in.

Vera's head snapped up, startled. She had been taking her new jade necklace out of the wooden box on the coffee table. "Excuse me! Did you just let yourself into my room?" She was piqued at the unexpected intrusion. "You may have taken it upon yourself to get a key to my stateroom due to my one-time forgetfulness, but that does not allow you to enter my room whenever you want."

"Do you want me to leave?" Justin was irked at her rebuke.

Vera drew in a breath, biting back the words she wanted to say. Instead, she turned her attention back to the extravagant necklace she held in her hands and, walking over to the mirror above the wet bar, fastened the piece around her neck.

"I've asked Mr. Parsons to join us for dinner tonight," she announced as she looked at her reflection in the mirror, admiring the six strands of oval-shaped jade beads that wound around her neck and cascaded over her collarbone.

"I'd like to talk with you about him. I sent a message to Inez and asked her to find out what she could about him."

Vera stared at Justin through the mirror. "You did *what*?" and whipped around to face him.

He held a piece of paper out to Vera. "He's not a horse trainer. He's an ex-con and served time for being a jewel thief."

"Really." Vera tried valiantly to keep a straight face while walking toward Justin. "First, you were concerned that he was a serial killer, and now you believe he is a jewel thief." She placed a finger on her chin. "Wasn't there a movie about a heist pulled off by a group of retirees?" She snapped her fingers as laughter bubbled up. "I remember watching it. One of them kept falling asleep at the most inopportune times."

She saw Justin's hurt face and bit her lips together to regain her composure. "My darling nephew," she stood before him and clasped her hands together, "I believe you have spent too much time out in the sea air today. While your new friend Diamond Jim is a colorful character, Mr. Parsons is a simple horse trainer from Kentucky who is an excellent dancer and has a friend in the cruise line's corporate office. Why don't you make us both a drink, and we can put this silly notion about Oliver behind us."

In exasperation, Justin shook the piece of paper at Vera. "Aunt Vera, it's right here in black-and-white. I must insist you not have dinner with him until you read this."

Vera gave him a patient smile and looked at the paper Justin held. "And isn't it possible that Inez did a quick search, and the first article that popped up was a man with the same name? I would think there is more than one Justin Jameson in the world, wouldn't you? Now, I am dining with Oliver tonight. You are welcome to join us or dine elsewhere."

"If you aren't going to take what I found out seriously, I *will* find somewhere else to eat." Justin stalked to the door and put his hand on the knob but suddenly pulled it back. He let out a breath and turned around. "I'd hate for the family to find out about this. It might make them question your ability to run the company." He saw her eyes flash as her mouth began to work to form a retort, and he softened his tone. "Sometimes, when older women find themselves suddenly attracted to someone after a long time," he paused, "well, their logic and common sense go out of the window. I'm only trying to do what is best…for everyone."

Vera looked down at her black satin pump, wishing she could plant it firmly in Justin's backside. His comments had enraged her, and she was trying to keep her emotions in check. "I'm sorry you won't be joining us this evening. It might have allayed your fears. As to sharing this information with the family, please feel free to do so." She looked him in the eye. "But as I told you earlier today, it is *my* company, and *no one* has ever questioned my judgment when they cashed one of the quarterly checks they receive. I doubt that a doddering old woman without common sense and logic could support the family in the manner they have become accustomed to. Good night."

Justin opened the door and walked down the corridor, deciding to lick his wounds in Sedna's View. When he opened the doors, he was delighted to see his friend Diamond Jim surrounded by a large laughing group, and he was introduced to the very pretty Ronnee Barrett and her five charges.

"Justin!" Diamond Jim bellowed. "I need a wingman while I wait for Trixie!"

The tales grew taller as the drinks flowed. Justin told a humorous story about the first and only time he had ridden on a

213

horse, and a bee had gotten under the saddle blanket. "It was just like you see in the rodeo." He hunched over as if on a horse, one arm flying back and forth as he pantomimed the bucking of the crazed horse. "And then," his arm went up wildly in the air and connected with the bottom of Ronnee's glass as she put it to her lips. The contents of the glass flew all over Ronnee, covering her hair, face, and dress. Justin quickly ran to the bar and grabbed a stack of towels to help wipe her off.

"I'm fine," she laughed as he apologized profusely and patted her arms with the bar towels.

"I think I accidentally busted your lip."

He handed Ronnee another towel, which she put to her mouth to stanch the blood. "My dears, I am so sorry, but I need to go back to my room to change. You'll have to go to dinner without me, but I'll join you as soon as possible." The five ladies began twittering amongst each other, looking worried. "I promise not to be more than thirty minutes," she reassured them. "Tell the person at the podium my name, and they will seat you at our table."

"Ronnee, I feel terrible about this." Justin motioned to her red dress covered in dark maroon splotches. "With their permission," he nodded at the ladies sitting with Ronnee, "may I escort your friends to the dining room? I'd hate for them to enter without a male chaperone." He waggled his eyebrows, "It could compromise their reputations," making the women cackle in delight.

"Ladies?" she asked, and five grateful heads bobbed in assent.

The main dining room looked lovely for the Captain's Dinner. The gold flatware and chargers gleamed against the green marble tables, and crisp snowy napkins stood pertly on the chargers while crystal glasses reflected the twinkling lights from above. Kennedy was in a long black dress, and as she passed the captain's table, she sent up a silent prayer that Captain Volare would show up, but in case he didn't, she had a backup plan. She gave Jonny a thumbs up, and Siku's doors were opened as servers stood at attention awaiting their guests. Jonny stood smartly at the podium, greeting the passengers bedecked in evening gowns and tuxedos. Kennedy was amazed at how twenty-four hours could make such a change in the atmosphere.

Justin entered the room with his five charges, and Jonny escorted them to a large round table near the center. Kennedy silently thanked Jonny for his foresight. While LaVonda was an important VIP on the cruise, Ronnee was as well, but didn't flaunt it like LaVonda. Justin and Jonny seated each lady personally, and when Justin took his seat, the five women looked down at their place settings, suddenly shy in his presence.

Justin cleared his throat. "Ladies, I am the luckiest man in this room tonight, and while I am sorry that I spilled Ronnee's drink on her, I am delighted that I can be in such magnificent company. The jewels you are wearing complement your beauty and outshine every other woman in this room." The ladies giggled like schoolgirls at his compliment.

"This brooch," Helen pointed to the garnet and pearl dragonfly on her shawl, "was a gift from my father on my wedding day," she whispered.

"I'm sorry?" Justin leaned forward. "I didn't hear you," he said to the stooped gray-haired woman on his left.

"Helen can only whisper," Mary Margaret flashed a large sapphire ring in front of Justin's nose. "My ring was a gift from my husband on our twenty-fifth anniversary. I only wear it on special occasions."

He turned to the woman on his right. "Estelle, does your neck hurt when you wear that necklace? That's a huge opal."

Estelle, the smallest but loudest of the group, shouted, "Twenty-two."

"Twenty-two?" Justin repeated, confused.

"Twenty-two diamonds around the opal," she clutched her hand around the large jewel.

216

Not to be outdone, Marge pointed to the pin at her throat. "Do you like my cameo? Left-facing cameos like this one are rare and, therefore, more valuable."

Justin nodded. "It's lovely."

"Stop that!" Estelle hissed at Irene, who had been touching her earlobes.

"I wanted to make sure they were there. I don't want to lose them." Irene looked apologetically at the others who were staring at her. "My earrings are clip-on," she explained. "I could never get up the nerve to have my ears pierced. I have a jewelry box full of single earrings because I lost one. So, I'm constantly checking my ears to make sure nothing is lost."

"A wise insurance policy," Justin said, thankful that the server had appeared to take their drink order. He hoped Ronnee would appear soon, as he was running out of things to talk about. "Would you ladies like to see some magic tricks?"

Their eyes lit up like candles as he turned a fork into a spoon with the sleight of his hand. They were astonished when he then bent the spoon in front of their eyes, and when he made a coin vanish and brought it through the table, they applauded.

"Justin," Marge, the boldest of the group, piped up, "are you a travel agent like Ronnee? Is that why you are on this ship?"

"No, I'm accompanying my aunt. She's a guest of the

217

corporate office," he answered.

"How exciting," Mary Margaret said, then her brow furrowed. "But why aren't you sitting with her?"

Justin smiled tightly. "My aunt and I disagreed this evening. I don't care for the man she is dining with tonight."

"How noble," Irene said in a hushed tone. "I don't think my nephews know I am alive."

Justin was seated so that his chair faced the podium. He had been half-listening to Estelle when he saw Ronnee slip in, searching for their table. He was about to stand and wave to her when he saw LaVonda arrive. Several other people also saw the two women standing like bookends on either side of the podium, wearing identical midnight-blue lace dresses, but that was where the similarities stopped. While one was tall and slender with tousled caramel hair, the other was shorter and heavier with black hair that framed her face and flipped up on the shoulders. And while Ronnee wore simple diamond studs in her ears, LaVonda had chosen a pearl choker with a sapphire the size of a strawberry at the center and grape-sized pearl earrings.

Kennedy was returning to the podium, having seated another group far across the room. She watched in fascination as the two women arrived simultaneously. If their eyes had been lasers, the death stare each gave the other would have left the elegant dining room to look like the remnants of a smoking battlefield.

Ronnee saw Justin and her dears and waved. She turned and told Jonny she did not need an escort to her table. "I'm not as needy as some of your other guests." She darted her eyes at LaVonda.

LaVonda gritted her teeth, and the smile she gave Jonny came across as a ghoulish grin. She drummed her fingers on the host stand loudly. "Young man, as I am a guest of the captain, I suggest that you escort me to his table, and I'd like you to make a point of walking me past where *she* is sitting." She pointed at Ronnee, who had almost reached the table where her clients and Justin sat. Jonny swallowed hard, remembering Kennedy's words about comment cards and bonuses. They took the circuitous route, and when they passed Ronnee's table, LaVonda's eyes drilled into Justin's.

While Ronnee was settling herself in her chair, her tablemates began speaking at the same time.

"That woman is wearing the same dress as yours!"

"Don't you think she's over-accessorized?"

"I suppose she never heard what Coco Chanel said."

"Jewelry should tell a story, but she's wearing a novel!"

Justin noticed that Helen was having difficulty removing the dragonfly pin holding her shawl closed at the shoulder. "May

I help you?"

"You are just a dear," she whispered, and although he couldn't hear her, he gathered that she wanted help when she presented her shoulder to him. "Ooh, look, something is getting ready to happen." Because his head was close to her lips, he could finally hear her whisper. She pointed at the captain's table where J. Mitchell stood holding a glass of champagne and a microphone.

"Sir, it's time for your toast and the introductions," J. Mitchell whispered. The captain sighed heavily and nodded, draining the contents of the rocks glass in front of him. The lights lowered, and the captain, his key officers, and select staff members rose and followed him to the center of the room. The captain began another long-winded toast, and when he finally raised his glass and said, "Salute!" the passengers, thankful the toast was over, drank greedily. He then turned and introduced those standing behind him, and they each took their seat after being presented.

J. Mitchell was the last member standing by the captain. He stood there, preening as he waited for his introduction. Captain Volare looked around the room as if searching for someone, and his eyes finally found Kennedy. "I want to remind all of you that we have the incredibly talented Kennedy Reeves on board tonight compliments of our sister ship, the *Helio*. Kennedy will be performing her one-woman show in the Aurora

Theater after dinner, and I am told that people line up to attend it." He raised his glass and offered a toast. "To the best and brightest of the Sunny Dayz Cruise Line, Kennedy Reeves, we are grateful that you are here with us on this voyage and wish you would stay." The passengers applauded, and the house lights came back up. Kennedy watched as J. Mitchell, red-faced and standing alone in the center of the room, stalked away.

"Oh boy," she whispered dismally and walked over to Jonny. "Listen, I need to get ready for my show. Have you got this under control?" He gave her a thumbs up.

Kennedy went to her cabin, pulled out her signature evening gloves and costume jewelry, and placed them in a bag with her makeup. She had decided to get ready backstage where the mirrors would not distort her features. She didn't want to look like a clown on stage, especially after the captain's introduction.

Ducking behind the stage curtains, Kennedy sat down at the makeup table, undid her chignon, and fluffed her hair. She put on her false eyelashes and painted her lips bright red. Satisfied with the reflection in the mirror, she rummaged in her bag and found a large pair of rhinestone earrings and a matching bracelet. She pulled her long, red satin gloves over her arms and slipped the bracelet over her wrist.

"Gorgeous as always!" Mila came up behind her and placed her head beside Kennedy's. "Break a leg tonight!"

221

"Smile!" Bert called out. The two women turned around, and he depressed the shutter.

"Have I mentioned how grateful I am for you two?" Kennedy asked, her eyes wet.

"*No crying!*" Mila hollered and began to fan Kennedy's eyes. "Quick, look up at the lights. We don't have time to redo your makeup, and the place is full after the captain's plug."

The theater was filling up quickly, and Vera and Oliver found themselves in a slow-moving line behind Ronnee and her charges. They made small talk, and one of the ladies in the group said she hoped the show would be good as it wasn't a musical.

"Kennedy's shows are always hilarious!" Ronnee assured them.

Vera looked at Ronnee in surprise. "You know Kennedy?"

"For years. I always book my conferences on the *Helio* because of her attention to detail."

When they found seats, Oliver asked if he could take the ladies' wraps to the coat check area.

"Such a gentleman," Mary Margaret said dreamily. "Just like that Justin. I wonder where he got off to, he was with us at dinner, and then he vanished." Vera's ears perked up. She had seen Justin sitting at the table and wondered why and how their

222

paths had crossed.

Oliver returned just as the house lights dimmed. The curtains raised, and a spotlight bathed Kennedy in a glow as she sang her first song. When she finished, Kennedy took a deep bow.

"Ladies and gentlemen, welcome to my one-woman show, or as my mother, Lolly, would call it," Kennedy pointed at imaginary words over her head. "Kennedy's Showcase of Disappointments." She sighed heavily into the microphone. "I don't mean to be a disappointment to her. Somehow it just happens…all the time." She put the microphone into the stand. "Mothers are kind, correct?" The audience applauded politely. "They will go out of their way to help their children, right?" The applause grew, and when it died down, Kennedy spoke again. "My mother has decided to do this by pointing out my flaws…alphabetically and categorically. Her biggest question to me these days is why I am still single. It baffles her."

Kennedy threw back her shoulders, turned sideways, and put her nose in the air. "Kennedy," she mimicked her mother's haughty tone, "you have all of my qualities, yet you still can't find a man. I don't understand it. You are pretty." Kennedy faced the audience, wiggled her head from side to side, and fluffed her hair. "Obviously intelligent." Kennedy pointed to her temple. "And creative." She danced a short soft shoe. "I'm simply at a loss as to why you aren't married."

Kennedy gave the crowd a knowing look, turned her body the opposite way, and sighed exaggeratedly. "Mother, let's face it. I'm overqualified."

The audience burst into laughter. Kennedy picked up a blank poster board, and when the room calmed down, she flipped it over. "Look, it's a picture of my love life!" The crowd went into convulsions, and when the laughter subsided, she continued speaking. "Honestly, I looked into online dating, but I was afraid it would match me up with those crazy California boys: Ernest and Gallo. Although my mother would have approved of their line of work...and the discounts."

She lifted the microphone from the stand and began pacing the stage. "She and my sister, Willie the Perfect," she grinned, "yes, folks, that is her name, just like Mary Queen of Scotts or Catherine the Great, my sister is known as Willie the Perfect. Perfect family, perfect house, perfect hair—perfect, perfect, perfect." Kennedy grabbed her throat and stuck out her tongue. "So, back to my story, my mother, Lolly, and Willie the Perfect like to set me up on blind dates. I swear, sooner or later, I'll be having drinks with one of the Four Horsemen of the Apocalypse."

She walked back to center stage and sat on a high-backed barstool. "So, when I go home, I am required to attend at least two special dinners per week." Kennedy held up her hand in protest. "The details are sordid, but let me tell you, if my mother ever makes a deal with the devil, he's going to scratch his head and wonder how he came out on the wrong side of that deal." The audience roared, and Kennedy smiled to herself. "These are dinners where she invites a starving man, who is somehow connected to the family, over and plies him with food and liquor in the hopes that sparks will fly between this unsuspecting man and me." Kennedy hung her head. "Folks, she's running out of men. When we were driving one day, I saw her take down the number for a billboard company."

Kennedy took a sip of water. "So, let me tell you how the last dinner went because they all go the same way. The evening starts with drinks in the solarium or as I like to call it," she dropped her voice an octave and said in an exaggeratedly slow, deep tone, "the solemn room." She got up from the barstool and began pacing again. "Now, before the enchanted evening begins, I make sure I have already had a head start on the liquid courage needed to get through what is about to happen. My mother enters the room laughing and clutching the man's arm in a death grip, you know, the way police officers do when they have a felon they have just chased for ten blocks. Then she introduces me to the victim, I mean, the gentleman caller. 'And this is Kennedy.'" Kennedy held up a finger. "Now, at this particular dinner, the man looked at me and then at my mother, and his face went through a series of expressions from confusion to amusement and settled on being straight-faced. Finally, he said, 'From your mom's photo, I thought you were too young for me, but now I see it's just an old picture. What, about ten years and fifteen pounds ago?' "

Kennedy grinned at the crowd, "Yeah…he's a keeper, isn't he? And it only gets better." Kennedy and the audience laughed so hard that she had to hold up an arm to compose herself. "My mother, who sees my shocked face, chooses that moment to explain to him that I am going to be on an Alaskan cruise and pats my stomach." Kennedy changed her voice back into Lolly's. "Now, Kennedy, Alaska will be just perfect for you. You can hide those rolls under your jacket."

Oliver leaned over to Vera. "She's hilarious," he chuckled.

"And most of it is true. Her mother is a viper, and someday, I'm going to cross swords with that woman, and I intend to leave her in tatters," Vera whispered back. Oliver blinked, startled at Vera's response, and looked back at the stage.

Kennedy went into her next song, and when she finished, she took a sip of water and began walking around the stage, shaking her head.

"I've been on many first dates…not a lot of second ones. My mother calls it the seven-year plague." She made a face. "In her mind, it's as bad as the ones Moses brought to Pharaoh." Kennedy paused for a moment as the audience's anticipation grew. "I don't know. Locusts and frogs might have been easier to handle than some of the dates I've been on. Although I remind myself and my mother that I am not at a point where I am pen pals with convicts." She cocked her head to the side. "It's close. I did go out with someone I thought was wearing an ankle weight. Yeah, he wasn't trying to build better calves, ladies and gentlemen. It was an ankle monitor he had to wear while awaiting trial. Can I pick them or what?"

Ronnee laughed along with the audience as Kennedy talked about her bad first dates. She felt like she had dated some of the same men and agreed with Kennedy when she said that dating was a lot like buying a used car. You really wished you could talk to the previous owner to find out why they didn't want the car anymore.

"There was the man who kept calling his mother each time he found something his mother and I had in common. I wondered if he was looking for someone for himself or his mom."

Kennedy laughed as she prepared for her next joke. "And then there is my absolute favorite." She held her hand up in the air. "True story, folks. I was on a blind date with Willie the Perfect and her husband. I felt like the date was going well, and right after we ordered drinks, one of my nieces called my sister. Whatever was happening on the other end of the phone required two referees, and Willie and her husband had to excuse themselves to deal with the drama. The man and I made small talk, and he suddenly leaned across the table and told me he had to tell me something important." The theater was silent with anticipation. " 'I'm a warlock,' he said." Kennedy looked blankly at the crowd and pointed her finger. "Yeah, that's the same look I was wearing. Honestly, I didn't know what to say, so I said the first thing that came to me, which was, 'I'm Episcopalian. So, I don't think this is going to work.' "

Kennedy took another long drink. The show was beginning to wind down. "But blind dates aren't so bad. My dear friend Mila likes to tell me there are no bad dates. Only funny anecdotes to share over margaritas." Kennedy cocked her head to the side. "She also likes to remind me that I have a better chance of finding a rainbow-colored unicorn than a husband," she deadpanned and went into her last song.

She stood before the audience as they applauded. "Ladies and gentlemen, thank you for an amazing night, and remember, my life is like a romantic comedy. Only there is no romance...but you have been laughing! Thank you, and goodnight!" The house lights came up, and the audience, who had just been on a wild ride, caught their breath and chattered as they left.

Two people had been standing at the rear of the theater watching the show. "She's good," Tammy said off-handedly.

J. Mitchell cut his eyes at Tammy. "If she was on fire and I had a bucket of water, I'd drink the whole bucket in front of her while she burned," he hissed, his eyes narrowing at the woman on the stage who was basking in the audience's applause.

Vera and Oliver were slowly walking up the theater's aisle. Vera had enjoyed the show and was thankful she was far removed from the trials and tribulations of dating. When Oliver asked if she'd like to go to the Quiet Distil for a nightcap, she politely declined. "I have a better idea," she said boldly. "I have a balcony, bourbon, and some lovely cigars if you'd like to come back to my cabin."

Oliver whistled as he walked around her stateroom. "This is one fancy cabin," he said, removing his dinner jacket and placing it on the back of the couch. "The funeral business must be good."

"Well, you know what they say about death and taxes," Vera called out as she went into her bedroom to change out of her evening gown. "Death never sleeps, and neither do I. There are too many opportunities to make money and too many new ideas to ponder." She came out in a beautifully embroidered caftan and walked to the wet bar. "How do you take your bourbon? Splash of water?" He nodded, and she began to pour the dark amber liquid into two cut crystal glasses. She handed him a drink, and they gave each other a silent toast as they clinked the crystal tumblers. "Shall we go out onto the patio and stink up the place? After being shown the smoker's igloo yesterday, I can get away with it."

Oliver smiled. He was enjoying Vera's brash sense of humor. "I'll bring the cigars," he said. "But which box do you want me to bring?" There was a wooden box on the desk and another on the coffee table. "I hope you don't plan to smoke that many on the cruise."

Vera let out a little chuckle. "Bring the one on the desk, please." She walked over to the coffee table and lifted the cigar box lid. "This one is my very fancy jewelry box. In fact, I should put these in there now." She took off her jade necklace and earrings. "These are lovely but very heavy."

Oliver looked at Vera in disbelief. "You keep your jewelry in a cigar box?"

"Yes," she answered bluntly. "People tend to ignore cigar boxes as they are out of fashion. And when I travel, I slip the box into my bag, and it doesn't leave my side." She placed her earrings and necklace inside. When she looked up, she saw Oliver's face. "Are you appalled by my taste in jewelry? I'll admit the necklace is a bit pretentious."

"No, not at all. I'm more surprised you don't put your jewelry in the room safe. These are expensive pieces."

For a split second, Vera remembered Justin's preposterous words earlier in the evening, and she shook her head to get rid of them. "I'm sure I should, but I don't trust hotel safes. I used one once and couldn't get the damn thing to open, and neither could anyone else. It wasn't until the next morning, when the general manager arrived with a locksmith, that it could be opened." She was quiet for a moment. "There is a second reason, but it's silly and embarrassing." She closed the wooden lid.

Oliver sat down in a chair with a thoughtful look on his face. "I love silly and embarrassing stories. They make us human, and you seem to be a bit superhuman." He inclined his head at Vera. "Go on. I'm looking forward to hearing this."

Vera took a deep breath. "Once, my husband performed a funeral, and in lieu of money, which the family did not have, he was given a piece of jewelry as payment for his services. I kept the books for the company, and when I asked him about the payment, he replied that he had worked something out in trade but didn't elaborate. Well, one day, I went into my husband's office to filch a cigar because I didn't have any—"

"Wait," Oliver held up a hand to stop Vera from speaking, "his and her cigars? How very progressive."

"That is another story," Vera smirked. "But back to this one. When I lifted the lid of the box, I found a lovely piece of jewelry in addition to the cigar I had gone in there to swipe."

231

"And…" Oliver's eyes had a look of amusement in them.

"And nothing, end of story. It gave me the idea of putting my jewelry in a cigar box," she said flatly and looked away.

"I don't think so," Oliver chuckled. "I think there is more to the story." He was enjoying needling Vera.

She looked up at the ceiling and huffed. "Fine. I tried the piece on, and of course, I loved it. So much that I tried it on several times over the next few weeks." She paused. "Until I got caught red-handed…wearing the piece." She took a sip of her bourbon and smiled. She could still see her husband's annoyed face in her mind, and she chuckled. "He was mildly perturbed that I was wearing the piece of jewelry. But he was more upset that I was sitting at his desk with my feet propped up and smoking one of his cigars."

"Kennedy, your show was fantastic!" Mila exclaimed.

"It was," Bert chimed in. "I don't know what entertainment they had planned before you and Alfred talked, but your show had the audience in stitches."

The three friends were walking the promenade deck with LaVonda's dogs. Although LaVonda had expressly asked J.

Mitchell to take over the duties, Kennedy had learned he had not walked them before their dinner, so she quickly changed after her show and went to their cabin to collect them. The three ordinarily snarling dogs were overjoyed to see Kennedy, and truthfully, Kennedy was finding a soft spot for the cantankerous canines.

"They look different here." Kennedy pointed at the hundreds of stars in the sky.

"Changes in latitudes," Bert said and began humming a song.

Mila blew out a breath in disgust. "Stop right now. If I never hear a Jimmy Buffet song again, it will be fine by me. We heard him across the entire state of Idaho."

"But we each got to listen to our music per state." Bert protested. "You had your turn through Arkansas, and we listened to headbanger music. Kennedy got Missouri."

"Ugh, don't remind me. Show tunes," Mila snorted.

"Now I know why we made it across Idaho in four hours versus six," Kennedy giggled. "So, tell us, how was your trip to the spa?"

Mila recounted her visit. Kennedy and Bert laughed when Mila held out her hands to show the size of the towels and her desire to run out of the room but not being able to because the towel she had been given did not cover her up.

"Honestly," she said, "it was the first time I have prayed for the end of a spa treatment. Even the worst techs I interviewed for the *Helio* were better than this group."

"The day seemed to fly by," Kennedy said. "It was good that we all pulled together to get some other activities for the passengers. The only major faux pas was showing the movie *Titanic*."

"Did either of you see Mrs. Jameson and her dinner date?" Bert asked. "They stopped at the photo area for a picture, and she even smiled. It was a real smile, not the fake, 'I'd like to cut your heart out,' one she normally reserves for me."

Kennedy agreed. "She seems happy."

"The strange part of the evening was her nephew, Justin, escorting those five ladies Ronnee brought. They insisted on individual photos with him, and it really backed up my line."

"Speaking of which," Mila turned to Bert, "I'm sorry I didn't get to see your class. Unfortunately, I was teaching an uncomfortable yoga session."

"Poor Bert," Kennedy sighed.

"We are not talking about it!" Bert hissed.

"Okay, okay, it's over," she said soothingly. "Although," Kennedy bit her lips together, and a small snort came out of her nose.

"Now I have to know," Mila whined.

Bert gave Kennedy a dirty look. "It was nothing. When my talk was over, I was in such a hurry to leave that when I grabbed my camera bag, it hit a bunch of chairs, and they fell, making a huge noise."

"And…" Kennedy was struggling to keep a straight face. "Wasn't there something with a microphone?"

"Kennedy," he whined. "Please don't tell her. I'll never live it down."

Kennedy turned to Mila. "Bert got part of the story right. He was in a hurry to leave, and the chairs did make an awful racket when they fell, but he doesn't want to tell you the part about forgetting to take off the wireless mic when he went into the men's room next door."

"Oh, Bert," Mila exclaimed.

"Yep, and everyone still in the room heard everything."

"They only heard me washing my hands," he protested.

"I will never hear the song, "We Will Rock You" the same way." Kennedy patted her legs twice and then clapped. "We will, we will, wash you," she sang, patting her legs again.

Mila sucked in her breath and turned her eyes to Bert.

"Promise me that we will never speak of this again," Bert

begged. "Promise me!" But Kennedy and Mila were too busy laughing to answer him. "I'll never live it down if Franklin, Tony, and Luke hear about this." And then a panicked look came over his face. "Or Rosemary, if Rosemary hears it, she'll sing the song whenever she sees me." He pointed his finger at Kennedy. "If you tell them, I'll tell everyone about your orange hair!"

"Orange hair? What's he talking about?" Mila asked innocently, and Kennedy shrugged her shoulders and shook her head.

"Sure, pretend it didn't happen. I see how you two are."

While the three friends were walking LaVonda's dogs, LaVonda, Justin, Trixie, Diamond Jim, and Cameron had decided to go to the disco.

The dance floor was in the center of the room, and round tables and bucket chairs bordered it on three sides, while a floor-level stage with drums, an electric keyboard, and microphone stands sat on the fourth side. Tall cocktail tables and barstools were scattered at the back of the room.

"Well, I guess this is my bachelor party," Diamond Jim said over the thumping music. "This should be fun!"

A song came across the speakers, and LaVonda's eyes lit up. "I haven't heard this in years."

"I've never heard it," Trixie said with a bored tone, and Cameron and Justin shook their heads as well.

"Come on, girl," Diamond Jim stood up and shot LaVonda with his fingers. "Let's show these youngsters how to cut a rug. Something tells me that you were never one to sit out a dance." LaVonda grinned and followed Diamond Jim to the dance floor.

Trixie turned to her cousin. "Cameron, would you please get me a SunRumbrella? And ask the bartender for a few extra paper umbrella straws. I want some to take home."

"Sure," he smiled. "Back in a flash."

Justin was amused that Cameron had not asked him if he wanted anything from the bar, and he wondered about the cousin's relationship. He watched Trixie take off the lanyard that was around her neck. "That's smart," he pointed to the lanyard with a keycard in the pocket.

"I'm always losing keys," she explained. "I set them down and forget about them. I can't tell you how many times I have had to go to a hotel front desk to get a replacement key, and I usually don't have any identification with me, which means hotel security has to follow me up, open the door, and look at my ID." She rolled her eyes. "Diamond Jim and Cameron insisted that I wear one." She pointed at the lanyard. "Jim even got a second key for our stateroom for Cameron in case I lost this one."

Justin nodded his head, and there was an awkward

silence. "Jim mentioned he brought a lot of jewelry with him on the trip," he said, trying to fill the void.

"He did," she answered offhandedly and looked around the room.

Trixie's nonchalant answers stymied Justin. He usually had women eating out of his hand, but getting answers from the pretty blonde was like pulling teeth. "What kind? When LaVonda asked earlier, Jim only mentioned women's jewelry. I might be interested if he has some pieces for men. I'd rather buy something from someone I know and trust."

Trixie shrugged. "I'm not sure. Some gold chains, a few rings, and bracelets, probably some cufflinks. He can tell you." She was looking around as if she would rather be anywhere but sitting with Justin. "He thought that if someone forgot a piece of jewelry or admired something he or I had, he could make a deal. It happens when we go on trips." Her dull eyes came back to Justin. "I've learned not to get too attached to my jewelry because he might be able to make a good sale. One night I searched for a sapphire necklace for hours only to find out Jim had taken it from my jewelry box and sold it two weeks earlier."

"That must be hard," Justin remarked.

For the first time, Trixie became animated and gave Justin her full attention. "As long as he doesn't take this," she flashed her engagement ring at him, "or the earrings I am wearing at the wedding. The earrings are worth more than I was making as a model when I met Jim," she laughed. He watched her eyes widen when she saw her cousin walking toward the table with two tall, red, frothy drinks.

When Cameron sat the drinks down, the table moved slightly, and both glasses wobbled. "Oh no!" Trixie cried out as they toppled to the floor, and while Cameron and Trixie bent down to pick up the glasses, Justin tried his best to mop up the red mess with the cocktail napkins Cameron brought with the drinks. "I'll go get some more," he said.

LaVonda and Diamond Jim came back to the table a little while later, and the group decided to head across the hall to the bar called Stake Your Claim.

"I'm sorry I didn't get to dance with you," Justin said as he walked beside LaVonda. "And I'm sorry about dinner. I got roped into sitting with those old ladies." He explained that he and Vera had argued, and he had gone to Sedna's View to cool off. When he arrived, Diamond Jim was holding court, telling tall tales. "Then it became a competition. First, Diamond Jim would tell a story, and then it was my turn until my last story when I ended up knocking the glass this lady Ronnee was holding and spilling her drink all over her. I also gave her a bloody lip."

"I wish I had seen it. Especially her bloody lip," LaVonda smirked. "I'd like to give her one."

Knowing both women were well-known in the travel industry, he assumed there was some friendly competition. So LaVonda's comment surprised him. The fight for travel dollars was evidently fiercer than he had thought.

They entered the bar and were amused to see it resembled a turn-of-the-century miner's watering hole. Tinny fiddle music played through the speakers, and they could smell the faint scent of sawdust. Scarred tables made from long wooden slabs and plank benches anchored the center of the room while three-legged stools fashioned out of barrels stood along the bar. Stern-faced bartenders in white shirts with garters on their sleeves kept their backs to the long, crackled mirror behind them and made drinks for the cocktail servers dressed in black and red striped corsets and frilly skirts. Above the bar, reproductions of moose heads with their broad, paddle-shaped antlers looked squinty-eyed at patrons, and the other walls in the bar were littered with other replicas: picks and shovels, an axe as tall as a door, and curly-horned rams whose expressions made you wonder if they were itching for a brawl.

Diamond Jim eyed the space appreciatively. He was intrigued by the smell of the sawdust. It was a theatrical touch, and he wondered if there was a scent that would make shoppers want to buy more in his stores. "Now, this is more like it!" He clapped his hands together and then rubbed them back and forth. They wound through the bar and found a large table under two wagon wheel chandeliers with oil lanterns.

Cameron looked around the room and chuckled. "Whoever designed this bar must have used what was leftover in your suite, Diamond Jim," he yelled over the din.

The drinks and stories flowed until well past midnight, and Diamond Jim became livelier with each drink he tossed back. When he climbed on the table and began doing a jig, two bartenders came over and asked them to leave. "Diamond Jim," Cameron shouted, clapping him on the shoulder, "I believe your bachelor party is over, my friend."

"Just one more thing," Diamond Jim said, hopping down from the table as two cocktail servers walked by. "Watch this," he said, and the two women suddenly felt an arm around their necks as Diamond Jim lifted his feet into the air. "Somebody take a picture!" he yelled and swung between them with his legs straight out in front of him.

Cameron threw a twenty-dollar bill at the servers, and he and Trixie hustled Diamond Jim out of the bar, leaving LaVonda and Justin alone at the table. "I guess that's it for the bride and groom," he shouted. The noise made it impossible to talk. "Want to get out of here?"

LaVonda nodded, and they went out into the corridor and waited for an elevator. "Let's go back to the bar on deck eight," LaVonda suggested. "I liked it in there."

The Quiet Distil was busy but not loud. "What are your

plans for tomorrow?" LaVonda asked when they got their drinks. Justin shared that his aunt had set them up for a dogsled trip. "That's too bad. I have a private car to see the sights in Juneau. I had hoped you could go. I still haven't thanked you for taking care of me on the first night."

"Unfortunately," Justin sighed, "when Aunt Vera snaps her fingers, I have to jump."

Two hours later, when the bartender came over and told them it was last call, Justin and LaVonda realized they were the only people left in the lounge. She stood up unsteadily. "I think I should walk you to your cabin," Justin said. "What room are you in?"

"There you go again," she braced her hand on the table to steady herself, "being my knight in shining armor." They walked out of the bar, and her finger wobbled in circles as she tried to point down the corridor. "I'm in Cabin 801, all the way at the other end."

When they got to her cabin, she fished around in her handbag for her keycard and tried to lay it on the lock, missing it each time, and she began to giggle.

"Allow me." Justin took the key from her fingers and placed it on the lock. When the green light appeared, he opened the door. LaVonda walked in, but Justin stood in the doorway, taking in the disaster of clothing and accessories strewn about the room. He heard her dogs barking next door and pointed. "Do I need to take them out? I don't think you are up for the task," he said as she weaved back and forth.

"No, someone is taking care of that, and thank goodness it won't be that awful Kennedy. She'd be here obnoxiously early, all bright and chipper. I told J. Mitchell I didn't want her anywhere near my sweeties." She smiled at him, leaning against the door jamb. "Would you like to come in for a nightcap?" She was enunciating her words carefully to mask her inebriated state.

"I think you've had enough," Justin said, "and it would be improper for me to take advantage of a lady. Now, off to bed." He turned her around, gently pushed her forward, and pulled the door closed.

The services desk received a call sometime later. "This is Justin Jameson in Cabin 906. Could I get a vacuum cleaner? With an unused bag?"

"Certainly, sir," the voice on the phone said.

Twenty minutes later, Cormac O'Shea quietly knocked on Justin's door. Due to the guest's VIP status, the agent called Cormac's room instead of the housekeeping office. Justin poked his head out and saw Cormac standing there with the vacuum. "You requested a vacuum cleaner, sir. May I come in and take care of the issue for you?"

"Ah, no," Justin said in a low voice. "I just need it for a

few minutes. Where can I put it when I am finished?"

"But sir—"

"Thank you," and Justin reached out his hand to shake Cormac's and, in the process, palmed a folded twenty-dollar bill into Cormac's hand. Cormac looked down at the green and white square and then back at Justin.

"You can leave it outside your door, and a member of my team will pick it up," Cormac answered.

Cormac took his leave, and when he heard Justin's cabin door shut, he opened his hand and looked again at the folded bill. He gave a little shrug and stuffed it in his pants pocket. Kennedy had mentioned that Vera Jameson had made odd requests in the past. Perhaps what just happened was the status quo on the *Helio*.

Sunny Dayz Cruise Line

THE MALINA

DAY THREE

JUNEAU, ALASKA, USA

ARRIVAL 12:00 P.M.

DEPARTURE 7:00 PM

The jarring ring of the phone in Kennedy's cabin startled her, and she stubbed her toe on the desk chair as she ran out of the bathroom to get it. "Ouch, Hello?"

Through the staticky connection, she heard the monotone voice of the guest services agent. "You answer the phone very strangely. J. Mitchell isn't feeling well. You'll need to make the morning announcements."

"But I—" and Kennedy realized she was talking to a dead phone line. She checked herself in the mirror to ensure no stickers were on her clothes, took the previous day's newsletter from the desk, and stepped into the corridor. She rapped on Mila's door.

"It's a good thing I was already up," Mila said, opening the door. "Your phone is obnoxiously loud." She saw Kennedy's look of irritation. "What's wrong? Hit your head on the bunk bed again?"

"J. Mitchell isn't feeling well, and I have to make the morning announcements. Mila, I have no idea what to say. If I had known earlier, I could have done some research."

"Did he give you the script?"

Kennedy shook her head. "No, all I got was a call from our helpful friend at the guest services desk."

"Do you think there are any notes in the old cruise director's office?"

"And risk asking if Officer Friendly could let me in there? No thanks. But I do need your newsletter from yesterday so I can write on the back of it."

"But Barney is so charming and helpful," Mila called over her shoulder as she returned inside to get the ship's bulletin.

Mila handed her the paper, and Kennedy rolled her eyes at her friend. "Thanks. I'll see you later." She started down the hallway and turned around. "Oh, and I'll be late for our unofficial morning meeting because of this little surprise. Would you let everyone know?"

As Kennedy made her way to the mess hall an hour and a half later, she gave herself a little pat on the back. Despite having to walk LaVonda's dogs and not knowing what to say, she felt the announcements had gone well. As the dogs sniffed around, Kennedy used the time to plan what she would share with the passengers. Locating the books that would help her, Kennedy scribbled as many facts as she could onto one of the pieces of paper and used the other to write the script. Then, taking the service elevator down to the lobby, she mentally rehearsed what she would say.

"We hope that while in Juneau, you see the Mendenhall Glacier, whose arctic beauty draws hundreds of thousands of visitors each year. And make sure to take the time to see Juneau's life-size sculpture of a whale bursting from the water and rub Patsy the Dog's nose for good luck." Although most of

247

the passengers had booked excursions, Kennedy shared other activities cruisers could choose from if they had not made plans for the day, including whale watching, panning for gold, and self-guided tours of the town. "We will be docking at twelve and departing Juneau at seven. And don't forget, we will celebrate our newlyweds, Diamond Jim and Trixie, with a wedding reception in the main dining room tonight."

After making the announcements, Kennedy zipped down the back staircase to the mess hall and was surprised to see Tammy and J. Mitchell sitting at the table with the others.

Tammy gave Kennedy a look of annoyance. "Nice of you to join us, especially as these little get-togethers were your idea. Shall we get started? I have a bride to deal with this morning."

"I'll start," J. Mitchell said brightly. "The onboard entertainers will arrive and need to be checked in and shown the disco and cabaret." He put his hand up to his brow. "Since I've been *so busy* preparing for this cruise and dealing with the passengers, I'll be off the ship. I need a little J. Mitchell time." He turned to Kennedy. "Will you take care of them? You do *everything* so well," he said with a syrupy voice, "and you *were* sent here to *assist*."

Kennedy took a breath. She, Bert, and Mila had made plans to do some sightseeing when Bert returned from taking the wedding photos. "Of course, J. Mitchell, and I'm glad you made such a speedy recovery," she said with veiled sarcasm.

He gave her a thin smile. "It was amazing. As soon as you finished the announcements, which were fine but not what I would have said, I felt like a new person." Mila stepped on Kennedy's foot to prevent her from responding.

"I want to talk about the reception tonight," Chef Sha said. "J. Mitchell, is there a timetable we need to follow?"

"Yeah," Jonny sat up straighter in his chair. "I don't want anything to mess this up. I'm already in hot water. Do you want them to sit somewhere special?"

J. Mitchell let out an irritated sigh. "Look, people, you are blowing this out of proportion, and I can only guess why." He rolled his eyes to look at Kennedy and then turned his attention to Jonny. "Sure, set up a table for them if it makes you feel better. The schedule will go like this: I'll announce them, we'll serve dinner, and when I see that it looks like the right time, we'll wheel out the cake, make a toast," he clapped his hands as if brushing them off, "and call it a night. And if *someone* can remember they are the *help* and not the *host*, we can avoid any awkward moments like we had at the captain's cocktail party. You know the old saying…too many cooks spoil the soup."

"Chuckie," Sha began.

"If you ask me one more time about the carpet," he growled and rose from the table.

"If you'd just take care of it, I wouldn't have to continue to ask," she retorted.

Tammy pushed her chair away from the table noisily. "As much as I'd love to stay and listen to you two bicker like a broken record, I have better things to do." She looked at J. Mitchell. "Come on. We need to check on bridezilla."

Cormac motioned for Kennedy and Mila to stay as the others left for their respective departments. "I didn't think this was for the group. We had an unusual call from Mrs. Jameson's nephew late last night." He shared what Justin had requested. "Given the nature of their business, perhaps…" he trailed off and gave Kennedy a knowing look and then left the room.

Mila eyed Kennedy. "Okay, you have to admit, even for the nephew of Vera Jameson, who has come up with some weird requests, it's a little unusual."

Kennedy shrugged. "Not really. I read an article about using a vacuum to retrieve small items. Maybe his cufflink fell behind the dresser or nightstand? You know as well as I do that the furniture is bolted to the floor for safety purposes, and Rosemary loves to show us what they find when they deep clean a cabin. Using a vacuum cleaner would suck it right up, and with a clean bag, you could dump it right out and rinse it off. Kind of ingenious if you ask me. I'll have to remember that trick."

"Or maybe…as Cormac inferred, he spilled Aunt Bessie," Mila said dryly.

Vera knocked on Justin's cabin door but received no answer. She tapped her foot impatiently and knocked again harder. After their harsh words last night, she was not looking forward to spending the day with her nephew. Vera was about to knock again when Justin poked his head out. "Hey, Aunt Vera." His voice was gravelly. He ran his hand through his hair which was darting in different directions and rubbed his stubbled cheek. "Sorry, I'm not feeling well."

"You look terrible." She took a step back. "Should we call for the ship's doctor?"

"It's just an upset stomach," he clutched his midsection. "I'm not sure if it's seasickness or over-celebrating Diamond Jim's last night of freedom." Vera looked at him, puzzled. "He and Trixie are getting married today. Kennedy just made the announcement about the reception."

Vera waved her hand dismissively. "I've been blocking those out whenever they come on. Do you mean to tell me that vulgar little man you introduced me to, who pretends his fingers are guns, is getting married? To whom? Certainly not that young woman I've seen him with. I assumed she was his nurse."

Justin couldn't contain his grin. His aunt had no filter. "I don't think I will be able to go dogsledding. I was looking forward to going, but I'm too sick."

A look of irritation crossed Vera's face. "This was a rather expensive excursion, and if memory serves me right, *you* were the one who insisted on it. Are you certain you won't be able to go?"

Justin placed a hand on his stomach and grimaced. "I don't think so. I also want to apologize for last night. I was out of line about Oliver, and you are right. There must be several people with that name. I overreacted, and I had no business saying what I did about telling the family." He hung his head down.

Vera thawed a little at Justin's apology. "Well, I suppose you should stay here and rest. I can stay on the ship and catch up on some paperwork."

Justin shook his head and then grabbed the door frame to steady himself. "Sorry, I got dizzy. I think you should go. How many times in your life do you get the opportunity to go dogsledding?" He looked thoughtful. "Why don't you ask Oliver to take my place?"

"I don't think so." Vera shook her head. "I'm sure he has plans. We also have Mr. Turner's ashes to take to the Shrine of

St. Thérèse. He was very specific about being spread over all fifty states and paid quite handsomely for us to carry out his wishes. And the timing was perfect with the invitation to go on the cruise. You did remember the scattering tube, didn't you?"

"Yes, Aunt Vera. Let me take care of delivering it to the church. I'll go as soon as my stomach calms down." Vera opened her mouth to say something, and Justin clutched his stomach again and winced as if in pain. "Aunt Vera, I have to go," and he slammed the door.

Vera turned around and began walking toward the elevators. While annoyed at Justin's overindulgence last night, she was pleased he had apologized, and she reasoned it wouldn't hurt to see if Oliver wanted to take Justin's place. She pressed the up button on the elevator panel to see if he was in the library or walking the promenade.

While Vera was searching for Oliver, Ismaeel was in Sedna's View helping to restock the bar while Cormac and his housekeeping team were vacuuming and wiping down the tables. Ronnee entered the room with her five ladies in tow. "I'm sorry, ma'am, we aren't open yet," he apologized.

She made her way through the tables and chairs to the bar. "Did anyone turn in a silver and diamond bracelet?"

Ismaeel shook his head. "No, ma'am, but when we find things, we turn them into security. Their office is behind the services desk in the lobby. Have you checked there?"

Ronnee let out a defeated sigh. "Not yet. We thought we would retrace our steps. Unfortunately, I'm missing my bracelet, and my dear friend Helen lost her dragonfly pin."

"I'll keep an eye out." He lifted a finger. "Could you wait for a moment? Let me check with our executive housekeeper." He walked over to where Cormac was working, and both men returned to the bar where Ronnee was standing.

"I haven't seen anything, Miss," Cormac said, "but we'll keep our eyes open. Did you lose both pieces in here?"

Ronnee shook her head. "I'm not sure where we lost either of them. We were in here, the dining room, the theater, and the casino."

"I remember you now," Ismaeel said. "You ended up with a drink spilled all over you when the two men were telling stories. Did you have it then?"

Ronnee shrugged her shoulders.

"I know I had my brooch in the dining room. That nice Justin helped me take off my shawl," Helen whispered in a tremored voice.

"I will make sure to alert my team, but I would make a point of checking with security," Cormac said. "A passenger may have found it and turned it in. Have you been to Siku? I'd be happy to help you look in there."

Ronnee gave him a grateful look. "Thank you, but I don't want to take you away from your work. We can check the dining room. I remember where we sat, so it won't take long to look."

Cormac nodded. "If we can be of any assistance, please let us know. I'll radio ahead to the casino and the dining room."

Ronnee and the ladies took the elevator down to the seventh deck. They looked around the slot machines where Helen, Mary Margaret, and Irene had sat but found nothing. "Well, onto the dining room and the theater, and after that, we have an exciting day in Juneau planned." She patted Helen's hand. "Don't worry. I'm sure we will find your brooch."

They walked into Siku and found Jonny on his hands and knees, searching around the table where they had been sitting. "I'm sorry, ladies," he said, getting up and brushing off the knees of his pants. "No luck."

Ronnee forced a smile. "Thank you for looking." She turned to her five charges. "One more stop, ladies, and if we don't find them in the theater, we'll stop at the services desk and file a report with the security department. "I am very sorry, Helen."

"It wasn't expensive, just sentimental," Helen whispered sadly. "A gift from my father. I always think of him when I wear it."

They trouped down to deck five, and when they reached the theater, they found the doors locked.

"Maybe we can ask security to open them," Ronnee said hopefully. They walked to the services desk and inquired if anyone had turned in a brooch or bracelet. Ronnee also asked if someone could unlock the doors to the theater so they could look where they had been sitting. The desk agent shook her head without looking up from her computer screen. "Mr. Phyfe is the only one who could let you in there, and he is in a meeting behind closed doors," she said in a monotone. "He's also the only one who would know if anything was turned in or take a report for lost items."

Frustrated, they stepped away from the desk, and Ronnee patted Helen's hand again. "I'll check with Kennedy. I'm sure she can help us. Now, let's get ready for Juneau."

Vera did not find Oliver on the promenade deck or in the library and reasoned that the best way to find him would be to have him paged to the lobby. She saw LaVonda standing at the canoe-shaped desk in a red tartan cape and had second thoughts about getting in line behind her.

LaVonda had been waiting to be acknowledged by the

bored-looking desk agent. *"Excuse me,"* she tapped a manicured finger on the desk.

"Yes?" the agent asked without looking up.

"I am in Cabin 801, and I have misplaced my keycard and need a second one made immediately. I'm one of your VIPs. Taylor. LaVonda Taylor."

The desk agent sighed heavily. "The machine is rebooting. You'll have to wait or come back later. There is also a twenty-five-dollar lost key fee that we will bill to your cabin."

"But I'm a VIP," LaVonda huffed.

"Yes, ma'am, but those are the rules, even for VIPs." The desk agent motioned for LaVonda to step to the side, and LaVonda looked annoyed.

"And it's a stateroom, by the way," she bristled.

"Noted. Next," the agent called out and blew her bangs up in the air.

LaVonda moved over and began drumming her fingernails on the counter impatiently.

"I'd like to have a passenger paged," Vera said.

"Is it an emergency?"

"Well, no, I simply need—"

The agent cut her off. "We only page in an emergency,

per the director of security." She motioned her hand for the next passenger to step up. "Next!"

Vera found herself suddenly standing beside LaVonda.

"Oh, it's you," LaVonda looked over at Vera. "Other than J. Mitchell, their customer service is deplorable."

"Certainly not what I am used to on the other ships," Vera agreed and turned to leave.

"Your nephew Justin has been my knight in shining armor on this cruise."

"Justin?" Vera turned around, puzzled.

LaVonda nodded. "The first night of the cruise, I got ill during the captain's cocktail party. Justin wouldn't leave until he knew I was well enough to make it to dinner. Then, when I got the run around from security about something I lost, he offered to speak with them, and last night, we had a lovely time."

"Perhaps too good," Vera looked down her hawk-like nose at LaVonda. "He's not feeling well this morning."

LaVonda's painted-on brows raised in surprise. "It isn't serious, is it? He was fine when he walked me to my cabin last night. Perhaps I should check on him."

"He'll be fine," Vera said dryly. "If you'll excuse me."

LaVonda pouted her lips. "I had hoped he would go with

me to see the sites in Juneau. I have some tours set up: the Glacier Gardens Rainforest, a salmon hatchery, and a private boat ride to see the whales, but he told me he had to spend the day with you."

Vera smiled tightly. "It sounds like you have a busy day planned, and as I said, he isn't feeling well, but I am sure he will be fine. Now, if you will excuse me, I need to find someone before we dock." She turned and began to walk away quickly, afraid that LaVonda would start talking again.

Eager to get off the ship after a long day at sea, the passengers began to mill about on the decks taking in the view of the majestic mountains they passed and searching the ocean for the flip of a large black tail. Finally, as the ship entered the harbor, the clouds, which had been hanging low over the mountains, began to lift, and a whale surfaced, blowing a stream of air and water into the sky, and vanished back into the ocean with a tremendous splash.

Kennedy made her way to the lobby to assist the passengers with any questions they might have as they left for their day in Juneau.

"Now, don't forget," J. Mitchell came up to her, "the entertainers will be here this afternoon. There are two guys and a girl. Give them a little tour of the ship, show them their muster stations, and get them settled in their cabins. So much to do, and now I have to pick up flowers for the cake *and* the lobby arrangement because *your* VIP keeps stealing them." He sighed. "With all these errands, I don't know when I'll find a minute for myself today."

"Aren't you going to see the bride off?" Kennedy asked.

"Mmmm, no, I was with her for a little glass of bubbly this morning while she was having her nails done. She's all *cutified*[12] and ready for her big day." He looked around birdlike. "Ugh, I need to get in front of these passengers," and he disappeared into the crowd.

Moments later, Oliver walked up to Kennedy hurriedly. "Ms. Reeves, do you know where I can get a taxi quickly?" He held up a thick padded envelope.

"Of course," and she pointed at a spot on her map.

"Thank you," he called out and jogged down the gangway.

Vera was disappointed she had not found Oliver. She chided herself. It would be foolish not to go, and she was used to doing things alone. "Mrs. Jameson," Kennedy called out and waved to her. "It's nice to see you this morning. It looks like you have some exciting plans for the day." Vera was dressed smartly in a fur-lined ivory jacket, black turtleneck, hiking pants, and fur-lined snow boots. Her sunglasses sat on top of her head.

---

[12] cutified: to make beautiful.

"Dogsledding," she replied.

"Your excursions always surprise me." She looked around. "Is Justin going with you?"

"I'm afraid not. He's under the weather. There was an impromptu bachelor party last night, and I'm afraid Justin overindulged."

"That's too bad. Would you like me to have the ship's doctor check on him?"

Vera shook her head. "Not necessary. He assured me that he will feel better soon and has plans to go into town to take care of a business matter for me." She paused and then looked at Kennedy. "You haven't seen Mr. Parsons, have you? I wanted to see if he would like to take Justin's place on the excursion. I tried to have him paged but was informed it was not allowed on this ship."

Kennedy pointed to the gangway. "I did. He left a few minutes ago with a package and needed a taxi. He was in a hurry, but you might catch him."

"Thank you!" Vera began to walk quickly down the gangway. She saw Oliver on the pier and called out to him. Unfortunately, one of the boats in the harbor chose that moment to blow its horn, and her words were lost in its bellow. She watched as he got into a cab holding a packet close to his body.

Most of the passengers had departed for the day, and Bert

was in the lobby with his head down as he paced back and forth, mumbling to himself. "I will not fall in the snow, I will not fall in the snow, I will not fall in the snow," he chanted.

"Bert?" Kennedy said softly, coming up to him. "Are you okay?"

Bert raised his head. "Psyching myself up for the rest of the wedding photos. I've been in the spa snapping shots of the bride getting ready, which wasn't easy between J. Mitchell fluttering around her like a moth and her cousin refilling her champagne glass every time she took a sip. He kept telling her to relax and that it would all work out. Weird, huh?"

Kennedy shrugged. "Probably just nerves."

He jerked his head at the double staircase, and Kennedy watched Diamond Jim skip down the steps. "Good, we have a groom," Bert said. "I was a little worried after hearing about his bachelor party last night down on four." Kennedy looked oddly at Bert. "One of the bartenders told me he was slamming drinks back like water, and at one point, he decided to do a tap dance on the table. When they finally got him down, he used two cocktail servers as a swing set. I wish I had gotten a photo of that!"

Diamond Jim made his way over to Kennedy and Bert. He wore a fringed white leather jacket, black pants, and a white ten-gallon hat. "It's a good day for a wedding, isn't it?" he asked, shooting his fingers out from his waist. "Have either of you seen the bride-to-be?"

Bert nodded. "Yes, sir, I just left them. She and her cousin were finishing up in the salon."

"Those crazy kids," Jim chuckled and pointed at Bert's camera. "You've got everything you need? I want thousands of photos."

Bert patted his backpack. "Yes, sir. Can you share with me how this will go? Do we go straight to the glacier?"

"Ice field," Diamond Jim corrected Bert. "The limo will pick us up and take us to the marriage license bureau." He pointed at Bert. "Make sure you get shots of us going in and coming out, okay?" Bert nodded, and Diamond Jim continued, "Then the limo takes us to the helicopter."

"A h-h-helicopter?" Bert stammered.

"Well, heck yes, how else do you think we were getting there?" He paused, seeing that Bert had lost all color in his face. "Are you okay, son?"

"I-I-I didn't know about the h-h-helicopter."

"Just like riding on a plane, and if we are lucky, we'll see mountain goats, deer, and hopefully, some bears. The location for the ceremony is about two thousand five hundred feet." Diamond Jim was getting excited. "The ice field—"

Bert interrupted Diamond Jim. His face had gone as pale

263

as a snowbank. "Sir, did you say we would be two thousand five hundred feet...up?" he squeaked. "In the air?"

Diamond Jim nodded his head vigorously. "Just me, Trixie, Cameron, the pilot, the officiant, and you!"

Bert gulped noticeably, and Kennedy worried that he might pass out.

"It sounds breathtaking," Kennedy said quickly. Then, looking over Diamond Jim's shoulder, she saw Trixie poised at the top of the stairs. "Speaking of breathtaking, I believe the bride has arrived." Bert quickly forgot about his nervousness and began to snap photos of Trixie as she came down the steps on her cousin's arm in a white ski suit with fluffy white fur that enveloped her wrists and edged the large hood. Kennedy could see she was glassy-eyed.

"Let's go get hitched!" Diamond Jim exclaimed and took her hand, leading her down the gangway.

"Good luck!" Kennedy called out after them.

"We're going to need it," Bert said as he passed by her and scrambled after them.

Disappointed that she had not been able to catch Oliver in time, Vera saw a white limousine pull up, and she watched the odd-looking wedding party get inside. She thought the groom looked like a stand-in for a bad western movie in his white hat and fringed jacket as he shot his fingers in the air before hopping into the long white car while the bride in her furry white ski suit resembled a petite polar bear. A third man dressed impeccably in a long suede coat helped the bride into the car, followed by the ship's photographer. Vera window-shopped while she killed time before being picked up by the tour company. She was contemplating a tram ride up the mountain when she saw Oliver getting out of a cab, and he waved to her.

"I'm glad I ran into you," she said when he reached her.

"I had an errand to run. Something hot to get rid of."

She raised a perfectly arched brow. "Sounds mysterious." Oliver said nothing but nodded. "Justin isn't able to go dogsledding with me. Would you like to take his place?"

Olive broke into a grin. "I would love to, but I'm not dressed for it." He was wearing a pair of khaki pants and loafers. "Do I have time to return to the ship and change?"

Vera looked at her watch. "If you hurry. Meet me at the dog statue in thirty minutes." There was a gust of wind, and she shivered. "I can't believe I forgot my scarf. I left it on the table in my stateroom." She looked at the row of stores. "Surely one of these shops has one."

"Nonsense, I'm happy to stop by your cabin and get it. But I'll need your key. Which table?"

Vera handed him her keycard. "The one at the entry, the scarf is black. Thank you." Oliver gave her a quick salute and took off at a jog, and Vera was surprised to feel a sudden lightness come over her in anticipation of the day.

An hour later, they were strapped into their seats on the helicopter. "Folks, we are going to fly over the Juneau Icefield and toward the Herbert Glacier," their pilot informed them. "You'll see rock formations and ice falls. Then we'll dip down and land on the Herbert Glacier."

"Is that where we will meet the dogs?" Vera asked, and the pilot nodded his head.

"First, we'll tour the site, and you can meet the mushers and dogs. Then we'll go on a ride you won't ever forget. After that, we'll walk the lower part of the glacier. Are you ready?" They nodded, and the helicopter lifted them into the sky.

A quietness settled upon the ship after the passengers departed, and the staff and crew were busy going about their duties. Justin stepped out of his cabin and adjusted the baseball cap he was wearing to cover his unruly hair. He began pushing the vacuum cleaner he had borrowed down the corridor and passed a woman walking in the opposite direction.

"Justin? Is that you?" Ronnee asked and looked curiously at the vacuum cleaner. "Doing some light cleaning?"

He grinned. "No, trying to find someone to return this to." He lifted the appliance by its handle. "I needed to borrow one last night. They told me to leave it outside my cabin, but doing that felt tacky. And I don't want my Aunt Vera to see it. She'd be like a dog with a bone asking questions. " He looked both ways down the corridor. "It doesn't look like anyone from housekeeping is on this deck yet."

"No excursion for you today?"

Justin shook his head. "I was supposed to go dogsledding with my aunt but didn't feel well this morning." He grimaced. "We had a small bachelor party for Diamond Jim last night, and it ended when he began dancing on the table. I'm still feeling a little squeamish."

"We wondered where you had disappeared to. The ladies

were sad you didn't go with us to see Kennedy's show."

"After Diamond Jim's bachelor party abruptly ended, I spent the rest of the evening babysitting LaVonda Taylor." Justin saw Ronnee raise an eyebrow. "She latched onto the group early in the evening," he explained. "When the others left to put the groom to bed, I got stuck with LaVonda. I felt sort of sorry for her."

"My goodness, you might need to spend some time polishing your halo today. I would have left LaVonda where you found her. She's like a mangy old alley cat who always finds her way home."

Justin quickly changed the subject. "Shouldn't you have a gaggle of little old ladies in tow?" he asked, looking behind her.

Ronnee laughed. "I parked them at the Red Dog Saloon. I forgot my camera and thought I would stop at the guest services desk to see if anyone had turned in my bracelet or Helen's pin. She's devastated that she lost it."

"It was in the shape of a dragonfly, wasn't it?"

Ronnee was taken aback. "I'm surprised you noticed it."

"She pointed it out to me at dinner." He chuckled. "They all had to tell me about the jewelry they were wearing. I now know that Irene wears clip-on earrings because she was terrified of having her ears pierced. Mary Margaret's ring was a gift from her husband on their anniversary, but I can't remember which one. Marge instructed me on cameos and left-facing ones are more valuable because they are rare, and Estelle's necklace weighs about the same as she does."

Ronnee put a hand to her mouth to stifle a giggle. "Oh, Justin, I am so sorry. Waiting for me must have been torture. But I will tell you they won't stop talking about you. I also heard you did some magic tricks to keep them entertained."

Justin gave her a warm smile and shrugged. "It passed the time. Your twinning moment with LaVonda was the real entertainment."

Ronnee shook her head. "Wasn't that awful?"

"I never knew a dress could look so completely different. Thinking about it now, I don't remember seeing your bracelet on your arm at dinner, if that helps."

Ronnee looked down at her watch. "I wish I could stay and chat, but my ladies will get anxious if I am not back right away. I think I'll forgo stopping at the services desk. The woman working there is less than helpful." She let out a little sigh and tilted her head. "And I doubt anyone will have turned anything in. It's a long shot."

"Listen, I'm going down there to return this." He pointed at the vacuum. "I would be happy to check for you while I'm there. I'll even wear my shiny halo to win over the guest services agent." Another grimace crossed his face. "Maybe after I lie down."

"Are you sure?" she asked, looking at her watch again. "I hate to impose."

"Go," he said, "don't keep your ladies waiting. I don't know if anyone there knows any magic tricks."

Kennedy, Bert, and Mila had planned to do some sightseeing in Juneau after Bert returned from taking the wedding photos. However, when J. Mitchell foisted the entertainers onto Kennedy, they had to change their plans again. She and Mila were in the mess hall having a cup of coffee.

"I'm sorry, Mila."

Mila gave her a little shrug. "It's okay. Maybe we can do something in Ketchikan. I thought about stopping by the spa to see if I could chat with the staff. I think some of them were on the ship before the shutdown. I'd like to see things from their perspective. I've tried to talk to some of them," she directed her eyes at a table where a few of them sat, "but the minute I try, they clam up."

"Tammy has probably painted you as a man-eating shark

with big sharp gnashing teeth who eats spa technicians as snacks."

Mila gave Kennedy a prim look. "I gave up snacking on spa technicians." She sat up straighter and flipped a long strand of hair behind her shoulder. "They gave me terrible indigestion." She looked down at her notebook. "I am coming up with some brilliant design ideas. But first, I need to find out from Alfred if there are plans to revamp the ship. I hope there aren't. I love the art deco design and think I could do something interesting."

"Why don't you start by getting Alfred to spring for some larger towels," Kennedy snickered. "Maybe the size of a poster instead of a postage stamp?"

"Oh, don't worry, one of those towels is going in my suitcase. I plan to use it as the opening for my presentation."

Kennedy heard her name over the intercom. "Duty calls," she sighed and left.

When she arrived at the guest services desk, the same agent she had spoken to several times during the cruise looked at her blankly. "Can I help you?"

Kennedy looked at her strangely. "Someone paged me."

"Oh, yeah, right. There are some people here to see you." She pointed at two men standing by the whale fountain. At their feet were two black cases: a long rectangular one which Kennedy assumed was a keyboard, and a guitar case. The men were polar opposites of each other. One was tall and gangly with strawberry blonde hair pulled back into a long, thin ponytail. He wore round granny-style eyeglasses and had a horseshoe-shaped mustache that drooped down the sides of his mouth. The other man was short and barrel-chested with bushy dark hair and a full beard. He reminded Kennedy of an elf, but the glare he gave his partner made him a very unjolly one. She could hear their conversation as she walked up.

"If you would stop flirting with every girl you meet, we wouldn't be in this mess," the dark-haired man said.

"I'm sorry, man. I really am." The taller man put his hands to his chest. "But the heart wants what the heart wants."

"Hi, I'm Kennedy. Welcome to the *Malina*." She held out her hand. "Are you the musicians that the corporate office set up?" She looked around. "Are we missing someone? I was told this was a trio."

"It *was* a trio," the short man said hostilely, "until somebody screwed it up." He looked at the tall man. "I needed this gig, Malone," he spat out. "I don't want to go back to working third shift at that crappy little hotel kicking drunks out at three in the morning."

"It's not my fault, Evan," the other man whined. "Darla was supposed to be out of town. I didn't know she'd get so steamed about me doing a gig with another girl."

272

"I don't think it was the singing Darla was upset about. It was more that you had your tongue down the other girl's throat. Darla *was* your girlfriend."

Kennedy listened to the exchange. "So, I take it our third person won't be joining us, and my trio is now a duo."

"We can leave," the short man said. "I'm sorry we wasted your time, but without Darla, there is no sense in us doing the gig. Darla was the vocals, and," he wagged a finger at the two of them, "we were the backup."

Kennedy looked at them thoughtfully. "No, stay. I think we can work this out. It's only for two nights, and we need some additional entertainment. Can you guys play big band and jazz?"

"We can play anything," the barrel-chested man said. "We just can't sing."

"Okay, let's go up to the Starlight Lounge and see if we can throw together some sets with me taking Darla's place. If we can, I'll get you some cabin keys, and you can fulfill your contract. If not, we aren't out anything. Deal?" They nodded and picked up their bags, following Kennedy to the lounge.

An hour later, Kennedy was standing at the services desk with the two men. "Well, I'm feeling confident. How about you guys?"

"Yeah, I think we'll be fine," Evan answered, looking sternly at his friend. "As long as I can keep this one on a leash for a few days. Do I have time to buy one before the ship departs?"

Kennedy smiled and mused that several people, including her best friend and the first officer, needed leashes on this cruise. She gave Malone and Evan their keycards and a piece of paper. "Here are your cabin keys and a map of the ship. I've put a star by your muster station. Please make a point of finding it. I'll take you on a tour of the ship a little later, okay?" They nodded, and she looked at them with relief. "I'm thankful we could work this out. I'll see you both tonight in the Starlight Lounge at eight."

Malone looked around the lobby. "Thanks. Elevators?"

"Oh, sorry, the elevators are that way…" Kennedy trailed off as she saw Bert limping into the lobby holding an icepack on his face. Another icepack was strapped to his knee with a bungee cord. "Excuse me," she said to the musicians and hurried over to her friend. "Bert, what happened?" she asked in alarm.

Bert pulled the icepack away, and Kennedy saw a large bruise forming on his cheek. "I got into a fight," he said miserably.

"You did? With who? Diamond Jim? Cameron? Please don't tell me the bride."

Bert let out a depressed sigh. "No, with the snow and my camera, and they both won."

"Oh, Bert."

"It was like junior high all over again, except this time the bullies weren't people."

"Bert, how did this happen?"

He placed his backpack on the floor and made a square with his hands. "I had a perfect shot, the bride and groom in the foreground, the snowy wonderland behind them. It was icy where I stood, so I wanted to move back just a little to have better footing." He let out a breath. "And that's when my feet went out from under me, the camera flew up in the air, I landed on my back, and the camera came down and sucker punched me on my cheek." He looked at her dismally. "Oh, and I got sick in the helicopter."

Kennedy closed her eyes. "On the way there or the way back?"

"Both," he said dejectedly. "Diamond Jim had them send for a second helicopter so I could be gross in private on the way back." He put the ice pack back on his cheek and winced when it touched the bruise. "I'm going to hide in my cabin and edit the photos. Maybe I can find a shred of dignity before the passengers return."

"Other than this," Kennedy pointed to Bert's cheek, "how was the wedding?"

He shrugged. "It was fine but creepy. You couldn't hear what anyone was saying, just the shrieking of the wind. You should see the bride soon. Before I got in my taxi, I heard Diamond Jim tell the limo driver to drop him off in town because Trixie and Cameron had massages scheduled."

Kennedy gave him a strange look. Bert saw her face and bent down to pick up his backpack. "I'm just the photographer. All I do is press the button and get sucker punched."

While Kennedy was working with the two musicians, Mila had gone to the spa and salon. She walked around the entry envisioning the new look. Three stylists dressed in mint green tunics were pulling items from the cabinets at their stations. They had not noticed Mila enter, and as the spa receptionist was not at her podium to shush them, Mila overheard their conversation.

"Did you see the bride put her hood on the minute I finished her hair?" the male stylist griped. He buckled on a nylon toolbelt and placed combs and scissors in the pockets. "Her hair will be as flat as a pancake when she comes back," he huffed. "It will be a complete redo, and I used so much hairspray that we will have to start from scratch."

"Remind her when she comes in that the long skinny thing in your hand is a comb and not a wand," a red-headed

276

woman at a nearby station said, pulling on a pink smock. She noisily chewed a piece of gum and blew a bubble. "You are a stylist, not a magician."

Her male counterpart looked in the round mirror in front of him. "But I do make magic," he winked at himself in the mirror. "Although she probably doesn't remember being in here this morning. She drank an entire bottle of champagne by herself."

"If you were getting married to a short old guy who thought his fingers were pistols, wouldn't you?" the redhead hooted.

"Did anyone see the woman I was working on yesterday?" a brunette with a pixie cut asked, spinning in the red leather chair at her station. "Her hairstyle should have been called, 'I tried.' "

"Ugh, I had one yesterday who I think has been cutting her hair with safety scissors," the man said, and there were cackles of laughter. Mila smiled, you could change the names, but it was always the same: savage and sarcastic.

She accidentally knocked a hairbrush to the floor as she walked by the bookcase that held the retail items. A throat cleared, and the male stylist popped his head around the corner. Mila waved. "Don't mind me. I'm just looking around."

The man returned to his workstation, and Mila pondered

the design she had in mind. She was deep in thought when a tap on her shoulder startled her. "I have an appointment for a massage," the new Mrs. Diamond Jim said, still wearing her furry white ski suit.

"Oh," Mila said, startled. "Let me see if I can find someone to help you." She walked into the salon area. "Does anyone know where Tammy is?" she whispered. "There is someone here for a massage."

"Who?" the male stylist mouthed. "The bride?"

Mila nodded.

"Let me check and see if the room is ready," he said in a low tone. "I think it's a couples massage. Was the groom with her?"

Mila shook her head in the negative.

"Have her take a seat in the reception area."

"Sure, but where is the receptionist?"

He put a hand on his hip. "My guess would be Chuckie's office making up for their fight yesterday."

"Tammy?"

"Probably in Mr. Phyfe's." He cocked his head and raised his brows, giving Mila a look that conveyed more than he said.

Mila walked back out and was surprised to see Cameron standing beside Trixie, not Diamond Jim. "It will only be a moment," she said brightly. "We are checking the room to make sure it is ready. If you'll follow me?" She ushered them into the reception area, and they sat heavily on the red vinyl chairs. "How was the wedding?"

"Other than the photographer getting sick and falling down in the snow, it was fine," Cameron grunted. "I hope the photos come out okay."

"Is there any champagne in here?" Trixie asked, picking up a magazine and flipping through it loudly. "I'm going to need to drink an entire vineyard to get through tonight."

Cameron saw the look that crossed Mila's face. "It's been a long day, and we have the reception tonight as well. That's why I booked massages. Right, Trixie?" Trixie ignored him and continued to ruffle the pages of the magazine.

Before Mila could turn around, two spa technicians entered the reception area and motioned for Trixie and Cameron to follow them. Mila noticed that one of the technicians was the same woman who had given her a massage and prayed she would remove her watch.

Mila walked back into the salon area. "Thanks. Strange that Tammy is in Barney's office, don't you think?"

The eyes of the three stylists chuckled silently. The male

stylist gestured for Mila to follow him, and while walking to the retail area, he whispered something in her ear that caused her to stop in her tracks. He continued walking until he stood in front of the cheap display case. "Tammy's probably watching us through the security cameras, so we're going to pretend you are interested in some product." He pointed to a bottle and pulled it from the shelf.

"Were you on the *Malina* before the shutdown?" she asked as he handed her the bottle.

He nodded. "Four years. I've been working in Seattle since then. I took the week off to do this cruise. I figured it was a free trip. I'd make some tips and see some old friends. Half of us are treating this as a working vacation. The others Tammy brought from wherever she is currently reigning as the Queen of Mean." His eyes traveled around the entrance of the spa. "I had hoped there had been a miraculous transformation. It's hard to get enthused about returning to this place when it looks like your grandmother's beauty parlor. I don't understand why they won't renovate."

Mila turned the bottle around as if reading the ingredients. "That's why I'm here."

He casually pointed at the writing on the bottle. "Now I understand why Tammy told us we couldn't talk to you if we wanted to come back. But honestly, it won't matter whether you renovate or not. Queen Tammy will still run this place and the ship, and one false move with her, and it's off with your head."

Kennedy was waiting in the lobby as the passengers began trickling back from their day in Juneau. Ronnee and her five charges were in the first wave. "How was your day?"

"Exhilarating, breathtaking, and wonderful," Ronnee answered, and the ladies behind her nodded in agreement.

"Tell her about the bear," Irene interrupted.

"A bear?"

Ronnee nodded. "On our hike, it crossed right in front of us without a care in the world."

"It sounds like it was a wonderful day."

"It helped to take our mind off things." Seeing Kennedy's puzzled face, Ronnee explained that she and Helen had each lost a piece of jewelry.

"I'm so sorry. Have you checked with security?" Kennedy pointed to the services desk, and Ronnee made a face.

"The first time I went, the woman there was less than helpful."

"Would you like me to check?"

281

"No, that's all right. I'll stop by after I get the dears settled. We've had a big day."

Kennedy then reminded the group about the wedding reception for Diamond Jim and Trixie and told them about the entertainment options for the evening. "You ladies might enjoy going to the Starlight Lounge tonight. We're doing big band music."

"That sounds perfect," Ronnee said, and they left Kennedy to get ready for the evening.

Kennedy stayed busy as people came up to her with questions and shared their adventures in Juneau. Finally, when the last wave of passengers came through, she saw Vera and Oliver.

"You two look like you had fun. I'm glad you were able to find each other. I take it that you enjoyed the dogsledding?"

"I have never had so much fun in my life!" Vera's eyes were still brimming with excitement.

"She could have a future as a musher," Oliver chuckled and showed Kennedy photos of Vera riding the rails of the sled, a pack of huskies in front of her, and another of Vera surrounded by several dogs and wearing a beatific smile. Kennedy wondered if the smile was for the person who took the photo or at the fun she was having. The aloof, hardened exterior Vera typically showed the world had cracked open a little.

A half-hour later, Vera called the guest services desk and demanded to have Kennedy paged to her stateroom. "I don't care about your stupid rules about paging people," she snapped. "This is an urgent matter. And send the director of security!"

There was a knock on her door, and Vera opened it to find her nephew standing there dressed for dinner. "I waited for you to open the door this time," he began and saw his aunt's face. Her complexion was ghostly white, and she was shaking. "Aunt Vera, what's wrong?"

"The diamond and pearl earrings I bought in San Francisco are missing, along with some loose stones and two of my rings."

"*What*? Maybe you mixed up the boxes."

Vera walked over to the cigar box on the coffee table and opened the lid. The jade necklace and earrings she had worn the night before were the only things in the box.

Kennedy knocked on the door, and Justin hurried over to open it. "Be warned, she is spitting nails," he whispered.

Vera was irate. Kennedy had seen her irritated, rude, and obnoxious, but never in a rage. "Kennedy, this is unacceptable," she thundered. "Especially on this cruise. A cruise that I am supposed to recommend to people. I was even considering it an

283

offering for our destination funerals."

Kennedy was bewildered. "Mrs. Jameson, what is wrong?"

"*This*!" Vera stormed over to the wooden box sitting on the coffee table and opened it. "Someone has stolen my jewelry! I want to speak with someone in the corporate office right now! And where is that *damn* director of security? Honestly, the incompetence." Kennedy and Justin stood in awkward silence as Vera vented her displeasure.

There was a knock at the door, and Vera threw it open. "I understand there is a little problem?" Mr. Phyfe said officiously as he walked past her.

"*A little problem*? Exactly who are you?" Vera spat out.

"Bernard Phyfe, director of security." He pointed to the nametag on his light brown shirt and puffed out his chest. Then, he began rocking back and forth on the balls of his feet, causing the keys on his belt loop to jangle quietly.

Justin hid his laughter behind a cough when he heard the man's name, and Vera shot him an angry look. She turned back to Mr. Phyfe, and her eyes narrowed. "You certainly don't look like a director of security. You look more like a backwoods deputy."

"Ma'am, you called for me," he said tiredly, "perhaps you can explain why I am here."

284

"My jewelry has been stolen," Vera said flatly.

Mr. Phyfe rolled his eyes and let out a sigh. "Are you sure you didn't misplace it?" He looked around the room. "You gals can get a little messy throwing things around when you are getting all dolled up," he chuckled. "I am sure it's here somewhere. You probably just need to look a little more carefully."

"It was more than one piece," Vera replied stiffly, "and I assure you that I am not a messy person, quite the contrary."

He walked into the bedroom, and Vera whirled around and followed him. "Excuse me, why are you in my bedroom?"

He opened the closet door and pointed at the square metal box. "Just as I expected. How do you know anything is missing if the safe is closed."

"I don't keep my jewelry in the safe." She marched back into the living room and stood beside the coffee table. "I keep it in here."

He followed her and gave her a patronizing look. "Well, that's your first mistake." He hitched up his pants and pointed at the box. "Keeping it out in the open like that is just begging someone to steal it. But as I said when I first got here, it's more likely that you have misplaced whatever you are missing. A lot of that going around on this cruise." He looked pointedly at the wet bar. "It happens when older people drink too much."

285

Kennedy sucked in her breath. Vera's lips had dissolved into a thin red line. "Mr. Phyfe, perhaps you could take a report for insurance purposes," Kennedy said quietly.

"If I do it for her, I'll have to do it for everyone else who said they were missing something on this trip, and that's a lot of unnecessary paperwork for me. As I said, I'm sure she misplaced whatever is missing."

"I want the lock interrogated." Vera pointed at the door. "Someone from this ship was in my room today, and whomever it was is the person who stole my jewelry. I want whoever had access to my room questioned, and their cabins searched."

Mr. Phyfe held up his hands. "Now, now, there is no need for a lock interrogation. That's a bit overly dramatic and will only cause more work for me."

"Perhaps if you were doing your job keeping the ship safe, my jewelry wouldn't be missing."

"There's no need to get personal," Mr. Phyfe bristled.

"Are you going to have the lock interrogated?" Vera demanded.

"Let's start with the basics." He pulled a small notebook and a pencil from his shirt pocket. He opened the notebook and licked the tip of the pencil. "What exactly is missing?" Vera described the pieces. "And who has had access to your room?"

"Only myself, my nephew, and the person assigned to clean the cabin."

"No one else?" he asked and sniffed the air. "Have you been smoking in here? You know it is against the—"

"Mr. Phyfe," Kennedy broke in, "may I speak with you?" He sighed and snapped the notebook shut. They stepped into the corridor, and she spoke in a low tone. "Mrs. Jameson is a very close personal friend of one of the members of the board of directors, and it would give the *Malina* a black eye if word got back to the corporate office that we were not helpful."

"Fine," he huffed and strode back into the room. "Mrs. Jameson, I will be back in a few minutes with my machine to see who has been in your room."

"I want my lock reprogrammed as well."

"Now, let's not get carried away!"

Kennedy interrupted Mr. Phyfe before he could say more. "We will reprogram the lock as soon as we complete the lock interrogation, Mrs. Jameson. Do you still want two keys?" Vera nodded and sat down heavily on a chair. Kennedy and Mr. Phyfe left the room.

Justin waited for the door to close. "Aunt Vera, was someone in your room last night?" He pointed to the half-full bourbon bottle. "You don't drink that much."

A thought snaked its way into Vera's mind. She remembered showing Oliver both humidors last night, and at one point, he had gone inside to refill their glasses and bring her a blanket from the couch. She had been too busy looking at the stars to notice how long he had taken. Her mind switched to a snapshot of his dinner jacket on the back of the couch. Then she replayed the argument she and Justin had last night and his subsequent apology this morning, telling her that she was right and that there could be several people with the name Oliver Parsons, one of whom had served time for being a jewel thief. She closed her eyes, and her thoughts whirled like a dog chasing its tail. She didn't hear Justin when he spoke.

"Aunt Vera," he said louder this time.

Vera opened her eyes. "I'm sorry, what?"

"I don't know if you had plans tonight, but perhaps it would be best if you and I dined alone. Then, if Mr. Phyfe or Kennedy needed to share any information, they could do it freely."

"Of course," she nodded distractedly. "Good thinking."

There was a knock on the door, and Justin opened it to find the security director with a maintenance man. The man held up a handheld device. "May I?" Justin nodded, and he stooped down in front of Vera's lock. He inserted a cable into the bottom of the lock and watched the screen. After a few moments, it beeped softly, and the maintenance man held the device up so Mr. Phyfe could see the small screen.

The security director looked at Vera smugly. "As I expected, the only keys that opened this door were assigned to you and the housekeeper who cleaned your cabin today. I will have her questioned and inspect her room, but I don't believe we will find the jewelry with her. We screen our staff very carefully, and I am always watching them. I still believe you misplaced whatever is missing. If you intend to file a claim with your insurance company, come to the services desk in the morning, and I'll prepare a form. I assume your jewelry is insured? I wasn't sure as you use a cigar box instead of a safe for your valuables." Vera ignored him and closed her eyes, hoping the pompous little man would be gone when she opened them. He hitched up his pants and rocked on his heels self-importantly. "We put safes in the cabins for a reason. If you don't understand how to use it, I'm sure your nephew can help." He nodded at Justin. "Goodnight."

"Aunt Vera, why don't we get out of here and have a drink before dinner?" Justin asked after Mr. Phyfe left, and Vera nodded absentmindedly, still staring at the wooden box on the coffee table.

"Before we go, I'd like to stop in the business center," she said. "I need to have Inez notify the insurance company."

"Of course, Aunt Vera, I should have thought about that.

I'm sorry."

After a drink in the ship's whiskey bar, Vera and Justin made their way to the dining room. She saw Oliver smiling widely, waiting in anticipation outside the entrance.

"You go on in. I'll meet you inside," Vera said to Justin. There was a touch of defeat in her voice, and he began to protest, but Vera was firm. "Wait for me inside, please. I need to break my dinner arrangements." She waited until Justin was gone. "Oliver," she said awkwardly, "I'm sorry, but I cannot have dinner with you tonight. Something has come up."

"I thought things were going well between us. Did I misunderstand?"

"Something has come up," she repeated and avoided his eyes. "If you will excuse me."

Trixie and Cameron walked down the corridor to her stateroom, giddy from the champagne they had drunk in the spa. She opened the door and called Diamond Jim's name but received no response. When they had arrived on the ship, Trixie had claimed the northern lights style bedroom and told Diamond Jim that he could have the other one until they were properly wed. Diamond Jim had chuckled at Trixie's sudden desire to be old-fashioned but went along with her request. He reasoned it was only for two nights, and he would do it to make her happy.

Cameron pointed Trixie in the direction of her bedroom. "You need to get ready for the reception."

"This is going to work, right?" she asked worriedly, and he nodded.

"You've already done the hard part. Think of tonight as playing dress-up." They entered the garish bathroom so Trixie could apply her makeup.

Moments later, they heard Diamond Jim. "Trixie? Are you here? Where is my beautiful bride?"

Trixie put a finger to her lips and motioned for Cameron to stay in the bathroom. She quickly pushed the bedroom door closed but left a small gap. "You can't see me!" she squealed, peering at Jim through the opening. "It's bad luck to see the bride before the wedding."

"But we're already married!" He pointed to the ring on his left hand.

"I don't want you to see me in my wedding dress," she cooed. "Why don't you find Cameron and get a drink? I should be ready in an hour, and then I can enter the dining room with both of my guys."

Diamond Jim looked up at the beautiful woman in front

of him. Her honey-blonde hair framed her heart-shaped face, and he wondered again how he had gotten so lucky. "Fine, I'll come back in an hour." He ran a finger down her nose and then pointed it at her, "One hour, that's it."

He left the suite, and when the lock clicked, Trixie breathed a sigh of relief. "Very clever," Cameron said, opening the bathroom door, "although I now need to find the old man and have a drink with him."

Trixie poured herself a glass of champagne and carried the bottle and her glass into the bathroom. "Didn't you have enough of that today?" Cameron looked at the bottle with disapproval.

"Liquid courage," she said defiantly and sat at the vanity. She raised her glass at her reflection. "They say money doesn't buy happiness, but it does buy champagne and jewelry, and that's close enough for me." She was about to say something else but was suddenly distracted. "Where are my diamond earrings?" she asked in a panic, immediately sober. "They were right here this morning." She began lifting towels and makeup containers. "I haven't even worn them yet." She looked up at Cameron, who was leaning against the doorway. "Don't just stand there. Help me find them!" she hissed. "I've spent the last six months earning those earrings. I nearly froze to death today during the ceremony, and now we have this idiotic reception."

Cameron laughed at Trixie's lament and gave her a slow

clap. "And the award for best actress goes to Trixie Dubois Adair." Cameron looked at his watch. "Relax. You have less than eighteen hours to go."

She gave him a murderous look as she brushed past him into the bedroom. "That's easy for you to say." She began lifting boxes and articles of clothing. "Cameron, help me find my earrings!"

Cameron waved a hand at her. "Just wear another pair. We'll find them later. They are here somewhere in this mess. Now, I'm off to have a celebratory drink with the groom. I'll see you in an hour."

J. Mitchell and Tammy stood at the back of the dining room, watching the passengers file in and take their seats for dinner. "And when I didn't show up with the flowers for the cake, Little Miss Perfect went down to the lobby and took some of the roses out of my arrangement," he complained and then looked at her. "Are you even listening to me?"

Tammy was inspecting her nails. "I'm sorry, hon, I was, but I tuned out when you started your rant about Kennedy. Oh my..." She turned slightly, and he followed her gaze.

J. Mitchell let out a snort. "It looks like she couldn't pull it up all the way. It's so *blobular*[13]."

"I wish you would use regular words instead of these made-up ones," Tammy snapped. *"Blobular, cutify, fantabulous, fantastical,* they sound pathetic."

"But it's my thing," J. Mitchell whined. "And you liked it when I described the bride's cousin as *hunkalicious.*"

Tammy gave J. Mitchell a small smile. "Okay, that one was good." She turned her attention back to LaVonda. "Do you think one of the housekeepers sewed her into the dress?" Tammy held a hand to her lips. "And that neckline is a bit risqué for someone her age."

"I'll be back." J. Mitchell sailed across the room to LaVonda's side.

LaVonda arrived at the podium wearing a fitted, black velvet, dropped waist evening gown. Black ribboned rosettes embellished the mermaid-cut skirt, and rubies and diamonds winked at her neck and ears. "You look lovely this evening, Ms. Taylor," J. Mitchell trilled and held out his hands. "Let me look at you. I love, love, love your dress, and those rubies are stunning."

"I had planned to wear my amethysts," she pouted.

"Well, of course, they would have matched your eyes

---

[13] blobular: a circular blob.

perfectly," J. Mitchell gushed, and she fluttered her eyelashes at him.

"Exactly," she sighed. "I thought they were with my other pieces, but I guess not." She leaned into J. Mitchell and whispered, "Honestly, I have so much jewelry I can't keep up with all of it."

"Well, you look fabulous anyway." J. Mitchell extended his arm to LaVonda. "May I escort you to the captain's table?"

Justin and Vera were sitting at their table. "I have something for you." Vera pulled a velvet box from her evening bag and slid it toward Justin. "Your official welcome to the company."

Justin opened the box. "Wow, thank you, Aunt Vera." He noticed Ronnee arriving with her five ladies. "Aunt Vera, would you excuse me for a moment?" Vera nodded distractedly, looking at the menu.

After asking about their day in Juneau, he shared that he had checked with security about their missing jewelry. "Unfortunately, no one has turned in a bracelet or a pin. I'm sorry." He looked earnestly at Helen and picked up her hand to pat it.

Ronnee let out a little sigh. "Thank you for checking, Justin. We had hoped for better news, and I appreciate that you took the time to check for us." She gave the ladies a brave smile.

"But the cruise isn't over, and they may still turn up. Are you feeling better?"

Before Justin could answer, the house lights dimmed. "I think they want us to take our seats," he said, noticing that the doors behind them were being closed. "The bride and groom must be here."

To make up for his disaster at the wedding ceremony, Bert was poised to capture the bride and groom's grand entrance. When the doors opened moments later, the couple entered the dining room to thunderous applause. Diamond Jim, dressed again in his white fringed leather jacket and white cowboy hat, made his signature move, took off his hat, and waved it to the crowd. Trixie stood beside him, a vision of loveliness in a white brocade wedding dress with white fur trim at the plunging neckline and sleeves, and a belt of rhinestones hugged her slim waist. She wore her blonde hair down, and on the top of her head, a tiara glittered in the lights. When she'd come out of the bedroom, Diamond Jim had asked why she wasn't wearing the chandelier earrings she had begged him for. Before she could answer, Cameron quickly explained that they seemed garish with the tiara and the glittering dress.

J. Mitchell appeared beside the couple and tapped on his microphone. "Ladies and gentlemen," he threw his hands up theatrically, and a shower of rose petals fluttered down on him, "I give you Mr. and Mrs. Diamond Jim!" He brought the microphone to his lips, and Kennedy cringed when she heard the Frank Sinatra song he had chosen for the couple's arrival. "Love is Lovelier," a song about getting married a second time, would not have been her choice. He guided the new couple to their table, throwing rose petals as he walked, and his voice strained to hit many of the notes as he belted out the lyrics.

J. Mitchell had timed the song's ending to coincide with their arrival at the bridal table, and as he finished the song's last notes, he positioned himself between the bride and groom and cupped his face in his hands. The applause from the audience was polite, but it was evident they were ready to get on with dinner. Jonny had worked with the servers so that the moment J. Mitchell finished his song, they would be poised to serve the salads.

Dinner passed uneventfully, and as Jonny visited with the passengers, he noticed the time. He walked over to Kennedy, who was standing at the podium. "Should we have the captain make his toast now?" he asked. "It's almost time to cut the cake."

"Yes, where is J. Mitchell?" She scanned the room. "I don't see him, do you?" Jonny shook his head. After J. Mitchell's comments this morning at their meeting, Kennedy wanted to make sure she didn't step on his toes, but they needed to get on with the evening. "Let's give it a few more minutes, but keep your eyes peeled for J. Mitchell. In the meantime, have the servers hand out the champagne and begin passing out slices of cake. I'll let Chef Sha and Chef Jordan know so they can put on fresh coats. Will you tell Bert?" Jonny nodded, and Kennedy slipped into the galley. Walking back to the podium, her eyes scanned the room again for J. Mitchell.

"Did you find him?" she asked Jonny when she reached him.

Jonny shook his head. "No. Kennedy, we need to move on. The passengers are getting restless," he whispered urgently.

She looked once more for J. Mitchell. "I don't see him anywhere. I'll tell the captain it's time for the toast. I told Chef Sha to wheel out the cake as soon as she heard him begin to speak." Jonny handed her the microphone from inside the podium, and she made her way to the captain's table, picking up a glass of champagne from one of the trays.

J. Mitchell had been standing with Tammy in the shadows by Jonny's office. He felt his performance had been the perfect touch to the wedding festivities and had made a mental note to add it to his repertoire. He had just taken a bite of salmon when Tammy tapped his plate with her fingernail. "Ummm, J. Mitchell, sweetie, it looks like your comment this morning about who was the *cruise director* and who was the *help* fell on deaf ears." She pointed at the captain's table, and they both watched Kennedy hand the captain a microphone and a glass of champagne.

The fork in J. Mitchell's hand clattered onto the plate. "All I wanted was a bite of dinner," he seethed. "She should have found me, but instead, there she is, swooping in and taking all the credit. I'm the cruise director," he stamped his foot, "not her!"

"What are you going to do about it other than stand there and pout?" Tammy crossed her arms and looked at him from the side of her eye. She enjoyed poking J. Mitchell when he was upset. It was so easy.

"I'm not sure, but I'll think of something," he fumed and flounced out of the room.

What happened next seemed to take place in slow motion. Chef Sha heard the captain begin his toast, and she slowly began to push the three-tier white wedding cake into the dining room. Chef Jordan followed her, carrying a silver tray with a cake knife and two plates for the ceremonial cutting of the cake. As the chefs walked toward the couple, Jonny picked up a champagne bucket and stand he had strategically placed against the wall. He wound through the tables and chairs to put it beside the bride and groom. Although the champagne bucket had ice inside, Jonny did not realize the bottle was not cold. Moments before, one of the servers had switched her bottle out with the one in the bucket when she realized the one she had been given was too warm to serve.

Suddenly, Chef Sha's foot hit the tear in the carpet she

had been begging Chuckie to fix, and she began to fall forward onto the cart. The momentum of her fall caused Sha to push the cart forward, and it rolled ahead until it collided with one of the dining room chairs. When the cart hit the chair, the cake soared into the air, landing on a table of stunned passengers. At the same moment, Jonny pulled the warm bottle of champagne from the bucket, untwisted the wire cage surrounding the cork, and positioned his thumb under the bulbous head to open it. As the wedding cake flew through the air, the champagne cork exploded from the bottle like a rocket, hit one of the dark green marble columns, and ricocheted into Diamond Jim's eye.

There was a moment of stunned silence which was quickly replaced by Trixie's screams as Diamond Jim fell to the floor. Kennedy saw Otto Armitage, the safety officer, run over to Diamond Jim. "Someone call for the doctor," he yelled.

"*Please* tell me you have photos of this!" Mila gripped Bert's forearm as she, Kennedy, Bert, Sha, and Jordan walked the promenade deck with LaVonda's dogs.

Bert smirked. "I have time-lapse footage on my computer, but here are a few for you to see." Mila greedily grabbed the camera from his hands and stared open-mouthed at the screen. "It was a perfect storm, and for once, it wasn't me in the center of the chaos!"

"I can't believe I tripped over that stupid tear in the carpet," Sha snarled. "Will you all please surround me tomorrow morning at our meeting? I don't want to go to prison for strangling Chuckie. Orange is not my best color, and stripes make me look fat."

"My poor cake," Jordan sighed. "It was beautiful, and the roses you found to put on it were perfect, Kennedy."

"It was a mad scramble. I panicked when J. Mitchell strolled through the lobby moments before we pulled the gangway and informed me he didn't stop at the florist."

"Is Diamond Jim okay?" Mila asked.

Kennedy nodded. "Yes, but it was strange. Once Trixie had recovered from her initial shock, she kept asking if he would be okay to go to Ketchikan tomorrow."

"Maybe she has something special planned," Jordan offered, and Sha snorted.

"Where was J. Mitchell in all of this?" Mila asked.

"Oh, I haven't gotten to that part yet." Kennedy was still irritated at what had happened next.

After Diamond Jim had been whisked away to the infirmary, the stunned passengers began to depart the dining room in search of their evening's entertainment. Several had gone to the casino, but many either sat in the lobby or went to one of the lounges to gossip about what they had witnessed at dinner, agreeing that it reminded them of a slapstick comedy routine. As soon as she felt safe leaving the dining room, Kennedy went through the service corridor that connected the dining room to the Starlight Lounge and the casino. She came through the curtains and onto the stage, taking her place on the barstool between the two musicians. "Sorry," she had whispered, "a little drama in the dining room."

"It's cool," the guitarist, Malone, shrugged. "No one has come in anyway. By the way," he leered, "has anyone ever told you that you look fantastic in green? The color really brings out your eyes."

"Malone!" Evan, the keyboardist, hissed. "Do not hit on her again, or I swear I will throw you overboard."

"Gentlemen, can we skip the bloodshed? I've had enough drama for tonight, and the passengers should be coming in soon."

Kennedy sighed as she recounted her story to her friends. "Unfortunately, we played the entire set to an empty room."

"What happened?" Sha and Jordan asked in unison.

They were in the middle of their fourth song, and Kennedy looked around the vacant lounge in confusion.

Typically, passengers would stop in the various lounges, stand in the back for a moment and decide if they wanted to stay for the entire performance. But tonight, the door had never opened.

"Is our playing that bad?" Evan whispered to her. Kennedy shook her head and furrowed her brow. The only other people in the lounge were the servers leaning against the wall with empty trays and two bartenders who stood behind the bar, polishing glasses. When they finished the set, she strode through the tables and chairs to the entry door and opened it. Outside the door was a notice on an easel that read, "Closed: Please join us in the Aurora Theater for karaoke!"

Mila sucked in her breath. "Oh, no! J. Mitchell?"

Kennedy gave Mila a sarcastic smile. "I can't prove it, but it's the only thing I can come up with." They took another lap around the deck, and LaVonda's dogs struggled to keep up with Kennedy's peeved pace.

"What did you do?" Sha asked.

Kennedy shook her head. "Nothing I could do. He *is* the cruise director and is in charge of the entertainment. So, I went down to the theater and stood in the back, and I hate to admit it, but he was terrific. People clamored to get on stage and sing with him." Kennedy described how J. Mitchell strutted and sashayed across the stage in a flamboyant silver sequined cape.

"After the show, I went backstage to congratulate him.

303

He was still wearing his cape, which, I think, should be registered as a weapon. I was afraid I would get knocked over when he twirled by me."

"That would make for an interesting accident report. Especially after Ismaeel's black eyes, Bert's bruised cheek, the cork incident, and the flying cake," Mila mused.

"When I asked if he had put the sign up in front of the lounge, he denied it and then laughed that stupid little woodpecker laugh of his." She sighed and looked at Mila. "How many more days?"

"Three," Mila said and stopped. "I did find out something interesting today, but it's something you will not be able to unsee after I tell you." Four sets of human and three sets of canine eyes looked at her in anticipation.

"There is more going on in Barney's office than paperwork when Tammy goes in there." She gave them a knowing look and nodded as they each formed a mental picture of the self-important king of khaki strutting out of his office, followed by Tammy, looking cool as a cucumber as she patted her tiger-striped bouffant back into place and refastened the straining buttons on her shirt.

There was dead silence, and then Bert snickered, and a snort escaped Sha's nose. The group looked at each other, and they burst into laughter. Minutes later, after trying and failing to compose themselves several times, they calmed down enough for Sha to ask a question. "Do you think he wears khaki underwear?"

The corners of Mila's lips turned up slightly. "Why don't you borrow my suit of armor tomorrow and ask Tammy at the morning meeting?"

Sunny Dayz Cruise Line

THE MALINA

DAY FOUR

KETCHIKAN, ALASKA, USA

ARRIVAL 12:00 P.M.

DEPARTURE 7:00 P.M.

"Good morning, everyone," J. Mitchell's voice trilled through the ship's speakers, causing a few passengers to wince. "It's your little ray of sarcastic sunshine. First, thank you to those who came to the Aurora Theater last night for our impromptu karaoke show. We had some wonderful singers, and I want to apologize to those who wanted to see the show in the Starlight Lounge. Unfortunately, someone put the closed sign out by accident." He gave a little trill of laughter. "But don't worry, we'll have a great show for you in there tonight." Kennedy rolled her eyes, hearing J. Mitchell's comments while she walked the dogs.

"We will arrive in Ketchikan at noon, and I'm sure you are eager to visit the salmon capital of the world. Ketchikan also boasts more standing totem poles than anywhere else in the state. I highly recommend that you take the time to visit them at the Heritage Center. And if you love dramatic waterfalls, make sure to see the Misty Fjords National Monument. Finally, for those interested in viewing the most popular native animal in Alaska, check out the Great Alaskan Lumberjack Show, where you can view hunky, bearded men in plaid shirts dancing with axes and saws." J. Mitchell let out a staccato giggle. "I'll leave you with that thought and will return soon with more announcements. This has been J. Mitchell, *your* cruise director. Toodles!"

The tension in the mess hall was thick. "Well, it looks like everyone important is here," J. Mitchell chirped, looking at those around the table, "but only two of our three corporate helpers. Hmmm…" He rested his gaze on Mila and Bert and gave them a half-smile. "First, we should discuss the wedding reception—what a *disastrophe*[14]. When I left, everything was fine, and everyone *loved* the song I sang. But I heard things went to hell in a handbasket when I walked away to prepare for the karaoke show." He shook his head. "Tsk, tsk, tsk. And to think it happened to a VIP—*so embarrassing*. I'm sure the corporate office will be all over the incident. Or should I say incidents?" He gave Sha a wink. "I'm just glad it wasn't me."

Jonny's elbows were on the table, and he cradled his face with his hands. "Well, it was nice knowing you guys," he sighed. "My Uncle Barry will probably kill me when he finds out I almost blinded a guy with a bottle of champagne."

"It was a freak accident," Ismaeel offered. "Just make sure you check that the bottle is cold before you open one in the future."

"And not point it at people." J. Mitchell fanned himself. "Those things are like loaded guns."

Ismaeel furrowed his brow in irritation. "He didn't point it at anyone, J. Mitchell. It was a freak accident. I certainly didn't expect this." He pointed to the skin under his eyes which had turned a sick yellowish green.

J. Mitchell gave a little smile. "I wish I had seen the flying wedding cake," he snickered. "Usually, it's the bride and

---

[14] disastrophe: a dramatic, disastrous event.

groom covered in cake, not the guests."

Sha crossed her arms and gave Chuckie an unfriendly smile. "Yes, Chuckie, let's talk about the flying cake. What's your excuse today? Because I would love to know how my foot got lodged in a tear you have been asked to fix repeatedly."

"Here goes the broken record again," Tammy griped.

"It's not my fault," Chuckie whined. "I've been busy."

Sha turned to Cormac. "We put the work order in how many times, Cormac?"

"Three."

"It must have gotten lost," Chuckie said sullenly.

"Well, your office *is* the Bermuda Triangle," J. Mitchell giggled.

"And throwing people under the bus can turn you into a speed bump, J. Mitchell," Chuckie snarled.

"Enough," Sha barked. "I have a roll of duct tape in the galley. I'll tape down the tear so you won't have to find another excuse, Chuckie." She turned her gaze onto J. Mitchell. "And a little less commentary from the peanut gallery would be appreciated. As the cruise director, it was your responsibility to oversee the reception. It's clear you can't fill Joy's shoes."

"Honey, no one could fill Joy's shoes," Tammy trilled.

"They were big enough to qualify as lifeboats!"

Kennedy walked in and made her way to the table where they were sitting. "Oh goodie, Little Mary Sunshine has decided to join us," J. Mitchell muttered, rolling his eyes.

"I'm sorry I was late. LaVonda's dogs took longer than expected. Did I miss much?"

"Just the reception snafu," J. Mitchell snickered. "Glad it wasn't on my watch."

Kennedy frowned. "I was hoping Mr. Phyfe might be down here. I left a message for him at the services desk asking him to join us."

A disgusted sigh came from Tammy. "Why? Do you think he'd drop everything because you left him a message? Honey, this isn't the *Helio*. Or maybe it is now," she raised her shoulders and held her palms up. "So, tell us, what was so important? I'm sure we'd be fascinated to hear about it."

"I wanted to follow up with him on some jewelry reported missing by a few of our passengers," Kennedy replied stiffly.

J. Mitchell waved a limp hand back and forth. "I seriously doubt there is a crime spree taking place. I haven't exactly seen anyone wearing a black-and-white striped shirt and a mask with a bag over their shoulder running around the ship." Then, a burst of laughter escaped his lips. "Oh my, I can see it in

311

my head! And the jewel thief is running around the decks on tiptoes."

Tammy let out a trill of laughter. "Oh, J. Mitchell, that's too funny. Switching subjects, I heard your show last night was wonderful. Congratulations."

J. Mitchell preened. "It was. And I was FAB-U-LOUS. I'm only sorry we didn't have more time." He gave the group a pout. "I felt terrible telling people we had to stop, but we would still be in the theater singing now if I hadn't ended the show."

"And how was *your* show last night, Kennedy?" Tammy asked, and a small snort escaped from J. Mitchell. "Oh, that's right, I forgot, someone put a closed sign in front of the door...accidentally."

Mila put her hand up to her mouth and let out a tiny cough. "Khaki," she said.

"That's a strange cough, Mila." Tammy narrowed her eyes at her.

"Just a tickle. I think I'll get a drink of water." She gave Tammy a big smile as Sha, Bert, and Kennedy looked down, suddenly fascinated by the pattern in the flooring.

Justin had gone to the business center to check his messages and was surprised to see one from his sister.

Justin,

I saw Aunt Vera's email this morning about her jewelry. What the heck is happening out there? Tell her I filed a claim with the insurance company but need a copy of the ship's security report. I'm working on something else for her too. Would you tell her I'll give her an update when I call her late this afternoon?

Oh, did you and Aunt Vera get Mr. Turner's ashes to the shrine? Forty states down and ten to go.

Inez

Justin checked his watch. He needed to meet Vera for breakfast in forty-five minutes. Oliver walked in as Justin got up from the desk, and both men nodded politely. Oliver looked around to make sure they were alone.

"Justin, I hate to ask this, but what did I do to upset your aunt?" he asked. "We had a lovely time in Juneau and had made plans to sit together at dinner. However, when I saw the two of

313

you outside the dining room, she brushed me off and said something had come up. She seemed rather upset."

Justin looked uncomfortable. "She'll be irritated that I told you, but last night, when she returned from Juneau, she discovered that some of her jewelry was missing."

"From the cigar box on the coffee table?"

Justin wrinkled his brow. "You know about that?"

Oliver nodded. "She showed it to me when we went to her stateroom for a nightcap. Vera must be furious. It's no wonder she was so upset. I don't know your aunt well, but I'm sure she demanded an investigation."

Justin gave Oliver a weak grin. "The security director was less than helpful. He first told my aunt that she had misplaced the pieces. Then he ridiculed her for not using the in-room safe."

"Is he still alive?" Oliver asked, and Justin grinned. "I wanted to see if she would like to do something with me in Ketchikan, but I suppose that would be out of the question now. Thank you for explaining things. I'll stay out of the way."

The two men shook hands, and as Justin reached the door, he stopped and turned around. "Oliver, I'm on my way to have breakfast with Aunt Vera. Why don't you stop by Sedna's View in a little while? Give me a little time to work on her."

314

Oliver broke into a wide grin. "I'll see you then. Thanks."

When Justin arrived in Sedna's View, Vera was enjoying her second cup of coffee. "You're late."

He gave her a winning smile, took off the light blue sweater he had tied around his shoulders, and draped it across the back of his chair. "But I'm consistent," he said, sitting down.

She narrowed her eyes at him and then smiled. He was a charming boy. His curly chestnut hair and tan played off nicely against his white shirt and khaki pants. "In the chaos of last night, I didn't get to ask, you got Mr. Turner's ashes to the shrine, correct?"

Justin blinked. "Did I do it?" he asked slowly and leaned forward, clasping his hands together. "Of course I did." He looked at Vera. "I'm a little hurt you felt the need to ask. In fact, the priest insisted on giving me a tour of the shrine. I told you, Aunt Vera, I'm turning over a new leaf." He sat back in his chair and moved his hands to cup the back of his head. "Now, what are your plans for the day? Are you going to ogle the men in the lumberjack show?"

Vera knit her brows together. "That sounds positively vulgar. No, I'm going to catch up on some business matters. I haven't attended to much in the past two days. Have you heard from your sister? She hasn't responded to my message from last night, which is odd. I expect something like that from you, not her."

Justin took Vera's hand. "Why don't you come out with LaVonda and me? See the sights. She has a full day planned and a private car."

Justin saw the slight flare of his aunt's nostrils. "Thank you, but no," she said dryly. "I don't want to spend my day with a woman who expects people to do what she says because she snaps her fingers and commands it." She paused and stared at him. "Why are you smiling?"

Justin leaned back in his chair and crossed his arms. "Just smiling."

Vera picked up her napkin and dabbed the sides of her mouth. "I don't want to be near that rude and disagreeable banshee. And the things she said about—"

Justin cut her off. "It was only a suggestion. I apologize for proposing it."

A server came over, and they ordered breakfast. "Aunt Vera," Justin began, "you know what they say about all work and no play."

"We can't play all of the time." She gave him a knowing look. "Work is how the bills get paid, Justin."

Justin had the grace to blush and was thankful when their

breakfast arrived a few minutes later. They chatted companionably, and when Justin saw Oliver enter the room, he said casually, "I ran into Oliver Parsons this morning, and he was asking after you. He was concerned after the abrupt change in your dinner plans."

Vera's movements were suddenly jerky. "Yes, well, it was for the best, considering the circumstances," and she took a drink of water.

Justin dabbed the corners of his mouth with his napkin. "You should know he's walking over here." Startled by his statement, Vera began to cough.

"Good morning, Vera, Justin. Good to see you both," Oliver said when he reached their table.

"And you too, sir, would you like to join us?" Justin gestured at an empty chair.

Oliver sat down and cleared his throat. "Thank you. I heard the wedding reception had some excitement last night. I hate that I missed it. I hear it was just short of a vaudeville routine."

"It was vile," Vera scoffed. "The cruise director pranced around like a chimpanzee."

Justin looked over his coffee cup at his aunt. "I've never seen a prancing chimpanzee, Aunt Vera. It must be something they only do for you," and his eyes were full of mirth. "Has anyone seen the groom?"

Oliver nodded. "I saw him a little while ago. He was sporting a patch over his eye. Coupled with his cowboy hat, he now looks a little dastardly." He cleared his throat again. "Vera, I was wondering if you had plans for the day?"

"I was going to catch up on some work and perhaps go into town at some point," she said stiffly.

"Hmmm. I wonder if you would allow me to reciprocate our time yesterday."

Vera wiped her hands on her napkin and placed it on the table. "That is kind but unnecessary. Justin couldn't go, and I hated to waste the open seat. And as I said, I'm behind on my paperwork."

"All work and no play," Justin murmured, and Vera snapped her eyes at him.

"I'm also expecting a call from my niece about some important matters that have come up," Vera added, "so I want to be available when she calls."

"Aunt Vera," Justin leaned forward on the table. "What if I take the call with Inez? You could go with Oliver, and we could meet in town at a designated time." Vera began to protest, but he continued, "If the information is urgent, I'll call you immediately, and you can stop what you are doing and call her back. You did say it was time for me to grow up and take on some responsibility."

"Yes, well…" Vera peered up at Oliver. "Before I say yes, what will we be doing?"

A smile came across Oliver's face. "You should wear clothing suitable for an active day."

"That's all you are going to tell me?"

"Yes."

Justin looked at his watch. "I have some time booked at the golf cage. Diamond Jim was going to watch to see why I keep missing the fairway. I hope he is still able to see." He turned and kissed Vera on the cheek. "Why don't we meet in the lobby when the ship docks? We can make our plans of when and where to meet."

The two men left, and Vera sat at the table, finishing her coffee. She was surprised at Justin's behavior but reasoned that perhaps the events of the previous evening had caused him to grow up a little. As for Oliver, she did enjoy his company and would have her answer about him soon enough.

When he reached the promenade deck, Justin was glad to see Cameron and Diamond Jim taking practice swings. They shook hands. "Heck of a party last night, Diamond Jim. Congratulations on the wedding." He removed his sweater, set it aside, and selected a driver. The eyepatch Diamond Jim wore was pushed up and sat on his forehead. "Nice black eye," Justin chuckled.

Cameron stepped up to the tee box and took a swing. Diamond Jim pointed at his eye. "This is nothing. I had two black eyes from some dental surgery once. I scheduled it exactly right, two days before my divorce was finalized. I told the judge I was so sad about the end of my marriage that my eyes were bruised from crying." He began snickering at the memory. "My ex-wife, Darlene, looked like she had sucked on a bag of lemons when she heard that."

"Very theatrical," Cameron said, returning to where Diamond Jim and Justin stood.

"It got me the sympathy I needed," Diamond Jim shrugged.

Cameron motioned for Justin to take his turn. "I got one once roughhousing with my dog, but no one believed me, so I changed the story and said I was in a bar fight. That one they believed. At least Jim has a good story to add to his tales. I wouldn't have believed it if I hadn't seen it with my own eyes. That crazy song the cruise director sang, the cake flying, the cork bouncing around the room like a wild bullet. Now it seems comical, but I must tell you I was worried when I heard the champagne cork pop and you hit the ground, Jim. I was afraid your ex had snuck on board."

"Did either of you see the bartender with the shiner? And

I saw the ship's photographer was sporting a large bruise on his cheek," Justin said. "Must have been a heck of a night in the crew bar."

The men took turns practicing, and Diamond Jim explained to Justin the adjustments he needed to make to his swing and stance.

"Plans in Ketchikan?" Cameron asked, and Justin shared that he and LaVonda were touring the town together.

Diamond Jim looked at Cameron from the side of his eye and smirked. "Unusual woman, but she talks too much," he said. Justin retook his position at the tee and swung the golf club. "Much better," Diamond Jim noted approvingly. "You just needed to make a few adjustments. I assume your aunt is not going with the two of you—there's no love between those two women. I'd think twice about crossing your aunt. She's tough as nails and has access to places to bury a body."

Justin smiled. "I always tread lightly around Aunt Vera. So, what are you doing today, Diamond Jim? I assume the bride is not out of bed yet?"

"Trixie takes her sweet time getting ready," Cameron answered. "It's why Jim and I had time to come up here and hit some balls before we go into town." Then, he turned to Diamond Jim. "Don't forget Trixie said we had to be off the boat as soon as it docks for our excursion."

Diamond Jim looked at Justin and grinned. "Not even married a full day yet, and she's already calling the shots."

The three men took a few more turns in the cage until Justin noticed the time. The ship would be docking in Ketchikan soon. He returned the driver to the box and picked up his sweater. "I can't thank you enough for your help," he said, shaking Jim's hand. I don't think I'll embarrass myself as much now at the club. Have fun in Ketchikan, and watch out for wild champagne corks."

"Welcome to the salmon capital of the world," J. Mitchell's voice crackled through the speakers as the ship docked. "We hope you enjoy your day in Ketchikan. Make sure to walk the waterfront of this artsy little frontier town. We'll see you back on board at six for our seven o'clock departure, and keep your fingers crossed for our northern lights show tonight."

When Kennedy arrived in the lobby, she saw that it was already full of passengers eager to get into town, and she was pleasantly surprised to see J. Mitchell engaging with a few of them. She visited with Ronnee and her ladies dressed in matching colorful warm-up suits and learned they had a full day planned, starting with a bear exploration in Herring Cove.

"Didn't you see a bear yesterday?"

"Yes, but that one doesn't count," Mary Margaret answered. "He was a bonus bear."

"Is it safe?" Kennedy asked.

Estelle pointed to the sneakers she was wearing. "I don't have to outrun the bear, just the slowest person, and it's every woman for herself if it comes to that," she cackled.

Ronnee nodded. "I'd never put my dears in harm's way." She looked at them in adoration. "I keep a close eye on these darlings."

"I suppose there has been no luck finding your bracelet or the pin?"

Ronnee shook her head. "No, we'll be back early today, and I'll pick up the security report and send it to Helen's son before we leave." Kennedy saw Ronnee make a face. "I'll see you later. Your favorite VIP just entered the lobby, and she reminds me of a linebacker searching for a quarterback to squash. Hope you don't have the football," she chuckled and motioned for her companions to follow her.

Moments later, Kennedy felt a finger poking her shoulder and turned around to find LaVonda standing behind her with her hands on her hips. "I suppose I'll tell you since I can't find J. Mitchell. My sweeties have not had their afternoon walk, and it's time. They shouldn't have to wait," she huffed.

Kennedy gave LaVonda a patient smile. "As soon as everyone going ashore is safely off the ship, I will attend to your dogs, Ms. Taylor."

LaVonda shook her finger at Kennedy. "I don't want *you* anywhere near them. Tell J. Mitchell to walk my dogs or find someone else."

"See what I mean about your friend?" Vera said to Justin as she watched LaVonda shaking her finger at Kennedy. "I'll be right back."

LaVonda continued to lecture Kennedy. "And another thing, I suppose I can give you the message to relay to the chef about their dinner service tonight, although, again, you have nothing to write on. Tell the chef—"

"Kennedy," Vera interrupted, her tone as cold as an icicle, "I must speak with you about an urgent matter." She gave Kennedy a quick wink, and Kennedy fought hard to control her facial muscles. "Excuse us," Vera said and took Kennedy's arm, walking away from LaVonda.

"Mrs. Jameson, you are my favorite person in the world." Kennedy stole a look over her shoulder and saw LaVonda looking murderously at them. "Where are you off to today?" she asked. Vera was dressed casually in hiking pants, a white button-down blouse, and a V-neck sweater.

Vera shook her head. "I have no idea. I had planned to

spend the day catching up on work, but I got shanghaied by my nephew and Oliver Parsons. Kennedy, I need a favor; would you send me the security report for my stolen jewelry? The insurance company needs it."

"Of course," Kennedy answered. "And again, please accept my apologies."

"Why? Did you steal the jewelry?"

Kennedy looked at her, startled. "Of course not."

"Then you have nothing to apologize for."

Kennedy looked over Vera's shoulder and saw LaVonda standing with Oliver and Justin. "Please tell me LaVonda isn't going with you."

Vera turned her head. "Thank goodness no." She saw Oliver and Justin motioning to her. "I need to go, and you'll take care of the insurance report?"

"Yes, ma'am, and enjoy your day."

Kennedy chatted with a few more passengers and noticed Cameron in the lobby on his phone. He quickly hung up when he saw Trixie and Diamond Jim come down the grand staircase and waved as if to hurry them.

The passengers began to walk down the gangway and onto the boardwalk, chatting about their plans. "Well, I suppose we should go," Oliver said to Vera, Justin, and LaVonda, and they got in line with the others.

Vera noticed the jacket in Justin's hand and was confused. "Justin, why do you have Oliver's jacket?"

Oliver was quick to answer. "Justin pointed out that it is quite warm outside and mentioned that I might not need such a heavy jacket. I didn't want to delay us by returning the jacket to my cabin, and he offered to hold onto it since he and LaVonda have a car. He and I both know how you feel about tardiness."

Vera eyed her nephew, who was trying hard to hide the look of laughter in his eyes at Oliver's comment. "Hmph, I suppose I should be grateful that *something* is getting through to you."

"I learn a little something each day, Aunt Vera," he grinned and turned around.

The glacial pace of the line in front of them annoyed Vera almost as much as being kept in the dark about whatever Oliver had planned. She turned to him. "Well, are you going to let me know where we are going, or do you intend to continue to keep me in the dark? I find the lack of information quite maddening."

Oliver was amused. "Patience," he answered and winked. Vera was used to being in control; however, today, she would have to throw caution to the wind and trust him.

They had almost reached the pier when the sun burst

through the clouds, blinding everyone. Oliver reached up to his head and then patted his shirt pockets. "My sunglasses! I must have left them on the table in the lobby. Go on down. I'll be right there." Vera nodded at him and continued down the ramp.

Justin and LaVonda were already on the boardwalk and had stationed themselves near a photographer snapping photos of the ship. Justin waved, and Vera walked over, explaining that Oliver had returned to the ship to retrieve his sunglasses. "Go on," she said. "I'll be fine. I'll see you at five o'clock at the welcome sign." She pointed at Oliver's jacket in Justin's hand. "And thank you for being so thoughtful…" she paused, distracted by five police officers standing on the walkway, and nodded at them. "If that's to make us feel safe, it's a bit overkill." Vera saw Oliver brush past Diamond Jim, Trixie, and Cameron as they descended the gangway and smiled. "Look, he's here. Now go."

"My watch," they heard a man's voice call out. "Where is my watch?" Several people turned around and saw Diamond Jim whipping his head around frantically. He tried to turn around to go back up the ramp but was unsuccessful as the crush of passengers trying to get off the ship blocked his passage. "My watch is missing," he shrieked.

"Diamond Jim," Cameron shouted anxiously and pulled at his arm. "We have to get off the gangway. We can't hold these people up. Let's go down, and as soon as the way is clear, we'll go back." He ushered Diamond Jim off the ramp.

When they reached the boardwalk, Diamond Jim, wearing his black cowboy hat and fringed jacket, looked through his one eye at the lengthy line of people still coming off the ship. He had put the patch back on because he felt it would make people remember him better. He danced from foot to foot in agitation, and a note of panic edged his voice. "I know I put my watch on this morning, and now it's gone. We have to check everywhere we've been, starting with the gangway."

"Excuse me, sir," a policeman came up and flashed his badge. "Are you Diamond Jim Adair?"

"Yes, are you here to help me find my watch?"

"No sir," the policeman said, "I'm here to arrest you." He pulled a set of handcuffs from his belt. "I have an order from the Honorable Judge Montgomery Maxwell in Texas to detain you." The photographer, who had been on the boardwalk, began to creep toward the police officers.

"What's going on?" Cameron demanded.

"Mr. Adair has been playing games in Texas, and Judge Maxwell is not amused. He's been skipping appearances and hiding assets in the property settlement with his ex-wife."

"Diamond Jim," Trixie looked at her husband in surprise, "is this true?"

"Now, don't you worry, sugar. I'll have this straightened out quicker than lightning," he said with false bravado. "Keep your phone with you, and we will figure out where to meet. This is all a little misunderstanding, and Darlene is trying to throw cold water on our wedding and honeymoon." He grabbed the sleeve of Cameron's jacket and pulled him down so he could whisper in his ear. "Call my lawyer. The number is in the notebook on the nightstand. Tell him we need to circle the wagons and tell him to reach out to the boys. He'll know what to do. And please, take care of Trixie. Don't let her worry."

The policeman read Diamond Jim his rights, including the right to remain silent. "You might want to remember that one, sir," he said.

The police officers turned Diamond Jim, handcuffed but still wearing his black ten-gallon hat, toward the waiting police car, and the photographer who had been in the background jumped in front of them. "How about a big smile for Darlene, Diamond Jim?" He depressed the shutter, and several flashes went off.

"That's enough," one of the police officers warned, and they walked down the boardwalk, passing Ronnee and her ladies, Oliver and Vera, and LaVonda and Justin. When they reached the car, one of the officers opened the back door while another removed Diamond Jim's hat. Whisps of fine white hair stood up from his bald head, and the crowd on the boardwalk watched in stunned silence as he was placed in the back seat of the police car.

J. Mitchell had gone up to the pool deck as soon as the passengers began leaving for Ketchikan and saw Tammy looking over the railing at the pier below.

"Ugh," J. Mitchell whined, walking up to her. "That was awful. Remind me never to make an appearance in the lobby when the *tourons* are there. I had to make small talk and pretend to be interested in their plans."

"Tourons?"

"Tourist and moron. It's one of my little words."

Tammy rolled her eyes.

"Don't be like that. It's funny and fresh, like me." He let out a trill of laughter. "*Funesh.*"

Tammy looked at him and shook her head. "No. Just no."

The commotion on the pier pulled Tammy's attention away from J. Mitchell and back to the scene below.

"Is that Diamond Jim?" J. Mitchell pointed. Leaning over the railing, they watched the arrest unfold. "What do you think that was about?" he asked after the police cars pulled away.

"Who knows?" Tammy waved her hand. "Maybe the fashion police busted him for wearing a hat that was taller than

330

he is? Or maybe the costumer from *Easy Rider* wanted their fringed jacket back."

"Well, we can be sure that the ever-perfect Kennedy will be in the lobby just waiting to rescue them," J. Mitchell said, his voice dripping with sarcasm. "It will give her something else to worry about."

Kennedy had stepped onto the gangway when she heard the commotion and watched the police car leave. She greeted Cameron and Trixie when they came back into the lobby. "I don't mean to pry, but is there anything I can do?"

Cameron shook his head. "Honestly, I don't know what to make of what just happened. but it appears we may have some legal issues to deal with," he said gravely, placing a hand on Trixie's shoulder. "We may need to get off the boat here. Can that be arranged?"

Kennedy nodded. "Of course, just let one of us know."

She watched them walk to the elevators. She thought Trixie's face had looked different for the first time since boarding the ship—almost relieved. Kennedy walked to the services desk and picked up the phone, requesting coffee and sandwiches for the Owner's Suite. She was sure the afternoon would be long for them as they made calls on Diamond Jim's behalf.

J. Mitchell was opening the door that led to the cabins

from the pool deck when he saw one of the pool bar servers pushing a cart with food, a coffee urn, and two bottles of champagne. "Room service?" he asked. "I figured everyone would be in town."

"It's for the Owner's Suite," the young woman answered. "Did you hear what happened? Everyone is talking about it."

J. Mitchell nodded. "I watched it happen. Can we say *awkwardalous*[15]?" He eyed the bottles of champagne. "That's a little strange."

"I know. The sandwiches and coffee were a last-minute request from that other cruise director just as I was going on my lunch break. And five minutes later, we got a call from the Owner's Suite asking for champagne."

An idea occurred to J. Mitchell. "You know, I can deliver that for you. I hate that this delivery will cut into your break."

"Really?" she asked wide-eyed. "That would be great!" J. Mitchell took the cart from her. "You know you are so much nicer than everyone says."

"Thanks," J. Mitchell said, perplexed by her comment. He was, after all, adorable and funny. So why wouldn't people like him?

He pushed the cart down the corridor to the Owner's

---

[15] awkwardalous: an event that is both awkward and scandalous.

Suite and had raised his hand to knock when he heard Trixie's voice come through the door. "Thank goodness that is over," she said with a relieved sigh. "I wasn't sure how much longer I was going to last. Do you think it will work?" Intrigued, J. Mitchell pressed his ear to the door.

"Perfectly," a man's voice responded. "Thanks to my egging him on, Diamond Jim kept dodging the judge and Darlene's lawyer about the property settlement. Darlene isn't going to say anything, she just wanted him served, and *we* made sure Jim was in the right place at the right time."

"But what about—"

"Relax. As soon as we get back to Texas, you'll file for divorce, and no one will blame you after they hear what happened and see the photos. I'm sure Darlene has already tipped off the newspapers. The prenuptial agreement Diamond Jim and I haggled over states that in the event of a divorce, you are allowed to keep any jewelry you received, your car, the new house, and the condo in Hawaii. It's why we had those things put in your name. Jim added the provision for a monthly stipend so you wouldn't sue him for half of the assets, and trust me, after Darlene and the judge are through with him, he won't have any assets. I couldn't have scripted this better if I had tried. The old fool played right into our hands." He let out a chuckle. "So, are we getting off the ship or going on to Vancouver?"

J. Mitchell could only hear murmurs but could not make

out the words, so he knocked on the door. "Room service," he called out.

"Finally!" Trixie said over her shoulder as she walked into the bedroom.

When Cameron opened the door, he found J. Mitchell standing behind a room service cart. "I saw what happened, and I am so very sorry for your troubles. And right after such a lovely wedding." He looked at the items on the cart. "I thought some sandwiches and coffee would help. I'm sure you will be busy with your, umm…legal matters." He frowned and looked from the bottle of champagne to Cameron. "Whoops, I think someone in room service goofed. I didn't order champagne. I'll just wheel this inside and take the champagne back. My apologies." He began to push the cart into the room.

"Pop open that champagne! I feel like celebrating." Trixie hollered, coming out of the bedroom Diamond Jim had been using. She was rolling a small suitcase toward the entryway. "Okay, I've got his jewelry in the nightstand, and there was a wad of cash. I thought there was more, but he must have made some deals I didn't know about, and I still can't find my diamond bracelet or earrings, and I'm not leaving this ship until I find them!" She heard Cameron clear his throat and saw J. Mitchell and the room service cart. Darting her eyes at Cameron, she stepped in front of the suitcase to hide it with her body. She put her hands over her eyes, "I'm sorry. It's been a horrible day, and I'm not up to seeing anyone." She ran back into the bedroom, leaving the suitcase in the entryway.

Before Cameron could offer an explanation, emergency lights flashed inside the cabin, and an alarm began to shriek. "Is there a problem?" Cameron shouted, putting his fingers in his ears. He walked around the room service cart and saw the strobing lights in the corridor.

"Nothing to worry about," J. Mitchell yelled back, waving his hand at the flickering lights. "It will stop soon. These things happen all the time. I'll leave you two alone." He gave Cameron a funny look and walked away briskly in the direction of the spa. He needed to find Tammy and tell her what he had seen and heard.

Kennedy, Bert, and Mila were sitting in the mess hall with the others when the alarm sounded, and the emergency lights flashed. Several people looked around uneasily, and Otto, who had been sitting with them, stood up immediately. "That's not a sound I like to hear." He was halfway to the door when Chuckie strode into the room.

"Nothing to be worried about," Chuckie called out, clipping his radio back on his belt. "Like I just told the captain, that thing goes off every now and then since they updated it." He lifted an orange plastic plate from the pile and tossed it on a tray, looking at the food on the buffet. "My lucky day—fried chicken!" He shook a glob of mashed potatoes onto the plate, ladled gravy on top, and then speared several pieces of fried chicken from the pan. Walking over to the table where an unperturbed Bernard Phyfe sat with the spa's receptionist, Chuckie pulled a chair out with his foot and sat heavily in his seat. "I'm not sure why everyone gets so worked up. The thing goes off whenever it feels like it," he grumbled loudly and began gnawing on a drumstick. "How much do you want to bet Little Miss Nosy Pants over there has already called the corporate office?" People in the mess hall fell into two camps: those who looked anxiously at one another and others who, like Chuckie, continued to eat, oblivious to the screaming siren.

Kennedy walked over to Chuckie's table with her fingers in her ears. "Chuckie," she shouted, "are you sure there is no cause for alarm?" And, as if someone had thrown a switch, the scream of the siren abruptly ended, and the flashing lights turned off.

Chuckie looked up at her, wiped his hands on his shirt, and adjusted his hat. "See? Everything's fine. It goes off like that ever since they updated it."

"How often?"

He tipped back in his chair. "Well, let me think. I don't

remember off the top of my head." He tugged on the brim of his hat and used it to scratch his forehead as if the memory would surface from the action. He snapped his fingers, and his chair fell forward. "It was a couple of weeks ago. There was a moth in the sensor chamber, and we had to evacuate everyone off the ship. No passengers on board, just crew and some staff, but it was still a pain. Before that, there was a problem with one of the circuits. When it went off that time, I smacked my head on one of the pipes and still have a lump."

"But you don't know why it's going off now?" Kennedy pressed.

The woman sitting at the table with them rolled her eyes at Kennedy. "Can't you see he's eating?" she said in her gravelly voice. "If he said it's fine, then it's fine."

"I'll check after I eat my lunch," and he took a large bite of mashed potatoes.

"We could stay in port a little longer to give you time to—"

Chuckie swallowed and gave her a warning look. "Look, I know you work with Franklin, and he's perfect and jumps whenever you say something, but as Tammy pointed out this morning, you aren't on the *Helio*. You are on *my* ship." He nodded his head at the director of security. "He doesn't look worried, and I'm not concerned. So, there's no reason for you to get all worked up about something that isn't your responsibility."

"Yes, but—"

"Look, everything was fine when I did my morning rounds. It's a bug or dust inside the sensor panel or another faulty circuit. These things are overly sensitive now." He pointed his fork at the table where Kennedy had been sitting. "Now, your lunch, like mine, is getting cold, and I'd like to have a few minutes to eat in peace." Tiny flecks of mashed potato flicked into the air as he shook his fork.

Summarily dismissed, Kennedy walked back to the table, troubled. "He said it was nothing, a moth or some dust, and that everything was fine this morning when he did his rounds," she reported. "Oh rats, I wanted to talk to Mr. Phyfe." She began to get up and saw the spa's receptionist glaring at her. "I think I'll skip it," she sat back down.

Mila turned around in her chair to look at the table where the security director sat. "What is so pressing that you want to talk to Barney? He's as dull as his uniform."

"The missing jewelry I mentioned this morning. Both Ronnee Barrett *and* Vera Jameson are missing pieces."

Mila raised an eyebrow. "And let me guess, the king of khaki is being less than helpful?"

"I'm surprised he's still alive after how he treated Vera last night."

"Could the pieces have slipped off?" Mila asked.

Kennedy wrinkled her nose. "Maybe Ronnee's and Helen's, but Vera swears her jewelry was in her room, and I believe her. I suppose it's good that no one else is missing anything."

"Other than Diamond Jim," Bert piped up, and Kennedy and Mila looked at him.

"Oh, that's right, neither of you were on the pier. Right before he got arrested, he was on the gangway hollering that his watch was missing."

"That's odd. I'll ask Trixie and Cameron about it when I see them. Speaking of watches," Kennedy looked at hers, "time to walk the beasts. I'll see you guys later."

After she had walked the dogs and put them back in their cabin to watch television, she saw Otto checking the straps holding up one of the lifeboats. "Did I miss the captain's message to abandon ship?" she grinned. "I think we could just walk down the gangway and onto the pier."

"I get paid to have anxiety when I hear alarms and see strobe lights," Otto said, tugging the strap. "Chuckie may have said everything was fine, but I'm not one to take chances with a ship full of people in the middle of the ocean. And since the passengers are off the ship, I decided to do a more detailed safety walk. I was a Boy Scout, so being prepared is imprinted on my brain."

Kennedy furrowed her brow. "Chuckie said the alarm had gone off before. Something about a bug in the sensor chamber and a faulty circuit."

"Hmmm, well, it doesn't hurt to check these." He pulled on another strap. " I know there is a northern lights reception tonight for the passengers, but would you like to watch them with me? I can show you some of the constellations, too."

Kennedy stumbled for a response. "Oh, I wish I could, but I'll be busy with the passengers." She saw Otto's crestfallen face. "I'm sorry, I make it a policy not to get involved with anyone I work with."

Otto swallowed. "I understand."

"But could we do something as friends tomorrow night? It's a sea day, so I won't be as busy with the passengers."

"Sure." Kennedy could hear the disappointment in his voice, but she didn't want to put herself in an awkward position. The humiliation of her breakup with Omar had left her gun shy.

Kennedy continued her walk to the Starlight Lounge. She, Malone, and Evan had agreed to a quick practice, and as they finished their last song, Mila walked in and began to clap. Kennedy took a bow and sat down at Mila's table. Malone and Evan left, telling Kennedy they were meeting Bert and Ismaeel in Ketchikan for a beer.

"I need your opinion, but I need you to remember I don't have a degree in interior design like you."

"Yeah, I use it so often these days," Kennedy said wryly, motioning for the file Mila was holding. Kennedy took her time looking at each page and laid them on the table one by one. It was clear Mila had spent a great deal of time picking up different details and nuances of the ship.

"Well, what do you think?"

Kennedy's eyes lifted from the pages on the table to her friend. "That I will miss you when you are here renovating this spa. Mila, Alfred is going to love this. Do you have a name in mind yet?"

Mila shook her head. "No, but I can leave that up to the marketing folks. I got to name Oaza. That's enough for me."

Kennedy wrinkled her forehead. "Really? You're comfortable leaving it to the people who came up with the company's signature cocktail after an afternoon of day drinking in the sun?"

SUNNY DAYZ SUNRUMBRELLA

2 PARTS PINEAPPLE JUICE

2 PARTS ORANGE JUICE

1 1/2 PARTS RUM

LIME JUICE

GRENADINE SYRUP

CITRUS SLICES

CRUSHED ICE

COMBINE ALL INGREDIENTS IN A LARGE CONTAINER. POUR OVER CRUSHED ICE. GARNISH WITH CITRUS SLICES AND PAPER UMBRELLAS.

"Thank goodness there was an umbrella nearby. Who knows what the name might have been?" Mila grinned.

Justin and LaVonda had finished their tour of Ketchikan and were poking around the quaint shops that dotted the harbor. "Oh, let's stop here," LaVonda said as they walked by a jewelry store. She went inside, perusing the items in the glass cabinets. "May I see this?" she pointed to a gold-marbled, white quartz brooch. Placing it in her hair, she looked in the mirror on the counter.

"What do you think?"

The salesman was staring at her eyebrows which sat like thick dashes above her eyes, and he wondered if she had drawn them on with a black marker. "There are matching earrings and a ring if you'd like to see them as well," he said smoothly, seeing a large commission in front of his eyes.

Justin walked around the store while LaVonda looked at the matching pieces with the salesman. Then, when she saw him standing by a display of paperweights, she hurried over to him. "Pick one."

"LaVonda—"

"Good for holding down papers," the salesman offered. "A real statement piece and a memento of your time in Alaska."

"What about that one?" LaVonda pointed at a gold-veined piece of quartz the size of an apple sitting on the top of the display, and Justin reached out his arm to get the rock.

"Sir, that is a remarkable watch." The salesman motioned at Justin's wrist, and Justin tried to tug the cuff of his jacket down as he began to hand LaVonda the paperweight.

"A watch? I want to see!" LaVonda pushed Justin's sleeve up before taking the paperweight. She gazed at the watch appreciatively. "I can't believe I didn't notice it earlier. Have you been wearing it during the whole trip?"

"It-it-it was a gift from my Aunt Vera last night," Justin stammered. "She gave it to me at dinner as a sort of welcome to the company gift." He pulled his sleeve down and placed his hand in his jacket pocket. "I shouldn't have worn it," he said, embarrassed. "And please don't say anything to her about it. She gets funny about private family matters. Now, isn't there some crazy red-light district with a brothel in this town that I read about?"

Oliver and Vera were also wandering the harbor. "Well?" Oliver asked worriedly. He and Vera did not know each other well, and she had said little on their walk.

"I'm still in shock," Vera turned to him, and he could see her eyes were bright with excitement. "Did you see the bald eagle soaring beside me? I still can't believe it."

Oliver grinned, relieved. "Getting out of your comfort zone can be a good thing." He had secured a last-minute zip-line tour through the Tongass National Forest, and he and Vera had sailed over the treetops while watching bears feed on salmon below, and birds flew in formation beside them.

Vera looked at her watch. "Unfortunately, it's time to meet my nephew. I believe the welcome sign where I agreed to meet him is around the next corner."

Twenty minutes later, Justin and Vera were sitting in a nearby pub. "You went zip-lining?" Justin looked at his aunt in disbelief. "I would have paid good money to see you trussed up like a Thanksgiving turkey," he chuckled. "I should ask Oliver if he has any photos he'll part with for some cash. I could frame them and hand them out at the company Christmas party."

"I assure you I did not look like a turkey," she said stiffly, "and there are no photographs." They were sitting alone at their table. When they met at the sign, Justin had given Oliver his jacket, and Oliver told Vera he would meet her back on the ship so she and Justin could discuss their business matters privately.

"Did Inez call?" Vera took a sip of water. "I didn't hear from you."

"She did, but it wasn't anything to interrupt your day." He saw Vera frown, and he pulled out a folded piece of paper. "She had some inquiries for some destination funerals. One involves spreading someone's ashes over an ice rink at the end of hockey season." He saw Vera motion for the paper. "I've got this, Aunt Vera. Remember? I'm turning over a new leaf."

"Did she say anything else?"

Justin gave his aunt a blank look. "No, oh wait, there was something else."

Vera looked at him expectantly.

"She had a strange inquiry. Someone wants an urn, but they want it to look like a bust of the deceased—something to do with 3D imaging. They don't need it now. They just wanted to know if we could do it."

Vera made a face. "How barbaric. I suppose we can find someone when we get back. Inez didn't say anything else?" she pressed, and Justin shook his head. "I suppose we should head back to the ship."

"Yes, I need to send Inez the report from that odious little man for the insurance company."

As they walked, she asked if he had heard any news on the commotion that had taken place on the dock earlier. "No, we—"

"Yoo-hoo, Justin!" They turned around to see the five ladies traveling with Ronnee. "Is this your aunt?" they asked as they approached Vera and Justin.

"Your nephew is just the most charming young man."

"He took us to dinner the night we met you in the theater."

The ladies chattered and reminded Vera of a flock of seagulls as they tried to talk over one another. Vera nodded politely, hoping she could disengage herself from them soon.

"Are you going to the northern lights show and reception tonight?" Mary Margaret asked. "It's supposed to be magnificent."

"Oh, and there are some old movies playing in the theater after dinner," Estelle called out, and Helen nodded. "*An Affair to Remember* with Cary Grant and one with Groucho Marx. Do you think we will have time to see a movie and the northern lights?"

"I'm sure we can," Ronnee chuckled. Since seeing Justin, her five traveling companions, who had been drooping daisies moments before, had perked up considerably.

"Did anyone find out what happened to the groom this morning? That poor, poor girl, to see her new husband carted off in handcuffs. She must be beside herself with worry," Marge sighed.

Several yards in front of them, a door opened, and a tipsy woman, laughing gaily, tottered out on high heels, pulling on the arm of the man behind her.

"Well," Vera said drolly to no one in particular as they all looked in shock at the couple in front of them, "it appears the bride is weathering her new husband's arrest rather well."

The *Malina* glided out of Ketchikan's harbor as the passengers entered the dining room for dinner. There were a few raised eyebrows when Trixie, wearing a sapphire blue, one-shouldered evening gown that clung to her figure, arrived on her cousin's arm. Diners murmured behind menus that only twenty-four hours earlier they had applauded as Trixie, wearing a snow-white wedding gown, had entered the room with her new husband, and wondered what the bantam-sized man with the larger-than-life personality would be eating tonight in his jail cell.

Kennedy was standing at the podium helping Jonny seat the passengers. Jonny didn't necessarily need help, but they were falling into a comfortable rhythm, and she used the time to plug the holes in the young manager's cruise ship education. She watched as Vera, dressed in a pewter evening gown, walked serenely through the dining room on the arm of Oliver Parsons as Jonny led them to the captain's table. Justin rose when his aunt arrived and pecked her on the cheek. As LaVonda's escort, he was also dining at the captain's table, and when Kennedy had seen the seating diagram earlier, she had pointed at the names.

"Orders from J. Mitchell," he sighed. "And it wasn't a big deal. I added two more chairs and a table, so it now seats eighteen instead of the original sixteen."

"Good thinking. I'd place Mrs. Jameson and Mr. Parsons

near the captain and LaVonda at the opposite end. Safer to keep those two women apart."

"How do you know to do stuff like this?" Jonny asked sincerely.

Looking up from the diagram, Kennedy smiled at him. "Years of observation, reading the notes on the VIP list, and picking up on body language. You'll get the hang of it."

As soon as the captain and his officers left the dining room after dessert, J. Mitchell picked up the microphone. "Ladies and gentlemen, I wanted to let you know that Mother Nature has decided to grace us with a perfect night to see her fabulous light show. We encourage you to meet us on the pool deck at ten o'clock and recommend that you dress warmly. We also have a wonderful collection of black-and-white movies playing in the Aurora Theater—"

The security lights flashed on and off, and an alarm let off a little chirp. "Nothing to worry about, folks," J. Mitchell waved his hand dismissively. "It went off earlier when you were in port, and I was told a moth had brushed up against a sensor. I guess he's back. So, as I was saying before I was so rudely interrupted, after last night's little mix-up, our own Kennedy Reeves will be entertaining in the Starlight Lounge." After he finished speaking, many passengers took his announcement as their cue to leave.

"Do you want to go?" LaVonda asked Justin as they stood up.

Justin shook his head. "To the movies? No, not at all."

"No, to see the northern lights."

He faked a smile. "I'm going to pass. I'm not much for looking at the stars. I'm heading to the casino. I feel lady luck calling my name."

"Oh," LaVonda said with dismay. "I had my hopes up to see them, and I need to take some photos to send to my clients."

There were a few moments of awkward silence. Justin had been trying to find a way to extricate himself from spending more time with LaVonda. "You shouldn't miss it just because I am not going. But, tell you what, if I run into some bad luck, I'll come up and find you."

"Maybe I'll go with you to be your good luck charm. I can always find some photos of the northern lights, and no one will be the wiser." She squeezed his arm, and Justin inwardly sighed. It seemed he would be stuck with LaVonda for another night.

Thirty minutes later, Kennedy was in the middle of a song when J. Mitchell, resplendent in a sequined suit featuring piano keys on the cuffs and lapels, burst through the doors of the Starlight Lounge, causing everyone to turn around and gasp. "Isn't this fun?" he called out, sashaying through the lounge, shaking hands with the passengers on his way to the small stage. When he reached Kennedy, he wiggled his fingers at her, and she dug deep to mask her look of annoyance and finish her song. J. Mitchell cupped his hand to whisper in Evan's ear, "Play 'Anything You Can Do,' then I'm going to talk, and when I say, 'Hit it, boys,' you start playing, 'There's No Business Like Show Business,' got it?" Evan nodded and leaned over to Malone. They bridged from the song Kennedy had been singing to the one J. Mitchell had requested, and J. Mitchell turned to the audience. "Do you guys know this one?" He turned to Kennedy, giving her an ingratiating smile, and whispered in her ear. "Now, let's not cause a scene," he hissed. "And, of course, you understand I'll take the lead."

When the song ended, J. Mitchell grabbed the microphone he and Kennedy had been sharing from the stand. "Wasn't that great?" He began to walk around talking to the audience. "Since Kennedy has had so much time with you, I'm going to let her take a break. She's been working so hard and just looks exhausted." He held his hand to the side of his mouth as if telling the passengers a secret. "Have you seen those bags under her eyes? Bless her heart. She's going to need a luggage cart to wheel them around soon." He let out a staccato laugh and turned to face Kennedy. "Now, off you go," he made a little shooing motion.

Seeing that J. Mitchell had upstaged her once again, she gracefully exited the stage waving to the audience. J. Mitchell, still weaving around the tables and chairs, zeroed in on a group of older ladies. He pushed an empty chair between a bewildered Marge and Mary Margaret and, crossing his legs, struck a pose hunching his shoulders forward and placing one of his hands on his knee. "Hit it, boys."

Dismissed from her show in the Starlight Lounge, Kennedy went to her cabin and changed out of her evening gown. She slipped her phone into her jacket pocket with the hope of snapping a photo of the northern lights. Before the sirens and alarms went off at lunch, she and Mila agreed to meet by the pool at nine, walk the dogs, and help the *Malina* team with the reception. As the three dogs pulled her down the deck, Kennedy saw Mila with Bert. He was setting up his tripod and camera to capture shots of the light show.

"Ready?" she asked. "Bert, do you want to go with us?"

He shook his head. "I'm going to pass. See you two in a little while."

Kennedy unleashed the dogs when they got to their special area several decks below, and they sniffed excitedly at the artificial turf. "It's so peaceful," Kennedy breathed, looking out at the inky darkness full of shimmering stars.

"I haven't seen nights like this since I lived in Las Vegas," Mila said. "I'd drive out to the desert and lose myself in the sky."

They turned when they saw a strobe light flicker and suddenly stop. There was no alarm, but they both felt a wave of apprehension.

"Must be that pesky moth again," Kennedy said uneasily.

"You know how sensors can be."

"Sensitive?" Kennedy asked dryly.

"I once had a temperamental smoke alarm. I was on a stir-fry binge, and it was always going off."

"What did you do?"

"I stopped dating the man who liked stir-fry." Mila brushed her hands together. "Problem solved."

"I love you, Mila. You have a unique way of dealing with

problems. Okay, beasts, time to go back to the cabin." She received three venomous glares full of canine hate and discontent. "Tough crowd tonight."

"Meh, they told me they like J. Mitchell better than you. Everyone does."

A few decks below, Chuckie stood in front of the fire panel, flipping switches. "That's it," he growled. "I'm turning this thing off until we get to Vancouver. Someone else can figure out what is wrong and why it keeps going off for no reason," he muttered, rubbing his baseball cap up and down on his forehead. "I'm going to my cabin. One more day and this overly sensitive piece of junk can be someone else's problem."

At ten o'clock, passengers began gathering on the pool and observation decks. They snuggled into the blankets Cormac's team had set out on the lounge chairs and searched the night sky with their binoculars. Half an hour later, someone called out,

"Look," and a wave of green lights began slowly swaying in the night sky.

Kennedy held the binoculars to her eyes and watched the

rippling green lights. Suddenly she saw a flash of red begin its dance. It reminded her of being mesmerized by the flames in the family fireplace as a small child.

While Kennedy and the others were watching the blazing undulations of the night sky, a member of Chuckie's team was dealing with flames of another kind. He had gone into the engine room to do his hourly check and smelled smoke before he opened the door. His eyes darted around the room full of white pipes and metal equipment until he saw fire licking a section of pipe. Smoke billowed out of the open door and alerted the secondary alarm. Thinking quickly, he grabbed the closest fire extinguisher and put out the flames. Satisfied that there was no further danger, he was perplexed that the alarm had not gone off, nor had the automatic fog system turned on when the fire started. He shrugged and, per protocol, radioed the fire team and others to let them know he had extinguished a fire. His last call was to Chuckie.

Chuckie was in his cabin when the shrill ring of the telephone startled him. He had been dozing in front of the television and was annoyed at the interruption. "This better be important," he growled.

"Had a little problem, Chief," the voice on the other end of the phone said. "Sorry I called, but I couldn't raise you on the radio. We had a fire on one of the pipes. It's out, but the fire team has to give the all-clear. Do you want me to call the bridge and let them know?"

"I will," Chuckie grumbled. "I'm sure they have their pristine tighty-whiteys all twisted up about it," he huffed.

"Sorry, sir."

Chuckie let out a sigh of disgust and hung up the phone. He closed his eyes for a few moments and then called the bridge. Andreas answered the phone in a clipped, businesslike manner.

"Surprised you are up there," Chuckie let out a forced laugh. "You've been following that spa lady from the *Helio* around since she got on board. I'd be—"

"We heard the code go out, Chuckie," Andreas said curtly, "and have been waiting to hear from you. Can you explain the situation? We're a little nervous after the alarms went off earlier today and after dinner. And why didn't the alarm go off?"

Chuckie ignored Andreas's last question. "Those were false alarms." His tone was dismissive. "Something screwy with the sensors. This was a tiny fire in the engine room. My guy put it out, and the fire team is inspecting the area. This is a non-event. You can go back to worrying about your hair and chasing after the lady from the *Helio*."

"I'll let the captain know," Andreas said crisply.

"There's no need to tell him, Andreas. It was a tiny flare-up," Chuckie griped. "The area affected was no bigger than a coffee can. You know, back in my day—"

Andreas, cut him off, "Chuckie, in your day, people made fires by rubbing two sticks together. I have to go. Otto is calling." He disconnected and answered the other line, sharing Chuckie's comments.

"The fire team says it was much bigger than a coffee can, and if the guy hadn't caught it when he did, we could have had a real situation. We have to follow protocol," Otto said. "Call the captain, and I'll put the word out to the Coast Guard and any ships nearby."

"Are we being overly cautious?"

"I'm not taking any chances."

After Andreas woke the captain and brought him up to speed, the captain demanded that Chuckie report to the bridge.

"What a bunch of unnecessary drama," Chuckie huffed aloud to the empty room, hastily putting on his uniform, and grabbed his radio. As he made his way to the bridge, he carried on a running monologue with himself. "They think they know everything because of their pretty uniforms. Well, it's like this. It's the guys like me that make sure these sardine tins float," he grumbled. He was still talking to himself when he approached the entrance to the bridge. "Sometimes we have to take some shortcuts to make things look smooth. A little duct tape is all you usually need." He patted the wall and opened the door to the bridge.

"Would you care to explain why I am here and not comfortable in my bed, Mr. McDermott?" Captain Volare's eyes pierced into Chuckie's like a hawk.

Chuckie paled, which made the freckles on his face stand out. "I won't know what's going on until I can get down there, and I can't do that until the all-clear is given," he said defensively.

Captain Volare closed his eyes, trying to control his temper. Years ago, the two men had almost come to blows after a heated argument about the uncleanliness of the engine room. Since that day, they had steered clear of each other. Finally, Captain Volare opened his eyes and glared at Chuckie. "Then I suggest you get down there immediately and find out what is wrong with my ship." He turned to Otto. "Mr. Armitage? Your report?"

"I've alerted the ships in the area of our coordinates and the trouble we recently experienced. I also spoke with the Coast Guard base in Ketchikan, sir."

The phone rang, and with a nod from the captain, Andreas picked it up. While he listened, Chuckie tried to fill in the silence, his words coming out high and in a rush. "You know, there wasn't much upkeep performed on the ship during the shutdown."

The captain crossed his arms and narrowed his eyes at Chuckie. "Wouldn't that have been your job, Mr. McDermott? You were one of the few who stayed on the payroll during the shutdown to ensure the ship stayed in running order."

Chuckie glowered. "I replaced a few sections of pipe in anticipation of the cruise, and everything looked fine when I inspected it."

Andreas frowned when he set the receiver in the cradle and then looked at Captain Volare, Otto, and Chuckie. "That was the fire team, and they apologized for the delay, sir. The fire is out, but they found cracks in a section of pipe above the original fire and further down the line." His face hardened as he looked at Chuckie. "The cracks were not seen earlier due to the dirt, grease, and oil on the insulation, which is what ignited."

"Mr. Armitage, full stop and lower the anchor until we can ascertain the ship is safe," the captain snapped.

"Answering all stop, Captain. Lowering the anchor."

When the light show Mother Nature had provided died down, J. Mitchell came across the speakers. "Now, who's ready for some *aftertizers*[16] before the next show?" Food stations had magically appeared while the passengers were busy watching the night sky. On one table, a popcorn display made to look like a snowy glacier stood before them. Dark chocolate and caramel had been drizzled down the creamy mountain of white kernels to a sea of roasted nuts, chickpeas, and dried fruits. At another table, wheels of Gouda and cheddar cheese sat beside wedges of creamy Havarti while rounds of warm brie, dribbled with honey, sat waiting to be cut. Chefs Sha and Jordan stood at the dessert table behind a selection of cheesecakes, gelato, and angel food cake dappled with cinnamon sauce.

"I've always avoided buffets in the past," Vera said to Oliver looking in hesitation at the mounds of blackberries, raspberries, orange slices, and pineapple chunks. "The thought of them has always horrified me."

"You've mushed huskies, soared beside eagles, and just saw the northern lights," Oliver chuckled. "You aren't the dainty flower you make yourself out to be."

Vera looked at him from the side of her eye and promptly

---

[16] aftertizer: a nighttime snack.

picked up the tongs in front of her. "Perhaps brusque blossom fits better," she smirked, placing several pieces of fruit on her plate.

They made their way back to their chairs and sat down. Vera leaned over to Oliver. "Is it me, or are we barely moving?" They saw several other passengers looking around, having noticed the same thing.

Kennedy and the others had noticed the slower movement of the ship much earlier, but the passengers had been busy filling their plates. Otto had appeared moments before the buffet opened and motioned for Kennedy and J. Mitchell. He told them in hushed tones what had happened.

"The passengers are going to notice. We need to make an announcement," Kennedy whispered. "It's easier to tell them calmly what is happening rather than allow for rabid speculation."

J. Mitchell had a panicked look in his eyes. "This is something the captain should announce. I'm Mr. Entertainment, not Mr. Bad News."

"Does the captain want to keep everyone on the two decks?" Kennedy asked, and Otto nodded his head. "J. Mitchell," Kennedy began, but he vigorously shook his head.

J. Mitchell had his arms folded across his chest. "Not me! I told you before. I'm here to entertain them, not play nursemaid.

And I certainly don't chat with them if I don't have to. I learned my lesson this afternoon when we docked in Ketchikan. Good grief, how they went on and on." He waved his hand. "Seriously—"

"J Mitchell!"

He pointed his finger at Kennedy and placed a hand on his hip. "You do it, Miss Perfect Cruise Director. You haven't had any problem taking over other things on this cruise—like the captain's cocktail party or the wedding, or the—"

Kennedy cut him off. His voice had begun to rise, and she didn't want to cause any unnecessary alarm for the passengers. "Fine, I'll do it." She went down to the services desk, where the public address system she had used earlier was stationed.

Her calm voice came across the speakers. "Ladies and Gentlemen, this is Kennedy Reeves, one of your cruise directors. The captain has asked all passengers to report to the pool and promenade decks. There is no cause for alarm. Unfortunately, we have experienced a small fire in the engine room. With your safety being our highest priority, we ask that you join us on the upper decks and enjoy the northern lights dessert reception while you pass the time. With any luck, we'll see another show from Mother Nature while we are waiting."

Questioning looks and murmurs passed between the

passengers as they made their way to the pool and promenade decks. In the casino, the blackjack dealer ended the game at LaVonda and Justin's table after hearing the announcement. "But I was on a streak," she said furiously, and the dealer looked at her blankly.

"Just following the rules, ma'am."

"But—"

"LaVonda, you can come back later," Justin rose from his seat. "This is temporary, and didn't you say you needed to take some photos for your clients at dinner?"

"I suppose," she huffed, and the dealer shot Justin a look that conveyed what they were both thinking.

Justin had been irked when LaVonda tagged along with him to the casino. He had hoped she would go to the northern lights reception and leave him in peace, but she had stuck to his side like glue. As they climbed the steps to the pool deck, Justin tried to block out LaVonda's never-ending chatter. He would have to find a way to duck her tomorrow, and then he remembered dismally that it was a sea day and the chance of hiding from her was between slim and none.

With the engines off, the passengers now heard the steady hum of the generator as it kicked in, and a festive party atmosphere took over the two decks. Thirty minutes later, the droning noise abruptly stopped, and the ship was plunged into darkness for a few moments until the battery-operated safety lights came on.

Standing on the bridge, the captain waited to hear the generator come back on, and when it did, the lights came on again, and he breathed a sigh of relief. Moments later, watching the lights flicker out again, he felt a flutter of fear in his stomach. He had brought his ships through many perils over the years: raging storms that had toppled furniture, pirates off the coast of Africa, and heavy waves, but the eerie calmness of the sea and the silence in the air gave him pause. He picked up his radio. "Mr. McDermott, I'd like to know why our generator has stopped."

There was static on the line, and he could barely make out Chuckie's panting nasal twang through the noise. "Overheated."

The line began to hiss and pop, and he heard Chuckie speak again. "I can't…generator…cool down…dampers won't…"

The captain closed his eyes. For the first time in his life, he was the captain of a ship that was dead in the water.

Many younger staff members became anxious when the lights went out the second time. A few passengers near J. Mitchell remarked that the cruise director seemed disconnected from what was happening and saw the more seasoned staff and crew happily engaging the passengers in conversations. They pointed out the battery backup lights, made light-hearted comments, and passed out more blankets. Kennedy noticed Mila helping to bundle Ronnee's five charges in additional blankets as they looked around nervously.

"I wonder how long we will be stuck up here," Cameron asked Justin as they filled their plates at the cheese display. "Trixie is already on edge after what happened earlier today."

"Yeah, what was that all about? We saw Diamond Jim taken away in a police car."

"An unfortunate legal matter involving hiding assets from his ex-wife," Cameron answered. "Although he was more worked up about missing his watch than about going to jail."

"We heard him yelling as he came down the gangway. You didn't find it?"

Cameron shook his head. "No, the last time I remember seeing it was on his wrist at the tee box this morning." He blew out a breath. "That seems like another lifetime ago."

"Try spending the day with LaVonda if you want to

know what endless feels like."

Cameron let out a bark of laughter and put a few more pieces of cheese on his plate. Justin furrowed his brow as if trying to remember something. "Maybe it slipped off his wrist. I remember it almost fell off at the cocktail party the first night. Remember? You pointed it out to him." He looked out and let out a frustrated sigh. "Excuse me. I'm being summoned."

Justin made his way over to LaVonda, who had buried herself under several blankets. She eyed the plate of food he was holding and wrinkled her nose. "I can't eat. I'm worried about the dogs, Justin. I'd feel so much better if my sweeties were with me."

Justin placed the plate on the table beside LaVonda. "You heard the announcement. We have to stay here until the captain tells us otherwise." Justin told himself that he would have loved to get the dogs for her if only to escape for a few minutes.

"But what if they are scared?" She selected a piece of angel food cake from the plate and stuffed it in her mouth.

"I doubt they have noticed anything. They are probably asleep in their bed. Listen, I'll be back in a few minutes. I need to check on my aunt."

"And without any power, their television isn't on," she fretted. "They can't sleep without their shows. Oh, my poor sweeties." She had not heard Justin in her ramblings and finally noticed him standing. A look of fear crossed her face. "Where are you going? Are you leaving me?"

"I'll be back in a few minutes," he said with feigned patience and left. Instead of searching for his aunt, he went to the pool bar for a drink. He reasoned he could extend his delay by looking for his aunt and praying she would ask him to stay with her.

The captain sent Otto to bring Kennedy to the bridge. "I know this is not what you signed up for, Ms. Reeves," the captain spoke gravely, and he shared the update from Chuckie with her. "We may need to evacuate the ship. Have you ever done that?"

Kennedy shook her head. "No, sir. I've done every training but never had to lead the passengers in an actual evacuation."

"We won't do it unless we absolutely must. And we certainly won't do it in the dark. It's too risky. We should be fine until morning. But will you quietly inform our senior staff of what may happen? I'd prefer that you did it. I don't need someone who might break out into a song and dance routine."

Kennedy nodded and swallowed hard. She left the bridge and returned to the pool deck. When she saw Bert and Mila, she walked up to them wearing a big smile.

"You should probably turn down the wattage on that smile, friend," Mila said. "It's a little frightening. You look like a television evangelist."

"Would you help me find the others and meet me in the pool bar kitchen?" she said through her smile. "I have information I need to share, but it needs to be somewhere we can't be overheard."

When they were gathered, Kennedy told them what the captain had said. "Please keep this to yourself until we receive our orders."

From his vantage point at the bar, Justin watched Kennedy speak to Mila and Bert and then saw them take off and start up casual conversations with several other members of the ship. His curiosity grew as he saw them enter the bar, one by one, and walk through a swinging door at the back. Making certain no one else was joining the group, Justin got up, casually made his way to the door, and leaned against the doorjamb so he could hear what was being said. Minutes later, when the conversation on the other side stopped, he walked away quickly and melted into the crowd.

A little while later, one of the senior crew members pointed his finger to the sky as the undulating lights began again in the distance, distracting the passengers.

"Justin, I need to know my sweeties are safe," LaVonda

whimpered when he returned.

He knelt down and whispered in her ear, and she pulled back and looked at him in fright. "Are you sure?" He nodded.

"I'll sneak down to your cabin and get the dogs. You stay here." He turned and began walking away.

Her eyes were still wide from what he had told her. "Wait, Justin…" but he was already out of earshot.

Justin crept down the outside steps to deck nine. After hearing what Kennedy had said on the other side of the pool bar door, Justin remembered the words he had vaguely listened to during the muster drill. They would not be allowed to return to their cabins in the event of an evacuation, and he needed to retrieve something important from his room. If the item were found in his cabin when the ship returned to port, his aunt would never forgive him. He opened the door to the corridor and looked both ways. The lighting was dim, and he thought about using the flashlight on his phone to make his way to his room but decided against it. He didn't want to draw anyone's attention with the light. Head down, he walked quickly to his cabin and was placing his keycard against the magnetic lock when he heard an authoritative voice call out.

"May I help you, sir?" First Officer Andreas Pritchard was walking briskly toward him. "For your safety, we've asked that all passengers stay on the pool and observation decks for the foreseeable future."

"I'm sorry, I just needed to get something for my friend." Justin offered Andreas a winning smile. "I promise I won't be a minute."

"I'm sorry, sir," Andreas said firmly. "You need to return to the pool or observation deck. I'd be happy to walk with you if you are unsure of how to get there."

Justin, furious, stalked back to the pool deck, followed at a discreet distance by the ship's first officer.

"Where are my babies?" LaVonda asked in a panic when she saw him arrive alone.

Justin nodded at Andreas, who had positioned himself in front of the glass doors. "See that guy right there? He wouldn't let me get them. He said it was the captain's orders."

"Excuse me?" LaVonda went from worry to outrage in a split second. She pointed at Andreas. "He told you that you couldn't bring my precious babies to me?" she spat each word out like a machine gun. "I'll take care of this."

LaVonda marched up to Andreas, wearing her blanket like a cape, and began to harangue the first officer. Passengers gathered loosely around them, and Kennedy, noticing the disturbance, walked over to see if she could defuse the situation. She had been grateful that, so far, things had remained peaceful.

Kennedy crossed into LaVonda's line of sight. "You! This is your fault," she jabbed a finger at Kennedy. "My friend, knowing that I was distressed, offered to get my precious sweeties, who are like my children, from my stateroom. And this," she whipped her head around and looked at Andreas with blazing eyes that should have turned him into a pile of ash, "this overzealous junior jet told him no."

"Kennedy—" Andreas protested, but LaVonda cut him off. She whirled around and pointed again at Kennedy.

"Is this some sick way to get back at me for demanding your termination all those years ago? If I had known you were on this cursed ship, you can be certain I would not have accepted the invitation. I still can't believe they didn't get rid of you. As it is, I will go out of my way to tell people not to book any cruise with this line." She stared icily at Kennedy, daring her to say something. "Well, what are you going to do about it?"

Kennedy swallowed. The crowd stared at her, waiting to see what she would say. "Ms. Taylor, First Officer Pritchard and I will go immediately to your cabin to get the dogs. In my concern for our passengers and their safety, I will admit I forgot about them, but I will be back with your dogs momentarily."

Andreas and Kennedy went down the back steps from eleven to ten. "Kennedy, he never said anything about the dogs." When he opened the door to the ninth-floor corridor, Kennedy looked at him strangely. "What are you doing?" she asked.

"LaVonda is on deck eight, Cabin 801."

"Are you sure?"

"Very. I walk those dogs four times a day."

"But I found him on deck nine."

"That's odd." They went down another flight of steps, their shoes making a tap dance on the metal treads.

Kennedy opened the cabin door and was met with sleepy growls.

"I don't think they want to go with us," Andreas offered, stepping back as the dogs rushed forward, baring their tiny fangs. "They look as grouchy as their owner."

"Their grumpiness is a small price to pay if it keeps her quiet. By the way, have you seen Mr. Phyfe?" she asked. "I assume he knows what is going on?"

"Yeah, he's securing the public spaces that aren't muster stations and helping us patrol the corridors so passengers can't sneak into their cabins."

Kennedy grinned. "A perfect job for him. He must be elated."

"Why are we down here?" J. Mitchell whispered over Tammy's shoulder as she put her key in the lock of the salon door.

She waved her hand under her nose. "What have you been eating? Your breath stinks."

"Cheese. I eat when I am stressed," he whined. "But why are we here? We could get into trouble if anyone finds us."

Tammy opened the door and walked inside with J. Mitchell close on her heels. "Relax, I told Barney we had some things to do before the evacuation. They've already checked the cabins on this deck for passengers, and he appointed himself guard for this floor and the lobby. And everyone else will think we are somewhere upstairs with the passengers,"

The battery-operated emergency lights offered little help in the darkened salon. "Ow!" J. Mitchell screeched when his knee collided with the reception desk. "Who moved that?"

"Shhhh," Tammy admonished him, relocking the door. "No one moved anything. Open your eyes."

"They are, but it's not exactly bright in here."

Tammy pointed at the chairs against the wall where the stylists worked. "Go over there and sit at the last chair, and for heaven's sake, keep your voice down. Barney's patrolling, but we don't need to advertise our presence to anyone else. I'll be right back."

J. Mitchell looked at the red glow from the emergency lights on the gold and red flocked wallpaper. "Now I know where the demons from hell get their hair done," he grumbled. "Why are we down here?" J. Mitchell asked again.

Tammy smiled widely. "Trust me. I have a plan, and after I'm done, *you* will be a star." She turned on her heel and left. J. Mitchell had no idea what she meant. A star? He was already one as far as he was concerned. He just hadn't been discovered yet.

She wound her way through the back of the spa and pulled three large battery-operated flashlights from a cabinet. J. Mitchell could hear the clack of her heels on the floor get louder as she returned to the salon and dumped the flashlights onto the counter in front of him.

"Ummm, *confuzzled[17]*," J. Mitchell cocked his head.

Tammy ignored him and looked around the room. She spied two folding tables leaning against a wall. "Bring me those," she pointed, "and put them behind the chair."

J. Mitchell picked up on Tammy's strange mood and did as he was told.

---

[17] confuzzled: to be confused or puzzled.

She gently patted the red and white striped seat, and he sat down cautiously. Tammy pumped her foot up and down on the lever under the chair to raise it.

"Tammy—"

"First, I'll trim your hair and maybe put a little gloss treatment on it to give it some shine. Then, we'll give you a facial." She pulled a plastic cape from the cabinet below the mirror and fastened it around his neck.

"You want to give me a haircut now?" He twisted in his seat and looked at her wide-eyed. "We might have to abandon ship! We might sink! Why are my hair and face so important now? We could die out here." He struggled to get up, and she pressed his shoulders down.

"Sit down!" She smacked him on the corner of his head with the hairbrush in her hand.

He turned his head and scowled at her. "Owww. Don't do that. It hurts. My mother always said I had a very tender head." He rubbed the spot and turned back to face the mirror.

"More like she wondered if you were dropped on your head. Stop being so melodramatic. We aren't going to die." She rested her chin on his shoulder and smiled. "But you heard Miss Goody Two Shoes. There is a distinct possibility that we will be evacuated."

"Okay…and?"

"And who do you think will be the first person in front of the news cameras? The heroic young cruise director who put the passenger's safety above his own." She stood up straight and began brushing his hair.

A light went on in J. Mitchell's eyes, and seconds later, he frowned. "But what if we don't evacuate?"

"But what if we do?" She turned his chair around so that he faced her. "These passengers will talk their heads off the minute their feet touch land. This is the most exciting thing to happen to them in their dreary little lives, and you can bet they'll still be riding on this story when they return home." She wheeled him back around, and J. Mitchell stared at his ghostly reflection in the mirror. Tammy leaned forward and snaked a hand over his shoulder. She gripped his chin tightly in her hand.

She stared at him in the mirror. "It was this face, *this face* that saved them when they were in peril." She released his chin, and he rubbed it gingerly. When Tammy's fingernails had dug into his chin, he had an unpleasant flashback to standing before his mother, who had held his face the same way when he got into trouble. "Think of the number of reporters and news shows that will clamor for our story."

"Our story?" J. Mitchell turned his head in confusion.

She took a pair of scissors out of the drawer. "Yes, *our* story. Your best friend, the beautiful spa director, Tammy, was beside you the entire time, risking her life to bring the passengers to safety. And once corporate sees our faces plastered all over the media, you and I will become the darlings of the company and not Miss Perfect." She snipped the air and held a hand up to her ear. "Did you hear that?" She cut the air again. "Kennedy, who? Mila, who?" She placed her fingers on his temples and turned his head.

"And then there is the matter of the hush money you are going to extract from the new Mrs. Diamond Jim. She won't want anyone to know what you overheard in the Owner's Suite. And if she doesn't budge, we'll go to Diamond Jim and tell him what we know in exchange for a nice fat reward. One of them will pay, trust me."

J. Mitchell looked at her in awe. "I do. I didn't know that under that creamy skin was such a crusty layer of evilness. I'm glad I'm on your good side."

Tammy offered him a sly smile. "Opportunistic, not evil. Now, after your haircut and glossing, I'll give you a turmeric facial."

"Turmeric?" he asked. "Isn't that the orange stuff in curry?"

"Yes, it will brighten your skin and give you a youthful

glow when they put the camera lights on you. But we'll do it last because you only want to leave it on for a few minutes, or it will stain your skin. If you leave it on for too long, you'll look like the inside of a cantaloupe."

He blinked rapidly. "Okay, you are the boss," he said in his singsong voice.

"Remember that!" She smacked him on the back of his head again. "Now sit up straight. I've never cut hair by flashlight."

After LaVonda's outburst and the arrival of her dogs, Justin excused himself to visit with his aunt. He was thankful Vera and Oliver had been standing at the railing engrossed in conversation and had not witnessed LaVonda's tirade at Kennedy. Where LaVonda behaved like a toddler having a temper tantrum that one could easily ignore, Vera preferred a stealthier approach so that the death by a thousand cuts was not apparent until you were bloodied and gasping for breath as you lay dying on the ground, pleading for your life. He had almost reached his aunt when he saw her rubbing her hands up and down her arms and watched Oliver remove his coat and help her into it.

"This is unnecessary, Oliver," he heard Vera say, "I can

get a blanket."

"Nonsense," Oliver tugged on the zipper and pulled the collar around Vera's neck.

"But what about you?"

"I'm fine right now, and if I get cold, I'll find a blanket."

"Well, thank you." Vera put her hands into the pockets of Oliver's jacket, and as she did, Justin saw curiosity cross his aunt's face as her fingers felt something. She pulled the object out and held it to the starlight to see better. Stunned, she turned to Oliver. "Why is my earring in your pocket?"

"What?" Oliver's forehead creased. "What are you talking about? Your earring?"

Vera lowered her hand. The diamond and pearl earring she had worn to the captain's cocktail party sat in her palm. "This is one of the pieces taken from my room." There was a mix of emotions in her voice—confusion, fury, and hurt. She stared at Oliver, and the hand holding the earring shook so hard she clenched it into a fist. "Answer me," she barked. "Why was my earring in your pocket?"

"Vera—"

"Aunt Vera, are you okay?" Justin had reached his aunt, and he looked at her with concern.

Vera's eyes snapped over to Justin. "You were right,

Justin," her voice wavered for an instant. Then, she looked back at Oliver, and her tone was glacial. "You were, unfortunately, very right."

Kennedy was passing out more blankets when she heard raised voices. She searched the deck and saw they came from where Vera stood.

"Vera, I don't know how that earring got into my pocket," Oliver protested.

Oliver's jacket suddenly felt tight and suffocating on Vera. She had to get it off. She angrily yanked the zipper and wrenched one shoulder back, struggling to pull her arm out. "I even defended you," she panted.

"Defended me?" A wave of indignation flooded through Oliver.

The jacket fell to the ground, and Vera looked from it to Oliver. "On the second day of the cruise, Justin pointed out that I didn't know you and begged me to be careful. I was furious at his accusations and told him to mind his own business." She gave Justin a look of apology, and her shoulders sagged for an instant. "I'm sorry, my dear. You had my best interests at heart, and I should have listened. I realize now you only went along with things to make me happy." Justin tore his glare away from the man who had stolen his aunt's jewelry to look at her.

Vera turned her icy blue eyes back onto Oliver. "What a

fool I was. Trusting you enough to invite you into my stateroom, naively telling you things…" Vera trailed off and then spoke again sadly. "I even gave you my keycard to get my scarf in Juneau. Did you take my jewelry then or the night before? Did you leave this piece in your pocket so you could feel it and laugh about how easily I played into your hand? What's the term? A mark?"

Oliver held up his hand. "Vera, I didn't take your jewelry," his voice was now angry and bewildered. "Why would I do something like that?"

Vera looked coldly at Oliver and then at the twinkling night sky as if searching for an answer. "What is the quote?" Her voice quavered with humiliation. "There's no fool like an old fool? Then I suppose the joke is on me." She brought her eyes down, gave Oliver a hard look, and then turned her attention to the crowd. Her eyes found Kennedy's. "Please find that excuse for a security director. While he couldn't find his ass with both hands, we now know who stole my jewelry." Kennedy nodded and went to the pool bar to call the operator.

A gust of wind blew across the deck, and Oliver crossed his arms. "Vera, before you say something you will regret." Vera silenced him with her stare. "Check my cabin," he implored. "I didn't steal your jewelry. If I did, it would still be in my room. I was with you all day today and yesterday."

Kennedy walked back over to Vera and Oliver. "Mr.

Oliver, perhaps it would be best if you didn't say anything else," she said quietly.

The crowd, who had had a front-row seat to the unfolding drama, murmured amongst themselves, and when they heard the rattle of keys, they parted to allow the security director through. "What seems to be the trouble here?" he asked with his hands on his hips.

Vera pointed a finger at Oliver. "I want this man's cabin searched. I believe he is the one who stole the jewelry from my stateroom."

Mr. Phyfe looked at Vera and shook his head. "Now, there you go again, demanding that someone's room be searched. I think I should be the one to decide whether—"

Justin interrupted him. "He was in my aunt's stateroom on at least two occasions, had access to her key, and knew where she kept her valuables."

"Well, now, that *is* interesting." Mr. Phyfe pulled his notebook from his shirt pocket and flipped the pages. "And I have several other reports of missing jewelry. A few of the pieces reported missing happened before we docked in Juneau. Plenty of pawnshops only a taxi ride away from the port," he mused.

Kennedy's head shot up, and something in Vera's mind clicked. "I saw you get into a taxi when I was trying to find you to see if you wanted to go dogsledding with me, and when I finally caught up with you, you were getting out of one. You said you had to get rid of something." The cords along Vera's neck were taut with anger. "I hope you at least got a good price."

Oliver looked around at the growing crowd. "Vera, I can explain," he said, "I had a set of documents that had to be sent out."

Kennedy remembered seeing Oliver with the padded envelope when he had hurriedly asked her where he could find a taxi. She had difficulty seeing him as a thief and wondered how he would have taken Ronnee's bracelet and Helen's brooch.

"And what about the fact that you are a convicted jewel thief?" Vera snapped.

There was a gasp from the crowd, and Oliver looked like he had been punched in the gut.

Mr. Phyfe cleared his throat. "Sir, I think you need to come with me."

Several hours passed. The ship's generator would come on, and the lights would flicker along with the passenger's hopes that they could return to their cabins, only to have them flutter out moments later. Kennedy was emotionally exhausted. The worry over the need for an evacuation, the verbal barbs from LaVonda, and her concern over Vera weighed heavy on her heart.

Bert and Mila found Kennedy at the railing, and the three friends hugged. "Certainly not like our normal evening promenade get-togethers," Mila said.

Kennedy nodded and looked at them both grimly. "I'm sorry I drug you two on this trip. You only came because of me."

Mila cocked her head. "It wasn't all bad. We saw Bert's mom, went to that wild sculpture park in South Dakota, and toured a brothel museum in Idaho with creepy mannequins dressed in 1980s clothing. Those are not things you see every day, my friend, even in Poland."

Bert snickered. "And then there was Kennedy's hair disaster."

"Bert! We swore on a carton of ice cream that we would never speak about that night."

When they were in South Dakota, Kennedy decided to change her hair color on a whim. Buying some hair dye in the drugstore across the street from their hotel, she had gone into the bathroom and, forty minutes later, shrieked Mila's name. Mila opened the door, looked at Kennedy's reflection, and quickly slammed the door, telling Kennedy she would be right back. She quietly left the room, went next door, and whispered in Bert's ear. He grabbed his camera, and the two friends crept back into the hotel room. When Mila opened the door, Bert, the shutter speed set on continuous, pressed the button and took multiple photos of Kennedy's bright orange hair. Mila and Bert collapsed on the beds in laughter as the bathroom door slammed shut. An hour later, Bert opened the door and, in a truce, waved a white towel and slid the cowboy hat he had bought earlier in the day toward Kennedy.

"Are we really going to have to evacuate? What if I fall out of the lifeboat? You know how clumsy I am. What if there aren't enough life preservers?" he worried.

"Bert, my friend," Mila put her arm around his shoulders, "I want you to know something," and her tone was solemn. Kennedy was giving Mila a strange look which she ignored. "If the captain orders us to evacuate, and we somehow run out of life preservers…well…know that Kennedy and I will miss you and think of you often. We might even light a candle in remembrance and float it off to sea in a life ring."

Kennedy let out a snicker, and Bert looked at both women and shook his head, wondering again how he had been convinced to go on this cruise and how these two women were his best friends.

"You know," LaVonda said in a voice loud enough to be heard clearly by those around her. "My sapphire tiara is missing. I wonder if security will find it in his cabin," she sniffed. "I'm also missing my amethyst necklace and earrings." She stroked the heads of the dogs in her lap. "Were you terrified when that scary man came into mommy's room and robbed her?" Panting, the dogs stared back at her with their bug eyes. "My poor babies," she said to those around her, "you can see they are traumatized."

Mary Margaret, Irene, Helen, Marge, and Estelle shared worried looks.

Marge cleared her throat. "Ronnee, perhaps—"

Ronnee cut her off, shaking her head. "No, I'm sure of it. We were never around him. How would he have taken my bracelet? Or Helen's brooch?"

"But we *were* with him and Justin's aunt. Remember? On the second night of the cruise, the night you both lost your jewelry. We sat together to watch Kennedy's show," Estelle whispered. "And he offered to take our wraps to the coat check. Maybe that was when he stole Helen's brooch. She remembered having it at dinner."

Ronnee furrowed her brow. Estelle did have a point, but she didn't want to believe it.

Vera, who could hear the comments around her, could take no more. She got up, and Justin stood to follow her, but Vera shook her head. She needed to be alone.

Cameron and Trixie were snuggled under a blanket, ecstatic that the whispers about Diamond Jim's arrest and their appearance in the dining room had been replaced by the drama surrounding Justin's aunt. Cameron was sure Trixie's earrings and bracelet were buried under the mounds of clothing and shoes in her room. Trixie was a slob, and he would make a point of doing a thorough search.

"I just don't see how he could have taken Diamond Jim's watch," Cameron said. "It was never off his wrist, and we were never around the guy."

"That's not true," Trixie said slowly. "He brushed past us going down the gangway today right before Jim began to holler about his watch. Maybe Jim felt him slip it off his wrist. We were so focused on getting Jim into the hands of the police that we weren't paying attention to anything else. Thank goodness the other passengers were trying to get down the gangway and prevented Diamond Jim from going back up, or he could have ruined the whole thing."

"It almost was," Cameron corrected her. "That weird little cruise director heard what you said when you came out of the bedroom with the suitcase, yelling about the jewelry. The only thing that saved us was the alarm suddenly going off."

"So, what happens with Jim's watch if they find it in the guy's cabin?"

Cameron shrugged. "We tell the security guy that in the uproar of today's events, we didn't realize what happened, and as Jim's wife, he should give it to you. But we won't sell it until we know what will happen to Diamond Jim. We'll call it our rainy-day fund."

"I do love rainy days." Trixie snuggled under the blanket with a smile. "Rainy days mean rainbows, and everyone knows there is a pot of gold at the end of them."

A gust of wind blew across the deck, and Kennedy tucked a stray lock of hair behind her ear as she tried her best to comfort the passengers. Unfortunately, she had little to offer them other than a warm smile. With no electricity, the coffee and hot chocolate had run out along with the liquor, and the mounds of food from the reception had been reduced to crumbs.

When the passengers had been told to wait on the decks, most had taken the captain's orders in stride, believing the forced containment would not last long. There was food and drink and the potential for another show from Mother Nature. They would treat their confinement as an impromptu cocktail party. Groups congregated merrily, sharing stories and telling jokes as they ate and drank with a spirit of adventure. However, their enthusiasm waned as the hours stretched and the damp chill settled in. Muffled whispers had replaced the boisterous laughter as somber passengers huddled under blankets and towels, trying to stay warm.

She saw Otto conversing with Ronnee and her charges as they shivered under their blankets and motioned for him to follow her. "It doesn't look good for our stargazing tomorrow night," he said.

Kennedy looked at him blankly.

"You don't remember?"

"Oh, right, I'm sorry. It's not that I wasn't looking forward to it. Blame it on my worry about the passengers."

His radio chirped, and he listened to the message. "Where's yours?" he asked.

"Never got one." He pulled his from his belt and handed it to her. "With everything going on, you are going to need one. I'll get another one from the bridge."

Kennedy pointed at the five ladies with Ronnee huddled under their blankets. "Otto, could we ask the captain to allow us to bring people inside for a little while? Just long enough to warm up."

"Not a bad idea," Otto agreed. "Let me check with the captain."

A few minutes later, Kennedy saw the captain come out with a bullhorn inviting the passengers into Sedna's View. "I can't offer you anything hot, but I can get you out of the night air for a little while."

The grateful passengers lined up quickly and walked down the steps. Once inside, they rubbed their arms and stamped their feet to regain their circulation. A few took seats around the tables while others stood at the expanse of windows, looking out into the inky darkness.

Several decks below, Chuckie grunted as he tried again to open the fire dampers so the cool air could get to the overheated generator when a terrifying thought crossed his mind. Were the air and fuel supply gauges shut off completely? He couldn't remember. A trickle of fear snaked down his spine. As he made his way to the engine room, he noticed the air was much warmer than it should be. He wiped away a drop of sweat running down the side of his nose, and when he placed his hand on the door handle, he snatched it back and yelped. "Code Bravo to the engine room," he screamed into his radio. As he was hollering, the door blew open, and the ship lurched violently.

The powerful pitch of the ship caused the passengers in Sedna's View to look at each other in panic.

"Code Bravo team members to the engine room," the radio on Kennedy's hip squawked.

Kennedy saw the terrified faces around her, and several people began walking to the entry doors. She walked in front of them and crossed her arms. "Everyone," she said in a firm, clear voice, "we don't know what that was. I know we are frightened, but we need to stay here until the captain issues his orders."

The room was thick with tension as all eyes watched the entrance to the lounge with anxiety. Mila was comforting one of the guests when seven long blasts cut through the night air, followed by one short one, and Otto, his face pale, pulled the door to Sedna's View open and walked in to face the passengers. "We are in Code Kilo," he said in a steady voice, and Kennedy and Mila's heads jerked up. "All passengers, crew, and staff are to report to their muster stations. Ladies and gentlemen, this is not a drill," and then he was gone.

"Okay, everyone," Kennedy swallowed as anxious eyes fixed on her. "We are going to prepare to evacuate the ship. I need everyone to go to their assigned muster station. That is the area you went to for the lifeboat drill before we left Seattle. Please walk, do not run, and *do not* go to your cabins. You will be given a life jacket at your muster station, and you will remain there until you are escorted to your lifeboat by a member of the ship. Please listen to all directions given to you."

There was confusion on some of the faces in the room. In the gaiety of starting the cruise, they had not paid attention to the evacuation directions. At the time, they had likened it to the safety instructions given by flight attendants before their plane took off. Important words said but generally ignored.

Mila squeezed Kennedy's hand as she left Sedna's View for her muster station. "Be safe, you. I'll see you soon," Mila whispered and was gone.

When the others had gone inside to warm up, LaVonda had elected to stay where she was. She was cozy under the mound of blankets, and her dogs, curled up on top of her, let out quiet snores. LaVonda had contemplated unclipping their leashes which lay draped over the arm of the heavy metal lounge chair but decided against it, not wanting to disturb them. LaVonda looked around the deck, noticing that only a few passengers had elected to stay outside. She was mildly annoyed that Justin had not returned from his aunt's side. At the thought of Vera, a smug smile replaced LaVonda's pout, and a tiny giggle escaped her lips. The man escorting Justin's snobbish aunt on the cruise was an apparent jewel thief. "Serves her right," she said to the three dogs in her lap. "She looked down her nose at me, but who's having the last laugh now? She won't be able to walk past me with that snooty nose up in the air."

Suddenly, an explosion ripped through the air, and the dogs leaped off her lap, barking wildly and running in circles. LaVonda tried to get out of her chair but found herself imprisoned by the cocoon that enveloped her. Finally, violently throwing the blankets off, she scrambled out of her chair. Her eyes looked wildly around the deserted deck. "Quiet!" she screamed at the dogs, but the deafening blasts of the ship's horn

suffocated her yell. Seconds later, people raced past her, screaming and shouting. The three dogs, excited and scared at the loud noises and the people running past them, yapped loudly and ran under her, trying to find safety. Like a salmon trying to swim upriver, LaVonda watched the terrified passengers come toward her, and she was pushed and elbowed on both sides. People shouted as they ran by, but she couldn't understand their words. The ear-splitting blasts of the horn made her feel like she was hearing things underwater, but as one man ran past, she watched his lips form the word—muster station. An unintended shove as a passenger ran past her caused LaVonda to lose her balance, and she tumbled to the ground, hitting her head on the heavy metal arm of the chair.

Kennedy waited until the room was empty before making her way to the Starlight Lounge, the muster station she had been assigned to when she arrived. She saw the two entertainers, Malone and Evan, and several passengers already inside and explained what would happen next. Soon after, a crew member came in with lifejackets and a list of the assigned passengers for their muster station. Kennedy quickly checked off the names of those already in the lounge and positioned herself at the door to greet the others when they arrived and mark their presence.

Twenty minutes later, Kennedy saw Ronnee run past her wild-eyed and then race back when she recognized Kennedy. "I can't find the dears!" She gripped Kennedy's arm in terror. "I've looked everywhere. You have to help me. We got separated, and they aren't where they are supposed to be." She tried to pull Kennedy away from the doorway.

"No, you are going to come inside and sit down, Ronnee," Kennedy said sternly and encircled Ronnee's arm with her hand and pulled her inside. "What muster station were you assigned?"

"I don't remember, and it doesn't matter," she moaned. "I have to find them!" She tried to pull away from Kennedy.

"Ronnee! Look at me!" Kennedy gently shook Ronnee to

394

get her attention and slowly walked her backward into the lounge while speaking to her in a soothing tone. "Ronnee, listen to me. They are fine. They can't get off the ship without being on one of the lifeboats, and we have plenty of trained personnel to take care of them until they find you." Ronnee's legs hit the seat of a chair, and she sat down in a daze. "Right now, we have to follow the captain's orders, which means you are staying put. Running around searching for them will cause distractions we don't need. Now, let's get you a life jacket, okay?"

Ronnee nodded and then burst into tears, placing her hands over her face.

Satisfied that Ronnee was calming down and understood she could not leave to find her charges, Kennedy repositioned herself at the door. She looked down at the papers in her hand. A few passengers still needed to check in, and she figured that, like Ronnee, they had not gone to their assigned muster station. Otto would check with each area and crosscheck the master roster against the handwritten additions. Andreas walked by hurriedly with a grim look on his face. Then, seeing Kennedy, relief replaced his worried frown.

"We need you," he said. "There is no one in the main dining room other than the dining room manager and a crew member, and the passengers are a little on edge."

"A little?"

Andreas gave her a grin and shrugged. "Okay, freaked out."

"Things are under control in here. I just need to hand off my list. But where is J. Mitchell? He had the dining room with Tammy," she whispered. "I haven't seen them in hours."

Andreas shook his head. "I wish I could tell you. We've checked all of the decks. They're here somewhere."

Kennedy found the crew member she had been working with and gave him the list of those in the room, explaining what she had been asked to do. As she reached the entrance to the main dining room, she could hear the loud rumble of voices, reminding her of the first dinner on the cruise. Walking inside, the rumble became a roar, and she saw that Andreas had been correct. The passengers in the room were in panic mode. She saw fear on Jonny's face as he stood there, attempting to calm passengers, check off names, and hand out life vests.

"I should have paid more attention when we were doing the safety classes," he said when he saw her.

"Think of this as more on-the-job training," she joked. "Who knows? You might get some good comment cards out of this." Jonny gave Kennedy a confused look and then broke into a grin as some of his fear dissipated. She patted him on the back. "It's going to be okay. Now, let's bring some order to this room."

Kennedy took position by the podium and put her two fingers in her mouth to let out a shrill whistle. The noise in the room instantly died as the passengers recognized her. She gave them a warm smile. "Wow! I can still do that! I know everyone is upset, but we need to focus on putting our life jackets on and finding out who is in here. So, first, we're going to maintain a whisper voice level. Next, if you are unfamiliar with how to put on your life preserver, please allow one of us to help you. Lastly, once you have your life jacket on, I want you to form a line and check in at the podium." She turned to Jonny. "You are in charge of checking off names. Only check the name of the person in front of you. If they say another name, like a spouse, don't mark it. You have to see the passenger." Jonny nodded, and Kennedy began to walk through the room, helping the passengers don their life vests.

She saw Trixie angrily tugging the straps on Cameron's vest. "We should have gotten off in Ketchikan," she said coldly. "I would have had jewelry and cash with me. Now, who knows? The ship might sink along with everything I worked so hard for."

"You didn't want to, remember?" Cameron snapped back. "You wanted to stay on the ship and drink champagne."

"Well, you should have made me!"

The line at the podium quickly melted away, and

Kennedy was pleased to see that everyone was safely belted into their orange vests.

"What happens now?" Jonny whispered.

"We wait until we are told to line up and get on the lifeboat," she answered. Twenty minutes later, several crew members arrived. One spoke with Kennedy, and she went to the podium and let out another loud whistle.

"Ladies and gentlemen, I need you to form a single file line so we can take you to your lifeboats."

The passengers left the dining room, and Kennedy heard nervous whispers as they made their way outside. Getting the group on the lifeboats didn't take long, and only a few people were left. Satisfied that she could leave and see where she could help next, she began to walk toward the door to go inside and saw a strange apparition.

"Out of my way Miss Goody Goody." Kennedy was pushed against a metal column as the figure continued down the deck.

"Stop!" she hollered, scrambling to her feet. The figure had almost reached the lifeboat and turned around. Kennedy was stunned to see J. Mitchell standing there but more stunned at what she was looking at. His face was an orangish-yellow, and as he began to shout at her, a sudden gust of wind blew his hair up. For a split second, between the black cape that hid his body, his hair blowing wildly in the wind, and the hue of his face, Kennedy thought she was looking at an angry floating pineapple. "Why haven't you been helping the passengers?" She limped toward him. "And what's wrong with your face? It's orange."

J. Mitchell tugged at the neck of the cape he was wearing and pulled it off, revealing his sequined piano key suit. He balled up the cape, threw it at Kennedy, and pushed aside the last two passengers who were waiting to get on the lifeboat. "You are going to have to find another boat."

He stepped into the lifeboat and turned to face Kennedy. "You see, Kennedy, I need to be on one of the first boats to safety to share the story with the reporters waiting for us. They need a face, and I," he framed his face with his hands, "am that face." He took a seat. "And the orange on my face is a mask to give me glowing skin." He let out a little sigh. "As I'll be on camera in front of millions of people, I must look *fantabulous*. It's also why I went to my cabin and changed into my outfit." His dream-like face morphed into a pout. "I just wish I could have gotten my silver sequined dinner jacket, but it was in the theater's costume room, and the doors were locked for some reason. A look crossed his face. "Was it you? The sequined cape I wore for karaoke night was in there too. I saw how jealous you were of my performance. You probably locked the doors out of spite." Kennedy was bewildered at his accusation, and J. Mitchell's face instantly brightened as a thought crossed his mind. "It doesn't matter. After I tell the world about this heroic rescue at sea, the networks will beg me to be on their talk shows, and I'll have all the sequins I could ever ask for."

The lifeboat jerked and began to descend. Kennedy took her eyes off J. Mitchell just long enough to realize that the two passengers he had pushed aside were Cameron and Trixie, who were gaping at J. Mitchell in disbelief.

"Looks like we are on our way," J. Mitchell cackled as the boat lowered, and he waved his fingers at Cameron and Trixie. "And I can't wait to tell the story about you two!" Kennedy, Cameron, and Trixie leaned over the railing and watched the boat hovering over the water. "The May-December romance," he hollered and puckered his lips, "the kissing cousins, the groom getting arrested because the bride was in cahoots with his ex-wife, and of course, the wedding reception gone wild." J. Mitchell let out a frenzied staccato laugh, and it drifted up from the lifeboat. "Toodles!" he hollered.

Kennedy heard the clattering of heels behind her. "J. Mitchell," Tammy screamed as she marched down the deck. "J. Mitchell! Where are you? I can hear your stupid little woodpecker laugh. Don't you dare leave without me!" She stomped up to Kennedy. "Where is he?" she demanded.

Kennedy pointed down at the lifeboat now in the water.

"You little twit!" she hollered down at him and shook her

finger. "You left me!"

"Yeah, sorry, *not sorry*," J. Mitchell yelled back. "But thanks for making me look good for the camera." He said more, but they couldn't hear him as the drone of the motor cut off his words.

Tammy pushed herself away from the railing and turned around slowly with a look of mystification. "I can't believe that little idiot left me. After all I did for him. I laid out the plan, took him down to the salon so he would look good, and this is the thanks I get." Tammy looked down at her watch and let out a little snicker. "Although the little fruit will probably look like a goldfish when he gets to wherever they are going."

Kennedy gave Tammy a quizzical look.

"He's wearing a turmeric face mask. It can dye your skin orange if you don't take it off by a certain time." She gave Kennedy a little smile. "Well, this has been fun, but I need to find a lifeboat and get off this ship before it sinks."

"But what about the passengers?" Kennedy asked.

Tammy gave Kennedy an ingratiating smile. "Your problem, not mine, Miss Perfect. This is a cruise director thing, not a spa thing" She turned around and began marching in the opposite direction, her high heels echoing noisily against the ship's steel walls.

Kennedy stood there as her mind tried to make sense of

what had transpired. She was snapped out of her fog when she heard yelling and watched an empty inflatable life raft fall when someone released the wrong line.

"Trixie, Cameron," she shouted and motioned for them to come close to her. "Follow me." Trixie didn't budge, and Kennedy saw her face was a blank mask. Cameron also noticed the look and put his hands on Trixie's shoulders to push her forward. As they hurried down the deck, Kennedy's thoughts turned to J. Mitchell. She saw his pumpkin-colored face, and his words raced through her head. It would be a disaster for the company if anyone from the media interviewed him. She opened the door to the casino and saw passengers anxiously awaiting their turn to get on their lifeboats. She ushered Cameron and Trixie inside.

Cameron was still steering Trixie by the shoulders. "We aren't cousins," he said as they passed Kennedy. "We just—"

Kennedy held up her hand to stop him from saying more. "I need to have your names added to the list for this group," and she walked away to find the crew member in charge.

Mila had been assigned to the Quiet Distill, the ship's whiskey bar on deck eight. She had been surprised to see the five ladies without Ronnee and decided to stick close to them. Helping them into their life jackets, she made idle chit-chat to distract them. One of the crew members waved and mouthed a word to her. "Ladies," she said in a voice she used during spa treatments, "it's time. In a few moments, we will put you on a lifeboat that will take you to a rescue boat."

Helen motioned for Mila to come closer. "Will you be there?" she whispered.

Mila shook her head. "No, I'm sorry, but you will be safe."

"But what will we do without Ronnee?" Irene asked. "Do you know where Ronnee is?"

"She'll be so worried about us," Mary Margaret said. "She looks after us better than our children."

Marge tried to cross her arms over her life vest and shook her head back and forth. "I think we should wait. We shouldn't leave without her knowing."

Mila took a deep breath as she looked into their frightened eyes. "I'll make you a deal. You get on the lifeboat." They began to protest, and Mila held up her hand. "If Ronnee is still on the ship, I will tell her you are together. When you get to land, there will be an emergency center and people to help you." She squeezed each of their hands and pointed to the line forming. "Now, let's go find your lifeboat." They nodded, but Mila could still see the worry on their lined faces.

When the door to the casino opened, Kennedy was checking the straps on a passenger's life vest and looked up to see who was walking in. She breathed a sigh of relief when she saw Bert barrel in.

"Bert," she waved, and hearing Kennedy's voice, the dogs lunged forward, and their leashes flew out of Bert's hands. They yipped and pawed at her legs for attention.

"Kennedy," he dropped his backpack on the ground and hugged her fiercely. "I've been all over the ship. I'm not leaving your side. I don't want to get on a lifeboat without you and Mila. We are the three musketeers, remember?" he babbled.

"Bert! You have to get on the next lifeboat."

He clapped his hands together. "Sounds like a plan to me, but where is Mila?" he asked, looking around.

"I don't know." Bert craned his neck as he continued searching for Mila. "Bert! Listen to me." Kennedy shook his arms to get his attention. "You are getting on the next boat, but without me. I have to stay with the ship until everyone is evacuated."

A crew member came over and handed Kennedy a life jacket.

Bert wrinkled his brow in confusion. "Why? J. Mitchell is the cruise director. Remember? We're the hired help. So let him stay on the ship." Kennedy held out the life vest and slipped the openings around Bert's arms. "Isn't there something about women and children first?"

"Yeah, well, he fell into the children category," she said dryly. One of the dogs barked sharply to get Kennedy's attention, and she bent down to scratch their heads. "Where did you find them?"

"In the kitchen behind the pool bar. I stashed my camera bag in there when I was setting up to take photos of the northern lights. After the horn blast, I ran in there to get my bags and found them."

"LaVonda must be out of her mind," Kennedy said, standing up.

Bert looked down at the panting dogs. "I stopped in as many places as possible but didn't find her. But I did get some amazing photos of people in their muster stations."

Kennedy gave a hard tug on one of the straps on Bert's life vest. "You were supposed to go to your designated spot, not run around the ship taking photos, but I don't have time to yell at you about that right now." She gave him a steady look. "As soon as possible, call Alfred and tell him what happened. Tell him we need food and hotel rooms for wherever they take you." Bert nodded, listening to her instructions. "Bert, it's important that you tell him they cannot allow J. Mitchell to make any statements to the media. He's yellow."

Bert made a face. "That's a little harsh, Kennedy. I know the guy has been a jerk, but to call him—"

"Bert!" Kennedy snapped and looked him in the eye. "He's yellow, as in the color yellow," and she quickly relayed what had happened on the deck while Bert listened in amazement. "He said he needed to be on one of the first boats because he was the face of the company."

Bert blinked and blew out a breath. "Okay. Wow. Yellow. Okay, I'll call Alfred as soon as I can." One of the dogs let out a yip, and they both looked down. "What are you going to do about them?" Bert asked and groaned when he saw Kennedy's face. "Oh, man. I got them here. Isn't that enough? And you want me to call Alfred, remember? I can't take care of them and…" He sighed. "Fine. But how do you expect me to get them on a lifeboat and keep them from jumping out?" Kennedy looked at the backpack on the floor. "No, no, no, no, no. Kennedy, that's my new camera bag," he whined. "I just got it."

"And the perfect carrier for three small dogs. Alfred will buy you a new one, I promise. And if he doesn't, I will." She dumped the contents of the bag onto the floor. "Good grief, you don't need half of the stuff you have in here."

A crew member called out for everyone in the room to line up for the lifeboat. Kennedy placed the dogs inside the backpack and helped Bert put it on his back.

"But, what about you?" Bert asked as it dawned on him that he would get on a lifeboat without Kennedy or Mila in a few minutes. "Remember one for all?"

"Yep." Kennedy felt a sharp tingle in her nose, and tears smarted her eyes. She stooped to pick up his camera, remembering something he had said minutes before. "Take as many pictures as you can. Tonight, you are not the ship's photographer. Tonight, you are a hero and a photojournalist." She lifted the camera over his head, letting it lie against his chest. "And watch out for dangerous stairwells." Bert sniffed and tried to grin as a tear rolled down the side of his nose, remembering how he and Kennedy met. She had saved his life when his camera strap had wrapped around a railing and had cut off his oxygen supply. Kennedy checked the straps of his life vest once more and kissed his bruised cheek. "Call Alfred and take care of these beasts. I've spent the whole cruise walking them. When I tell LaVonda you have them, she'll probably yell at me for not putting them on their own special lifeboat with her jewelry." She grinned, "I also need to find Mila. She's probably in one of the empty muster stations making out with Andreas!"

While the passengers were being led to the lifeboats group by group, a Coast Guard rescue vessel arrived and pulled up alongside the *Malina*, and several members of the boat jumped onto the distressed ship.

"We got a call about a marshmallow roast," one of them shouted, and seeing Otto's confused face, he chuckled. "Do you still need help putting out the fire?" Otto nodded and motioned for them to follow him. As they trotted behind the safety officer, they saw the wild eyes of a few young staff members who looked scared and overwhelmed. Noticing there were still many people to evacuate, a seaman in an orange jumpsuit depressed a button on the radio at his shoulder and relayed a message. More help was needed. He motioned with his fingers at two of his team members, and they nodded and jogged off. "They are going to help get passengers on the lifeboats," he explained to Otto. "I have more people coming to help, and we'll get some rescue helicopters in the air if we need them." Relief flooded through Otto. The cavalry had arrived to save the day.

One of the men who had peeled off opened a door to find a room full of people in their life jackets. Andreas had been explaining the need to stay together and was startled when the door opened. He gave a quick nod to the man when he saw the Coast Guard insignia on his hat and jumpsuit. "Ladies and gentlemen, do whatever this man tells you to do."

They began shepherding the group out of the room, and a few minutes later, the passengers were helped onto a lifeboat, including a very distraught Ronnee. She had been in the Starlight Lounge, but after Kennedy left to assist in the dining room, she had slipped away, trying to find her traveling companions. When she was found searching for her clients on another deck, a crew member promptly escorted her to another muster station. "I should wait for the next boat," she said, getting out of the line. "My ladies, the ones I was traveling with, I should wait for them." Mila, who had just helped Mary Margaret, Estelle, Irene, Helen, and Marge onto their lifeboat moments before, heard Ronnee's voice. She walked over and nudged her back into the line.

"Your dears are fine," Mila said in a calm voice. "I put them on one of the lifeboats myself a few minutes ago, and two of our senior staff are on the boat with them, the dining room manager, Jonny, and our beverage director, Ismaeel."

"Ma'am," Andreas called out, motioning for Ronnee to step forward.

"This whole trip has been a mess," Ronnee, ignoring Andreas, sniffled. "Helen's brooch is missing, and my diamond bracelet is gone, and now this." She let out a heavy sigh. "Maybe I should stick to bus tours and cruises on the *Helio*. It's just been a disaster."

"Ma'am," Andreas called out impatiently, and Ronnee felt herself lifted in the air. Andreas had picked her up and handed her to another man in an orange jumpsuit.

"My goodness," she said, startled, looking into the man's

dark brown eyes, "you meet the most handsome men in disasters. I should have them more often. I'm Ronnee."

The grin he gave her caused her heart to pound. "Pleasure to meet you, ma'am, but I'd advise against using calamities to meet men."

One of the rescue team members was fighting with LaVonda as she tried to get off the lifeboat while other passengers were trying to board. "I can't go without my dogs," she wailed. "They are like my children."

The rescuer placed two hands on her shoulders and forced LaVonda back into her seat. "Ma'am, if we can find them, we will rescue them. But right now, I need to get a few more people on this boat, and you are causing unnecessary distractions." He pointed a finger at her. "Now sit down and don't move."

LaVonda shook her shoulders in indignation. "You can be sure I will call my congressman and tell him how you manhandled me and refused to save my dogs. He always takes my calls because I handle his travel arrangements, and he'll have you court-martialed!"

The man sighed inwardly and looked at LaVonda. The large gauze pad stuck to her forehead pushed her hair up. With the orange life vest around her neck, her mouth constantly open as she complained, and the fan of hair sticking up, he suddenly pictured her as one of the spiny wide-mouthed orange rockfish he had recently reeled in on a fishing trip. He turned away from LaVonda and motioned with his hand for the next person to board while he wondered how many years he had left in his enlistment.

Bert kept allowing others to go in front of him as they boarded the lifeboat, hoping Mila or Kennedy would join him. The first boat filled up quickly, and a crew member escorted Bert and a few other passengers to another lifeboat that still had room. When it was Bert's turn to get on, he grasped the hand held out to him. Before taking a seat, he removed his backpack and placed it on the floor. As soon as he sat down, he pulled the bag onto his lap and unzipped the top to give the dogs some fresh air. Three black snouts pushed out greedily, sniffing the air and licking his fingertips. Amused by their faces, he took a quick picture.

LaVonda raised her head when she heard the snuffling. The noise sounded just like her dogs, and she told herself her ears were playing tricks on her. She stood up again to complain to the man overseeing her boat when she heard a muffled bark come from a few rows behind her. She turned around and saw Bert with his hands inside the large backpack on his lap. Three furry faces poked out, panting.

"Oh, you wonderful, wonderful, wonderful boy," LaVonda cried out, crawling over the seats. When she reached

Bert, she threw her arms around him and planted a big kiss on his cheek, making him turn a shade of red, often only seen when the northern lights began to dance. "You are my hero." She pulled the backpack onto her lap, and the three dogs jockeyed positions to lick her face. "Oh, my babies, I was so worried about you," she crooned. She turned to Bert. "I knew you were an animal lover when you took their pictures on the first day, and now look, you've rescued them. When we get to land, I'm going to call the cruise line's corporate office and tell them about your heroism. They've always listened to me, except when I told them to fire that horrible little cruise director," she rambled. "I'm also going to have my congressman give you a medal or whatever they do for heroes!"

The rescuer on LaVonda's lifeboat, who had spent years training in search and rescue and had saved many lives, overheard her words and shook his head.

Mila and Kennedy finally found each other, and Kennedy shared that she had put Bert on a lifeboat with orders to call Alfred as soon as possible.

"Excuse me," a woman in an orange jumpsuit said. "Can you direct me to someone in charge?" Kennedy pointed at Otto, who was nearby.

"He's the closest unless you want to go to the bridge to find the captain. He's the safety officer."

412

"That will work. I need to give someone an update." She jogged over to Otto, and Kennedy and Mila joined them.

"The lifeboats have been successfully launched," she said. "By your count, how many people are left?"

Otto looked at the sheets in his hand. "About fifty plus the firefighting crew."

A few others from the Coast Guard boat joined them, including the lead rescuer who had boarded the ship first. He shook Otto's hand again. "I'm still waiting for my toasted marshmallow," he complained.

Otto grinned. "How about a beer in Ketchikan."

"We are very grateful for your assistance," Kennedy said. "We were lucky you were nearby."

One of the men flashed Kennedy a dazzling smile. "Semper Paratus," he said. "Always ready! Three hundred and sixty-five days a year."

"How will the firefighting crew get off the ship?" Kennedy asked.

"If we don't like them, we'll let them bob in the water." He saw the look on her face. "I'm kidding. We have boats nearby for them. The helicopter will pick the rest of you up on the top deck."

Suddenly the ship moved, and Kennedy sucked in a

breath. She had held it together for quite a while and only lost her composure when she said goodbye to Bert. "I guess we need to round everyone else up," she said.

"Already on it, ma'am," the lead rescuer said. "My people are scouring the decks, which means you three need to get up there and hold down the fort."

They followed the man to the promenade deck, and Kennedy saw several people already there, having been escorted upstairs by members of the Coast Guard team. She saw Vera standing at the railing with Justin, and Vera appeared to be yelling at her nephew.

The man in the orange jumpsuit pointed at Justin. "Your team found that one coming out of his cabin. He claimed he had to get something important from his room."

"I simply do not understand why you felt the need to go to your cabin," Vera railed. "You were told to report to your muster station, which was the same as mine, and you weren't there. This meant I had to explain, quite forcibly, that I was not getting on a lifeboat until we located you. And then, you were found coming out of your cabin? Help me to understand this, Justin!" She sighed exasperatedly and crossed her arms against the cold. "At least you were smart enough to get your jacket."

"I wouldn't want to be that guy," the man said, pointing at Vera and Justin.

"He deserves it," Andreas said, coming up to them. "He caused a lot of wasted manpower when his aunt couldn't find him."

Kennedy and the others turned their heads when they heard Vera begin to tongue-lash Justin again. They saw him try to move past Vera, but she blocked his path. "Don't you dare walk away when I am speaking to you. I've dealt with more than enough tonight!" They stared furiously at each other for a moment, and then Vera closed her eyes and sighed. The events of the evening suddenly felt like one-hundred-pound sandbags on her shoulders. She pinched the bridge of her nose. "Had you gone to our muster station, we could have been taken to safety by lifeboat. But you don't believe the rules apply to you, and now I'll be lifted into the air, trussed up in some ridiculous harness. It's undignified. Your parents will certainly hear about this."

"Wearing a harness wasn't so ridiculous or undignified earlier today," Justin spat out. "You thought it was fun when you wore it with your cruise ship lothario, and look how that turned out," he scoffed. "You can be certain I'll make sure *everyone* hears about what happened on this cruise when we get home." He gave her a look of amusement. "You may be out of a job by the time we get back."

Vera sucked in her breath and then let it out. "Well, where is it?" she asked in a defeated tone. "What was so important?"

Justin gave her a furious look. "Mr. Turner's ashes. That was what was so important. I didn't take them to the shrine. But I didn't want anyone to turn them over to you with our luggage when they tow the boat to land." He shrugged. "Honestly, it's not like the guy will know." Vera clenched her jaw as she digested Justin's explanation.

The man in the orange jumpsuit directed Kennedy and the other's attention to the opposite side of the deck. "You also have a prisoner, according to your director of security." He pointed at Oliver and Mr. Phyfe. They had not seen either man since Oliver was led away for questioning. "The security director wouldn't let us put him on a lifeboat. He said the other man was a dangerous criminal and had to be kept under watch." He gave the group a quizzical look. "Aren't these pleasure cruises?"

One of the rescuers walked over to check the harnesses that Oliver and Mr. Phyfe were wearing and tugged on the cable above their heads. Oliver was lifted first, without incident, and the moment Mr. Phyfe's feet left the ground, he began to scream and kick out his khakied appendages like a marionette.

"It's always the ones you don't expect," the lead rescuer said. The helicopter took off, and a second appeared.

Two slings landed with a thud on the deck, and the man who had harnessed Oliver and Mr. Phyfe motioned for Vera and

416

Justin to come forward. He put the harness around Vera and began to insert various clips into their holders. Then, he turned his attention to Justin.

"Whatever you have inside your jacket is making it hard to buckle the harness," he yelled over the whir of the helicopter blades. So, you either have to remove it or push it down. If it isn't necessary, take it out. We can get it to you in Ketchikan."

Justin shook his head vehemently.

"Justin, for the love of God, do whatever the man says so we can get off this ship," Vera shouted irritably. Justin reached under his jacket and pulled whatever was inside toward his hips. Then he put both hands in front of his stomach protectively.

"You can't do that," the rescuer hollered. "You have to keep your arms on the straps up here." He lifted Justin's hands from in front of his stomach and placed them onto the straps by his ears. "Don't move until they get you inside the helicopter. Got it?" The man yanked the ropes, and Justin gave him a dirty look, and a second later, he was lifted into the air.

Vera was thankful the nightmarish ordeal was almost over. She could deal with the fallout when they landed. Looking up, Vera saw that Justin had almost reached the helicopter's landing skid. He would be safely inside soon, and she would be next. Vera suddenly heard a scream from above and jerked her head up. She drew her brows together, wondering what Justin could be yelling about. She realized she would find out soon enough as she felt the ropes tighten and her feet left the ground.

Justin had almost reached the safety of the helicopter when the item inside his jacket slipped out. Kennedy and the others watched as what looked like a small paper bag dropped to the deck with a hard splat while a trail of dust particles followed it down like the tail of a comet. Kennedy rushed over to retrieve the bag. It was obviously important to Justin, and she would ensure he got it in Ketchikan. But as she got closer, her brow furrowed. What was lying on the deck didn't make sense. It was nothing more than a flattened but full vacuum cleaner bag. She knelt to pick it up, and, as she did, course gray silt poured out onto the deck from a large rip on the underside, followed by a clatter. Kennedy quickly turned the bag sideways to stop the flow, but not before three items tumbled onto the deck: a filthy chandelier earring snagged on the tine of a bejeweled hair comb and a man's watch covered in dust.

A few hours later, Alfred's deep sleep was interrupted by his phone ringing. He answered it, not recognizing the number or the voice on the other end of the line.

"Alfred, it's Bert Benson from the *Helio,* but right now,

I'm on the *Malina*. Well…not exactly. Everyone is fine…well, no, actually, nothing is fine. It's a huge mess. There was a fire and some explosions, and everyone had to get on a lifeboat. And J. Mitchell is the color of a pumpkin or a pineapple. I can't remember which one she told me, but J. Mitchell told Kennedy he would be the company's face. And Kennedy and Mila are still on the ship, and I don't know if they got off," he rambled and took a deep breath. "I guess what I mean to say is…Alfred, there's been a problem."

Sunny Dayz Cruise Line

THE MALINA

DAY FIVE

~~AT SEA~~

KETCHIKAN, ALASKA, USA

U.S. COAST GUARD STATION

KETCHIKAN POLICE STATION

The last rescue helicopter landed at six o'clock carrying Kennedy, Mila, Andreas, Otto, and Captain Volare. As they walked across the tarmac, Kennedy felt her jacket vibrate and realized it was her phone. She had placed it in her pocket to take pictures of the northern lights the night before, but that seemed like a lifetime ago. She pulled it out and pressed the screen to disconnect the call. She wasn't ready to speak to anyone yet.

"Corporate?" the captain asked, and Kennedy could hear the fatigue in his voice. "I'm afraid I will spend most of the day answering their questions." He turned his head to Otto. "Mr. Armitage, were there any injuries other than Mr. McDermott? I know he suffered from smoke inhalation and burns when we had the second explosion."

"No fatalities and only a few minor injuries, sir. Chuckie, I mean, Mr. McDermott is at the medical center," Otto replied, "along with J. Mitchell." The captain looked at him questioningly. "He was taken to the hospital for observation. Apparently, he was speaking erratically. He kept babbling about being the face, and those on the rescue boat thought he might be having some kind of allergic reaction with hallucinations. I understand his face was the color of a goldfish. Oh, and he was wearing his sequined piano key suit. I'm just glad none of the reporters saw him when they arrived in Ketchikan."

The captain stopped walking and fought hard to keep a stern face as he pictured a talking goldfish wearing a sequined suit. "The hospital is probably the best place for him. He seems to be as emotionally stable as a cheap do-it-yourself bookcase which is not what you want in a cruise director." He nodded at a group of people waiting in front of a hangar. "Before we get to *them*, can someone tell me about the passenger who may have been stealing jewelry?"

Kennedy spoke up, "What I can tell you, sir, is that a vacuum cleaner bag containing jewelry fell from the jacket of one of our VIP passengers when he was airlifted into the helicopter."

The captain looked at Kennedy for a moment and then up at the sun. "I know I should ask about the vacuum cleaner bag, but I'm too tired. Where is the jewelry now?"

"When I saw what was inside, I gave it to the Coast Guard and explained that we had several reports of missing pieces during the cruise. They said they would radio ahead and alert the police to detain the passenger for questioning and deliver the evidence." The captain nodded thoughtfully, and the group began walking again. "Captain, I know they," she inclined her head at the group of people they were walking toward, "want my statement, but I need to check on our passengers and do a little damage control. These are travel agents and other VIPs."

The captain nodded. "I'll take care of it. Miss Reeves. You will always have a soft and snuggly place in my heart," he chuckled, and Kennedy blushed, remembering the sticker he had pulled from her dress. "My friend on the *Helio* is fortunate to have you as his cruise director, and I was even luckier to have had you on this cruise," he paused, "such that it was. I am not sure what the corporate office will do now." He let out a sigh and washed his face with his hand.

They reached the group standing in front of the hangar. "Captain," a man in a suit said and held out his hand, "you are the last five people we need to debrief. It seems you've had quite an exciting cruise: a fire and explosion, a jewelry heist, and a groom who got married at your port of call in Juneau only to be arrested yesterday in Ketchikan."

Mila tried to stifle a yawn. "Sorry, but if you want anything coherent out of me, I'm going to need coffee. In fact, my coffee is going to need coffee."

"It's pretty awful, ma'am. It's been likened to motor oil."

"Then we may have to skip forward and go straight to wine," Mila yawned.

After giving their statements, Kennedy and Mila were given a ride to the hotel where Bert and the others had set up a command center to help the passengers. When Bert saw them walk into the lobby, he jumped up from where he was sitting and ran to them.

"I am so glad to see you," he hugged them both fiercely.

"You need to call Franklin and Rosemary. Tony is freaking out and wants to talk to one of you. And Kennedy, please call Alfred. He is beside himself. He says he has tried to call several times, but it goes straight to voice mail. But can we *please, please, please* get back to Florida and the *Helio*? I miss our boring little ship and my mundane life taking canned photos of our passengers."

"Excuse me," Mila said. "Did you say boring ship? Have you been on the *Helio* lately?"

Bert shrugged. "Well, okay, we've had a kidnapping and a murder, but we haven't had to evacuate."

"Did anyone else call, Bert?" Kennedy asked. Mila and Bert knew exactly who Kennedy was referring to, and their hearts broke for her when he shook his head.

Kennedy let out the mental breath she had been holding. "I need to take a shower." She paused, and a look of panic crossed her face. "I have no clothes. No one has anything other than what they were wearing last night."

"Easy lass," Cormac's brogue called out as he walked over to her with a grinning Jonny and Ismaeel. "Everyone has been taken care of." He handed Mila and Kennedy a bag. "The store owners heard what happened and sent things to the hotels, and the hotels called in their staff to help launder clothing. You might see a lot of these T-shirts," he grinned and pointed at the matching shirts he, Jonny, and Ismaeel were wearing. Kennedy looked around the room and suddenly noticed that most of the people in the lobby were wearing purple shirts featuring two salmon playing guitars. "A souvenir from a cruise they won't forget anytime soon," Cormac laughed. "And before you ask, the corporate office is sending a team to deal with the passenger's luggage."

Kennedy let out a sigh of relief, and two police officers passed the group and stopped at the large silver urn of coffee that had been set up in the lobby.

One of the cops placed a paper cup under the urn's spigot. "Glad that's over. That woman was a real piece of work. I can't imagine having to work for people like that every day. What an attitude. I think I like dealing with obnoxious drunks and breaking up bar fights now."

The other cop snickered. "Do you think that good-looking woman who was waiting on her earrings will still be there?" His co-worker looked at him strangely. "The one asking about the man's watch?" he prodded, and a look of recognition came across his partner's face. "She's the wife of the funny little guy in the holding cell," Kennedy heard him say.

"The one who points his fingers like pistols and dances the jig? Get out of here!"

"That's what I heard."

The other cop shrugged and poured himself a cup of coffee. The conversation between the two men drifted away as they walked out of the hotel and onto the street.

"Well, on that note, do we have any updates on our newlyweds?" Kennedy asked.

Jonny cleared his throat. "We don't know anything about Diamond Jim, but Trixie Dubois, I mean, Adair, is at one of the hotels down the street. When they got here last night, she and her cousin were having a huge argument. He wanted to get on the first flight out of Ketchikan, but Mrs. Adair was adamant about staying here. She wanted to know where the *Malina* would be towed so she could get her luggage. When Cormac told her we could have it packed and shipped to her, she freaked out and said she had to get her stuff herself." Jonny wrinkled his brows together. "I thought brides were only supposed to be nutty before the wedding, not after."

Kennedy heard her phone chirp. She pulled it out and sighed when she saw the screen, "Alfred," she said and pressed the red button to decline the call.

"You are going to have to talk to him at some point, Kennedy," Bert said. "He's trying to piece together what happened."

"I think we all are," Chef Sha Finch said. She pulled Mila and Kennedy in for a bear hug and kissed them on the temple. "Hello, my friends! Do we know how to end a cruise or what?" she grinned. "At least we went out with a bang!" The group groaned at Sha's pun.

"Where is Jordan?" Kennedy asked, and Sha rolled her eyes.

"In the kitchen making comfort food. When we saw J. Mitchell right before they loaded him into the ambulance, Jordan said she had a strange desire to make curried chicken."

"Has anyone heard from Tammy?"

"Oh, boy, did we ever! She was waiting for a taxi to take her to the airport, and guess who she was with?" Sha's eyes danced merrily. "The king of khaki!" Sha, Mila, Kennedy, and Bert began to laugh hysterically.

"I think we missed something somewhere," Ismaeel said to Jonny and Cormac. "The king of khaki?" The group burst into laughter again at his question.

"We need to find these people some beds, Ismaeel. They're slap-happy," Jonny said.

Mila glanced up and saw Andreas and Otto speaking with the front desk agent. She let out an exaggerated yawn. "Well, I am feeling a bit tired." She walked over and stood next to Andreas. "Fancy meeting you here. Do you come here often?"

"Only when I catch a flight to Ketchikan by helicopter after my ship has an explosion," he said with a wolfish grin. "What about you?"

"Strangely, the same."

Kennedy smirked and let out a silent chuckle as she watched them depart and get onto the elevator. "I'll be right back."

"I'm surprised to see you and Andreas so soon," she said to Otto, who was still standing at the desk.

Otto turned and gave her a tired smile. "The captain had us give our statements right after you and Mila and told us to get some rest, but I want to check on the crew and staff." The desk agent slid a keycard and piece of paper over to Otto, and he signed the document and handed it back to her. He turned to Kennedy. "Since you aren't with the *Malina* anymore, I wondered if you would like to have dinner?"

"Well, sure, if we can get Mila and Andreas to—"

Otto shook his head. "I mean you and me. We don't work together anymore, and I did promise to show you the constellations."

"Oh," Kennedy stammered, looking around the lobby.

"If you are too tired, I understand," he said in a rush.

Kennedy took a breath and looked up at Otto. "No, that would be great and a nice change from the last few days."

"What? You didn't like the elementary school cafeteria food?" he let out a nervous chuckle, which brought a small smile to Kennedy's tired face. "There are some good restaurants within walking distance. Meet here at seven?" Kennedy could hear the hope in Otto's voice.

"Sure, sounds great."

Otto gave Kennedy a long look. "See you at seven," and he walked toward the elevator.

Kennedy returned to where Bert and the others stood. "Okay, I'm going to get cleaned up and check on some of the passengers," she said.

"You need a lie-down, girl," Cormac said. "You've been up for over twenty-four hours. The passengers are fine."

Bert sighed and shook his head at Cormac. "She won't rest until she has checked on each of them. Kennedy is our resident mother hen on the *Helio*."

"Kennedy Reeves!" LaVonda's loud voice carried across the lobby as she came toward Kennedy and the others like a bulldozer, and Kennedy noticed the large bandage plastered to her forehead.

"I was going to skip her," she said under her breath.

"I think I have something to check on in the kitchen," Sha said.

Jonny gulped. "I've got to go help some passengers."

"We'll help," Cormac and Ismaeel said in unison.

"Cowards," Kennedy hissed to their turned backs, and she grabbed Bert's arm as he was also trying to get away. "Please don't leave me. I need backup in case I lose it." She plastered a smile on her face before turning around. "Yes, ma'am, how may I help you?"

"I haven't seen J. Mitchell, but I suppose I can tell you." She pointed at Kennedy's hand, which was holding a plastic bag. "Although, again, you have nothing to write on or with. Honestly, you just don't learn, do you?" she sighed. "I want someone to know how wonderful this young man is." She leaned forward, planting a big kiss on Bert's cheek. Then, she turned her head to scowl at Kennedy. "My dogs could have perished on the ship. No thanks to you. But this sweet boy," she beamed at Bert, "rescued them and kept them safe until he found me." LaVonda picked up each dog and placed them in Bert's arms. The dogs squirmed and let out low growls as LaVonda spoke loudly about the promotion and reward that Bert deserved. "The corporate office will listen to me this time!" She poked her finger at Kennedy. "He was a true hero. My babies and I might

431

have died if it hadn't been for him. I should have known this cruise would be a disaster when I saw you on the first day. It had catastrophe written all over it."

"I'm happy you and your dogs are safe, Ms. Taylor, and I am sorry the cruise took an unfortunate turn of events. Were you able to recover your jewelry?"

LaVonda sniffed. "I'm glad you brought that up. The officers told me I could pick it up at the police station when they took my statement, but I'm sure it is terribly far away." She put a hand near the bandage on her forehead. "I'm quite fragile after everything that happened. To think I was in the company of a jewel thief during the cruise. It makes me wonder what kind of people Sunny Dayz allows on their ships. And then the explosion. Do you know I was almost thrown from the ship? After everything that happened and the poor customer service, I highly doubt I will write an article promoting this cruise. My experience has just been terrifying."

She narrowed her eyes and shook her finger at Kennedy. "As an assistant cruise director, albeit a poor one, you should have had the foresight to pick up my jewelry from the police station, have it cleaned, and then brought to me personally, especially as I am one of your VIP VIPs." LaVonda let out another dramatic sigh and clucked her tongue. "I cannot believe I have to continue to tell you how to do your job, but then again, you just aren't a very good cruise director, are you?" She took a breath. "I had hoped you would improve under J. Mitchell, but I can see it's hopeless. Perhaps when I call the corporate office to commend Bert, I'll reiterate my demand to have you fired."

"Ms. Taylor!" Bert thundered, causing LaVonda to turn to him with her eyes wide and her thickly crayoned brows raised to the middle of her forehead. "You are not going to be a bully anymore, and if you insist on being one, you will have to deal with me. Kennedy has just arrived in Ketchikan, having ensured that everyone on the ship was evacuated safely. *She* insisted that I bring your dogs with me on the lifeboat because *she* knew you would be distraught and was worried about your well-being. Although why I can't imagine as you have been nothing but petty and mean toward her." He drew a breath and continued, "If you want your jewelry, I suggest you take yourself to the police station and pick it up yourself!"

LaVonda's eyebrows were now close to her hairline. Bert placed the three, now silent, dogs on the ground. He thrust the leashes at Lavonda. "To get to the police station, go outside, turn onto Water Street, and make a right on Grant." LaVonda began to shuffle away slowly, turning around to look at Bert with every few steps. "And I suggest you write a glowing piece about your cruise for the Casual Living Network *and* a letter to the corporate office commending Kennedy!" he called out.

Kennedy turned her head and blinked at Bert. They were both silent as they watched LaVonda depart the hotel.

"I think I've had too much coffee this morning." He shook out his hands and let out a large breath. "What did I just do?" he said slowly. "I'm suddenly feeling very weak." He gripped the arm of the sofa and sat down.

"I believe it's called standing up to a bully."

"Nooo, I'm the kid who is scared of his own shadow. The one the wimpy kids beat up after school." He pointed at the bruise on his cheek where his camera had hit him two days earlier. "Even inanimate objects take swings."

Kennedy sat down beside him and nudged his arm. "Look at all you did in the last twenty-four hours. You carried those dogs to safety in a backpack, got things organized here so the passengers could get home, and turned LaVonda Taylor from a snarling, fire-breathing dragon into a gecko. Are you sure you aren't a superhero?"

He chuckled. "Well, have you ever seen Superman and me at the same time?" He let out a yawn. "I sure hope there are no other heroic deeds I need to perform today. I'm exhausted."

"I wouldn't put your cape away just yet," Kennedy grinned. "I think I hear a beer calling. It's trapped inside a bottle and needs to be rescued."

A few hours later, an exhausted Kennedy found herself on a tram taking her to the last hotel she needed to visit. She was the only person in the car, and she relished the silence as it crept up the mountain, giving her a view of Creek Street and the harbor. The passengers she had visited had been gracious, assuring her they would not hold what happened against the cruise line and felt the Alaskan trips should be restarted. Several mentioned that they would now explain to their clients the importance of paying attention during the muster drill.

As the tram rose, Kennedy took in the view outside the window and smiled sadly. She was sure she would have received a message from Omar by now. He would have heard about what happened, and it spoke volumes to her that he had not reached out. With no word from him in months, it was time to put him in a tiny box and close the lid. She wondered if she was doing the right thing by going to dinner with Otto and smirked when she heard Mila's exasperated voice in her head telling her to stop overanalyzing and enjoy the distraction. "Put your toe in the pool, Kennedy," she heard her say. "It's dinner, not a midnight swim in the swamp with alligators."

She got out of the tram and felt the beginning of a smile cross her face in anticipation of the evening's plans. She walked into the hotel lobby and paused when she saw Vera sitting near the large rock fireplace, staring at the fire.

"How long has she been sitting there?" she whispered when she reached the front desk.

The agent looked kindly at Kennedy. "She was there when I came in. According to the night manager, she arrived around five this morning, sat in that chair, and hasn't moved. I was afraid to disturb her."

"Where can I get some coffee?"

"I can get it for you."

Kennedy nodded, and the man returned a few moments later and handed Kennedy a heavy white mug.

"Vera," Kennedy said softly. Receiving no response, she said Vera's name louder this time, and Vera looked up. The impeccably dressed and coiffed woman who could command a room with a single snap of her fingers was now the husk of the vibrant woman Kennedy knew. Her flawless ivory complexion had hard lines etched into it, and the laser-like eyes that could slash and burn with a single glance were now dull and lifeless.

"Kennedy," Vera exhaled.

Kennedy handed her the steaming cup, and Vera wrapped her hands around it and stared into the dark brown brew. She took the chair across from Vera, and both women stared at the flames in the fireplace.

Finally, Vera broke the silence. "I am so embarrassed. I don't know what to say. I heard Justin yelling about something, but when I got in the helicopter, he wouldn't speak. He just looked out of the window. Not that it mattered. I couldn't hear anything anyway with all the noise. When we arrived in Ketchikan, they took Justin off first, and he was whisked away in a police car."

Vera's shoulders sagged, and she was quiet for a few moments. "He'll stay here in custody until the FBI arrives. I need to call Justin's parents, but I don't have the energy. They will be furious to learn he will be facing federal charges. What he did can't be swept under the rug."

"Vera, did he offer any reason?"

The woman sitting in the chair let out a ragged sigh. "Justin was well-liked in our circle. He was charming, witty, and fun to be around. Over the years, my husband would mention something about cleaning up after Justin, but honestly, I listened with half an ear. I tolerated his side of the family and had no interest in them. I never understood until today how Justin always had money to burn when he constantly floated from job to job. I assumed his parents were still giving him an allowance." She laid her head back on the chair and stared at the ceiling. "He even confessed to taking jewelry from some of our...our clients," she said painfully.

"Oh, Vera," Kennedy murmured.

Vera shared how she had arrived at the police station in a fury, demanding explanations. Having recently witnessed Vera's rage when she discovered her jewelry missing, Kennedy felt sorry for the police officers who had experienced the tornado of her wrath and sharp tongue. Vera told Kennedy how the police chief had quickly ushered her into his office and, explaining the charges that Justin was facing, showed her the evidence.

"We're questioning him now," the police chief said.

Vera looked evenly at the chief. "Take me to him," she replied icily.

She turned her attention back to Kennedy. "He took one look at me and confessed to everything."

Vera thought back to the room. Four metal chairs sat around a scratched wooden table as a fluorescent bulb overhead flickered and emitted long buzzes. The officers had stepped outside to get coffee, and she and Justin were alone.

"How did you do it, Justin?" Vera asked, her voice devoid of emotion. "You were with people the entire time."

He held up his hands, shackled to the table, and twiddled his fingers. "Magic," he winked. When he saw Vera's perplexed expression, he explained. "When I was ten, I got a magic set for

Christmas, and it changed my life. The sleight-of-hand trick was my favorite, and the grown-ups thought it was funny when I made things disappear. No one said anything when they didn't reappear, and asking would have been considered gauche." He gave a low chuckle. "I never did get the hang of making things reappear." He took a breath and continued. "But I kept practicing and graduated from making cards and coins vanish to smaller, more valuable items. I was a teenager by then and had stopped performing my little party trick, but I still used my skills. Lifting a piece of jewelry at a party was a cakewalk because, after a few cocktails, the person thought the piece had slipped off and was lost or forgot they even wore it."

Vera stood up from her chair in front of the fireplace. As she paced back and forth, she explained how Justin had removed LaVonda's tiara when she was bent over the railing fighting seasickness and kept her room key after escorting her to her cabin, the way he slid Ronnee's bracelet off her arm by staging an accident, and caused the table to wobble so he could slip Trixie's lanyard containing her keycard into his pocket while she and Cameron cleaned up the spilled drinks.

Vera's thoughts went back to the room with the buzzing lights. "Lifting Diamond Jim's watch was my pièce de resistance," Justin said proudly. "I wanted that watch so badly I could taste it, and for a few hours, it was mine. It's all in finding the opportunity, Aunt Vera, and honestly, I hadn't planned to steal anything on this trip." Justin gave her a boyish grin and nodded his head to the side. "Well, that's not true. LaVonda's tiara practically begged me to take it. Then Oliver came along. And let me be honest, in the beginning, I was upset that you were spending so much time with him. I had planned to use the cruise as a way to convince you I was right for the company. You see, stealing jewelry from dead people requires no finesse, and the deceased's family is so wrapped up in their grief that they don't notice if something goes missing." He watched his aunt shudder in disgust. "Then, when Inez sent the information about Oliver's relative with the same name, it was like an ironic, funny gift. I had the perfect scapegoat." He let out a chuckle. "You believed me. And planting the earring was easy since I had his jacket. I simply transferred it from my pocket into his."

Vera stared at the young man sitting across from her. "I don't find your sense of humor amusing." She was quiet while she mulled things over in her head. "Justin, I still don't understand something. They wouldn't have found anything in Oliver's room, and when they intercepted the package he said he mailed in Juneau, it would have contained nothing more than paperwork."

Justin tilted his head and looked at Vera kindly. "But *we* would have been long gone before anyone knew what was in that package. By that time, Aunt Vera, your missing jewelry would have been an unpleasant memory tied to your shipboard

Casanova kept just between us because you would announce that you were grooming me to take over the company in exchange for my silence over such an embarrassing matter."

Kennedy sucked in a breath at Vera's last statement. "He was going to blackmail you?"

"Charming, isn't he? After he told me about his plans to blackmail me, I got up and walked out. I couldn't be in the room with him for another second. He had framed an innocent man and almost got away with it."

"So, now what?" Kennedy asked.

Vera crossed her arms. "Well, the good news is the jewelry he stole will be returned to the rightful owners." She paused, searching her mind for the answer to an elusive question. "I still cannot fathom how or why he put the pieces in a vacuum cleaner bag. I was so angry with Justin about his plans to blackmail me that I forgot to ask that question."

"I think I can clear that up," Kennedy answered uncomfortably. She explained how she had told the *Malina* staff to bend over backward for Vera and accommodate whatever she requested without question. "When Justin called the guest services desk the night before we docked in Juneau and requested a vacuum with an unused bag, our executive housekeeper brought one up immediately. He assumed, given the nature of your business, it was to clean up a spill from someone's ashes." She looked at Vera. "Honestly, I didn't think anything of it either."

Vera stared into the flames in the fireplace as she pieced things together. "Minutes before we evacuated, Justin and I argued. I was angry about the helicopter and demanded to know what he had gone back to get when he was caught coming out of his cabin. When he admitted it was the ashes of a client, I was furious. Justin assured me at breakfast that he had delivered them. Going so far as to make up a story about touring the shrine with the priest."

A look of stunned comprehension came across her face. "I assumed what was inside his jacket was the scattering tube." She turned to Kennedy. "But he needed a way to hide the jewelry. If he had removed his jacket, he had a plausible excuse for the lumpy bag—he had accidentally spilled the ashes of a client during the cruise. No one would dare look inside." Vera shook her head in disbelief. "He almost got away with it. His only mistake was allowing it to fall out of his jacket." She let out a heavy sigh. "I'll call the police station and tell them not to get rid of the bag. The least I can do is return to Juneau and take care of the client's last request."

Emotionally exhausted, Vera sat back down. "One good thing about the evacuation is that I don't have to face Oliver. I'll send him a note of apology if I can find something in this town that doesn't have a fish or a bear on it," she huffed. "Would you

442

deliver it for me?"

Kennedy nodded, and as she reached into her jacket to pull out her list of where the passengers were lodged, she caught her breath. "Vera," she whispered, moving her eyes to the left. Oliver was staring at Vera from the entrance of the hotel bar.

Vera's eyes followed Kennedy's. "He can't see me like this," she whispered. "I refuse to apologize to him wearing this ridiculous T-shirt. Despite everything that has happened, including my nephew trying to frame him for theft, I still have a modicum of decorum." Vera looked at Kennedy. "Quick, give me your jacket."

Kennedy knit her brows together. "My jacket?"

"Are we playing twenty questions?" Vera hissed. "Yes, give me your jacket. If I have to apologize, at least I won't be standing there wearing a ridiculous purple shirt with two fish on it."

Vera had almost gotten the jacket zipped up when Oliver reached them.

"Oliver," Vera turned to face him, and Kennedy crept away to the front desk.

"Would you please call Ronnee Barrett's room?" Kennedy asked. "She's traveling with five other ladies."

"Oh, those ladies are a hoot!" the desk agent grinned. "I

don't need to call Ms. Barrett's room. You'll find them in there."
He pointed to the bar entrance where Oliver had been standing
moments before.

Kennedy entered the hotel bar and found Helen, Mary
Margaret, Irene, Marge, and Estelle sitting at a table drinking
Bloody Marys. "Okay, sweetie, I must go. I love you too!"
Estelle said into her phone.

"Ladies, I wanted to check on you and offer my most
sincere apologies for what happened on the cruise," Kennedy
said sincerely.

"You're sorry? Why?" Estelle asked, placing her phone
on the table. "We had a delightful cruise. Of course, we were
frightened by the explosion and getting on the lifeboats, but
everyone took wonderful care of us."

"I've heard from every single one of my children and
grandchildren!" Marge offered.

Mary Margaret pointed to her T-shirt. "And we have
plans to wear our matching shirts on the next bus tour. Our tale
should double Ronnee's bookings!"

"Oh, and then there is our next cruise," Irene said
excitedly. "Ronnee's taking us on a Caribbean cruise to make up
for this one. We told her it had to be your ship so we could watch
your show again." She leaned forward. "Ronnee told us all of
those stories are true. Do you still talk to the warlock? What

about the guy wearing the ankle monitor—is he in jail?"

"Kennedy," Ronnee called out, joining the table. "I didn't see you come in."

"I doubt you would have seen her if she had marched in with a brass band behind her," Mary Margaret rolled her eyes, causing the ladies to cackle. Ronnee had been at the bar talking quite animatedly to a man in a Coast Guard uniform.

"Well, I had to thank him for saving my life," Ronnee turned, giving the man a little wave. Then she returned her attention to the group, blushing. "We have dinner plans tonight."

Her statement caused crows of laughter and a slew of raucous comments from her traveling companions. Finally, when they had settled down, Kennedy asked if the police had contacted them. Ronnee shook her head quizzically. "Why would they want to talk to us?"

"We found your missing bracelet and Helen's brooch during the evacuation."

The ladies stared at her in stunned silence, and then they heard Helen sniffle. "It was?" her voice just above a whisper. "How?"

Kennedy hesitated. "Let's just say it fell from the sky."

Ronnee stood up and held out her hand to Helen. "Helen, would you like to go now? We can get your brooch and come right back to celebrate."

Helen nodded, dabbing her eyes.

"Kennedy," Ronnee began as they got up from the table, "I know we didn't get to talk about the group I want to book on the *Helio*. I had planned to do it today when we were at sea, but now is as good a time as any."

Kennedy saw the crestfallen look on Helen's face. "Why don't you send me a message with the details." The ladies shuffled out of the room, and Ronnee and Kennedy strolled behind them.

"You are going to love this group. They need a place to take a few continuing education classes and blow off some steam. So, I thought a cruise would be perfect."

"Sounds great! What do they do?"

"Oh, I didn't tell you? They are personal injury lawyers. My friend Copper is in charge of the meeting this year." Ronnee saw Kennedy's panicked face. "What's wrong?"

"It's a group of personal injury attorneys, Ronnee…on a cruise ship. The whole scenario screams disaster, and I can already see the lawsuits coming."

Ronnee waved her hand. "Don't worry. I'll have them sign disclosure forms before they set foot on the ship. And you are going to love their names: Bennie the Brawler, Strongarm

446

Sam, Ponytail Paul—"

Marge appeared at the doorway and saw that Ronnee was still talking to Kennedy. She marched over and grabbed Ronnee's arm. "Put it in an email. Helen's probably halfway to the police station, and they won't be able to hear her when she starts talking." She squeezed Kennedy's hand with her other one. "Goodbye, Kennedy, and thanks for a cruise we won't ever forget."

On her way back to the hotel, Kennedy stopped by the police station and asked to speak to the officer in charge. After explaining that the bag with the jewelry had also contained ashes to be interred in Juneau, he assured her he would keep it secure in the evidence locker until Vera could pick it up.

Closing the door to her hotel room, she exhaled and realized she had time to call Alfred before meeting Otto for dinner. She pulled out her phone, and when he answered, she apologized for not calling him immediately. Her priority, she explained, had been to make sure the passengers were okay. They chatted about the cruise, and then, as they were ending their call, she suggested that he beg Joy, the former cruise director for the *Malina*, to come out of retirement for the next cruise season.

"That's my thought exactly," he said. "I don't know what I was thinking. I got a lot of things wrong about this cruise. Bert sent me the photos he took of the spa. Vintage is one thing, but that place was dreadful. But, because of this little mishap, Mila can move forward with the spa and salon renovation. I've tried to call her, but she isn't answering her phone."

Kennedy smirked but didn't say anything.

"Kennedy, I am sorry you didn't get to relax on this cruise. You will probably think twice before you offer to help me out again."

"It wasn't all bad, Alfred."

While Kennedy was on the phone, a van pulled up outside the hotel, and a dark-haired man hopped out. He jogged to the passenger side, opened the door, and lifted a vase of flowers out of the cardboard box on the front seat. The man didn't notice that the envelope with the flowers had fallen out when he lifted the bouquet, and it now rested under the van in a pool of dirty water. He went inside, handed the vase and a clipboard to the front desk agent, and told her the flowers were for Kennedy Reeves.

Kennedy was trying desperately to get off the phone with Alfred when there was a knock on her door. "Alfred, I have to go," she said. "Someone is here. We'll be in Ketchikan for a few more days while we wait for our stuff to get off the ship and will be back on the *Helio* in a few weeks. I'll call you tomorrow." She disconnected and walked to the door. When she opened it, she was looking at a beautiful bouquet of Alaskan wildflowers. "These just came for you," a blushing young man said, holding out the flowers, and Kennedy took the vase in her hands.

"Was there a note?" she asked, admiring the purple irises, fireweed, lupine, and chocolate lilies. The young man shook his head. "Thank you," she said and smiled. She thought she knew who had sent the flowers. It was a sweet, romantic gesture, and it fit his personality.

Two hours later, she entered the lobby and saw Otto. They began laughing when they saw they were wearing the same "Jammin' Salmon" T-shirt.

"Great shirt," Otto grinned.

"I hear only the coolest people are wearing them."

"Ready to go?"

Kennedy inhaled. "Ready as I'll ever be," and gave him a smile that lit up the room. Otto held the door open, and they walked outside into the misty moonlit night. They talked about the passengers and crew members they had checked on. Kennedy shared that she had borrowed Mila's jacket after Vera Jameson had commandeered hers when she had to apologize to Oliver Parsons but refused to do it wearing the purple T-shirt. Mila, she said, had left the jacket outside her door with a "Do Not Disturb" sign hung prominently on the doorknob.

Otto smirked. "We never did find those leashes or muzzles."

"Nope."

"It seems like things have ended well despite what happened last night," Otto said quietly.

"I think so."

They walked in step, each in their own thoughts, and Kennedy bravely took Otto's arm. "Oh, and the flowers were lovely, Otto. Thank you. They really brightened my day."

Otto stopped in his tracks and turned to her. The moonlight highlighted his puzzled face. "What flowers?"

AUTHORS NOTE

I don't know about you, but I need a SunRumbrella after that book. So many questions that now require answers. I suppose I should start writing book four, *A Sleaze on the Seas*, so we can find out what happens next. The cocktail book Ismaeel references is called *The Savoy Cocktail Book* and makes for some interesting reading. Thank you for reading *A Heist on the Ice*, the third in the Kennedy Reeves series. If this is your first Kennedy Reeves Mystery, I hope you enjoyed meeting Kennedy and her friends as much as I loved bringing them to life. If you've read the previous books, *A Boat for a Goat* or *A Cruise for Sous*, I hope you enjoyed reconnecting with the gang and meeting a few new people.

Stay tuned…MJ Mac

www.mjmacauthor.com

✉ mjmacauthor@gmail.com

Facebook – MJ Mac

Linked In—MJ Mac

Instagram – MJ_Mac_Author

www.amazon.com/author/mjmac

www.goodreads.com/author/show/22910684.MJ_Mac

OTHER BOOKS BY MJ MAC

A BOAT FOR A GOAT
Kennedy Reeves Mystery Series Book 1

Kennedy Reeves, cruise director for the *Helio*, has been called back to work after being on land for the last year. She looks forward to greeting her passengers: the business world's newest mega-millionaire couple, the Club Diva Boys, the Ladies from Harmony Lakes, and Vera Jameson (a businesswoman who could make a drill sergeant cry). Everything looks shipshape until the consultant hired by the corporate office arrives, and he has a very different course charted. Join Kennedy, her friends, and their zany passengers as they navigate the turbulent waters of their first cruise in *A Boat for a Goat*.

Available in paperback and e-book on Amazon, Barnes & Noble, and Indigo Bookstores

OTHER BOOKS BY MJ MAC

A CRUISE FOR SOUS
Kennedy Reeves Mystery Series Book 2

Secrets and scandal are the spices of this cruise when Classic Style Network chooses the *Helio* as the location for a cut-throat cooking competition, and it's up to Kennedy to keep things from boiling over. Old and new friends are also on this mouth-watering cruise: the Gents from Breezy Bayou, David from Club Diva, Jones and Terri Butler, and Emily Abbott, the great-granddaughter of the cruise line's founder. In between taking care of the passengers and making sure the competition goes smoothly, Kennedy is also in charge of decorating the ship for the holidays. "It's just a few trees," Alfred, her boss, wrote. And when travel writer Monique Patrick begins stirring the pot by asking uncomfortable questions, it could become a recipe for disaster.

Available in paperback and e-book on Amazon, Barnes & Noble, and Indigo Bookstores

COMING SOON

A SLEAZE ON THE SEAS

Kennedy Reeves Mystery Series Book 4

COMING SOON – FALL 2023

Q: Why won't sharks attack lawyers?

A: Professional courtesy

Kennedy has her hands full as the *Helio* will host a conference for a group of attorneys. With names like Ari the Anvil, Ponytail Paul, Strong Arm Sam, and Benny the Brawler on the manifest, what could possibly go wrong? Plenty!

ACKNOWLEDGEMENTS

The author gratefully acknowledges the assistance of many, many people who help keep this dream alive: Dan McCarragher, for his extreme patience, love, and support as I continue on this journey; Elvis for giving me silent encouragement with her soulful brown eyes and reminding me that we stop writing no matter where we are in the book at 5:30 for our walk. To my beta readers, thank you for trusting me when I sent you the rough draft of the alternate ending. (You have to admit it was better than the original.) To Denise and Sue, who wave their pom-poms from 3,000 miles away, and a massive shoutout to my friend Donna who listens to my prattling when I have an idea. Michelle Krueger, my fabulous editor, thank you for polishing another rough diamond.

But most of all, I want to thank you, the readers. Meeting you at book signings and reading your comments on social media keep me going! Please keep them coming!

The author also acknowledges Gettys Images, VectorStock, Weape Studio, and Dharma Type for the use of images and fonts.

ABOUT THE AUTHOR

Before embarking on a writing career, MJ Mac was a "Jill of all trades" in corporate America for forty years. MJ was a master juggler in her three-inch heels and lipstick, pulling the ropes from behind the curtain to seamlessly make magic happen. In 2021, a story about a cruise director, her coworkers, and their zany passengers began to formulate in her head. She traded in the corporate world of useless meetings, meetings about meetings, high heels, and suits for the sand, flip flops, and a sarong to pursue writing full-time and hasn't looked back. MJ and her husband Dan (her biggest supporter next to their adorable albeit scruffy dog Elvis) are living their best life on the beach, where she spends her time plotting what drama Kennedy and her friends will find next.

Made in the USA
Monee, IL
02 June 2023

34737205R00252